W9-BVH-975

Hum

If You

Don't Know

the Words

Hum

If You

Don't Know

the Words

❦

BIANCA MARAIS

G. P. PUTNAM'S SONS

New York

G. P. Putnam's Sons
Publishers Since 1838
An imprint of Penguin Random House LLC
375 Hudson Street
New York, New York 10014

Copyright © 2017 by Bianca Marais
Penguin supports copyright. Copyright fuels creativity, encourages diverse
voices, promotes free speech, and creates a vibrant culture. Thank you for
buying an authorized edition of this book and for complying with copyright
laws by not reproducing, scanning, or distributing any part of it in any form
without permission. You are supporting writers and allowing Penguin to
continue to publish books for every reader.

Library of Congress Cataloging-in-Publication Data

Names: Marais, Bianca, author.
Title: Hum if you don't know the words / Bianca Marais.
Description: New York : G. P. Putnam's Sons, 2017.
Identifiers: LCCN 2016043197 (print) | LCCN 2017006944 (ebook) |
ISBN 9780399575068 (hardback) | ISBN 9780399575075 (Ebook)
Subjects: LCSH: South Africa—History—Soweto Uprising, 1976—Fiction. |
South Africa—History—1961-1994—Fiction. | Apartheid—South
Africa—Fiction. | Family life—South Africa—Fiction. | BISAC: FICTION /
Literary. | FICTION / Coming of Age. | FICTION / Family Life.
Classification: LCC PR9199.4.M3414 H86 2017 (print) |
LCC PR9199.4.M3414 (ebook) |
DDC 813/.6—dc23
LC record available at https://lccn.loc.gov/2016043197
p.   cm.

International edition ISBN: 9780735218260

Printed in the United States of America
1   3   5   7   9   10   8   6   4   2

BOOK DESIGN BY AMANDA DEWEY

This is a work of fiction. Names, characters, places, and incidents either are
the product of the author's imagination or are used fictitiously, and any
resemblance to actual persons, living or dead, businesses, companies,
events, or locales is entirely coincidental.

For

Maurna,

my beloved Old Duck,

and for

Eunice,

Puleng and Nomthandazo

who taught me that even though human beings can be segregated,

their hearts cannot

because love is color-blind and can walk through walls.

Hum

If You

Don't Know

the Words

One

ROBIN CONRAD

❦

13 June 1976
Boksburg, Johannesburg, South Africa

I joined up the last two lines of the hopscotch grid and wrote a big "10" in the top square. It gave me a thrill writing the age I'd be on my next birthday because everyone knew that once you hit double digits, you weren't a child anymore. The green chalk, borrowed from the scoreboard of my father's dartboard without his knowledge, was so stubby that my fingers scraped against the concrete of the driveway as I put the final touches on my creation.

"There, it's done." I stood back and studied my handiwork. As usual, I was disappointed that something I'd made hadn't turned out quite as good as I'd imagined.

"It's perfect," Cat declared, reading my mind as she always did, and trying to reassure me before I washed the grid off in a fit of self-doubt. I smiled even though her opinion shouldn't have counted for much; my identical twin sister was easily impressed by everything I did. "You go first," Cat said.

"Okay."

I pulled the bronze half-cent coin from my pocket and rubbed it for luck before flipping it into the air from my thumbnail. It arced and spun, glinting in the sunlight, and when it finally landed in the first square, I launched myself forward, eager to finish the grid in record time.

I finished three circuits before the coin skittered out of the square marked "4." It should have ended my turn, but I shot a quick look at Cat who was distracted by a hadeda bird making a racket on the neighbor's roof. Before she could notice my mistake, I nudged the coin back in place with the tip of my canvas shoe and carried on jumping.

"You're doing so well," Cat called a few seconds later once she'd turned back and noticed my progress.

Spurred on by her clapping and encouragement, I hopped even faster, not noticing until it was too late that a lace on one of my *takkies* had come loose. It tripped me up just as I cleared the last square and brought me crashing down knee-first, my skin scraped raw on the rough concrete. I cried out, first in alarm and then in pain, and it was this noise that brought my mother's flip-flops clacking into my line of vision. Her shadow fell over me.

"Oh for goodness' sake, not again." My mother reached down and yanked me up. "You're so clumsy. I don't know where you get it from." She tsked as I raised my bleeding knee so she could see.

Cat was crouched next to me, wincing at the sight of the gravel embedded in the wound. Tears started to prickle, but I knew I had to stop their relentless progression quickly or suffer my mother's displeasure.

"I'm fine. It's fine." I forced a watery smile and gingerly stood up.

"Oh, Robin," my mother sighed. "You're not going to cry, are you? You know how ugly you are when you cry." She crossed her eyes and screwed up her face comically to illustrate her point and I forced the giggle she was looking for.

"I'm not going to cry," I said. Crying in the driveway in plain sight of the neighbors would be an unforgivable offense; my mother was very concerned with what other people thought and expected me to be as well.

"Good girl." She smiled and kissed me on the top of my head as a reward for my bravery.

There was no time to savor the praise. The trill of the ringing phone cut through the morning and just like that, one of the last tender moments my mother and I would ever share was over. She blinked and the warmth in her eyes turned to exasperation.

"Get Mabel to help clean you up, okay?"

She'd just disappeared through the back door into the kitchen when I became aware of whimpering and looked down to see that Cat was crying. Looking at my sister was always like looking into a mirror, but in that instant, it felt as though the glass between my reflection and me had been removed so that I wasn't looking at an image of myself; I was looking at myself.

The misery etched onto Cat's scrunched-up features was my misery. Her blue eyes welled with my tears and her pouty bottom lip trembled. Anyone who'd ever doubted the veracity of twin empathy only had to see my sister suffering on my behalf to become a true believer.

"Stop crying," I hissed. "Do you want Mom calling you a crybaby?"

"But it looks like it hurts."

If only it were that straightforward in the eyes of our mother. "Go to our room so she won't see you," I said, "and only come out when you feel better." I tucked a strand of brown hair behind her ear.

She sniffed and nodded, and then scurried inside with her head bent. I followed a minute later and found our maid, Mabel, in the kitchen washing up the breakfast dishes. She was wearing her faded mint-green uniform (a coverall dress that was too tight on her plump frame, the buttons gaping apart where they fastened in the front) with a white apron and *doek*.

My mother was on the phone in the dining room using the carefree, happy voice she only ever used with one person: her sister, Edith.

I left her to it, knowing that if I asked to speak to my aunt, I'd be told either to stop interrupting grown-ups' conversations, or to stop being so in love with the sound of my own voice.

"Mabel, look," I said as I lifted up my knee, relieved that it wasn't one of her few Sundays off.

She cringed when she saw the blood, and her hands flew up to her mouth, sending suds flying. "*Yoh! Yoh! Yoh!* I'm sorry! I'm sorry!" she exclaimed as though she'd personally caused my suffering.

To me, this litany was better than all the plasters in the world and an immediate balm to my pain.

"Sit. I must see." She knelt down and inspected the scrape, wincing as she did so. "I will fetch the first-aid things." She pronounced it *fest-aid* in her strong accent and I savored the word as I savored all Mabel-English. I loved how she made regular English words sound like a totally different language, and I wondered if her children (whom I'd never met and who lived in QwaQwa all year round) spoke the same way.

She fetched the kit out from the scullery cupboard and knelt down again to tend to the graze, the cotton ball looking especially white against her brown skin. She soaked it with orange disinfectant and then held it to the wound, murmuring words of comfort each time I tried to pull away from the sting of it.

"I am sorry! *Yoh*, I'm sorry, see? I am almost finished. Almost, almost. You are a brave girl." *You arra brev gell.*

I basked in her focused attention and watched as she blew on my knee, amazed at how the tickle of her breath magically eased the pain. Once Mabel was satisfied that the broken skin was clean enough, she stuck a huge plaster over it and pinched my cheek.

"Mwah, mwah, mwah." She placed lip-smacking kisses all over my face, and I held my breath waiting to see if this would be the day I finally got a kiss on the mouth. Her lips came as close as my chin before returning to my forehead. "All better now!"

"Thank you!" I gave her a quick hug before heading out again, and I'd just reached the back door when my father called me.

"Freckles!" He was sitting in a deck chair next to the portable *braai* he'd set up in the bright patch of sunlight in the middle of the brown lawn. "Get your old man a beer."

I ducked inside again and opened the fridge, pulling out a bottle of Castle Lager. My inexpert handling of the bottle opener resulted in a spray of foam across the linoleum floor, but I didn't stop to wipe it up. Mabel clucked as I made a run for it, but I knew she'd clean it without complaint.

"Here you go," I said, handing the still-foaming bottle to my father who immediately used it to douse the flames that had leapt up beyond the barrier of the grill.

"Just in time," he said, nodding for me to sit in the chair next to him.

My father's blue eyes twinkled out at me from a handsome face that was mostly hidden behind a thicket of hair. Wavy blond curls flopped over his eyebrows in the front, and grew long at the back so that they dipped over his shirt collar. He'd also cultivated long mutton-chop sideburns that fell just short of meeting up with his bushy moustache. Kissing him was always a ticklish undertaking, and I loved the bristly texture of his face against my skin.

I sat down and he handed me the *braai* tongs as if he was passing me a sacred object. He nodded in a solemn way and I nodded back to show I acknowledged the transference of power. I was now in charge of the meat.

My father smiled as I leaned into the smoke rising from the grill, and then he glanced at the plaster on my knee. "You been through the wars again, Freckles?"

I nodded and he laughed. My father often joked about having a son in a daughter's body. He especially loved to tell the story of how I'd come home from my first and only ballet lesson when I was five years old with ripped tights and my leg covered in blood. When he'd asked me how in the world I'd managed to get so roughed up in a dancing class, I confessed that I'd injured myself falling out of the tree I'd climbed in order to hide away from the teacher. He'd roared with laughter, and my mother had lectured me about wasting their money.

Teaching me how to *braai* was something my father should've taught a son. If he felt cheated that he never got one, he never said so, and he encouraged my tomboyish behavior at every opportunity.

Cat, on the other hand, was a sensitive child and in many ways, my complete opposite. She was also squeamish about raw meat. There was no way my father would ever have taught her the subtleties of cooking meat to perfection, or how to hold your fist when throwing a knockout punch, or how to bring someone down with a rugby tackle.

"Okay, now turn the *wors*. Make sure you get the tongs under all the coils and flip them together or it's going to be a big mess. Good. Now, nudge the chops to the side or they're going to be overdone. You want to crisp the fat but not burn it."

I followed his instructions carefully and managed to cook the meat to his satisfaction. Once we were done, I carried the meat in a pan to the table Mabel had set for us on the flagstone patio. The garlic bread, potato salad and *mielies* were already there, protected under a fly net that I sometimes used as a veil when I played at being a spy disguised as a bride.

"Tell your mother we're ready," my father said as he sat down. He didn't trust the giant hadedas with their long beaks not to swoop down and steal the meat; they often swiped dog food left outside in bowls and had been known to go for bigger prey like fish in ornamental ponds.

"She's on the phone."

"Well, tell her to get off. I'm hungry."

"We're ready to eat," I yelled around the doorway before stepping back outside again.

I'd just sat down next to my father when Cat trailed outside to join us. She'd washed all evidence of tears from her face and smiled as our mother sat down next to her.

"Who was that on the phone?" my father asked, reaching for the butter and Bovril spread to slather over his *mielie*.

"Edith."

My father rolled his eyes. "What does she want?"

"Nothing. She's got some vicious stomach bug that's going around and she's been grounded until it clears."

"I suppose that's a huge crisis in her life? Not being able to serve shitty airplane food on overpriced flights to hoity-toity passengers. God, your sister can make a mountain out of a molehill."

"It's not a crisis, Keith. Who said it was a crisis? She just wanted to talk."

"Wanted to suck you into the drama of her life, more like it."

My mother raised her voice. "What drama?"

Cat's eyes were wide as they darted between our parents. She pulled her gaze away from them and stared at me. Her meaning was clear. *Do something!*

"Everything's a drama with her," my father said, matching my mother's increased volume. "It's never just a small hiccup; it's always the end of the world."

"It's not the end of the world! Who said it's the end of the world?" My mother thwacked the serving spoon back into the salad bowl. She glowered at him and the vein in her forehead began to bulge, never a good sign. "God! Why must you always give her a hard time? She just wanted to—"

The doorbell rang.

Cat's expression of relief said it all. *Saved by the bell!*

"Oh, for God's sake!" My father threw down his cutlery so that it clattered across the table. "Look at the time. Who has no bloody manners rocking up at lunchtime on a Sunday?" My mother stood to go but my father held her back. "Let Mabel get it."

"I told her to take the afternoon off and said she could come in tonight to do the dishes."

As my mother disappeared into the house, my father called after her. "If it's the Jehovah's Witnesses, tell them to piss off or I'll shoot them. Tell them I have a big gun and I'm not afraid to use it."

"I wonder who it is," Cat said, and I shrugged. I was more interested in the gun.

When my mother returned a few minutes later, she was flushed and carrying two books, which she thumped down on the table in front of Cat.

"What's that?" my father asked. "Who was at the door?"

"Gertruida Bekker."

"Hennie's wife?"

"Yes."

"What did she want?"

"To complain about Robin who's apparently corrupting her daughter."

"What?" My father looked at me. "What did you do, Freckles?"

"I don't know."

My mother nodded at the books. "You gave those to Elsabe?"

"I didn't give them to her. I borrowed them to her."

"Lent them," my mother corrected.

"Yes, lent them."

My father reached across the table to pick up the books. "*The Magic Faraway Tree* and *Five Go Adventuring Again*," he read. "Books by Enid Blyton?"

"Yes, apparently Gertruida took exception to the characters' names and told me, in no uncertain terms, that Robin is a bad influence and she doesn't want her playing with Elsabe anymore."

"What names? What is the bloody woman talking about?"

My mother paused before answering. "Dick and Fanny."

"Are you being serious?"

My mother nodded. "Yes, she said they're disgusting names that shouldn't be allowed in a Christian household."

My father guffawed and that set my mother off. They were both in fits of giggles and it was my turn to look to Cat in mystification. I didn't know what was so funny.

I hadn't meant to upset Elsabe or Mrs. Bekker; all I'd tried to do was start my own secret society like the children in the books. I wanted to solve mysteries and have hidden clubhouses; I wanted to think up exotic passwords about cream buns and jam tarts that no one else would ever guess. Unfortunately though, all the other girls in our whites-only suburb of Witpark in Boksburg were Afrikaners and, from what I could tell, were only interested in playing house. All that cooking, knitting, sewing, baking, looking after screaming babies and yelling at drunken husbands who came home late from mine parties didn't appeal to me. I wanted, instead, to broaden their horizons and introduce them to a whole new world they were missing out on.

"I just wanted her and the other girls to read the books so they'd join my Secret Seven Club," I said. "So far, it's just me and Cat and we need five others."

"Bugger them," my father said, reaching over and fluffing my hair. "You girls can have a Gruesome Twosome all on your own. Or better yet, forget the girls and go play with the boys."

My mother rolled her eyes again, but she was still in a good mood and I didn't want to ruin it by complaining about how none of the boys would play with me. She didn't like whining and always said that instead of dwelling on the negative, I should try to think up solutions. Which is what got me thinking about what my father had said earlier.

"Where's your big gun, Daddy?"

"What?"

"Your big gun? The one you said you'd shoot the Jehovah's Witnesses with?"

"I was just joking, Freckles. I don't have a gun."

"Oh." This was disappointing. I was hoping to use it as a conversation starter with the boys. "Maybe you should get one."

"Why?"

"Piet's dad said the *kaffir* black bastards are going to kill us in our sleep because we're sissies. He said if we don't own guns, we may as well just bend over and take it up the backside like the *moffies* do."

"Oh yes, when did he say this?" my father asked just as my mother told me not to say *kaffir* and *moffies*.

"The other day when I was there playing with the dogs. What do the *moffies* take up the backside?"

"That's enough questions for one day, Robin."

"But—"

"No buts." He shot my mother a look and they both snorted with laughter. "End of conversation."

It had been an ordinary Sunday in every way. My parents fought and then made up and then fought again, switching from being adversaries to allies so seamlessly that you couldn't put your finger on the moment when the lines were crossed and recrossed. Cat perfectly acted out her part of the quiet understudy twin, so I could take my place in the spotlight playing the leading role for both of us. I asked too many questions and repeatedly pushed the boundaries, and Mabel hovered like a benevolent shadow in the wings.

The only difference was that, without my knowing it, the clock had started ticking; in just over three days, I'd lose three of the most important people in my life.

Two

BEAUTY MBALI

❀

14 JUNE 1976
Transkei, South Africa

My *daughter is in danger.*
  This is my first thought when I awaken and it spurs me on to get dressed quickly. Dawn is still two hours away and the inside of the hut is black as grief. I can usually move around the room and skirt the boys' sleeping mats in the darkness, but I need a light now to finish the last of my packing.

The scratch of the match against the rough strip of the Lion box is grating in the confines of the silent room, and my shadow rises up like a prayer when I light the candle and place it next to my suitcase on the floor. The lingering scent of sulfur, an everyday smell that has always made me think of daybreak, feels portentous now. I breathe through my mouth so that I do not have to inhale the smell of fear.

I am quiet but there is nothing to help muffle my movements. Our dwellings are circular and entirely open within the circumference of the clay outer wall. No ceilings crouch above us, bisecting the thatch roofs from the dung floors. No partitions cut through the communal space to separate us into different rooms. Our homes are borderless just as the world was once free of boundaries; there would be no walls or roofs at all except for the essential shelter they provide. Privacy is not a concept my people understand or desire; we bear witness to each other's lives and take comfort in having our own lives seen. What greater gift can you give another than to say: I see you, I hear you, and you are not alone?

This is why, no matter how quiet I try to be, both my sons are awake. Khwezi watches as I roll up my reed mat; the reflected light of the candle's flame burns in his eyes. Thirteen years old, he is my youngest child. He does not remember the day, ten years ago, when his father left for the gold mines in Johannesburg, nor the agony of the months of drought that came before. He does not remember the gradual slump of a proud man's shoulders as Silumko watched his family and cattle starve, but Khwezi is old enough now to be fearful of losing another family member to the hungry city.

I smile to reassure him, but he does not smile back. His thin face is serious as he reaches up absentmindedly to rub the shiny patch above his ear. The mottled pink tissue, in the shape of an acacia tree, is what remains from a long-ago fall into an open fire. There was a reason God placed the scar in a spot where Khwezi cannot see it but where I, from my height as a mother, cannot overlook it. It serves as a reminder that the ancestors gave me a second chance with him; one I was not granted when I failed to protect Mandla, my firstborn son, from harm. I cannot fail another of my children.

"Mama," Luxolo whispers from his mat opposite his younger brother. His gray blanket is wrapped around him like a shroud to ward off the morning chill.

"Yes, my son?"

"Let me go with you." He posed the same plea soon after my brother's letter arrived yesterday.

The crumpled yellow envelope bearing my name, Beauty Mbali,

has traveled a circuitous route to get here from my brother Andile's home in Zondi, a neighborhood in the middle of Soweto.

Our village is so small that it does not have an official name that can be found marked on a map of the Transkei, and so there is no direct mail delivery to the foothills of this rural landscape in our black homeland. Once the letter left my brother's hands, the postal service carried it out of the township of Soweto—on potholed and sandy roads—into Johannesburg, the heart of South Africa, and then south across the tarred arterial highways of the Transvaal, over the Vaal River, and into the Orange Free State.

From there, it traveled south still over the fog-cloaked Drakensberg Mountains and then down, down, down zigzagging through hairpin bends to reach Pietermaritzburg, after which it branched off into the veiny, neglected side roads that would officially deliver it to the post office in Umtata, the Transkei's capital city.

Its journey not yet complete, the envelope still had to be passed hand to hand from the postmaster's wife to the Scottish missionary in Qunu—a distance of thirty kilometers that would take six hours for me to walk, but takes the white woman forty minutes to drive in her husband's car—and then onwards still from the missionary's black cleaning woman to the Indian *spaza* shop owner. The final leg of its journey was made by Jama, a nine-year-old herd boy, who ran the three kilometers over dusty pathways to my classroom to proudly hand it across to me.

I do not know how long the envelope took to travel the more than nine hundred kilometers from black township to black homeland to bring its warning; the post stamp is smudged and Andile, in his haste, did not date his letter. I hope I will not be too late.

"Mama, take me with you," Luxolo entreats again. It is only his desire to prove himself as the man of the house that spurs him on to challenge a decision I have already made. He would not risk disrespecting me for any other reason. Only fifteen years old, Luxolo tries to fulfill the duties of a grown man in our household. He believes that protecting the womenfolk is as much his responsibility as tending the cattle that is our livelihood; by accompanying me on the journey, he will help keep his sister safe from harm and ensure that we both return safely.

"The village needs you here. I will fetch Nomsa and bring her home." I turn away from him so that he cannot see the worry in my eyes and so I cannot see his wounded pride.

My bible is the last of my possessions I pack. Its black leather cover is careworn from hours spent cradled in my hands. I slip my brother's letter between its hope-thin pages for safekeeping though I have already memorized the most worrying parts of it.

You must come immediately, sister. Your daughter is in extreme danger and I fear for her life. I cannot guarantee her safety here. If she stays, who knows what will happen to her.

I blink away the vision of Andile writing in his cramped scrawl, the wave of ink blowing back over his sentences like ash from a *veld* fire as his left hand smudges over the words he has just written. With it comes the memory of our mother superstitiously hitting him over the knuckles with a sapling branch every time he reached for something with the wrong hand. She could not torture his left-handedness out of him no matter how hard she tried, nor could she quench my thirst for knowledge or my ambition. Just as I could not rid Nomsa of her obstinacy.

Once I've wrapped a *doek* around my head, I slip the shoes on. They are as unyielding and uncomfortable as the Western customs that dictate the donning of this uniform. Here in my homeland, I am always barefoot. Even in the classroom where I teach, my soles connect with the dung of the floor. However, if I am to venture out into the white man's territory, I need to wear the white man's clothes.

I unzip my beaded money pouch and check the notes folded inside. There is just enough for the taxis and buses as I journey north. The return fare will have to be borrowed from my brother and it is a debt we can ill afford. I slip the pouch into my bra, another constrictive Western invention, and say a silent prayer that I will not be robbed during my journey. I am a black woman traveling alone, and a black woman is always the easiest target on the food chain of victims.

A cock crows in the distance. It is time. I hold my arms out to my sons and they rise silently from their beds to step into my embrace. I hug them fiercely, reluctant to let go. There is so much I want to say to them. I want to impart both words of wisdom and remind them of trivial matters, but I do not want to scare them with a protracted farewell. It is easier to pretend that I am leaving on a short journey and will return before nightfall. It is also important for Luxolo to know that I have complete faith in him to take care of his brother and the cattle while I am away; I will not belittle his efforts with entreaties for caution and vigilance. He knows what needs to be done and he will do it well.

"Nomsa and I will be home soon," I say. "Do not worry about us."

"And you, Mother, must not worry about us. I will take care of everything." Luxolo is somber. He wears this new responsibility well.

"I will not worry. You are both good boys who will soon be great men."

Luxolo steps out of my embrace and nods as he accepts the compliment. Khwezi is reluctant to let go. I kiss his head, my lips touching his scar. "Try to get another hour of sleep." Like the good boys they are, they obey me and return to their mats.

I step out into the dawn with a blanket wrapped around my shoulders and make my way down the narrow hillside trail. The scents of wood smoke and manure rise up to say their farewells. Crickets chirp a discordant good-bye. My breath is visible in the cold moonlight; ghostlike puffs of air lead the way ahead of me, and I trail them just as I trail the phantom of my daughter down this sandy path. My feet fall where hers did seven months ago when she traded our country life for a city education.

I try to recall how she looked on the day she left but what comes to mind instead is a memory of her at the age of five. Our thatch roof needed repairing, and for that, I had to use the panga to cut the long grass. Fearful of the children getting in the way of the blade, I sent them to the *kraal* to see the lamb that had been born in the night. Three-year-old Luxolo ran off trying to keep up with his sister and I set to work harvesting the thatch.

Later when the cry tore through the fields, setting a flock of sparrows in flight, I dropped the panga and started running. By the time I neared the *kraal* behind two other women who were racing ahead of me, the cry had turned to shrieking. Another more ominous sound threaded through the noise though I did not register what it was until I cleared the last hut.

There Nomsa was standing with her stubby legs apart in a fighter's stance. She had inserted herself between Luxolo and a low-slung jackal that was snapping and snarling at her with foam frothing from its muzzle. The jackal was rabid and out of its mind with aggression.

Nomsa's small fist was raised and she shook it while shouting at the beast that was sloping towards her. Before I could begin running again, Nomsa reached for a rock and threw it with such force that it hit the jackal square in the head, sending the animal staggering off to the side. When I got to them, I grabbed both Luxolo and Nomsa and pulled them up into my arms while the village women chased the jackal away. Nomsa was trembling with fright. My daughter, only five years old, had bravely fought off a predator to protect her younger brother. I expected to see tears in her eyes but what I saw instead was triumph.

I force the memory and the accompanying uneasiness from my mind. There are still six kilometers of dusty paths to walk before I reach the main road near Qunu. A rural village like ours, sunken into a grassy valley surrounded by green hills, Qunu is inhabited by a few hundred people, which has accorded it a proper name. It is rumored that Nelson Mandela grew up in those foothills so the soil is said to foster greatness. Perhaps touching it along my journey will bring me luck.

From Qunu, I must catch the first taxi to take me out of the protection of the Bantustan of the Transkei into the white man's province of Natal, specifically four hundred kilometers northeast through sugarcane and maize fields to Pietermaritzburg via Kokstad. After that, I will need to make my way north past the Midlands, through the Drakensberg Mountains and then on to Johannesburg.

My journey will take me from this rural idyll where time stands still to a city that is rocked from below its foundations by the dynamite blasts used in the mining of gold, and assaulted from above by the fierce Highveld thunderstorms that tear across its sky. Almost a thousand kilometers stretch out between here and Soweto in a thread of dread and doubt, but I try not to think of the distance as I hold my suitcase away from my body to stop it from drumming into my thigh.

I follow the morning star and look forward to sunrise, which is my favorite time of day, though Nomsa prefers sunset. There is no lingering twilight in Africa, no gentle gloaming as day eases into night; a tender give-and-take between light and shadow. Night settles swiftly. If you are vigilant, and not prone to distractions, you can almost feel the very moment daylight slips through your fingers and leaves you clutching the inky sap that is the sub-Saharan night. It is a sharp exhalation at the closing of day, a sigh of relief. Sunrise is the opposite: a gentle inhalation, a protracted affair as the day readies itself for what is to come. Just as I now must ready myself for whatever awaits me in Soweto.

I have just turned into the valley to follow the meandering path of the river when a thin voice calls out to me.

"Mama." The word expands in the hushed sanctity of the morning and is absorbed by the mist blanketing the riverbed. I think I have imagined it, that I have conjured up my daughter's voice from across the country calling to me for help, but then I hear it again. "Mama."

I turn and look back upon the trail I've walked and a figure bounds down the path towards me. It is Khwezi, sure-footed as a mountain goat. Within a few minutes he is next to me, our breaths mingling in puffs of exertion as we face one another.

"You forgot your food," he says, holding up the bag in which I wrapped the roasted *mielies* and chicken pieces the night before. "You will be hungry."

He looks so much like his father—the boy his father was before the gold mines took his joy and crushed it—and he smiles an unguarded smile, proud of himself for having spared me from hunger. My heart swells with love.

"You will bring Nomsa home?" he asks and I nod because I cannot speak. "You will come back?"

I nod again.

"Do you promise, Mama?"

"Yes." It is a strangled sob, a fire of emotion robbed of air, but it is a promise. I will bring Nomsa home.

Three

ROBIN

❦

15 JUNE 1976
Boksburg, Johannesburg, South Africa

Something tickled as it made its steady way up my arm, but I didn't want to interrupt my surveillance to see what it was. I didn't consider it a threat to my top-secret spy mission until it stopped to take a chunk out of my skin.

"Ouch!" I dropped the binoculars and held up the soft inner flesh of my forearm to find a red ant feasting on me.

I flicked it off and turned to look at Cat who was lying belly-down in the sand, resting on her elbows in the exact same pose as me.

"Look what you did," I hissed. "You made us lie down on a red ant nest."

She looked at the roiling mass of movement in the dirt beneath us and turned to me, her eyes widening in panic. "Sorry!"

"Sorry doesn't help, dummy. Look at this, we're under attack! Quickly, let's move before the boys get here."

Brushing ourselves off, we crouched and sprinted to another spot that would give us an equally good vantage point though it would place us closer to the action than I wanted to be.

We were at the boys' meeting spot up in the huge mine dump that was situated right across the road from our suburb. Witpark was a community where mine workers from the nearby Witbok Mine lived; housing was subsidized, and so we all lived together in a neighborhood that bordered the mine property. The mountain of sand was what remained after gold was extracted from rock, and living next to it was part and parcel of the whole mining way of life, my father said. Apparently it wasn't enough that the mine sank men like him deep into the guts of the earth, he complained, they had to make him look at its innards from his backyard too.

In the winter months, the dump—which rose up eight stories high—was merely a tsunami of sand threatening to drown us all. In the spring, when the wind blew and blew, the scraggly grass and bushes that grew over the dump like barnacles weren't able to hold on to the soil no matter how fiercely they clung to it. During those months, a fine white powder was swept off it in waves; it coated our houses and lawns and cars—nothing left outside was spared the onslaught—and then it crept into the cracks of our windowpanes and came to rest in the corners of our sleeping eyes.

Only the summer rains could wash the dust away, and then the heat made the dump shimmer like a mirage so that it took on a golden and magical quality. That's when the dump called to us most loudly, a siren luring us to come and explore the mysteries of its caves and shafts.

Of course, we weren't officially allowed to play on the dump. We actually weren't allowed anywhere near it; it was strictly forbidden because of the danger. There were regular cave-ins in which you could break your neck or die of suffocation. We told each other urban legends about children who'd disappeared down a tunnel never to be seen again, and about the ghosts of miners who'd died underground and now haunted the dump looking for revenge. Our parents warned us about the black vagrants who slept on the dump and had no qualms about murdering white children. None of the stories kept us away. The children in Cape Town had Table Mountain; we had the East Rand mine dumps where the most exciting parts of our lives unfolded.

"Quick, hide! I hear them," I hissed at Cat.

We threw ourselves down in a clump of long grass and kept our heads lowered as we listened to the boys make their way along the path towards the clearing.

They met there almost every day after school and I was dying to know what they got up to. There were six of them ranging between eight and twelve years old and they called themselves *Die Boerseun Bende*, which translated loosely to "the Afrikaner Boy Gang." I was desperate to join their group and figured that if I at least knew what their membership entailed, I could support my application.

I knew my chances weren't that great because the only times I was ever included in their games were when I was invited to be the wicket (not the wicketkeeper, mind you) in a cricket match, and when I served as their crash-test dummy to try out one of their inventions: in that instance, it was an oversized skateboard with a hand brake. It turned out not to be a well-conceived contraption as the scars on my knees can attest to.

I hadn't shown my true mettle in both those instances; I just needed the right circumstances to truly shine, so I'd been trying to find out for weeks what they did when they disappeared onto the dump. Following them hadn't worked, because they'd wised up to me and were constantly on the lookout to make sure I wasn't behind them. Finally, inspired by my literary heroes, the Secret Seven, I decided that a stakeout was the best way to spy on them.

I'd allowed Cat to tag along on the condition that she was quiet and didn't whine too much. I should have added finding non-life-threatening hiding places as another stipulation but you live and learn.

As we lay there trying to blend in with the landscape, Piet Bekker strode out from the path to the huge rotting tree trunk that took up most of the leveled-out clearing. He was barefoot and wearing white shorts and a long-sleeved green rugby jersey; the rest of his posse was dressed similarly. Afrikaner boys never seemed to feel the cold and would remain barefoot throughout the winter months.

"Where did you put everything?" Piet asked his second-in-command in Afrikaans. I understood the language because we were forced to study it in school, and also because most of our neighbors in the mining community were Afrikaners.

"It's all in the log," Wouter replied, also in Afrikaans. "About an arm's length in on the far side."

"So, what are you waiting for? Get it out."

I dared raise my head and rest it on my palm so that I could see better. My father's binoculars (that he said he used for looking at ships when we went to Durban on holiday, but actually used for looking at ladies on the beach) wouldn't be of any use because we were too close.

Wouter lay on his stomach and reached into the log. He pulled out a white packet and handed it to Piet who opened it and took out a *catty* before passing the bag to the next person. *Catties* were the Afrikaner handheld catapults they carved from the Y-shaped forks in branches. The slingshots were dangerous enough when acorns were used as ammunition and deadly when paired with stones.

"Set up the targets," Piet instructed.

One of the other boys, Marnus, set down a heavy-looking bag he'd carried in and started pulling out various empty containers. Most of them were either Lion or Castle beer tins and bottles; the rest were Gordon's gin and Smirnoff vodka dinkies.

I gasped as I recognized the little tot-sized bottles as ones that we'd thrown away. My aunt Edith worked as an airhostess for South African Airways and she brought my parents the little bottles of alcohol that she'd filched from planes and hotel minibars. I was scandalized that Marnus had gone through our rubbish and stolen them.

He lined a row of ten bottles and cans on the log and the boys then took up their positions. That's when I realized how unfortunate our vantage point was. Cat and I were lying a few meters behind the tree stump; they'd be shooting their stones in our direction as they tried to hit the targets.

I darted a look at Cat and mimed for her to duck. She didn't need to be told twice and tucked her head under the cover of her arms. There was an ominous silence as the elastic of Piet's *catty* was pulled back and then an almighty thwack as the catapult was released. From the eerie whistling noise, I knew the stone was airborne, and then glass shattered as the ammunition found its target. Cheers went up and within a few seconds, stones began raining down all around us as the other boys joined in.

Cat was lucky and managed to avoid any direct hits, which was fortunate because she wouldn't have been able to stifle her yelps of pain like I did. A pebble landed on the sole of my one *takkie* and then skittered off, and another stone, sharper and more irregular, nicked my knuckle. The sting was terrible and it took every ounce of willpower to stop myself from crying out as a droplet of blood welled up. I refused to let a few wounds prevent me from completing my mission.

The boys thankfully ran out of targets pretty soon and the noise and dust died down.

"*Wat gaan ons nou skiet?*" Wouter asked. What are we going to shoot now?

"We can see who can shoot the farthest."

"No, that's boring. We need something more challenging."

"Like what?"

They were all silent for a few moments as they thought about it.

"Birds," Piet said, "let's shoot birds."

But there were no birds. For once, the trees and heavens were free of feathered creatures and I was thankful for their reprieve. The boys had just grown bored of looking up when there was a rustle of movement along the path they'd come in through.

"Shh, *wat is dit*?" Piet asked. What is that?

A mangy-looking cat burst into the clearing and darted towards the log. A dog barked from somewhere nearby and the cat swung around, its fur raised as it prepared for attack. It hissed wildly and when its pursuer didn't materialize, it turned and scampered towards the log again, dashing into the hollow.

I saw the idea occur to Piet and how he slowly raised his *catty*, aiming it at the other end of the trunk where the cat would exit through. He closed one eye as he pulled back the elastic, yanking it taut.

"No!" I was up and running before I even realized that the person shouting was me.

Piet, surprised by the yell and the figure hurtling towards him, let go of the stone, flinging it ineffectually over the log. Just as the stone landed, the cat made a break for it, and Piet cried out in frustration as the cat careened off out of the clearing.

By the time I got to Piet, carried along by the momentum of my anger, there was nothing left to protect, and I was suddenly an easy target in a circle of angry boys.

"She was spying on us!" Wouter shrieked in Afrikaans and the other gang members joined in expressing their incredulous outrage.

I tried to speak to them in their own language as I hoped this would temper their anger. *"Ek is nie 'n sampioen nie!"*

The boys regarded me as one would look at a mental patient and then they all started laughing and spluttering. I thought this was because I was so brazenly lying to them, but I realized too late that I'd gotten the Afrikaans words for "spy" and "mushroom" confused.

I spoke to be heard above all the laughter. "I want to join your gang."

Piet was so incensed by this statement that he stopped chortling at my stupidity and even swapped over to speaking English. "A member of dis gang? I don't fink so!" He spoke with the strong accent of a staunch Afrikaner, rolling his *r*'s and sharpening his *th* sounds into *v*'s, *d*'s and *f*'s.

"Why not?"

"You is a *meisiekind*." He said this as though being a girl was one of the worst things you could possibly be. "You must go play wiff da udder girls."

"No, I don't want to play with girls. I want to join your gang and be one of the boys." I didn't point out his own mother had forbidden me from playing with his sister.

"But," Piet spluttered, "you is a *rooinek*." The way he said it made it clear that being English was way worse than being a girl.

I knew the Afrikaners hated the English because of something called the Boer War, but I didn't give much weight to it. Considering almost a hundred years had passed since the Brits and the Afrikaners tried to kill each other, the mutual hatred should've died down by 1976, but it hadn't.

Apparently the Afrikaners never got over losing the war, nor did they get over their women and children being imprisoned in the world's first-ever concentration camps at the mercy of the British, and if there's one thing I learned early on in my childhood, it was this: the Afrikaners had long memories and they could hold a serious grudge.

"Go now before I frow you wiff dis stone," Piet instructed sternly while reaching for another projectile.

"You mean you're going to throw the stone at me, not pick me up and throw me with the stone."

All the boys suddenly reached for stones and I decided that the English lesson was over. I started running, the dust from the dump billowing up around me and coating me in incriminating powder, which would have to be washed off. It was only once I was almost home, out of breath and burning with humiliation, that I remembered

Cat. She'd stayed out of sight while I'd almost been lynched. I wasn't surprised. That's why I called her Fraidy Cat.

I considered turning around and going back for her but figured that would only give her away. She'd be fine. No one could be as invisible as Cat when she set her mind to hiding.

Four

BEAUTY

❁

15 JUNE 1976
Pietermaritzburg, South Africa

How much longer, Mother?" The girl, Phelisa, sighs and turns away from the taxi window, which she has steamed up with her breath.

She reminds me of Nomsa though she is plumper and wears a re-signed look that I have never seen on my daughter's face. Perhaps the only similarity is their age or perhaps my daughter is so much on my mind that I am projecting her onto any canvas that is blank enough to absorb my memories.

A child lies draped over the girl, his head resting against the pillow of her breasts while his arms wrap around her neck, clinging to her. He kicks out with surprising strength and his foot connects with my stomach as he wrestles with his dreams. I am envious of the child. I wish I could sleep. I wish also that I could slow the drumbeat of my frenzied heart or tame the wild flight of my thoughts that swoop and circle like bats at dusk.

"More than two hours we have been sitting here," Phelisa says as she pats her son's back, soothing him so he will not awaken from his fussing. "How much longer until we go?"

"I do not know, my child." I sigh. "We must resign ourselves to the wait as impatience will only make the time pass more slowly." It is not the first time I have told her this.

It has been twenty-eight hours since I watched Khwezi scamper up the hill back to the village, more than a day since I traded the wide-open space of home for the cramped and stale interiors of one minivan taxi after another. We are parked on the side of the road near a petrol station just outside Pietermaritzburg, already packed together like cattle as we wait for the vehicle to be filled even further. The driver will not depart until another four passengers squash into the space at the back that could comfortably seat only two. This has been the way of the entire journey, more time spent waiting than in motion.

The girl frowns at me as though I am a problem she must solve. "I have been thinking . . . you are not really one of us, Mother, are you?"

"What do you mean, my child? I am from here just like you." We are speaking in Xhosa, our mother tongue, and are both traveling from the Transkei, which is the Xhosa Bantu homeland. I know I could trace her clan's ties to my own with just a few questions if I had the energy for the usual pleasantries.

"I mean only that you are not like the rest of us, Mother. There is something that is different with you. The way you talk and the things you say."

She means that I speak like an educated person whereas most of our people cannot write their own names. I have heard this many times before, this assessment that, although I am black and poor and as oppressed as the rest of my people, I am not one of them; sometimes it is said with admiration and respect but more often as a criticism. I will never understand why we hold each other in contempt like this, why we are all so scared that one of us will rise above their station when the white man has appointed himself the guardian of making sure that never happens. If there is one thing a black woman knows from the moment she is born it is her place; she does not need anyone reminding her of it.

"I am a schoolteacher," I say by way of explanation.

"*Hayibo.*" Phelisa smiles. The thought of a woman teacher is amusing. "My teacher was a man. I have the standard two."

From her shy smile, I can see that she is proud of this achievement. She managed to stay in school until the age of nine, which means she knows the alphabet, how to write simple words and how to do basic arithmetic. This is the only education she will ever have.

I pat her knee, too sad to give her the praise she seeks, and change the subject. "Why are you going to Johannesburg?"

"The father of the child works in the mines, but he does not send the money. I am worried."

I nod and do not say what I am thinking. If she finds him, he will probably not have money to give her, nor will he come home to look after her and the child. There is no work for young men in the homelands and the mining industry takes them far away from their culture and clan and customs. For eleven months of the year, they live and breathe the darkness underground; it has a way of seeping into their souls. What little money they have is often spent on distractions like women, gambling and alcohol.

"And you, Mother? Why are you going?"

"My brother sent me a letter about my daughter. She is living with his family in Soweto this year while she completes her schooling there. There must be some kind of terrible unrest in the township because he said she is in danger. I am going to fetch her."

She nods. "I have heard the township is a dangerous and ungodly place. There is talk of shebeens where people get drunk illegally and also of dancing halls. Gambling and prostitutes. I have even heard—"

I cut her off and change the subject, because I have enough to concern me without hearing the full extent of Soweto's depravity. "Would you like me to hold the child?"

"Yes, thank you, Mother." She accepts the offer gratefully, handing the sleeping child across to me before stepping out of the van to stretch her legs.

Another hour passes and two more passengers pay their fare. The child awakens and I pass him back to his mother to be fed. I need the toilet but do not want to wake the old man sleeping on my other side. His thin arms and legs are folded in upon himself as he tries to take up as little space as possible. His ribcage expands and contracts against my arm, and a dry whistle—like the wind through reeds—escapes his lips. Just when I cannot wait any longer, he snores himself awake.

"Excuse me, *tat'omkhulu*, but I need to get past you."

He shuffles over to let me pass and tips his hat at me as I step out of the van.

Two eighteen-wheeler trucks fly past kicking up gravel and leaving me in a cloud of exhaust fumes. A *bakkie* towing a boat follows; it is probably on its way to Durban. The sea is approximately a hundred kilometers east of here, and it is a well-known fact that the whites in Johannesburg make the journey to the Natal coast at least once a year to holiday there. They spend their three-week vacation time lying on the beaches, swimming in the warm Indian Ocean and fishing for free food when they could afford to buy it in shops. Why they lie for hours in the sun trying to get brown when they find our own skin color so displeasing, I do not know.

I have never seen the ocean and the idea of it I have is one that I have taken from photographs in books and newspapers. I have never lived close enough to the sea to make easy travel arrangements to see it, and since blacks are not allowed on the beaches or in the water, there seems little point in going. I cannot swim, but it would be nice to wade into the water up to my knees and feel the salt of it against my skin.

One newspaper article I read a few years ago told a story of Transvaal families who pitch tents in camping grounds for their holidays. Apparently, it is something they enjoy doing, which tells me a lot about white people. Only those who live in proper houses and are safe from the elements will find novelty in sleeping outside under the cover of a piece of cloth.

As I trudge along the road to the petrol station, which is a hundred meters away, a banana plantation flanks me on the left and a sugarcane field stretches out on the right. The year-round tropical temperatures of Natal are good for these kinds of crops, which we would never be able to cultivate in the Transkei. It is no coincidence that the parts of the country given to the blacks for their homelands are the parts where nothing of value grows.

When I get to the station, I skirt around the pumps where cars pull in and out at regular intervals.

"Excuse me, my son, but where are our toilets?" I ask a young petrol attendant who is waiting for change from the cashier.

He smiles and removes a matchstick from between his teeth. "They are round the back, Mother, but you cannot use them."

"Why not?"

"They have been broken for a week. The owner here will not spend the money to fix them."

"Where do you go then?"

He nods to the fields behind the station and then excuses himself.

I do not want to squat in the fields where the people in their cars can see me. I will not act out the role of savage that is expected of us. Instead, I approach the whites' toilets and stand in the shadows by the pay phones and watch. Two women exit the lavatories as an old woman shuffles her way through the doors. Another two girls follow after her; they all emerge together a few minutes later. There is a lull. My bladder is going into spasm. Now is the time for me to dart inside; if I time it correctly, no one will see me.

I have just taken a step towards the entrance when a mother and daughter turn the corner. The little girl looks to be six or seven and has curly blond hair that needs to be brushed. She sucks her thumb, a habit she is too old for, and the mother smokes a cigarette. I freeze at the threshold, pretending to be disoriented. A stab of pain shoots through my pelvis; I pray that I will not wet myself.

"Mommy, that black lady is not coming to our toilets, is she?" The girl speaks around her thumb and it slurs her speech.

"No," the mother says as she drops the cigarette on the concrete and stamps on it. "She's not allowed in our bathroom and she knows that." The woman looks at me with a raised eyebrow.

They disappear through the doors and the little girl turns back to ensure that I stay outside. Once she is certain that I know my place, she smiles and waves with her free hand. I force myself to smile and wave back.

Five

BEAUTY

❁

I t takes another twenty-two hours, two buses and four taxi changes to get to Soweto. By the time we arrive, I have been in transit for more than two full days and have barely slept. I have worn the same clothes for the entire journey, and have not been able to find a place to wash myself or change my underwear. I stink not only from the smell of my own body, but also from the sweat of the many passengers who have been pressed up against me in close quarters.

When we turn off the highway from Johannesburg, my fatigue sharpens into curiosity. I have never been to Soweto, I have only heard about it in the tales of others and I am eager to see if it lives up to its reputation. On the Old Potchefstroom Road, we pass Baragwanath Hospital on our left. It is one of the biggest hospitals in Africa catering to the black population though the doctors are all said to be white. I would not like to discover firsthand the kind of care a white doctor would take with a black life in a country like this. I wonder if their oath to care for human life is stronger than their prejudice.

Once the hospital has disappeared behind us, I try to get a proper look out of the window next to me, but the breathing of too many people in the taxi has steamed it up. I clear a viewing hole on the fogged-up glass with the sleeve of my jersey and am surprised by the sea of humanity outside. I was told that Soweto was big but I never imagined it could be this sprawling. Logic, more than the tales I have heard, should have prepared me for the size.

Johannesburg is a huge city filled with hundreds of thousands of white people, and what white people need more than anything is black people to labor for them. What white people do not need, however, is to have those same black people living near them threatening their way of life. This is how the township of Soweto came to be in the first place. Close enough to the city so that the workers can commute there, but far enough away so that the white man does not have to smell the black man's stench. And as the demand for labor grows—as our villages are drained of men who head for the city to seek employment—so, too, does Soweto grow.

I have never seen so many of my own kind as here. The street is full of taxis, cars, buses and pedestrians, and all the faces are black. In between the chaos of cars trying to make their way down the street are donkey carts and cyclists, half-starved dogs and free-roaming livestock. A *bakkie* driving next to us is piled full of cages holding chickens. A single untethered pig sniffs the morning air from next to them.

Mothers weave through the traffic, babies tied to their backs with towels or blankets. Schoolchildren mingle with women in maids' uniforms. Men in overalls stop to talk to those in three-piece suits. Fires burn in braziers with *mielies* roasting atop them, and peddlers call out their wares for sale. Cinder-block houses sit wedged between hostels, and car washes flank churches, making me realize that the old saying is true: cleanliness really is next to godliness. Two huge cylinders rise up into the sky along an otherwise flat landscape; they are the cooling towers of the Orlando Power Station.

The noise is overwhelming. Gospel and kwela music are turned up loud and filter out of vehicles, dogs bark as they chase cars, hooters blare in both warning and greeting, voices call out in a babel of tongues and taxi drivers yell out their windows to attract passengers. It is an electric atmosphere that relaxes my neck and shoulder muscles. Despite the frenetic pace and the noise, I am back in the protection of my people and I feel safe.

That feeling lasts only as long as it takes to turn onto Klipspruit Valley Road and see the huge army trucks parked on the side of the road.

The taxi driver whistles an exclamation of surprise.

"Is this not a usual sight then?" I ask.

"No, *sisi*. Something bad must be happening."

We slow down. White men in army uniforms with big guns slung across their shoulders wave us past. A tremor of fear grips me as I recall Andile's words from his letter: *You must come immediately . . . Your daughter is in extreme danger and I fear for her life. I cannot guarantee her safety here . . .*

I pray that these army trucks are not linked in any way to the danger Nomsa is in.

When I look at my watch, I know that she will have already left for school. I have waited long enough to see my daughter and do not want to wait another full day until she returns home. Instead of getting dropped off at Andile's house, I instruct the taxi driver to go straight to the school. If I am lucky, I will see Nomsa before the bell rings for the first class. All I want is to hold my daughter and know she is safe.

When we jostle to a stop outside the Morris Isaacson High School, the gates are open; they gape like the toothless mouth of a sleeping *madala*, and the grounds are deserted except for a few startled-looking teachers who mill about uselessly, ants separated from their colony.

I approach one of them, a woman who looks to be my age, and say, "*Molo*." The rest of the customary greeting dies on my lips; she looks so worried that I cannot bear to waste time with pleasantries. "Where are the children, *sisi*?"

"*Andazi*. They have all left."

"They have left? For what reason?"

"They are all going on a march."

"They are protesting?"

The woman nods.

"What are they protesting against?"

"The new Afrikaans curriculum the government wants us to teach."

"And you do not know where the children are marching to?"

"No, but there are rumors that it is not just the children from this school that are protesting. We have heard that many thousands of students will join them."

Many thousands of students. I go cold with dread.

A man comes running up to us from a nearby group. His glasses glint in the morning light and his suit jacket flaps open. "There have been sightings of army trucks along the Klipspruit Valley Road."

The woman gasps. "Army trucks?"

He nods. "And police vans on the Soweto Highway. It is worse than we thought."

Before we can ask any questions, he jogs off to share his news with others.

Army trucks and police vans. This protest has attracted the attention of the military, and the white government and its soldiers are prepared to use great force against our children. My stomach clenches with fear and it mobilizes me. I clutch my suitcase and break into a run out of the gates.

Up ahead, stragglers head east along Mputhi Street. My legs are stiff and sore from the commute, and they cramp as I quicken my pace. Each step makes me feel much older than my forty-nine years, but I ignore the pain and keep moving.

I catch up and then overtake the students at the back of the march as I try making my way to the heart of the group. Someone bumps into me and almost sends me tumbling. I turn back to see a boy who cannot be older than ten years old.

He smiles as he rights himself, dimples sinking into his cheeks. "Sorry, Mother. I tripped." He indicates his shoelaces that have come undone and scampers off to the side to retie them while his friends laugh at his clumsiness.

Three girls ahead of me in skirts and stockings link arms and begin to skip. A group of boys in blazers and hats posture and wave their fists in the air. Their faces are shiny with expectation and their eyes flash with merriment. They may be fighting an adult's cause but they are still just children.

The air is cold. A chill bites at my bare hands as the weak winter sun struggles to penetrate the layer of smog that still hovers after last night's fires. Wood smoke lingers in the air; it is a smell that warns of the possibility of violence and death. I push myself from one group of children to the next and scan the older girls' faces for my Nomsa's features. My heart stutters with hope each time I spot Nomsa's profile: the proud jut of her chin or the high peak of her forehead, but it is never her. As my gaze jumps from face to face, the crowd swells and surges. I tighten my grip on my case.

We pass through Mofolo heading into Dube and the school uniforms start to vary in color and style. The teacher was right. Thousands of students from other schools have joined the march. I am borne along and nudged by children waving placards with slogans haphazardly scrawled across them: "To Hell with the Boer" and "Afrikaans Is Terrorism." I try to temper my annoyance that the boards obstruct my view of the sea of young faces and fight the urge to swat them out of my face.

I approach some of the older children who look to be Nomsa's age.

"My child, do you know Nomsa Mbali?"

"My child, can you tell me where we are going?"

I am either politely ignored or kindly told to leave.

"Mother, you are going to get hurt."

"You will be safer at home, Mother."

Eventually, it becomes too loud to be heard over the roar as the crowd breaks into song. The refrain *"Masibulele ku Jesu, Ngokuba wasi-fela"* washes over me, and my skin prickles and responds like a living thing with feelings of its own. Their youthful voices are fluid and their rapture flows through me. "Let us thank Jesus, for He died for us."

I used to sing this song to Nomsa when she was a baby. Please, God, please keep her safe. She has the heart of a lion, but even lions cannot stand up against the white man's guns.

When one song ends, a new voice rises up with the opening lines of another, and the crowd joins in to fill the silence: "Lord, bless Africa. May her spirit rise high up. Hear thou our prayers. Lord bless us."

I start to sing along. The resistance song is, after all, as much in my blood as it is in any of these youths'; even more so, as I have been singing "Nkosi Sikelel'iAfrika" since long before any of these children were born.

Then, suddenly, the forward motion of the crowd is halted and everyone lurches to a stop. Frustrated, I try to peer over the heads of the children in front of me, but the protest signs limit my view. I can hear shouting magnified through bullhorns, but cannot hear what instructions are being given; the sound is too distorted.

A tall boy next to me cranes his head over the crowd. *"Ke mapolisa."* It's the police, he reports.

Another boy who has climbed up on the shoulders of a friend calls down to us. *"Bazama ukusivimbha singafiki la esithe kuhlanganwa khona."* They've set up a barricade. They're trying to stop us getting to the assembly point.

"Ba batla regutlele morao." They want us to turn around.

The words are uttered in multiple languages. Even if I did not understand Zulu and Sotho, I would understand the angry tone. My breath catches as I spot two yellow-and-blue Casspirs. The presence of the dreaded armored trucks says more than any placard ever could.

Grumbles turn to shouts. The tension rises. Those who are coming from behind strain forward against the barrier of bodies in front of them; they are impatient to start moving again. I am caught in a rising tide. Violence is a muzzled brute walking among us, and it is just a matter of time before it is set loose.

A voice rings out. A boy in a school uniform stands on the bonnet of a car; he is one of us. He is composed and has a calming effect on the crowd as he gives a spirited address. "March in an orderly fashion. Do not provoke the police or give them reason to use violence against us."

Thank God someone is trying to keep this peaceful. Please let them listen to him.

The crowd starts to move again and they split into rivers that stream around the police barricade onwards towards Orlando West Junior Secondary School, which appears to be the meeting point. Thousands upon thousands of young faces blur around me. Any one of them could be Nomsa. None of them is Nomsa.

I just think I have caught sight of one of Andile's sons and am about to push through the crowd to get to him when we all turn sharply into Vilakazi Street. The energy level rises again. Children raise fists in the air and start shouting.

"*Inkululeko ngoku!*" Freedom now!

"*Amandla!*" Power!

We surge forward.

Then: a loud pop. Chanting turns to screaming. The air is stained with sour smoke. A canister bounces off a shoulder in front of me, skitters away. *Tear gas.* I try to shield my eyes and nose with my jersey, which I pull across my face. The tears stream down my cheeks and their salty bleakness makes me gag. I stumble blindly to get away from the streaming, poisonous can. Shoved from behind, I lurch forward and fall over other bodies and sprawl onto the road.

The last thing I hear before the world goes black is the sound of gunfire and the barking of dogs. The white man's silver bullets and black beasts have been set upon us. Only God can help us now.

When I awaken from the merciful darkness, I can no longer hear the baying of dogs or the asthmatic rattle of guns. Those sounds have died away, replaced by the requiem of children screaming. Terror and panic surround me; they wrap me in a blanket of knives. My eyes are open but I cannot see. I am still in danger and struggle to my feet but a hand on my shoulder pulls me back. A voice is talking to me, its tone is urgent, but I cannot make out the words amid the sounds of a beautiful morning ended in bloodshed.

I reach a hand up to wipe my eyes and my fingers come away wet and feeling strangely like the sticky sap of the *ikhala* leaf. This time, I use my whole forearm to wipe at my face and when I look at the sleeve of my jersey, it is stained red. With the blood from my eyes cleared, I can see again, though when the world comes into focus, I wish that I had remained blind.

I am not in the middle of the street where I fell. I have been dragged clear of the road to a patch of sand twenty meters away. The air is thick with smoke and people run through it in every direction trying to get out of the way of the policemen and their batons and beasts. The few who are not trying to escape surge forward with glass bottles and bricks. They fight back, their faces made hideous by rage.

Two sets of hands reach out, pulling me to my feet, and I look up to see if I am being rescued or arrested. The hands belong to Langa and Dumi, my brother's sons who are only thirteen and fifteen years old, and I thank the Lord for this deliverance. They are still trying to tell me something, but there is such a ringing in my ears that there is no hope of my being able to hear them.

Instead, I shout to be heard above the noise. "*Uphi uNomsa?*"

They cannot hear me. I pull Langa close and speak directly into his ear. "Where is Nomsa?"

He looks close to tears. *"Andazi."* I do not know.

He pulls at my arm again, wanting me to go with them, but I cannot turn my back on the vision of hell that has opened up before me. There is a river of blood in the street and the children are floating in it. They lie in unnatural shapes, limbs bent at awkward angles. Some of them are facedown, drowning, while others lie on their backs gazing up at the sky; they are human debris swept along in a flood of destruction.

Discarded shoes, placards, tear gas canisters, hats and bags are littered between the bodies. My suitcase, lying in the middle of all the carnage, looks like a relic from some bygone era; a time before it was acceptable for white armies to harvest black children's lives like crops. I note with detached interest that the case has split apart; my clothes are strewn across the road and one of my dresses is covered in blood. My bible lies open next to it, the soiled pages fluttering gaily in the dirty breeze.

Is God watching?

Dumi links his arm through mine while Langa pushes me from behind. I know they want to get me to a place of safety but I cannot leave. I pull away from my nephews and try to find my balance as I make my way towards the body that is lying closest to me.

It is a girl. Her school dress is torn and raised up over her buttocks so that her white cotton underwear is showing. I gently roll her over and pull the dress down to give back the dignity taken from her. Her eyes are open and she is staring fixedly up at the heavens. She no longer sees the blood and violence of this world, and for that, I am grateful. She is seeing a better place, one in which singing voices are not greeted with bullets; a world in which innocent children are not murdered because their skin is a color that white people find offensive. I touch her eyelids with my fingers, drawing them closed.

Rest, my child. Go with God.

From there, I keep moving from one body to the next. Some of the children are still alive; they are either too injured or too terrified to move. They clutch my hands and ask for their mothers. I tell them that their mothers are coming soon and that they are loved. I make the promises they want to hear, the ones I would want Nomsa to hear, and wipe the blood and the dirt and the tears from their faces. I ask names and bear witness.

Zanele. Twelve years old. She is bleeding from the ear.

Goodness. Her lips tremble and her tears are hot against my skin but she still manages a smile.

Kidebone. Fifteen years old. Her lips are shiny with Vaseline.

Jabu. Fourteen years old. He is the man of the house after his father died in a rockfall underground.

Fumani. Wonders if I am an angel.

Thandeka. Asks if I have seen her younger sister.

Sipho. Has never met his father.

Kleinboy. Says he is late for school.

Six

ROBIN

❈

16 JUNE 1976
Boksburg, Johannesburg, South Africa

I was in a tight race for first place, pedaling furiously. I knew I had the best bike in the neighborhood; no other set of wheels could measure up to my candy-apple-red Raleigh Chopper with its distinctive banana seat and monkey handlebars. All I had to do was prove that I deserved to be the one riding it.

My adversaries were neck and neck as we neared the finish line. I'd have to reach deep to find the energy to claim victory. I was already tired—the circuit had taken us around the neighborhood twice—but I refused to be beaten. There was no second place; there was only the first person who'd lost. I pumped my legs as hard as I could; they felt independent of my body, spinning like the arms of a windmill. The multicolored streamers attached to the handles fluttered in the breeze as I picked up speed, and the scent of burning rubber wafted up to greet me.

I pipped my closest rival at the post, winning by a hair's breadth, and the crowds went wild. I celebrated my victory by popping a triumphant wheelie and was nearly unseated by the patch of loose gravel beneath my tires. When the twenty-inch back wheel almost gave out from under me as the bike bucked like a startled horse, I lost my concentration and the ability to maintain the fantasy. The crowds and competitors all vanished and I made my way home alone at a slower pace.

Flecks of ash, like torched snow, began to drift down all around me. I realized that the smell I'd thought was burning rubber from my tires was actually the stink of a *veld* fire. They were common in winter when all the open land surrounding our suburb became dry and parched from the lack of rain, and a cigarette butt flicked from a car window could set it all alight in a few seconds. I sometimes worried about our houses—and our lives as we knew them—going up in smoke when the flames got too close, but my father assured me the fire trucks would put them out way before they reached us. The fire department even sometimes started the fires themselves to burn controlled breaks.

It was nearing 6 p.m. when I parked the Chopper in the garage and headed into the kitchen where I found Mabel ironing and listening to her "story." South Africa had finally lifted its ban on television that year, but we didn't have a TV set because my father said we weren't the Rockefellers. So we listened to programs on the radio though ours were very different from Mabel's. My favorite program, which was on at 7:30 p.m. every Friday, was "Squad Cars," a cracking series about detectives at the Brixton Murder and Robbery Squad who solved crimes no one else could.

The opening sequence made my pulse race: the wailing of a lone police siren, the slamming of brakes, rapid gunfire and the heralding of trumpets followed by Malcolm Gooding's deep voice intoning, "They prowl the empty streets at night . . . in fast cars and on foot . . . living with crime and violence . . . these are the men of 'Squad Cars.'" I tried to solve their cases as I listened, and was sure that if I could just get to the Brixton police station, they'd hire me as part of their elite squad.

I couldn't understand any of Mabel's stories because they were all in Sotho and sounded mostly like a lot of people fighting. When I asked her why black people shouted so much, she said they had a lot of reasons to be angry, but she wouldn't say why. When my own pestering made her start yelling, I took her at her word and dropped the subject.

I left Mabel to it and walked down the passage to my parents' bedroom. I didn't know where Cat was; she'd gone off in a sulk when I'd refused to give her a lift on my bike's sissy bar. (Cat refused to race on her own bike because she was scared of getting a scarf caught in the spokes and crashing and losing all her front teeth like a girl in our school had done. "Oh for heaven's sake," my mother had said, "you don't even own a scarf!" But Cat couldn't be swayed and would only go for rides as a passenger on mine. It slowed me down in the races so I wasn't always prepared to humor her.)

My father was pulling on a pair of shoes and sitting on their bed to do the laces up when I swung through the door. I caught the scent of Sunlight soap combined with the Johnson's baby powder he used on his feet to stop his rubber boots from chafing after hours of trudging up and down the underground stopes. My father always showered at the mine before coming home, shedding the layers of sweat and grime from a day spent with men before returning, clean and fragrant, to his household of females.

"Daddy!" I cannoned into him and he laughed.

"That's quite a tackle you've got there, Freckles. I think we have a rugby player in the family."

"Why are you getting dressed again?"

"Your mother and I have a function tonight."

I went into the bathroom where my mother was getting ready and greeted her with a hug before I pulled the lid of the toilet seat down to use as a chair. I loved watching my mother get "dolled up," as my father called it, though I didn't enjoy being left behind when they went to their functions.

"Hurry up, Jolene. Stop faffing around." My dad ducked around the bathroom door with a dark green tie, which he started knotting.

"I'm sorry, but two hours' notice is a bit ridiculous. If I'd known about this yesterday, I could have arranged to come home earlier."

"*Ja*, sorry about that. Hennie was supposed to go to represent the proto team, but he has gippo guts. He spent the whole day on the bog stinking up the place. The *okes* eventually told him to piss off home and clog up his own toilet instead."

"Sounds like he has the same stomach bug as Edith."

My mother was pumping a mascara wand in and out of the tube before applying another layer to her sticky lashes, and my dad stilled his own activity to stare at her. We were both mesmerized by how her mouth gaped in a large *O* whenever she carried out this ritual, and I sometimes discovered my own mouth to be open in unconscious mimicry.

My dad shook his head and smiled. "You look like a demented goldfish when you do that."

My mother closed the mascara and launched it at him, laughing when he pretended to be mortally wounded as it bounced off his chest. She undid the knot he'd made and pulled him close for a kiss. "Let me do this for you or else we'll be here all night."

He studied her face while she was distracted with the tie. "You look beautiful, Jo."

I squirmed with pleasure as I watched them be all lovey-dovey with each other for a change. My father wasn't lying; my mother was beautiful. She had wispy brown hair that fanned from her face like a dandelion, drawing attention to her arched eyebrows and high cheek-bones. Her large brown eyes contrasted with my father's blue ones, and although hers were pretty, I was glad that mine were like his. I also would have preferred his blond hair to the dark brown I got stuck with, but as they both frequently reminded me: life wasn't fair.

When she was done with the tie, my mother swatted him away,

bent to pick the mascara up off the floor and returned to the mirror. "You always say that no matter what I look like. Is this dress okay? Those women have already got a lot to say about my working and my delinquent daughter," she said as she shot me a rueful look. "I don't want to give them more to talk about."

"You look perfect. The dress is perfect. Can we go now?"

"Just give me a minute." She picked up a necklace from the counter, one with a delicate gold chain and a gleaming black onyx pendant, and clasped it around her graceful neck. "Where's Mabel?"

"She's in the kitchen finishing the ironing. I'll go tell her she needs to stay in."

Mabel's duties as our maid included cleaning the house, washing, ironing, cooking and taking care of us, duties she was expected to perform every day except on some weekends when she had a Sunday off. On weekdays, she'd fetch us from school and keep an eye on Cat and me until our parents came home from work. If they were going out and couldn't take us with, it was understood that Mabel would stay inside and look after us until they came home. I'd never heard my parents ask Mabel if she would be free; it was just presumed that she'd do it and wouldn't be paid extra for it.

As my father swung out of the bathroom, I hopped off the toilet seat and followed him down the passage, my *takkies* squeaking on the polished wood, towards the kitchen. A pot of water simmered unsupervised on the stove, and he pulled it off the element before he opened the back door and called, "Mabel?"

There was a faint reply, but I couldn't make out what she'd said. We stepped outside and headed for the maid's quarters, a tiny room with a separate toilet that was attached to the house but had its own entrance. I could make out the voice of the newsreader on Springbok Radio, coming from inside.

"—over twenty thousand black school pupils from Soweto high schools went on the rampage this morning, rioting and throwing stones at armed police forces. The riot began as a protest against the introduction of Afrikaans as the language of instruction in local schools. The angry mob attacked the police, and over—"

My father banged on the metal door and the commentary from the radio stopped abruptly. He pushed the door open and stepped into the threshold of Mabel's darkened room while I peeped around him. I made out her silhouette as she stood up from her single bed. She was tying her *doek* around her head as she slipped past us and pulled her door closed once we'd followed. I caught the faint scent of Vaseline and snuff that was so particular to Mabel.

"How many times must I tell you not to leave food cooking on the stove when you're in your room? If it's not the oven, it's the iron left on. You burn my house down, Mabel, and you see what I do to you."

"Yes, *baas*. Sorry, *baas*."

"Don't 'yes-*baas*-sorry-*baas*' me! Listen to me the first time when I speak to you. You're worse than a child."

Mabel pulled the pot back onto the element, switched it on and reached for the packet of Iwisa from under the kitchen sink. The white maize meal was the staple of her diet. She ate it with a tomato-and-onion gravy, and a vegetable dish called *morogo* that came from wild spinach picked in the neighborhood, but she'd make mine with sugar and butter when I asked for some.

"I heard you were listening to the radio now. Did you hear what those *kaffir* kids did today in Soweto? Running around, throwing rocks at the police, necklacing innocent people, starting fires—"

"Why were they giving necklaces to people?" I asked. My father ignored my question so I tried again. "Giving necklaces is a nice thing to do, isn't it?"

"Robin, 'necklacing' means they put a car tire over your neck and then set it alight so you burn to death. It isn't a nice thing."

"*Baas*," Mabel said before I could ask why anyone would do something so horrible, "the march was peaceful and then the police, they come and they shoot at the children." She spoke to the pot as she added the white Iwisa powder to the boiling water and reached for the wooden spoon.

Mention of the police gave me a fluttery feeling in my stomach because when Cat and I were younger, Mabel would sometimes tell us she was phoning them to come get us when we misbehaved. This was her only way of enforcing any discipline; she wasn't allowed to smack or punish us in any way no matter what we did and we knew it.

The thought of cops shooting at children made me nervous, but before I could ask my father if the police would come to Boksburg to shoot us as well, my father raised his voice in reply. "They're lucky they even have schools, which is where they should have been this morning instead of in the streets looking for shit."

My mother clattered into the kitchen on a pair of strappy heels, shrugged into a coat and dropped her lipstick into her handbag. "Who was looking for shit?"

"Those coon kids rioting today. Twelve- and thirteen-year-olds went on the rampage in Soweto. They've had to call the bloody army in with tanks and everything because of the little savages. Didn't you hear the helicopters overhead from your office?"

"No, the typing pool makes such a racket, you can't hear a thing. What about the mine? Are you guys safe there underground with all those miners? What is there? Like one white guy to every hundred blacks?"

My dad started answering but was drowned out by Mabel hitting the wooden spoon against the pot to dislodge the sticky *pap*. He nudged her arm to still the activity. "They said we've got nothing to worry about, but the mine security will be stepped up from tomorrow just to be on the safe side. These bastards will just as soon slit your throat as look at you."

Mabel jerked the pot from the stove and turned the heat down.

"Well, can you blame them?" my mother asked.

My father shot her one of his dirty looks and waited for Mabel to leave the room. "You sound just like your bleeding-heart sister. Today was a big fucking deal, Jolene. Word is they've never seen an uprising like this before. The blacks are getting cheekier by the day, and the government is finding it harder and harder to control them. Today will just get the rest of them riled up. Do you want to live in a country with all the *kaffir*s running loose, doing whatever the hell they want, feeling like they're entitled to help themselves? Soweto is only fifty kilometers away from here. That's nothing!"

Cat had come out of our room, probably drawn by my father's raised voice, and was standing next to me. She tugged at my elbow, though it wasn't necessary; I already knew what she was thinking. Cat got scared when my father spoke this way. She worried that a black man would slip into our house one night and kill us or, even worse, take us away for some unspeakable purpose. From what my father and Piet's father said, it was clear that the blacks were dangerous, though Mabel wasn't that scary. I'd told Cat it was probably just the black men who were evil, not all blacks, and so she lived in constant fear of them; though to be fair, she lived in fear of almost everything.

"I don't want you to go tonight. Please don't."

"You'll be fine here with Mabel, don't worry."

"But Cat's scared."

My mother sighed. "Cat's scared or you're scared and you're just putting words in her mouth?"

I glared at Cat wishing she'd speak up for herself. "She's scared."

"What of?"

When Cat still remained resolutely silent, staring at her feet rather than at our mother, I spoke on her behalf. "She's scared of the *veld* fire. What happens if it gets near the house?"

"I passed it on my way home. It's just a small one and it's way over by the main road. The fire trucks were already there putting it out."

"She's also scared that you won't come back."

My mother laughed. "Don't be silly, of course we'll come back."

"You promise?" Cat and I asked at the same time.

"I promise."

I already knew that when the time came to go to bed, Cat would go through the motions of pretending to sleep in our room. She'd climb into her bed, wish me a good night and switch out the light, but just as soon as she thought I was asleep, she'd sneak off to our parents' room where she'd climb into their big bed. That was the only place she felt safe when they were gone, and that way when they came back, she'd be the first to know.

My mother bent down to hug us good-bye. She wore Charlie perfume and despite my need for assurance, the floral scent was overpowering and I struggled to pull away. She picked the car keys up from the kitchen counter and tossed them to my father.

My mother turned to Mabel. "We'll probably be home close to midnight, so just sleep on the floor in the lounge if you get tired."

I watched as my father ushered my mother out the door, his hand on her elbow. He blew us kisses and then turned to Mabel. "Lock all the doors, Mabel. This fucking country has gone mad today."

It was the last thing I ever heard him say.

Seven

ROBIN

❁

16 JUNE 1976
Boksburg, Johannesburg, South Africa

The pounding on the door started up just before midnight. I jolted awake, alone; as expected, Cat had snuck off to our parents' room as soon as I'd fallen asleep. I tiptoed to my bedroom door and peeked out to see Mabel standing frozen in the lounge.

"*Maak die deur oop!*" Open the door!

Bang, bang, bang.

It's the firemen coming to save us. The veld *fire's reached the house and they've come to get us out.*

Before I could voice this thought to Mabel, the shouting started up again, this time in heavily accented English. "It's the police. We know you're in there. Let us in."

Mabel beckoned me with a trembling hand and I rushed to her side. The police didn't come for fires. She pulled me in tightly against her and I wrapped my arms around her hips. We shuffled to the door, which Mabel unlocked and opened, and then stepped back to let the men inside. I peeked around Mabel and saw police vans in the street.

Their flashing lights lit up our yard and the surrounding houses like a disco ball, making the familiar suburban landscape oddly festive.

The two policemen loomed in the entrance hall; they wore the distinct blue South African Police uniforms and their guns were holstered at their sides. One of them was tall and thin with tightly cropped red hair and a beard that covered most of his face and neck. His partner was older with darker features, and he wore his blue cap pulled low over his forehead. It cast a deep shadow over his face while the gold badge above the peak glinted when it caught the light.

The tall redhead was the more aggressive of the two and he did most of the talking. "Why don't you make the door open when you see the police?"

"Sorry, *baas*." Mabel's voice was a tightrope on which her quavering words struggled to find purchase.

"What are you doing in this house? You sleep here?"

"No, *baas*. The madam and the *baas* have gone out, and I am staying in here to watch the child."

"Come, we're taking you to the police station."

"You cannot leave this child alone, *baas*."

His voice rose with impatience. "She'll come with us."

"But the madam and the *baas*, they will be worried when they come home and see she is not here."

"The madam and the *baas* aren't coming home," he snapped. He had no patience with Mabel answering him back; he was clearly a man who was used to being obeyed.

"Why, *baas*? Where are they?"

"Who do you think you are talking to, *kaffir meid*, huh? I ask the questions here, not you." He jabbed his finger at Mabel's nose, and she flinched as his spittle landed on her cheek though she did not make a move to wipe it off. The policeman stepped forward and stared her down. Mabel did not step back or look away. He wanted to intimidate her and she would not be cowed.

Don't do that, Mabel, I thought. *He wants you to be scared. Show him that you're scared.*

Their eyes remained locked, neither of them prepared to be the first to look away, and I spoke to divert their attention, and also because I couldn't keep the questions in any longer. "Where are my mommy and daddy? Are we going to meet them?"

The other policeman spoke to me in a softer tone. "Just come now." He reached out for my hand, but Mabel stepped back and pulled me with her.

"You are not taking this child."

The backhanded slap connected with the side of Mabel's head, and her jaw snapped shut as she stumbled back against me. I couldn't stop her fall and she crumpled to the floor, hitting her head against the polished wood. She lay there for a few seconds, whimpering and dazed, and then eased herself up on her elbows.

"Get up," the man instructed but Mabel didn't move.

I reached down and tried to pull her up, but she was a deadweight who wasn't yielding to my efforts.

"Get up now!" the policeman barked again.

There was no way I could move Mabel by force or protect her using my body; I was too small and too weak. Still I tugged at her.

Please, Mabel. Help me. Get up!

I was just beginning to panic when my mother's voice came to me, cutting through my fog of terror and calming me.

Stop dwelling on the negative. Try to think up solutions, she instructed.

It occurred to me that if I couldn't move Mabel with my might then perhaps I could move her with my words. Dropping to my haunches, I whispered into her ear. "Come, Mabel. Please stand up. Please. Let's just go. It's fine. We'll go together. Mommy and Daddy will find us."

Mabel looked at me blankly for a moment and then her expression cleared. She nodded and struggled to her feet, and I slipped my hand into hers. The policeman frowned at the sight of our fingers entwined like that.

"Where are my mommy and daddy?" I asked again. "I want them."

"You can't have them," the redheaded policeman spat. "Do you know why?"

I shook my head.

He nodded at Mabel. "Ask your friend why. She'll tell you."

Mabel squeezed my hand. I looked at her and waited for her to say something but she didn't. She only squeezed harder.

"You can't have them because the black bastards slit their throats from ear to ear leaving them almost headless like chickens," the policeman said. "Your mother and father are dead."

Eight

ROBIN

❀

17 JUNE 1976
Brixton, Johannesburg, South Africa

C*at!*
      As we were being shoved into the back of a police van, I finally thought of my sister. I hadn't forgotten her; it's just that with everything else happening, she hadn't been foremost in my mind.

"Mabel," I whispered. "What about Cat?"

She blinked but didn't say anything; her eyes were open but she looked like a sleepwalker.

"Cat was sleeping in Mom and Dad's bed. We need to go back and—"

"No." Her voice was a desert landscape, flat and desolate.

"But we need to tell them—"

"No," she repeated, more emphatic that time.

"But—"

"I said no!"

It was the first time I'd ever seen Mabel lose her temper. Over the six years she'd worked for us, I'd sometimes seen her annoyed, flustered and impatient, but I'd never seen her truly angry.

"You must not speak of her to these men. Do you hear me?" Her eyes glowed with fervor as she glared at me. There was something feral about her expression, something I didn't dare challenge, and so I just nodded.

"You must not speak of her!" she repeated and I nodded again. If Mabel thought Cat was safer at home, then that's where we'd leave her.

Your mother and father are dead. The policeman's words nicked at my consciousness like a tiny blade.

It can't be true, it just can't. He has to be confused or lying, I thought desperately.

All I knew of death was that it was a mysterious force that came for baby birds and hamsters and people like my Ouma. Dying was what happened to the sick or the weak or the old, and my parents were none of those things; they were young and strong and healthy.

They have to still be at their party. There's been a mix-up, that's all.

My dad was a joker who'd do almost anything for a laugh, although people didn't always get that he was kidding around. My mom often said that not everyone understood his weird sense of humor, and the policemen didn't look like people who enjoyed laughing. They just didn't understand whatever prank it was my father had pulled.

Of course they're not dead. Of course not.

It was a ludicrous thought and even entertaining it was disloyal. So I shook the evil notion from my mind and looked around the van's cabin instead. Two benches ran the length of the space, facing each other, and I sat on one and Mabel sat across from me. The metal of the seat was cold under my pajamaed thighs. Crisscrossing metal grates that looked like *braai* grills covered the glass of the side windows and back door. There was a cage between where we sat and the front-seat cabin where the driver was, and as I slid up to it, something stirred inside.

It was a dog, an Alsatian by the looks of it, and as it got to its feet, my spirits rose with it. I loved dogs but hadn't been allowed to get one of my own. I reached out to try to pat it.

"No," Mabel cautioned as she swatted my hand away from the cage.

She was almost too late. I'd already managed to fit two fingers through the metal bars and the dog was quick to react. It lunged just as I snatched my hand back and its hot breath sliced against my wrist. The dog started barking viciously, and I backed away from the cage just as the redheaded policeman banged on the partition from the front.

The van rumbled to life, the floor rattling beneath my feet, and we pulled off with a lurch. There was no light in the back, just the sweeping arcs of streetlights as we passed under them, and with each splash of light that fell on Mabel, the swelling on her face got worse. We were jostled around on our seats each time we hit a rut in the road, and I crossed over to sit next to Mabel so we could lean against each other for support and so I wouldn't have to look at her.

I looked out of the window instead and saw what appeared to be thousands of tiny red eyes staring at me from the darkness. It took a second to realize they were the dying embers of the *veld* fire. My mother had been right: the fire had been far enough away from us to not be a threat and the fire trucks had gotten it under control.

After another few minutes, I noticed that we'd passed the turnoff we should have taken for the Boksburg Police Station.

Where are they taking us?

The question had barely formed in my mind when the one cop radioed in that we were en route to Brixton.

Brixton! The Murder and Robbery Squad. They're taking us to the "Squad Cars" team.

Mabel started trembling. I could feel the vibration of it against my shoulder, and I thought she must be cold. I huddled up against her to warm her with my body.

"Don't worry," I whispered. "The 'Squad Cars' team will find Mommy and Daddy. Everything's going to be fine."

Mabel, though, did worry because she knew something that I didn't. She'd heard the rumors about the station that was notorious for its torture of blacks, and probably sensed in that moment what lay ahead for her in the long hours before dawn. She didn't stop trembling all the way there.

L ater, I wasn't sure how much time had passed, we arrived at the station and entered a large open room that stank of cigarettes. The tall cop pulled Mabel aside and took her away as soon as we arrived, while his partner led me to a long wooden bench.

"Sit here and wait for me, okay?"

"Okay." I sat on the bench as instructed, my legs dangling above the green linoleum floor. He hitched his navy pants and squatted so we were at the same eye level.

"Where are you taking Mabel?" I asked.

"We are just going to ask her a few questions."

"Can I go with her?"

"No, you must not move from here, all right?"

"All right."

"Not even a few steps. You must stay right here."

I nodded that I understood and he patted my head and then stood to go, but hesitated before turning back again. "I know you feel very alone right now, but I want you to know that you don't need to because your parents are here with you."

His words confirmed what I'd been thinking.

Mommy and Daddy are here! The "Squad Cars" team solved the mystery of what really happened to them and now we're all going to be together for the closing credits of the show.

I craned my neck as my eyes darted around the room.

The policeman must have realized his mistake because he quickly added an amendment. "What I mean is, your parents are now in heaven, with God, and they are looking down on you and watching over you. You will never be alone because they will be with you. Always."

"But where are the 'Squad Cars' team?"

"Who?"

"The guys from the radio? The crack team of detectives who work here?"

His confused frown turned to a smile. "*Ag*, no, man. That is just made up. Those guys do not exist in real life. They are just actors who pretend to be detectives." And with a wave, he was gone.

The safety net of denial I'd built for myself was slowly unraveling, but still I refused to harbor the thought that the policemen were right about my parents. My entire relationship with my mother and father was built on the faith—the unquestioning, all-consuming, unwavering faith—that they were infallible.

If they truly always knew what was best, if they could drive and have jobs and drink alcohol and smoke cigarettes, if they could come and go as they pleased without asking for permission, if they could make hundreds of decisions about my life and their lives and only ever have to justify themselves with "because I said so," then I had to believe them worthy of that exalted position. Without blind faith, the whole illusion of the child-parent relationship fell apart, because what is a parent more essentially than a child's God? I would not lose faith in my Gods. And so, I waited for them to come get me.

Every now and again, a door opened somewhere and the sounds of metal clanging, angry shouting and pitiful crying escaped. Sometime later, the kind officer brought me a blanket when he came back to check on me. Dozens of black people were brought into the waiting area throughout the early hours of the morning and were pushed through the same doors Mabel had disappeared behind. Many of them looked like teenagers and most were bleeding or injured in some way.

One girl was wearing only a bra and panties covered by a long-sleeved man's shirt. The buttons were all ripped off and the shirt only came to mid-thigh; she had her arms crossed over her chest and was shaking. When I leaned over and held out my blanket to her, she looked at me wildly like a rabid dog I'd once seen at a garbage dump. Despite the cold, a sheen of sweat coated her skin and she gleamed in the fluorescent lighting. A whitish blemish, either a burn mark or a birthmark, spread out from below her lips, down her chin and disappeared below the shirt's collar. She smelled bad, like sweat and smoke, and I had to wave the blanket in front of her for a few seconds before she understood my intention. She snatched it from me. Within seconds, she'd wrapped it around herself to fashion a dress and then she was led away.

Another hour passed.

Has Cat woken up yet? I wondered. *Does she know she's all alone in the house? Is she scared? Maybe Mommy and Daddy are at home with her. When are they going to let Mabel out?*

I was desperate to wee, but I'd been told not to move from the bench. *I'm not a child anymore. My age is almost in double digits. I can hold it in.*

But I couldn't and a wet warmth seeped across the bench as the acidic smell of urine saturated the air. I flushed with shame. As my wee dripped down the bench and pooled under my feet, my aunt Edith turned the corner. She was running and out of breath, frantic as she searched through the crowd. When she didn't see me, she turned to retrace her steps.

My voice was shrill as I called out to her, "Edith!"

She turned back and her face was pale and pinched with anxiety. She shoved her way through the throng of people, and when she reached me, she collapsed on my bench and clasped me to her chest.

Edith is here. She's here and everything is going to be okay.

When she finally let me go, I searched her face for answers. If there was one person I could count on to not lie to me, it was Edith. I opened my mouth to ask the question, but then I closed it again because I could see no questions were necessary. The truth was there in her tear-puffed eyes and her swollen nose. It was there in the bleakness of her gaze and the grayness of her skin. She did not wear her despair well, and all of a sudden, I didn't want to hear it. A few seconds ago, all I'd wanted was the truth, but in that moment, I knew I couldn't bear it.

I started to babble. "Edith, we need to go get Cat."

"What?"

"Cat was sleeping in Mommy and Daddy's bed. She was asleep when the policemen came and she didn't wake up and I wanted to tell them to bring her but—"

"Robin—"

"She's there all alone and we need to go get her—"

"Robs, honey—"

Don't tell me Mommy and Daddy are dead. "She'll be scared. You know how she is." *Don't tell me Mommy and Daddy are dead.* "She'll be really, really scared and she shouldn't be alone and we have to go get her. Now! Right now. We have to get her. Let's go! Cat will be wondering where we—"

"Robin," Edith shouted as she gripped my shoulders to steady me. "Cat isn't real," she cried. "Cat isn't real, you know she isn't real. Your sister isn't real."

No, of course she wasn't.

Nine

BEAUTY

❀

Sunrise struggles to penetrate the haze of smoke that has settled over us like a collective sadness. I sit outside on an old tree stump in Andile's patch of yard and greet the day. It is a ritual I have undertaken every dawn since I can remember; it helps me forget now that I am wearing borrowed clothes in a foreign city and that my child is missing.

"*Molo, sisi.*"

Andile stands behind me holding two mugs. Steam rises into the cold morning air obscuring his face. When it clears, I can see from the pouches under his eyes that he has slept as little as I have.

"I brought you tea. Three sugars, the way I like it. I hope you like it that way too."

Of course my brother does not know how many sugars I take because men do not serve women in our culture. The kindness of the unfamiliar gesture, and his awkwardness in carrying it out, make me want to cry. He hands the mug across and puts his own on the ground before going back inside. He returns after a few moments carrying a rusting white garden chair, which he sets down beside me. "You sit here. The tree stump is my chair."

It is another kindness, but he tries to disguise it as staking his claim on what is his. I know that thanking him will only embarrass him and so I say nothing. We exchange places and I wrap my hands around the tin mug. Its heat is a balm. My fingers regain feeling, and when I take a sip, the warmth seeps through me settling into my stomach. Its sweetness gives me strength.

This is the first time Andile and I have had a moment alone together to have a proper conversation. Yesterday was spent in constant motion with us all splitting up to look for Nomsa. We were certain we would find her; it was just a matter of looking in the right place. I searched at the schools and gathering points where the children had retreated once the violence broke out. Andile and the boys went to the homes of Nomsa's friends and classmates. Lindiwe, Andile's wife, searched the hospitals and clinics.

At first, I put the same question to every child I encountered. "Do you know Nomsa Mbali?"

I expected to repeat the question many dozens of times before I might get one affirmative answer, but I was surprised by how many of the children nodded.

"Yes, I know Nomsa."

"The Nomsa Mbali who goes to Morris Isaacson? She is seventeen years old."

"Yes, Mother."

"Do you know where she is now?"

They shook their heads and returned to their conversations.

I tried a different question with the next children I asked. "When last did you see her?"

A girl furrowed her brow as she thought about it. "I saw her this morning, Mother. She was handing out placards to some of the students to carry."

"And after that?"

"She was one of the first people out of the gate after the bell rang for assembly and we all followed. I did not see her after Mputhi Street once the children from the other schools joined us."

After hours of searching and asking, I found many other children who relayed similar accounts of the morning, but I could not find anyone who had seen Nomsa after the confrontation with the police. It was hours after dark when I stopped my frantic movement and forced myself to be still and think. I had been so focused on finding Nomsa that it had not occurred to me that she might be at Andile's house waiting for me.

Of course, I thought, *that is where she is. They have found her and she is waiting there.*

It took an hour of walking to get to Andile's house, and when I opened the gate, the boys ran out to greet me.

"Is she here? Did you find her?" I pushed past them and rushed inside, searching the faces for my daughter's features. When the hope drained from Andile's face, I knew. They had not found her. They had waited for my return, hoping that I would bring Nomsa with me.

I collapsed then, drained of all hope and strength, and Andile rushed to steady me. Lindiwe bathed me with cold water as I sat, paralyzed by anxiety, on my mattress. I prayed as she wiped the encrusted blood from my face. I prayed still as she removed the filthy, torn clothes from my body and pulled her own cotton nightgown over my head, raising my arms and guiding them through the holes as if I were a child. The bitter tea she brewed helped ease me into a deep, dreamless sleep so that I was able to find oblivion for a few hours.

Now, I am stronger. I am ready. "Tell me," I say. "Tell me everything."

Andile clears his throat. "A few weeks ago, Langa came to me. He said he was worried about something and he needed to speak to me in confidence."

I nod for him to continue.

"Nomsa had invited him to a Soweto Students' Representative Council meeting where he heard about a protest they were planning. She swore him to secrecy, but when he heard how many children would be involved, he began to worry. He knew that any march of that size would attract the attention of the police."

"The Students' Council? Is Nomsa a member of that?"

Andile frowns. "You did not know?"

"No. When she begged me to let her come here for her final year of study, I made her promise she would not get involved in politics or any of these organizations. She promised."

"But she wrote you letters every month. She did not tell you then?"

"No, she told me she was studying hard and enjoying school." His frown deepens at my reply. "Are you telling me, *bhuti*, that she was lying?"

Andile sighs and rubs his chin. "Nomsa said she told you about it and that you had given her permission."

"So she was lying to me. She was a member of this council?"

Andile shakes his head. "Not just a member, *sisi*, but one of the leaders who arranged the march. One of the main organizers."

His words settle like stones on my chest. Yesterday, all the children seemed to know who Nomsa was, and the young girl's words ring in my mind: *She was one of the first people out of the gate after the bell rang for assembly and we all followed.* I thought it was bad luck that Nomsa was at the front of the group, but it was not bad luck, it was by design. She was leading.

"What happened then?" I ask.

"Langa tried to speak to Nomsa about his concerns of the dangers involved, but she called him a coward and told him she was embarrassed to be related to him. She would not allow him to come back to the meetings or tell him anything more. When he started to hear rumors at the school, he came to me again and then I spoke to her."

"What did she say?"

"She did not deny that they were planning something, but she would not tell me the details. She was defiant and that is when I wrote to you. I had to take care with my wording in case the security police intercepted the letter. You can never be too careful."

Defiant. The word echoes in my ears and I burn with shame to think that my daughter would disrespect her uncle and guardian in this way.

"The night before the march on Tuesday," Andile continues, "Lindiwe overheard a conversation between Nomsa and a friend of hers, Phumla Ndlovu, and understood from that the march would take place the next day. That is why Lindiwe and I did not go to work yesterday. We stayed home in case Langa was right and the children were in danger, but Nomsa got dressed for school in her uniform like it was a normal day. She said she had a test to write and was determined to do well, so we let her go. We did not think they would leave for the march after going to school first. We thought Lindiwe had misunderstood." Andile hangs his head.

I know from speaking to teachers and other parents that most elders did not know what was planned. Before the sun even rose yesterday, they had stood in lines for the green Putco buses that would take them to their jobs in the city, away from the march, and also away from any chance of protecting their children. By the time they heard what was happening and had fought their way home, the acrid smoke was blanketing the horizon and hundreds of children were already dead.

"I have let you down, *sisi.*" Andile's voice is raw with emotion. "I promised to look after your child and take care of her and I have failed you." His voice breaks. "If anything has happened to her, I will never forgive myself."

Ten

ROBIN

❦

17 JUNE 1976
Boksburg, Johannesburg, South Africa

When I was six years old and spying on the grown-ups, I eaves-dropped on a conversation I should never have heard, and in that moment of my shame, my twin sister, Cat, was born.

I knew she was a figment of my imagination. I didn't actually see her standing there as I would a real person; it wasn't as if I was hallu-cinating. On the contrary, it took a lot of time and practice to conjure her into life; creating her took a great deal of effort.

For the first while, mirrors were essential to her survival. Cat was my reflection and that was where she lived, confined to the looking glass. I would go there to find her, and we would have long conversa-tions that ended abruptly when I was forced to turn away. Soon though, any reflective surface was enough. If I could catch a glimpse of myself in a window or a pool of water or on a newly waxed wooden floor, then I could see Cat. In this way, she followed me out of the mirror and into the world.

My parents humored me at first. My father said it was the sign of a creative mind and that he'd spoken to his dog all the time when he was a child.

"It's wonderful to have two of these faces running around," he said as he pinched my nose. "You know how much I love your freckles."

That was the day Cat's complexion miraculously cleared up, not a freckle to be found. My face remained beloved, while Cat's became a blank slate.

We were each defined by the other: when I wanted to cry, Cat shed my tears; when I had to be brave, Cat became a coward; when I did something wrong, Cat took the blame. It wasn't long at all before my parents grew tired of tedious Cat and I became the favorite. You can't be the preferred child when there's only one of you, and so Cat served her purpose; just as she would've in that moment at the police station if Edith had only let her.

"Robs, Cat isn't real," Edith cried. She shook me as though trying to shake some sense into me. "Why do you keep pretending she is?"

It was a good question but one I couldn't answer, not then and certainly not for many years until I finally understood how fractured I'd become in my quest to be lovable. In trying to be everything each of my parents wanted me to be, I dissected myself to excise the parts that weren't acceptable. I sloughed off bits of myself—the gangrenous, unlovable aspects of my personality—and like Frankenstein, I built a monster.

But I didn't have the language then to explain that to Edith, and since she wouldn't let me use Cat as the shield she was, I steeled myself instead to deal with what couldn't be put off any longer.

"Mommy and Daddy are dead." I uttered the words as matter-of-factly as I could, testing the weight of them.

Edith took my hands and bent her head, a tear dripping onto me as she nodded.

"Black people slit their throats," I said.

Edith's head snapped up. Her eyes were red, as red as her nose, which leaked unattractively. She pulled a crumpled tissue from her pocket and dabbed at her nostrils. "Christ. Who told you that?"

"The policeman," I said.

"Oh, Robs, I'm so sorry. I didn't want you to find out that way. What else did he say?"

"He said 'Squad Cars' isn't real."

Edith grimaced. She knew how much I loved the program as I'd made her listen to it every weekend she'd ever visited.

"Is Mabel dead too?"

"No, she isn't," Edith said. "She's here somewhere and we're going to find her."

I would find out later that Edith was meant to be headed to China that day and was scheduled to be away for more than two weeks. The virulent stomach bug that she'd called my mother about had forced her to book off sick and the airline had replaced her. I tried not to think about what might have happened if the police hadn't gotten hold of Edith that morning, and how long they would have kept me there. Or what they would have done to Mabel.

Edith opened her handbag and pulled a wad of pastel-colored tissues from it. She plucked out a few for herself and then tried handing me one. I shook my head and left it in her hand. Edith looked at the tissue and then looked at me. She seemed to see me, properly see me, for the first time since she'd arrived.

"Robs, I know it's been a terrible night, you must have been frightened out of your mind, but I'm here now. You don't have to be strong anymore."

Edith's empathy tugged at the knot of sadness that had been building in my throat until it had formed a lump of emotion so huge, it made it difficult to swallow. The adrenaline had petered out, the shock dissipating with it, and I was left feeling hollow. My parents truly were dead. There hadn't been a misunderstanding and it wasn't some kind of sick joke. The thought closed up my windpipe and made it difficult to breathe. Tears began to sting my eyes and I waited for the release they would bring, but with them came the memory of what the policeman had said.

"Edith?"

"Yes, kiddo?"

"Is it true that Mommy and Daddy are in heaven and that they're watching over me and that they're with me all the time?"

Edith paused for a second and I could see her thinking things over. After a moment, she nodded. "Yes, absolutely."

My parents are watching me. They can see me now just as they always could. And then something alarming occurred to me. *Now there is nowhere to hide.*

Before, when I couldn't stop the tears from falling, I'd run to my room so I could cry where my mother couldn't see me. That wasn't an option anymore. *Mommy can see me all the time so I can't be a crybaby anymore.* It was the first time I'd ever envied Cat her invisibility.

Edith checked me to see if I'd need the tissue after all but I remained resolutely dry-eyed.

"I want Mabel," I said.

Edith nodded. "Then you shall have her."

Mabel was shoved into the waiting room an hour later, after Edith threatened the station captain that she would contact the *Rand Daily Mail* to give an interview about their officers' treatment of me. We didn't have much time to register Mabel's appearance as we hurried outside, wincing in the face of the harsh winter sunlight. Once we were far enough away from the station to feel safe, Edith slowed and came to a stop in the parking lot. We turned to look at Mabel. I gasped at the sight of her. She looked even worse than the night before.

Mabel's right eye was swollen closed and would have been a vivid purple if her skin had been white. Her nose was crusted with blood and her lip was split and puffy. What startled me most was the sight of Mabel's hair, something I'd never seen before as it was always covered with a tightly woven *doek*. It was mostly braided into cornrows but a few tufts had been pulled loose and stood up haphazardly.

Edith dropped the cigarette she'd been about to light and reached for Mabel's face, but Mabel flinched and backed away from her touch. The one bloodshot eye that was functioning darted around the parking lot.

"Oh my God, Mabel, what happened to you?"

Mabel wasn't listening. She was taking in her surroundings and looked heartened by the number of black people milling around the parking lot.

"Come, Mabel, I'll take you to the hospital. We need to have a doctor look at you."

Mabel shook her head and cringed. The movement caused her pain.

"You're hurt. I don't know what those bastards did to you, but we need to get you treated."

"No," she rasped. "No."

Edith flung up her arms in despair. "So what do you want to do?"

"I am going home. To my homeland."

"Your homeland? Where is that?"

"QwaQwa."

I normally delighted in the explosive clicks of the Sotho language. Mabel could make certain words sound like a champagne cork erupting from a bottle, and though I often tried to imitate her, my tongue was lazy and disobedient. This time, the sound of her uttering the name of her homeland, speaking in the dialect of her people, elicited nothing positive, only a nameless dread.

"That's way too far for you to travel in this state." Edith looked like she wanted to argue more, but could see that it was hopeless. Mabel had made up her mind and there would be no stopping her.

Before any further words could be uttered, I stepped forward to hug Mabel. I raised my arms, wanting to wrap them around her waist so she could pull me up against the sturdy, reassuring warmth of her, but she stepped back outside of my reach. I looked up at her, surprised. I could see by her vacant expression that something had changed between us during those long, lonely hours as night turned into day.

Mabel was the one who always knew how to fix my pain, and I'd never been in so much pain in my life. Each time I pictured my parents' necks slit, the blood gushing from them, I wanted to be dead too. And if I couldn't be dead, then the only person who could take my misery away was Mabel.

I reached out to her again, lunging before she could step away, and I wrapped my arms around her hips as tightly as I could. I inhaled the familiar, comforting scents—Vaseline, tobacco, soap and onions—but there were other smells too, new ones overlaying the old ones, the offensive tang of fear and sweat. Mabel reached her arms around her back to unclasp my grip, but I held on tighter. I needed her to tend to my wounds. I needed her to kiss it all better.

Instead, she yanked at my arms and, in doing so, twisted the skin of my wrists; it hurt and forced me to loosen my grip. It was the first time Mabel had ever caused me pain. Within a few seconds, she was out of my grasp and looking around wildly for an escape.

"Mabel." I knew what was about to happen. "Mabel, please don't go."

She turned and looked in the other direction, searching the crowd.

"Mabel." Her name snagged on the despair gathering in my throat and I fought to hold the tears back. "Please don't leave me."

Edith tried to pull me to her, but I yanked away.

As Mabel turned, I tried again, a desperate plea to keep her bound to me. "I love you, Mabel. Please. I need you."

Without looking back, Mabel headed for the throng of people who were scattering out of the way of the police van pulling into the parking lot. In no time at all, she was absorbed by the crowd, enfolded by her people and pulled into their midst. I watched helplessly as she, too, disappeared from my life.

Eleven

ROBIN

❀

17 JUNE 1976
Yeoville, Johannesburg, South Africa

Edith lived on the eleventh floor of a high-rise in Yeoville, a central suburb in the city of Johannesburg, and though the building was old and shabby from the outside, it had an air of quiet nobility to it. Weathered and proud, it stood like a matriarch watching over the younger blocks of flats, as well as the comings and goings of the neighborhood's inhabitants. The building, named Coral Mansions by someone with severe delusions of grandeur, shared its block of land with a leafy park on one side and a small grocery store on the other.

It was the first time I'd ever been to Edith's home, and being allowed into the inner sanctum of her life gave me the opportunity I needed to focus all of my attention outward. I knew instinctively, somehow, that dwelling on the horror of the past few hours would push me into the chasm of loss that had opened up inside of me, and I suspected that being distracted would be a whole lot easier than being brave.

If not a healthy strategy for coping, it was at least one that Edith could supplement with her own brand of denial. She had no clue how to console a grieving child. She didn't even know how to deal with her own feelings of pain and loss, as her whole life had always been structured around the pursuit of pleasure. Edith got over her heartbreaks and disappointments not by accepting them or working through them, but by distracting herself from them with alcohol, men, parties and adventures. If I was an emotional magpie, then Edith was the most glittering and shiniest of objects. In our dysfunction, we were perfectly suited.

"Here we are," Edith trilled as she opened the door. "I always said I'd have you over for a slumber party one day, didn't I?" She said it with such conviction that I could almost believe this was a social visit.

And so the charade had begun.

"Wow," I said, playing my part, as I stepped inside the Aladdin's cave of treasures that was Edith's flat.

One long wall that ran the length of the apartment was covered with shelves that were densely packed with books, records and curios from across the world. Metallic blue-and-green peacock feathers from India languished next to a dried and spindly puffer fish from the Philippines. A red-and-gold-glass clock from Venice ticked serenely next to a grotesque clay effigy from Ghana. It had never occurred to me before how very immense the world was until I saw its footprints in Edith's home. The opposite wall was covered in framed posters, wall hangings, masks, tapestries and paintings; in some instances, their edges overlapping one another as they vied for space. The entire wall was like a patchwork quilt sewn together from Edith's vibrant memories.

At the very end of the room, to the left of the large window, was an elaborate gold coop that looked like a miniature version of St. Paul's Cathedral. It was made up of three separate cages that were fused together, and the center cage—the largest of the three—towered over my head and culminated in a great domed roof. It was a magnificent bird mansion that housed Edith's African gray parrot, Elvis, who was named after Edith's idol.

As I stepped closer, Elvis greeted me with the first few lines of "Are You Lonesome Tonight?" while his little head bobbed enthusiastically. I reached for the miniature door.

"Can I let him out?" I hadn't seen Elvis since Edith's last visit and that had been months ago. She'd had the bird ever since I could remember; he'd been a gift bestowed by one of Edith's many wealthy suitors. "He can sit on my shoulder."

"You and Elvis can catch up later. I'm sure you'd prefer to spend some time with your sister anyway."

"My sister?"

"Yes." Edith smiled. "I sent a friend to fetch her from your house. She's been waiting here for us." She turned away from me and called out in the direction of her bedroom. "Cat! Come on out!"

I was touched by both Edith's willingness to pretend that my sister was real, as well as her compassion in sensing how much I needed Cat. The small kindness brought on an unexpected wave of gratitude and, with it, the sting of tears.

Don't cry. Don't cry. Don't cry.

Edith rescued me by ushering Cat and me into the bathroom where she started to fill the huge claw-foot tub. She held up two different kinds of bubble bath. "Lavender or rose?"

I couldn't decide. "Can I have both?"

"Why not? We'll make our own concoction and call it 'Eau de Brothel.'"

"You're standing on Cat by the way," I pointed out. She wasn't really, but I was compelled to fill the silence with chatter. The tiled, humid space amplified sound so that it reverberated through me, filling up my chest so it felt less empty.

"Sorry about that, Cat," Edith said as she made an elaborate show of sidestepping. "Is this better now where I'm standing?"

"Yes."

"Good!" Edith emptied a generous amount from each bottle into the stream of water. "There you go. That ought to do the trick. Bubbles, bubbles and more bubbles. I'll just step outside to give you both some privacy while you undress. Call me once you're in the tub."

I waited for Edith to leave the small space before I shot a quick look at Cat. She was faint, more a memory than a vision, and a flutter of panic rose up in me, scraping against my ribcage like a baby bird testing its wings.

Cat?

I couldn't lose her as well, not now when I needed her more than I ever had before.

"Just look in the mirror," she whispered weakly—so softly that I almost didn't hear her—and that faintness, too, made me nervous.

I turned and looked in the mirror. There I was: scrawny chest, long brown hair, blue eyes, and a nose and cheeks covered with freckles; I was pale and had purple smudges under my eyes. At first, all I saw was myself, nothing more, and then the girl in the mirror's freckles started to fade as the steam from the hot water clouded the glass, and that's all it took for things to shift into place. The girl in the mirror was me and it also was Cat. I blinked and she blinked back. I grimaced and she grimaced back.

"Hello," she said, her voice as clear as it ever was.

"Hello," I said, taking her hand as we stepped into the bath. Once we got used to the heat, we submerged ourselves until the frothy bubbles reached almost higher than our heads.

"Edith!"

Edith stepped inside and scooped up my pajamas, panties and socks from the floor. "I'm not even going to try and wash these. Out they go!"

It only dawned on us once I got out of the bath that I had absolutely nothing to wear, but Edith refused to retrieve the blood-and-urine stained clothes from the bin to wash. Instead, she dug around in her huge closet and found a small T-shirt. "Here you go. This might work."

It hung off my slight frame comically. "It's too big."

"It will be fine for sleeping in. Pretend it's a nightgown."

"What about underwear."

"Underwear? Pfft. Who needs underwear for sleeping in? I, myself, like to go commando."

"What about clothes for Cat?" I asked.

"Can't you do a reverse version of 'The Emperor's New Clothes' and imagine clothes onto her?"

I considered that for a moment. "Okay."

"Excellent! I'm glad we've solved that little conundrum. Now, hop into bed while I go heat you a glass of milk."

I waited for Edith to leave and then wandered around her room instead. It didn't contain a princess canopy bed as I'd always imagined, but it was still very feminine. A large queen-sized bed with an ornately carved headboard stood against the wall facing the window. The walls were bare except for two large framed paintings of Elvis (the icon, not the bird), both of which were rendered in black and white.

An oversized dressing table dominated the room, taking up the whole area in front of the window where the afternoon sun filtered through the white netting gently stirring in the breeze. A thin layer of glass covered the wood's surface, protecting it from the dozens of containers lined up like a cosmetic army. I'd never seen so many different colors of nail varnish, lipstick, pencil, rouge and eye shadow, each of which was neatly stacked in its own designated section.

I randomly opened one of the drawers and peered inside. It was filled with assorted bottles of perfumes, moisturizers and other colored lotions, their fragrances rising up like scented ghosts. The exploration of another drawer revealed hairbrushes, curlers and hairpins, and I ran my fingers along their prickly bristles, enjoying the ticklish sensation until it made me think of my father's moustache and I snatched my hand back.

My mother never had a dressing table; she kept all her cosmetics in a single bag in the bathroom cupboard, so I was fascinated by the potions and elixirs Edith employed in the alchemy of her beauty. She wasn't as pretty as my mother. My mom had a softer quality, whereas Edith was all sculpted edges with a longer, harder face. Her hair, usually worn up, was a vivid shade of what she called fire red, and her makeup was always applied with great care. Edith was both artist and creation, and her bedroom was her studio.

When she switched off the kitchen light, I hopped off the bench and padded back to the bed where Cat was already fast asleep. Edith sat on the edge of the mattress and gave me the hot milk, watching as I blew on the surface to cool it down. She kept staring at me as I sipped and it made me nervous. I poked the film of skin floating at the top and sucked it off my finger.

"Robs?"

"Hmm?"

"Are you okay? I mean, I know you're not okay, but I'm concerned that—"

"What am I going to wear tomorrow?"

I knew what Edith would've said if I'd let her. She was going to ask me why I hadn't cried, and I knew that trying to explain it to her would make me sad. I didn't feel strong enough to fight back the tears again, and I was disappointed with her for breaking our unspoken rule. If we stopped the charade, even for a moment, the entire illusion would disintegrate and the chasm would beckon once more.

My question worked; it diverted her. Edith smacked the palm of her hand against her forehead and hopped up to go to her cupboard. "I almost forgot! I got you a few things on my travels that I was going to give you the next time I saw you."

I put the mug down on the bedside table. I'd always loved getting Edith's gifts, and it had been a while since my last haul. During her travels, she had access to a wide range of expensive merchandise that wasn't available in South Africa because of corporate sanctions or censorship. She'd always been generous and I enjoyed being spoiled, but now the gifts served the even greater purpose of being further distractions when that was what I needed most.

Edith craned up on her tiptoes and pulled a big packet down from the top shelf. "I can't remember exactly what I bought, just a few bits and bobs each trip, but I'm sure some of it will be helpful." She handed it across.

"Thank you." The bag was stuffed full and I yanked it open. The first thing to spill out was a stuffed toy. "It's a dog!"

"Not just any dog, it's Lassie."

"Who's Lassie?" I stroked its long fur against my cheek.

Edith shook her head at my ignorance. "Sorry, I keep forgetting how isolated we are here without television. Lassie's a famous dog and there have been movies and TV shows made about her. She's a collie."

"I love her. Thank you." I set the dog aside and reached inside the packet again.

"Let's just empty it all out," Edith suggested, grabbing the bag from me and upending it so all the contents tumbled out onto the duvet. "Okay, this is a Bugs Bunny AM radio. He's a Looney Tunes character," she said, holding up a plastic rabbit chewing on a carrot. "He says things like, 'What's up, Doc?' And these ones are Charlie Brown, Snoopy and Linus. They're from the Peanuts cartoons." Edith handed across three stuffed toys that looked like drawings. "I wanted to get you Lucy, because she's the most kick-ass character, but she was sold out. Oh, and look, this is a Mickey Mouse watch. Mickey's a world-famous Disney character."

I didn't know who any of the characters were or who Disney was, but that didn't stop me from loving the gifts. I put the watch on, marveling at how the mouse's hands moved to tell the time.

"Aha, I knew I bought you some clothes." Edith snatched up something. "This is a bell-bottom denim overall. See? The top and the bottom are all in one and look how the pants flare out. It's all the rage."

"Are they dungarees?"

"No! Dungarees are what farmers wear, Robs. Overalls are what fashion-conscious nine-year-olds wear."

I nodded, but before I could take a proper look, I was distracted by two shiny silver objects that had been buried under everything else. "What are these?"

"Oh, I forgot about those! They're platform disco shoes in faux snakeskin. You like?"

I'd already hopped off the bed and was putting them on. They were a bit too big so I tied the laces extra tight and stood up.

"Pretty snazzy, hey? I bought them to piss your father off . . ." Edith trailed off looking stricken.

She went quiet and the silence made me nervous. I wanted the chatter back because the chatter filled up the time with trivial diversions. Each minute that passed without my crying or thinking or remembering was an achievement, and I knew that if I strung enough minutes together, it would keep getting easier because it had to.

"I love them!"

Edith shook her head as though to clear it and then smiled. "Okay, take them off and get back into bed. You can wear them and the overall tomorrow, and I'll borrow a T-shirt and jersey from a friend's son. Everything is unisex these days anyway, so it hardly matters. After that, I'm afraid we're going to have to go back to your house to fetch your stuff."

Edith didn't question me any further about my feelings and I didn't ask about hers. We were each alone in the bubble of our grief, and while it's true that misery loves company, sorrow is not reduced or diminished in any way even when it's shared.

Twelve

BEAUTY

❦

17 JUNE 1976
Soweto, Johannesburg, South Africa

A s we latch the gate behind us, a child calls out from the darkness of the house. Her voice is reed-thin and tremulous. "*Ufuna ntoni?*" What do you want?

"It is me, your father," Andile identifies himself in a whisper and the front door is wrenched open.

Eleven-year-old Buyiswa scampers out. She throws herself at her father, wrapping her arms around his waist. "I have been waiting for you. I was scared."

"I am here now," Andile assures her as he gently loosens her grip. "Where is your mother?"

"She went back to check the clinics just after she got home. She told me not to open the door for anyone."

The boys lead the way inside and we follow.

"Why is it so dark in here?"

"I was afraid to light a candle in case someone saw I was alone."

Buyiswa's voice is quivering. "I have been sitting on the floor behind the door. The noise frightened me."

Even from here in Nkosi Street in Zondi, there is no respite from the din. The muffled sounds of explosions and shouting tear through the night. There is looting throughout the township and the sound of glass breaking has become as commonplace in this city of suffering as the sound of birdsong in the hills of my homeland. I have not seen one bird since I have been here and I understand why. If the Lord had given our people wings, would we not all have flown away from here?

I am homesick and want to return to the rural landscape and the green pastures of the Transkei. I miss my sons and my hut and the school I teach at. I miss the *tsee-chee-chee* of the *umvetshana* bird—its call so like a herd boy's whistle—and I miss breathing air that does not feel as though it has been scorched. I have a pain in my chest that will not go away. Is this what heartbreak feels like?

Once we are all inside, Dumi leads me to the living room and helps me into a seat.

"Buyiswa, go fetch candles," Langa instructs his sister before turning to me to pose a question. "*Ufuna into yokusela?*"

When I accept his offer, Langa nods to Dumi. "Bring *udadobawo* a glass of cold water." He takes a candle from his sister and pulls it close to me so he can inspect the gash on my forehead. It has swollen since yesterday and started weeping again. "You need stitches, Aunt."

"It will be fine. We just need to clean it again and cover it."

Langa pulls away so that he can meet my eyes. "What if the wound festers?"

"It will not fester. Bring hot water."

It takes ten minutes to get the water boiling on the coal stove and the boys tend to the cut. As Langa gently dabs at my skin with a cloth and Dumi is careful not to drip wax on me, I feel an overwhelming tenderness for these boys who are almost the exact same ages as my two sons at home.

Buyiswa cuts slices of bread and opens two tins of bully beef and passes the food around on scratched yellow tin plates. I am too nauseated to eat and give Andile my share, but he sets it aside and heads out into the night again to look for his wife.

Once the children are finished eating, they lie on their mattress on the floor, pulling their blankets up to their chins, and soon they are snoring. The boys have brought the smell of fire and conflict inside with them. They should have a bath to wash off the stink of the day, as should I, but it would take five trips to the communal tap that is half a kilometer away in order to pump enough water to fill the small zinc bathtub. Another hour would be spent heating the water up sufficiently for one of us to have a tepid bath. It is simply not viable.

Langa murmurs in his sleep and I worry what dreams the boys will have this night and all the nights to come. Children should never see what these children have seen: the darkness in men's souls, the infinite capacity to hate.

I have spent the past forty hours searching for my daughter in every place I can think of, but it is like searching for a ghost. She has left nothing of herself behind, nothing at all except the many lies she told me over the past few months. It pains me to admit the extent of her deception, but I will be honest with myself even though my daughter did not believe me worthy of the truth.

I will try now for a few hours of sleep, and when I wake, I will wash my face and I will begin the search anew.

Thirteen

ROBIN

❀

18 JUNE 1976
Boksburg, Johannesburg, South Africa

Two days after my parents died—two days of constant chatter as Edith and I tread water—we made the only trip we'd ever make back to my childhood home.

A maroon-and-blue blanket lay on the floor in the lounge where Mabel had cast it aside, and the covers from my bed lay where I had thrown them. Footprints littered the hallway where the police had dragged dirt and misery into our lives.

Edith was watchful, alert to any sign that I wasn't coping, but I was even more vigilant than she. If my parents could watch over me in places that they'd never been to, like the police station and Edith's apartment, then they were definitely going to be present in their own home. I couldn't risk dropping my guard for a second.

I wanted so badly to go into their room, to open their cupboards and inhale their particular scents, to lie on their bed while snuggled up to their pillows. I'd sought comfort in there so many times when nightmares woke me up and terror wouldn't let me go back to sleep. If they could see me, maybe it wouldn't be that difficult for them to make the leap to reach out and touch me.

I thought back to the night of their deaths when my mother had hugged me for the last time. If I'd known that was the last hug I'd ever get from her, I would have pulled her close and clung to her; I would have grafted myself to her skin so we could never be separated. As the memory of my careless rejection rose up to taunt me, my traitorous nose started to run—a precursor to tears—and I knew with absolute certainty that being in their room for longer than a moment or two would be too overwhelming. So I made a calculated decision.

I'm going to run as fast as I can and I'm going to get it.

I took my platform disco shoes off.

"I want to come with you," Cat said, also reaching down to take her own shoes off.

"No, wait here for me." I took a deep breath and headed for their bathroom, sprinting as fast as I could. My mother's mascara was exactly where I knew it would be, on the counter where she'd left it. I snatched the pink-and-green tube up, not daring to exhale until I was out the door again.

Edith was making coffee in the kitchen and heard the commotion of my footfalls. "Robs? Are you okay?"

"Yes. I'm fine!"

"Are you sure?"

"Yes!"

I quickly shoved the mascara into my overall's pocket, then thinking better of wearing my new outfit while packing, I took the overall as well as the borrowed T-shirt and jersey off, and got dressed in a pair of corduroys and a long-sleeved shirt instead. It felt good to have underwear on again. Once the mascara was transferred to my pocket, I was able to relax and allow my breath to slow before setting to work.

As I packed up suitcases and filled garbage bags with everything from flip-flops to the old shoeboxes that I'd kept my silkworms in,

Edith chain-smoked and tried not to get in my way in the small room. Being there couldn't have been easy for her, but she remained stoic throughout the visit. She hadn't tried to break our pact again, and she hadn't cried in front of me since those first few moments in the police station. She fixed a smile on her face and coated her words with a brittle cheer. I tried to do the same. The more hours that passed, the easier it became.

The bags piled up and Edith made multiple trips to her car, even making a big show of carting Cat's possessions along with mine.

"This is the last thing," I said, wheeling my bicycle around from its spot in the garage.

Edith, distracted, looked up from where she was wedging a bag into the backseat, and did a double take at the sight of it. "A bike?"

I nodded.

"But, Robs, the car is already chockablock. Where will we put it?"

I shrugged. "On the roof?" My dad always found space for everything. He said that's what rope was invented for.

Edith scratched her head as she looked from the bike to the roof and back again. "Maybe with a normal car roof, but this one's curved, see? It'll fall off."

I just stared at her. She didn't expect me to leave my cruiser behind, did she?

"Also, Robs, the city streets aren't the same as the suburbs. It's not safe for you to ride that in Joburg. You'd get knocked over by a bus or something. Those guys drive like bats out of hell."

My lip started to quiver.

"Okay, how about you put it away in the garage for now, and then we'll make a plan to come and get it another time? When the car's empty and we can fit it in?"

"You promise?"

"Yes, of course."

"Okay." I wheeled the bike back, gave it a quick kiss on the seat and whispered that I'd return soon and that it shouldn't be afraid.

When we were ready to leave, Edith locked up using the spare key my mother had given her for emergencies, and I headed for Mabel's room at Cat's jabbering insistence.

"Maybe she came back and she's hiding in there because she's scared of the police," Cat said.

I tried the door, but it was locked.

"She wouldn't leave us. She just wouldn't."

I peered through the keyhole; there was no movement inside.

Cat still wouldn't accept the proof of our abandonment and wanted to linger in case Mabel returned later, but I told her we had to go. We turned to walk to the car and saw a group of children gathered at our gate. They were shuffling around uncertainly, and I could make out most of the members of Die Boerseun Bende as well as Elsabe and Piet.

Piet was standing a few feet in front of them, holding something and looking important. He'd changed from his school uniform and was wearing dark gray knee-high socks and white *takkies* that had been scrubbed clean. It was an unusual sight as the Afrikaner children were almost always barefoot. His snow-white hair was wet and combed to the side as if he'd prepared for a formal visit.

Piet would normally just let himself into our garden so I was confused by his hesitation, until I remembered that he only knew Edith by sight and probably wasn't sure of the welcome he would receive. The Afrikaner culture was a curious mix of formality and affability, boorishness and courtesy. They could be as abrasive as sandpaper one minute and then blindside you with their gallantry and graciousness the next.

Edith spotted them a minute later and looked to me for guidance.

"It's Piet. His dad works"—I stopped to correct myself—"worked with my dad."

Edith nodded and held out her hand, which I took as we walked to the gate. The children stopped shuffling and stood to attention, looking to Piet to be their spokesman. Most of them hadn't followed his lead with the shoes, and dust caked their feet and shins. Their eyes were lowered and I couldn't read their expressions. None of them would meet my gaze.

Piet passed the Corningware dish he was holding to a boy behind him, reached down to pull up his socks and then turned to grab it back. "Hello, *Tannie*," he addressed Edith, clasping the dish to his chest with one hand and reaching out the other for a formal handshake. Edith took his small hand and shook it.

Piet flushed and his large buck ears colored to a red so deep that it bordered on purple. "I are very pleased to meet *Tannie*. My name are Bekker, Petrus Bekker, and we stay over va road der."

I knew Piet didn't like speaking English and it was a touching gesture, his being prepared to embarrass himself as he mangled our language when he could have just saved face by using his mother tongue. His obvious struggle made me want to hug him and so I hugged myself instead.

Edith greeted him and introduced herself by her first name, not prefacing it with *Tannie*, or "Aunty." It sent a murmur of surprise through the group behind Piet and he turned and shushed them. When the formalities with the adult were out of the way, Piet turned to me. He had startling dark blue eyes that were framed by long white lashes. The contrast was disconcerting.

"Hello, Robin." He inserted an *h* sound into my name, dissecting it in the process. *Rob Hin.*

"Hello, Piet. What's that?" I asked, pointing to the container.

"My ma did cook a stew for you," he stammered, and then reached out to hand it to me over the fence. "Is *blouwildebees* meat, very *lekker.*"

I thanked him, holding the dish awkwardly. I had no idea what *blouwildebees* was, but figured it was some poor animal they'd killed on a hunting trip. Piet's house was filled with trophies that proved their prowess as great hunters. Animal heads were mounted on all the walls in the lounge and dining room, and zebra and leopard skins were used as carpets. All those dead eyes following my every move gave me the creeps. They had two white bull terriers and I wondered if their heads would be joining the macabre mounted zoo one day.

Seemingly in a rush to deliver his message so he could leave, Piet said, "We is very sorry to hearded what happened. Wiff your ma and pa." His expression was earnest and out of place on his freckled face. "They was good peoples and did not deserved to be killed by *kaffirs*."

I'd once listened as Piet's father expounded on the many reasons why you couldn't trust a *kaffir*, the greatest one being something they'd done in the early 1800s. Apparently Dingane, the king of the Zulus, had invited the Boers and Piet Retief, the Voortrekker leader, to the Zulu royal *kraal* for a party to celebrate a treaty they had just signed. The Boers, in good faith and at the request of Dingane, had left their weapons behind. During the peak of the party, Dingane leapt up yelling, "*Bambani abathakathi!*" which was apparently Zulu for "Seize the whities" and all the Boers were then executed.

His speech had bewildered me at the time because it was delivered in front of their black maid, Saartjie, who nodded along agreeing with everything he said. Everyone knew, though, that Saartjie was entrusted with the care of their home and its contents whenever the Bekker family went on holiday to Durban. She'd also bragged to all the maids in the neighborhood how much more she was paid and how well the family looked after her. When I'd asked Piet about it later, he couldn't understand my confusion. He'd simply shrugged and said, "Saartjie are not a *kaffir*. She are a part of da family."

"Thank you for the stew," Edith said. "It looks delicious. Please extend my thanks to your mother for the lovely gesture."

"Ja, I will, *Tannie*. She say also vat she are sorry. Vey will be by va funeral and she are baking cakes for vat." Seemingly satisfied that he'd fulfilled his duty, Piet reached out to shake her hand again. He then turned and, with the subtle flick of his head, commanded his posse to follow him.

The street was set up for one of their day/night cricket matches; the streetlights would act as their floodlights once darkness fell. A metal dustbin stood in the middle of the road in place of proper wickets, and a cricket bat rested against it waiting for a batsman. The mine dump rose up behind the tableau, absorbing the light so that it seemed to glow golden from within. Piet kicked off his shoes and, removing his socks, started to split the boys up into two teams. The girls filtered to sit under the trees where they would serve as rowdy spectators, calling out encouragement to their brothers and cousins, or boys that they secretly fancied. A wicketkeeper took his place behind the dustbin and Piet took up the bat, signaling to the opposing side's bowler that he was ready for the first ball.

As the game began, I thought that if life was fair, Piet's dad, Hennie, would've attended the party instead of my father, and his parents would be the ones who were dead instead of mine. But my parents had been right all along. Life wasn't fair and it amazed me how everything was the same as it ever was. It was only my world that was unrecognizable.

Fourteen

BEAUTY

❀

18 June 1976
Soweto, Johannesburg, South Africa

I t has been two days since Soweto started burning and yet I do not
know where Nomsa is or even if she is still alive.

It is after dark on Friday night and men from the community have
gathered in Andile's house to trade information. They have been careful not to attract attention and arrived one by one in ten-minute intervals. The police are nervous of gatherings and will not hesitate to
arrest anyone they suspect of holding a meeting to conspire against the
government.

Lindiwe and the children have gone out. I should have gone with
them, but I am too weary for an evening spent making conversation
with Lindiwe's family in Meadowlands. It is not customary for a lone
woman to be in a room full of men, but they overlook the intrusion
because I am a visitor in my brother's house and because my daughter
is one of the missing.

Smoke uncurls from pipes wadded with tobacco and some of the
men sip from bottles of beer they brought with them. There is a sour

stench—stronger than sweat—that permeates everything; I am offered some of the sorghum beer but the smell of the *umqombothi* turns my stomach. The only light comes from the burning tips of cigarettes and the few candles I have lit out of the way of shuffling feet and gesturing arms.

"It is fitting that the next generation are the ones to rise up," Odwa is saying in that singsong preaching way of his, "because it has all been for them." He grew up with us in our village in the Transkei and always liked the sound of his own voice.

Andile's neighbor, Madoda, agrees. "All these years of struggle have been so that our children can one day have a future in this country."

"A future!"

"They deserve a future that is not sunken into a mine shaft or measured out in hours of hard labor."

"Amen!"

"Viva freedom!" a few of the others call out.

I say to hell with their freedom if it means the spilling of the blood of my firstborn child. When Nomsa left the protection of our hut in the Transkei seven months ago, I did not want her to go. Nomsa, who was always so special from the day she was born, a gift bestowed by the ancestors. She, who survived the flooding of the river when even the cattle were swept away along with her beloved brother, Mandla. She, who listened at the knees of the elders to the *imbongi*'s poetic words of our wars and our victories. Her eyes burned with the fire of vengeance and it scared me. I did not want her to fight the battles that needed fighting.

I wanted her to stay home with her brothers and me. I did not want her following in the footsteps of her father to Johannesburg, because I feared that, like him, the only way she would return was in a casket. I tried to keep her safe, but safety was always a prison to Nomsa. I spent my life trying to lock her inside, but she said I was locking her outside of the world. So I relented. I allowed her to come to this city to study so long as she promised she would not get involved in anything dangerous, but I should have known she was lying. The only thing a warrior cannot fight is her own fierce nature.

And now Soweto is under siege. The army patrols with tanks, fire has razed buildings to the ground and the stench of tear gas is a constant reminder of the war waged against us. Helicopters circle overhead; they are the army's vultures searching for human carrion while violence flares like *veld* fires across the township.

"I have heard the security police are hunting the leaders of the uprising," Odwa says.

"Let them root around in dark places like blind pigs, trying to sniff out the scent of our heroes. They will not find them."

Odwa continues, oblivious of Madoda's attempt to stop this kind of talk from taking place in front of me. "They say they are being dragged to secret locations where they are tortured and—"

Andile cuts him off and I am grateful. "There are rumors of those who are being protected, hidden away until they can be taken across the borders of Rhodesia, Mozambique, Angola and Botswana and sent into exile."

I hope with all of my heart that Nomsa is one of these people. If not, we will find her in the morgue.

"You should be proud." Odwa turns to me. He adjusts his glasses and nods to emphasize what he is saying. "You should be very proud of Nomsa. The ripples of their actions here are being felt across the country." His voice rises and falls as though he is delivering a sermon. "People are waking up and they are fighting back because of what our children have done." He says "our children," but Odwa is not a father, though I do not point this out to him.

"It is true," Xolani says. He lives three houses down and his two sons participated in the march though they both returned home safely. "The youth across all provinces are striving to make the country ungovernable. Riots are breaking out everywhere and there have been reports that many of our people have taken the uprising as a call to arms."

"The time for speaking is over," another man says as he thumps his fist into the palm of his hand. "Now we will talk with fists and spears!"

"And knives and fire!"

"Maybe now they will listen!"

The men cheer and Andile quickly stands up. "We must keep our voices down." The volume drops but the fire in the men's voices burns strong.

It is not my place to speak in this setting. Even if it was, there is no point in telling these men that I do not condone violence. I have always believed, and still do, that violence begets more violence. We are relics of a bygone era, those of us who support passive resistance. The younger ones do not believe that the meek shall inherit the earth. They insist the struggle must be an armed one because the only way to overthrow the white minority who keep the black majority in chains is with force.

But what quality of freedom will it be if it is won with blood? And after that? Once our rage has boiled and we have taken the life force of our enemies, have we not become the very people we have fought against, the ones who use violence against us? If we ever taste victory, will our fighters lower their fists and live in peace or will they always be looking for the next conflict? I despair that we are all becoming murderers, white and black alike, and that we will never be able to wipe this blood from our hands. I pray that I am wrong.

The young people are singing a song, one that is accompanied by the beating of a thousand drums and makes my heartbeat quicken. Yet, as much as I want to sing along with them, I do not know the words. Perhaps that is what it means to get old: you must let the young ones sing their own songs.

Fifteen

BEAUTY

❋

19 JUNE 1976
Soweto, Johannesburg, South Africa

When I heard the rumors of what happened at the church, I thought they had to be false. No matter how evil the white government is, it is inconceivable that its police force could chase fleeing children into a church and open fire at them inside.

Yet, here I am, sitting in one of the pews of the Regina Mundi church in Rockville—the largest Roman Catholic Church in South Africa—and all around me is proof of the attack that took place here three days ago. The marble altar is cracked down the middle, the wooden statue of Christ is split apart and the bricks have chunks torn from them. Six women are on their hands and knees with buckets of water and scrubbing brushes trying to remove the stain of blood from the floors.

How is it that the apartheid government claims to be such a religious government? How can they assert that South Africa is a Christian state when its police officers attempt murder in a church? What kind of men fire bullets at terrified children in a house of God?

I was hoping to find answers here, but instead I have found something I have needed far more than information: I have found sanctuary. That is why I linger under the pitched roof and the light that floods inside, trying to find some calm in the center of this war zone.

There is much to look at, but what keeps drawing my gaze is the portrait of the Black Madonna. It depicts a beatific black Virgin Mary holding a black baby Jesus, halos of light flare from both their heads. It is a wonderful thought that the Messiah could have been black, but that is just a fairy tale. If Jesus were black, surely we, the children of Africa, would not be suffering as much as we are.

I begin to pray. *Lord, please take this hatred from me. Anger is a self-administered poison and I want no part of its contagion.*

"Was your child one of the injured?"

The voice startles me from my prayer. Those of us sitting here have mostly been silent while taking comfort from the wordless sense of community. I turn to look at the woman who has spoken. She is younger than me as all the other mothers are. That is what happens when you are one of the very few of your kind to pursue an education before having a family. She holds a photograph of a young girl in her lap, one who is about twelve years old by the looks of her, and I try not to stare at it.

"I do not know," I say. "My daughter is still missing."

"What school did she go to?"

"Morris Isaacson."

"Her age?"

"Seventeen." I try not to get my hopes up. The woman is interested and is making conversation, that is all.

"What is her name?"

"Nomsa Mbali," I say, beginning to hope that my daughter's name will be the key that unlocks information that will spill forth from this woman's lips.

She is quiet and appears to be thinking. Finally, she shakes her head no. I stand, ready to leave—not surprised that this trip did not provide any new information but disappointed nonetheless—but she reaches out and grabs my hand.

"You need to go to the house of my neighbor, Nothando Ndlovu. Her child, Phumla, is the same age as your daughter and she went to the same school. She, too, is missing. Maybe Nothando has information that can help you."

Sixteen

ROBIN

❀

20 JUNE 1976
Yeoville, Johannesburg, South Africa

A few days after Piet and the neighborhood children receded from the back window of Edith's car, the terrain of my life changed so utterly that I became a foreigner in it.

I no longer had my own room or my own bathroom; Edith and I now shared her bedroom as well as her bed. She tried to clear cupboard space so I'd have somewhere to put all my stuff, but it wasn't an easy task since Edith's closets were already bursting at the seams with all her clothes, shoes, bags and accessories.

I'd managed to carve out one tiny place of my own; a secret compartment at the bottom of Edith's dressing table where I placed my mother's mascara tube. It was the only space that was wholly mine and that I didn't have to share with Edith or Cat.

Edith decided she was keeping me out of school until the dust settled, and I didn't argue; I was getting away with something most children only dreamt about. It hadn't fully occurred to me yet that since Edith lived in Yeoville, a suburb in the city center that was miles away from Boksburg, I wouldn't be going back to my primary school, the place I'd happily attended and taken for granted for the past three and a half years. I had a few friends in my class and had I known that I wouldn't see them again or even get to say good-bye, I would have put up more of a fight.

Along with attending classes, after-school activities fell away too. I was never very good at sports, so I had no qualms about letting any of my teams down. My library membership was greatly treasured, though, and my pink lending card was one of my most prized possessions. The thought of not being taken to the library, where I would spend hours browsing the shelves, was distressing.

Also books had always helped me make sense of the world and given me answers when I needed them.

"Edith?"

"Hmm?"

"Can we go to the library, please?"

"The library? But there are lots of books here." She waved her hand in the direction of her shelves where all her travel books were stacked.

I didn't know how to tell her that those books would only be useful if I found myself embarking on a world tour; instead, I found myself in a parentless new reality that I desperately needed to come to grips with.

"I don't really like picture books," I said instead.

"Picture books?" Edith looked pained. "Those aren't picture books. They're travelogues put together by some of the world's finest travel writers and photographers."

I could see I'd have to play along and humor her if I had any hope at all of getting what I wanted. I went over to the shelves, pulling books out and flipping through the pages, sighing loudly every few minutes until Edith asked what the problem was.

"These books are beautiful," I quickly assured her. "It's just that there don't seem to be any orphans in them."

"Orphans, hey? That's what you're looking for?"

I nodded.

"Okay, I see where you're coming from. We'll get to the library soon, I promise."

I wanted to explore my new environment, but Cat was reluctant to venture out. We'd grown up in Witpark, a tiny suburb in the sticks, where hardly anything ever happened. Cat wasn't used to city life. She was overwhelmed by its hustle and bustle, the constant activity and noise, the wail of sirens, the stench of garbage and the clusters of buildings that were even taller than the mine dump. All those thousands of people of different colors milling around like ants scared her and so I chose to stay inside with her instead.

During that week, Edith fielded various calls from senior mine officials updating her on the investigation. Their general consensus was that the murder hadn't been personal and that my father wasn't specifically targeted. Edith was convinced by their assurances, but I wasn't. I'd seen the expression on our garden boy's face once when my father called him a "useless *kaffir* with less sense than a mule" for digging up chrysanthemums that he'd mistaken for weeds. I didn't know how my father spoke to the blacks at work, but if it was the same as the gardener, it wasn't difficult to imagine that they hated him.

When I voiced my doubts, Edith said that murders like theirs had occurred throughout the country on the same day as certain groups of blacks took the uprising in Soweto to be a sign that the revolution had begun.

"Your mom and dad were just really, really unlucky, Robs. They were at the wrong place at the wrong time. The police are doing everything they can to catch their killers."

Since finding out the truth about the "Squad Cars" team, and after my own horrible experience with the police, I didn't have that much confidence in their ability to find my parents' murderers.

"Can we go to where my parents died?" I asked Edith.

"Why? Would you like to lay some flowers down?"

"Flowers? No, I want to go look for clues."

"Clues?"

"Yes, something that the killers left behind that could help us find them."

Edith sighed. "Like what?"

"Like lots of things. A monogrammed handkerchief, or a lighter that's been engraved, or a calling card, or a rare cigar butt or monocles made up to an unusual prescription."

"Kiddo, you do realize this isn't nineteenth-century England?"

I couldn't understand her skepticism; those were the kinds of clues literary sleuths found all the time and I told her so.

"Robs, the men who killed your parents are almost certainly dirt-poor and uneducated, and couldn't afford handkerchiefs or cigars or monocles."

"Oh," I said, considering this for a moment. "But there might be gum-boot prints that are in a very large size or a particular kind of snuff that very few miners use."

"Hmm, well, those are better things to look for, but the police have already looked over the crime scene."

"But maybe they missed something. And if you just take me there, I could use a magnifying glass—"

"Robin, no! This isn't a game or something that's happened on the radio or in a book. This is real life and these men are dangerous and you're just a child—"

"But—"

"No buts! This isn't something you'll hear me say very often because it makes me sound like my mother, and quite honestly, there's nothing I hate more, but I'm afraid I'm going to have to put my foot down with this. We'll leave it up to the professionals to find the killers and we absolutely won't be sticking our noses in. Do you hear me?"

I mumbled something inaudible.

"I said, 'Do you hear me?'"

"Yes," I sighed, "I hear you."

Over a series of phone calls, the mine also informed Edith that the ERPM Benefit Society was arranging and covering the cost of my parents' funeral and she agreed it was the least they could do. A woman from the society, who introduced herself as Mrs. van der Walt, phoned Edith one night to discuss arrangements for the funeral. She spoke so loudly that Edith held the receiver away from her ear, and I could hear every word the woman said.

"Shall we begin by deciding on the hymns? Most people like 'Amazing Grace,' but I am particularly partial to 'Morning Has Broken.'"

"Keith and Jolene weren't religious people," Edith said, "and I, myself, am an agnostic. Could you play Elvis's 'Crying in the Chapel' instead?"

Mrs. van der Walt sounded scandalized. "The church is no place for rock 'n' roll music!"

"Excuse me, but Elvis Presley has also recorded many, many gospel songs!"

"*Ag*, those songs are even worse than rock 'n' roll. You really cannot underestimate the evils of *kaffir* music—"

Edith cut her off. "Look, never mind. Pick whatever hymn you prefer, anything except 'The Lord's My Shepherd.'" Apparently, when Edith and my mother were children, they had two maids who pinched and hit them whenever they thought they could get away with it. Their names were Goodness and Mercy; Edith said the thought of them following her all the days of her life gave her the screaming willies and she was sure my mother would feel the same.

That out of the way, they moved on to flowers. "How about yellow roses for the church? They're cheerful and were Jolene's favorites," Edith suggested.

"But yellow is not the color of mourning," Mrs. van der Walt said. "I think we would do better with white lilies instead."

"I'm not sure why you've bothered to consult with me at all," Edith complained, twisting the cord around her index finger.

"I am just trying to help, Mrs. Vaughn—"

"It's Miss. Miss Vaughn."

I couldn't hear what Mrs. van der Walt said after that, because she'd lowered her voice enough that Edith had to hold the receiver back up to her ear. There was a moment of silence as Edith listened, and then she raised her voice in annoyance. "Of course Robin will be at the funeral. She is their daughter, you know."

More silence ensued. I assumed from Edith's raised eyebrows, and the deep crease that cleaved her brow, that she did not like what she was hearing. She started tapping her long nails on the dining room table and took a deep drag from her cigarette. Finally, it looked like she couldn't listen to another word. "I don't care that you people think children shouldn't attend funerals. She is their daughter, their only child, and I will not, do you hear me? I will not keep her from her own parents' funeral. It's bad enough the poor child has had to endure this whole ordeal, but not to get to say good-bye to them is completely and utterly ridiculous. She will be there and you can, quite frankly, shove your sanctimonious objections up your big Dutchman arse!"

Edith slammed the phone down and Elvis started yelling, "Up your big Dutchman arse! Up your big Dutchman arse!"

My aunt took a final drag of her smoke, stubbed it out viciously and told me to get dressed so we could go shopping for the funeral.

"God, could those people possibly be any more conservative and uptight? Well, we'll just have to show them, won't we? We're both going to be in the brightest fucking yellow we can find. So fuck Mrs. van der Walt and the horse she rode in on."

I didn't like the sound of the yellow outfits; they sounded too much like my school uniform, but I perked up at the mention of the horse.

"Do you think she'll bring it with?" I asked.

"What?"

"The horse. Do you think Mrs. van der Walt will bring it into the church?"

Edith was quiet for a beat and then started laughing. "You crack me up, kiddo."

I wasn't sure what was so funny, but I remained hopeful about the horse.

Seventeen

BEAUTY

✿

21 June 1976
Soweto, Johannesburg, South Africa

My eyes take a few moments to adjust to the darkness of the room. At first, circles of light are the only things I see after the brightness of the yard, but then the halos fade and are replaced by faces—worried faces—coming into focus. They sit in a row facing the door through which I have entered; it looks as though they are keeping vigil.

I can tell that I have interrupted a conversation in which my name has been mentioned by the way the room falls silent after I cross the threshold. This is not the way of African people. We talk and talk and laugh. Our voices are layered one on top of the other, always; even in mourning, we talk or wail or lament. Silence is foreign to us—it is the way of the white man, not the black woman—so it is never a good omen when the sight of your face can make a dozen voices die within their throats.

I greet the room in the customary way, *"Molweni,"* and then I make my way to sit next to the woman of the house, Nothando Ndlovu.

She is the one I was told about at Regina Mundi, the mother of the missing girl. When the churchwoman mentioned the girl's name, I knew it was familiar. On my way home to my brother's house, I recalled the conversation he and I had had the morning after the uprising when he mentioned Nomsa's friend. Andile confirmed that Phumla Ndlovu is Nomsa's best friend and she, too, went missing after the police started shooting. She has also not been found in any of the hospitals or other children's houses.

I greet Nothando Ndlovu and introduce myself. *"Molo. Igama lam ndinguBeauty."*

"Ndiyakwazi." Nothando says she knows who I am. I reach out to take her hand so that I can hold it in my own, but she is clutching a piece of paper, which she hands across to me. I hold it up so the light from the window can fall on it; it is a photograph of a pretty girl of seventeen with a white birthmark seeping out from below her lips to her neck. She is smiling with her mouth closed as though she is embarrassed about her teeth, but her eyes are alive with laughter.

Before I can tell Nothando that her daughter is beautiful, and that I will not rest until we find her, an agonized moan tears through the room. All eyes turn to the corner where the darkness has gathered itself so tightly together that very little light penetrates. I peer into the gloom and can make out a shape lying on a mattress on the floor; it is covered by many blankets and yet it is shivering. The bundle groans again, louder than before, and I look to my host for an explanation.

"That is Sipho, the son of my friend Lungile. He was shot in the leg by the police."

I go to the bed to pull back the blankets so I can look at the boy's face. It is as I thought.

"He's in a lot of pain."

The voice startles me; I did not see the boy sitting on the other side of the bed leaning against the wall, still as a statue. His resemblance to the boy in the bed is striking. It is like looking at a reflection of the same person.

"You are his brother?"

He nods. "His twin." The boys look to be about thirteen. They still have the cherubic faces of babies, but this boy's voice sounds as though it is breaking into manhood.

"What is your name?"

"Asanda," he replies. "I should have been there with him to protect him."

"You got separated?"

"No, I didn't attend the march. I thought it would be too dangerous, but he wouldn't listen to me. He insisted on going after he was bullied into it." He is quiet for a moment and then continues. "I just keep thinking that after he was shot, he was lying there in the street, bleeding for a long time. He was alone and a twin should never be alone." His voice is heavy with pain and regret. "I should have been there," he repeats.

"He was not alone."

"How do you know?"

"I was there with him." I recognized the boy immediately. He was one of the children I spoke to as he floated before me in the river of blood.

"You? You were there with him?" I am not offended by his skepticism. I still cannot believe that I was there. It feels like a dream.

"Yes, I was looking for my daughter who I could not find. I found him instead. He told me his name was Sipho, and I held his hand and stroked his forehead. He said that he had never met his father, and I told him that his mother loved him and would be there soon."

At this, the boy begins silently weeping, and I turn my face to the room full of women. I can see he is proud and does not want me to witness his tears.

"The police have instructed the doctors at the hospitals to report anyone who comes in seeking treatment for a gunshot wound so they can arrest them for being involved in the protest," Nothando says. "That is why they could not take him to the hospital. They brought him here because Lungile's house is too far."

"I have heard that the doctors are refusing to make these reports," I say. I place my hand on the boy's forehead. It holds the heat of a hundred fires. "He needs medical treatment."

"You think the security police will not just walk into the hospitals and pull these children from their beds? You think white doctors can be trusted?"

She says the words that I, myself, thought when I first arrived in Soweto and we drove past Baragwanath Hospital.

The child cries out again, his eyes rolling back, and I stand up to face Nothando. "I think this child has an infection and he needs to see a doctor."

"The *nyanga* has been here. He removed the bullet and prepared a poultice for the wound."

"The poultice is not working. He has a fever."

"We have brewed the *nyanga*'s herbs for that. We feed it to him every hour."

"How much of the tea does he keep down?"

Nothando averts her eyes, confirming my suspicion.

"If you do not take this child to the hospital, he will be dead by nightfall," I say. The words feel like sand in my mouth but I must speak the truth.

"And whose fault will that be?" A woman walks through the door and rushes over to the bed. I do not need an introduction to know that she is Lungile, the boys' mother. "If he dies, it will be your daughter's fault. She is the one who made our children do this. She is the one with blood on her hands and you, her mother, did not stop her. If he dies, you are just as much to blame as Nomsa is."

Of course, she is right. If it is true that the sins of the father will be visited upon the child, then the sins of the child must be visited on the mother tenfold.

Eighteen

ROBIN

❀

22 JUNE 1976
Yeoville, Johannesburg, South Africa

E dith handed me the freshly laundered T-shirt and jersey. "Go take that down to the Goldmans in 302, and say thank you to Morris and his mother for lending them to you."

"Can't you come with?"

"Nope, I'm planning to soak in the tub for an hour and read the latest Jackie Collins."

"What's it called?"

"*The World Is Full of Divorced Women.*"

"Can I read it after you?"

"You're a bit young."

"When will I be old enough?"

"We'll talk again when you're thirteen and I'm teaching you how to stuff your bra."

I crinkled my nose. I'd never wear a bra! "Come on, Cat," I called as I headed out.

"No, leave Cat behind."

"Why?"

Edith sighed. "Robs, I've tried to be understanding, I really have, but aren't you a bit old for an imaginary friend?"

"She's not a friend, she's my sister."

"Fair enough, but aren't you a bit old for an imaginary sister?"

I considered this and then, remembering an unkind remark my father had once made about Edith's obsession with the rock legend, I asked, "Aren't you a bit old for an imaginary boyfriend?"

"Ha! You got me there. Touché!" Edith laughed for a moment before growing serious again. "I just wonder why . . . I mean, where she came from. As I remember it, I was there one weekend visiting you and Cat wasn't around, and then all of a sudden, there she was the next time I saw you. Did . . . did something happen to make her appear?"

I thought back to the conversation I'd overheard between Edith and my mother, the one that had forever changed the way I saw myself, and remembered the surprise on my mother's face when Cat was born fully grown a week later. My mother had been spooked at first, then slightly amused; the annoyance only came later when Cat's true nature showed itself.

"No," I lied. "She just decided to come. Why can't I take her with me now?"

"It's important to limit the amount of crazy you show people the first time you meet them. First impressions are important. You can spring your sister on them once they know you better."

I sighed and turned to Cat to explain. "I won't be long, okay?"

Cat smiled and nodded. "I understand." And that was the thing about Cat, she always did.

"Bye," I said, and turned to go.

After waiting too long for the elevator, I took the stairs the eight floors down. I found a boy sitting in the stairwell on the third floor, staring dejectedly at the contents of a Tupperware container that was laid open on his lap. Peeking over his shoulder, I caught a glimpse of diced brown stuff that didn't look very appetizing. It didn't smell appealing either. Crackers and a butter knife were spread out on a napkin to his right and a big, lumpy backpack sat on his left.

"What's that?"

He jerked around at the sound of my voice, and I skirted him, careful not to step on any of his stuff. Heaving a sigh that was too weary for such a young soul, he said, "It's my lunch."

"Why are you eating it here?"

He shrugged in reply.

"What is it?"

"Chopped liver and onion."

"It looks horrible."

"It's not as bad as pickled herring."

I had no idea what pickled herring was, but it sounded just as awful. "Are you going to eat it?"

"I don't know. I could throw it away, but I'm actually quite hungry." He poked at it as though he was expecting it to magically turn into ice cream.

Before I could stop myself, I ventured, "I could get you a peanut butter and jam sandwich if you want."

His face brightened. "You could?"

I sighed. "Well, I can't let you starve, can I?"

I knew from what Edith had told me that Morris Goldman was eleven years old. That made him two years older than me even though he looked two years younger. Olive-skinned and gawky, he had an unruly mop of hair that was whipped up into a black meringue, which topped off a generally disheveled appearance. He was wearing full-length brown pants that looked like something formal you'd wear to church, and he'd paired them with a snow-white T-shirt (identical to the one I was returning) and leather sandals.

Besides being odd-looking, Morris spoke with a deep voice that was disarming. By the look of him, you expected him to chirp like a cricket; instead, sound boomed from his tiny chest so that whispered conversations with him would pretty much be impossible. Being able to whisper and keep secrets was high up on my list of traits I looked for in friends, as was being a girl. He failed miserably on all accounts, but I figured I couldn't be too picky.

"Do you want to be my friend?" I asked.

He smiled and nodded. "I don't have any friends so you'd be my first one."

"You don't have any friends?"

"Well, my mom's my friend, so I guess I have one. My dad says he can't be my friend, because he's my dad and the disciplinarian in the family, so I need to respect him."

"What about school? Don't you have any friends there?"

"I don't go to school. I'm homeschooled."

"Why?"

"One of the kids in grade one called me a dirty Jew boy and a Jesus killer so my parents took me out. My dad says school in this country is an incubator for fascists."

Most of the words that came out of Morris's mouth confused me. "What's a fascist?"

"I'm not sure. I think it's a rat or something like that. My dad hates rats."

I hadn't seen any rats at school, but I wasn't going to argue with his father. "What about family? Don't you have cousins who can be your friends?"

"I have two cousins; they're twelve and sixteen. They live in Cape Town and I only see them on holidays, but they don't want to be friends with me either because they say I'm weird."

"Good grief, I thought I had it bad."

"Because your parents are dead?"

"Who told you that?"

He shrugged. "I heard my parents talking." He held out his hand formally to shake mine. "My name's Morris."

"Yes, I know."

"You can call me Morrie if you like."

"I'm Robin."

"Yes, that's what I heard, but I thought it couldn't be right."

"Why?"

"Because Robin is a boy's name."

"No it's not!"

"Yes it is. Robin Hood was a boy."

"Who's Robin Hood?"

"A guy who stole from the rich to give to the poor."

"Why?"

Morrie scratched his head. "I'm not sure."

"He sounds stupid. Stealing is wrong, everyone knows that. Is he a friend of yours?"

"No, he's not a friend of mine. Didn't I just tell you that I don't have any friends?"

"Oh yes. Sorry."

"Anyway, he has your stupid name."

"It's a girl's name!"

"The goyim are weird."

I wasn't going to give him the satisfaction of asking him another question, so I pretended to agree. "Stupid goyim. So let's go."

Morrie bundled up all the food and slung the backpack over his shoulders. Whatever was in there must have weighed a ton because he tottered a bit before he regained his balance and followed me. Once we got back to the apartment, we called out greetings to Edith who was already in the bath. Cat was in the lounge and she smiled at me and I winked back. Once she could see I didn't need her, she waved and disappeared into the bedroom.

Morrie upended the Tupperware over the bin and all the chopped liver came tumbling out. He stared at it for a moment—the brown mess settled on top of congealed white porridge that Edith had burnt on the stove that morning—and then reached for his backpack. He pulled out something big and bulky and started fiddling with it as he held it up to his face.

"What's that?"

"It's a Kodak EK6."

"A what?"

"It's an instant camera."

I was impressed even though I didn't show it. "Where did you get it?"

"My grandfather gave it to me at the end of December. He got Edith to bring it back from America."

"For Christmas?"

"No, definitely not for Christmas! Just for the end of December." He was very adamant about this and stopped fiddling with the thing just so he could glare at me to be sure I understood this point.

"Okay."

"He's a photographer and he's been teaching me because he says genius should be cultivated from a young age." Morrie clipped something onto the camera and then turned back to the bin and opened the lid again. He held the boxy silver camera up to his face and looked through the hole, pointing it down at the garbage.

"What are you doing?"

"I'm going to take a picture."

"Of that horrible mess?"

"Yes."

"But why? Why don't you take a picture of something pretty instead?" My father had had a camera and he'd been very particular about the kinds of things he'd take pictures of: sunsets, misty mountain ranges and my mother when she was all dressed up. He said film was expensive and so you had to be a hundred percent sure you had a good shot of something beautiful before taking it; he'd sometimes make my mother and me pose for half an hour until our jaws got sore with smiling before he was satisfied enough to press the shutter.

"My *zayde* says—"

"Your who?"

"My grandfather. He says that the world is a cruel place and it's our job to record its ugliness."

I thought his grandfather was crazy, but Morrie was so fixated on taking his picture of the disgusting bin that I chose not to express my opinion about his relatives. A bright flash lit up the kitchen and then a square of something was ejected from the bottom of the camera. Morrie plucked it out and then waved it around before putting it gently on a clean surface. By then, I'd fanned a few slices of bread out in front of us and Morrie looked at them as if he'd died and gone to heaven.

"Do you keep a kosher kitchen?" he asked.

"Of course, doesn't everyone?"

He seemed satisfied with that and then sat looking at me, expecting me to serve him. I wasn't Edith's niece for nothing; she'd taught me a thing or two. "Make your own damn sandwich. I'm not your concubine, you know."

"What's a concubine?"

It was something I'd heard Edith say to my father on more than one occasion, but I wasn't sure what it meant and didn't want to admit it. Instead, I rolled my eyes and sighed. "It's a small animal that shoots quills out at people. Everyone knows that."

"Oh." If Morrie wondered what a quill-shooting animal had to do with being self-sufficient, he didn't say. Instead, he set about making his sandwich, using the same knife in the peanut butter and jam jars and making a gloppy mess.

Half an hour later when Morrie had finished the sandwiches and packed up to leave, he picked up the piece of thick paper he'd taken from the camera and held it up to the light to peer at it. He handled it like it was a holy object; there was reverence on his face.

"Look." He held the photo out to me.

"It's developed already? My dad's pictures usually took two weeks."

"I told you. This one is instant."

I looked at the picture. "It's garbage," I said.

He sighed. "Everyone's a critic."

Nineteen

BEAUTY

❀

23 JUNE 1976
Soweto, Johannesburg, South Africa

Today is Nomsa's eighteenth birthday and instead of celebrating her birth, Andile and I are standing in line outside the South African Police morgue waiting to identify her body. We have been waiting outside the ugly face-brick building since 4 a.m., and despite the early hour, we were not the first to arrive; there are at least ten families ahead of us.

The temperature is just below freezing. I have two blankets draped over my head and wrapped around my shoulders, and still I tremble; it is as much from dread as it is from cold. Someone has built a fire in a metal drum, and the flames cast leaping shadows on the faces of the people around me. We look like poor, damned souls who have been sent to hell to suffer. Perhaps that is where we are.

Andile leaves my side to talk to a woman who is in front of us in the queue. I recognize her. Nothando Ndlovu is here looking for her daughter, Phumla. At least she and I have some hope, threadbare as the thinnest of blankets, but still something to cling to which is more than what Lungile has. I heard that her son Sipho died. Never have I wished so much that I would be wrong as when I looked upon that child and felt his life burning itself out. I cannot meet Nothando's eyes. I cannot face the anguish in them and I turn away, waiting for Andile to return.

When he does, he has some news.

"Sipho's twin brother, Asanda, has been asking around for information. He told Nothando there was a man seen regularly with Nomsa and Phumla."

"What man?"

"He does not know. Some believe he is with the African National Congress while others say Pan Africanist Congress. He has not been seen since the march. The boy says the man lives in Mofolo. We will send someone to check."

I nod and try not to get my hopes up.

A few hours after sunrise, a murmur ripples through the line and Andile places his hand on my shoulder. The morgue is about to open for the day. Soon we will know if Nomsa's body is one of the many waiting inside to be identified.

The door opens and a voice calls out from inside.

"One family at a time. Wait until you are called."

It is only 9 a.m. and already we have been waiting for five hours. The queue has grown so long that it snakes around the building. It is going to be a long day.

The first family steps inside. Progress is slow and no words are exchanged between those who are at the front of the line still waiting to go in and those who exit the doors once their business there is complete. No words are necessary. Some mothers are weeping, their eyes unseeing with horror and disbelief. Others are mute; the shock of their loss is too much for them. Some have to be carried out; their legs unable to hold them up under the crushing weight of knowing that their children will not be coming home, not ever again. Nothando, when she walks out the door, is dry-eyed. She shakes her head at Andile. Phumla's body has not been found.

When it is our turn, Andile tries to wrap his arm around my shoulders, but I gently shake him off. I will bear myself with dignity. I walk inside and go to the counter. Behind the glass, a white policeman stands with his head bent. I clear my throat, but he does not look up. He does not appear to know I am there.

"Good morning, sir, my name is—"

Without raising his head, the man holds up his hand. "I haven't addressed you yet. You'll wait until I'm ready for you." He shakes his head and then mutters, "*Geen fokken maniere, hierdie kaffirs.*"

I understand Afrikaans. It is one of the six languages I speak. *No fucking manners, these kaffirs.*

I fall silent. He is writing on a piece of paper, taking his time with each word. He pauses between sentences, and even as I read them upside down, I can see he has spelled three words incorrectly. I do not dare correct him. The clock overhead ticks away a minute and then another two as the man continues writing at his snail's pace. When the document appears to be done, he reaches for an ink pad and spends another minute stamping and signing the document.

Finally, he sighs and puts the paper in a folder. He looks up though he does not meet my gaze. His eyes hover just above me. "Name?"

"I am Beauty Mbali."

"Who are you looking for?"

"Nomsa Mbali, she is my—"

Again, he holds up his hand. He extracts another piece of paper from a drawer in his desk and begins writing. Dark hairs sprout like spiders on the pale flesh of his fingers. Another minute passes before he looks up again.

"Age?"

"My age?"

"No, man, the age of the missing person."

"Eighteen years old."

"Sex?"

"Female."

"Description?"

"Black hair, brown eyes—"

He snorts. "*Ja, ja.* That's the same for all you people. We know she's a black, okay? What was she wearing? Does she have any distinguishing features like scars or birthmarks?"

"She was in her school uniform. Gray skirt, white shirt and gray jersey. Stockings and black shoes." Andile runs through the description.

"She would also have had her silver stud earrings in," I add, knowing that Nomsa never took the earrings out. "And a silver cross on a chain around her neck."

"Okay, go sit down. We'll call you if we find anyone matching that description."

We walk to the back of the room and sit on orange plastic chairs. We wait. Each minute stretches into an eternity. I have heard Catholic missionaries speak of a place called purgatory. This is what I imagine it to be like.

After half an hour, a door opens and a tall man in a military uniform steps inside. His polished black boots squeak on the floor. He beckons me to follow. "Come, we have found a girl matching the description."

The room and everything in it tilts and shifts out of focus. I am no longer rooted to the ground by my feet. Instead, I am floating above it, above the ugly room with its ugly chairs, above myself and Andile and the man. The ceiling keeps me trapped inside, my head butting against its broad whiteness, and I want to tear a hole through it with my teeth. I want to float away.

"Come! Hurry up!"

The man's impatient command returns me to myself and though I am light-headed, I stand and Andile stands with me.

"No, just her," the man barks. He has already turned away and is heading back through the door. Andile makes a sound of protest, but I pat his arm and nod at the chair for him to sit down again. I follow the man down a long, bright corridor that smells of bleach. My own shoes squeak on the floor, and I try to focus on that sound rather than the pain growing and expanding in my chest. The soldier reaches another door and I trail him through it.

I have never been in a morgue before. In our village, we prepare our own dead for burial and then we perform the *umkhapho* rituals. I am not sure what to expect, but it is not the rows and rows of tables to hold the dozens of bodies that take up every inch of surface space. The tables are pushed so close together that it looks like one large bed on which all the corpses sleep.

The man squeezes his way through the tables, muttering about African women with their fat black asses who aren't able to fit through the narrow passages. He turns and seems to see me properly for the first time. He nods, apparently satisfied that my black ass will be able to comfortably navigate the cramped route behind him. Finally, he stops in front of a table and indicates that I should join him there.

I try to block out the bodies on either side and focus on the shape under the white sheet. It does not seem real that this could be Nomsa, my only daughter, the child who has brought such light and joy to my life. How could it truly be that she may be dead? If that is so, I will never see her smile again. I will never enjoy an intelligent argument with her quick mind while pretending to scold her for being disrespectful to her mother. If she is dead, I will never see her become a wife. I will never see her pregnant belly swell with a child of her own. It does not seem possible that I will not bear witness to her life, share in her joy and triumphs, and console her in her misery.

I am not ready but the man does not care. He reaches for the sheet and I murmur a prayer to both God and the ancestors as he pulls it back. Silver stud earrings catch the light and my knees weaken as I avert my eyes. I take a deep breath, ignoring the twinge of pain in my chest, and force myself to look at her face.

I exhale a quivering breath. The girl is someone's daughter, but she is not mine.

Twenty

ROBIN

❧

23 JUNE 1976
Boksburg, Johannesburg, South Africa

T he funeral was held at an austere church in Boksburg. All the
men wore long-sleeved shirts, suits and ties, and they fidgeted in
jackets that were bought for their own weddings. There were a lot of
straining buttons battling to close over stomachs that were rounder
than they'd been ten years before.

The women wore dresses in dark shades and the air crackled with
the static electricity of polyester blends rubbing against each other.
The only thing more shocking than their synthetic materials was the
scandal Edith created by arriving in a sunflower-yellow tailored pantsuit, with matching handbag and heels. She also sported a yellow pillbox hat with a veil that was bordered with yellow trim. Looking at her
was like looking directly at the sun.

I was in a yellow polka-dot sundress. I wore a matching yellow
ribbon in my hair, which had been curled into ringlets that bounced
when I shook my head. We couldn't find yellow shoes for my outfit, so
I was wearing shiny black Mary Janes with frilly white ankle socks.

Since it was the middle of a South African winter, the sundress wasn't very practical and had to be paired with a long-sleeved knitted jersey. Edith also made me carry a dainty yellow umbrella despite my protests that there wasn't a cloud in the sky, and even if there was, it wouldn't rain inside in the church. She explained that the umbrella was an accessory worn purely for effect, and promised I could use it as a fencing sword if I got bored.

We arrived exactly as the service was scheduled to begin because Edith wanted to make an entrance. "There's no point in spending all that money on our outfits if we don't give everyone the opportunity to gawk at them!"

As we walked down the long red-carpeted aisle of the packed church, a murmur rose from the congregation. It rippled behind us and only trailed off a few minutes after we sat down. I realized, when Edith smiled faintly at the scorn directed at her, that she didn't share my mother's obsession with what people thought of her. She looked glamorous and completely relaxed in the spotlight.

I'd had no control over what I was wearing since Edith had decided to use me as a weapon in her "war on repression," and I knew my father would've hated my ridiculously girly outfit. It was only through Cat that I was able to exert some force of my own will, and so I dressed her in jeans, *takkies*, and a red-and-white rugby jersey because Transvaal was my father's favorite Curry Cup team.

A man waved to us from the front pews where he was sitting. "Edie! Over here, I saved you a spot."

He had a shiny, bald head and a cherubic face, and was immaculately dressed in a three-piece suit; none of his buttons were straining to remain closed.

"Robin," Edith said as she sat down next to him, "this is my friend Victor."

Victor shook my hand across Edith. "Dear heart, I'm so terribly sorry for your loss. Please accept my heartfelt condolences." He had kind hazel eyes and he squeezed my hand softly before I pulled it away. I wondered if he was Edith's boyfriend and watched to see if they'd kiss or hold hands, but they just leaned in close and spoke in whispers, which I was still able to overhear.

"How is she holding up?"

"Okay, I think. It's hard to tell."

"And you, Edie, how are you holding up?" Victor asked.

"I've packed a hip flask. That should tell you."

"That's my girl," Victor said. He was quiet for a beat and then leaned over again. "Don't you always feel like you're going to burst into flames when you set foot inside a church?"

Edith laughed and I could see that had been Victor's intention. He had to be a very good friend of hers, because he knew not to fawn over her or focus on the negative. "Is Michael coming?" he asked, craning his head to look at the rows behind us.

"No," Edith replied.

"Why not?"

"He's in China, but even if he wasn't, I don't think Lotharios generally make a habit of attending their lovers' family funerals."

Edith's voice dropped too low for me to hear anything after that, and so I tuned their whispers out and took in my surroundings. The church was cavernous. Up until then, our school hall was the largest building I'd ever been in and this dwarfed it in comparison. The air smelled of pine wood polish and flowers.

A scrawny woman decked out all in black scurried over to where we were. She had small piggy eyes and a thin-lipped mouth that was puckered in disapproval. She made me think of kids I'd known in school who couldn't color in the lines, because her orange lipstick was applied well beyond the confines of her lips' natural contours.

"Good morning, Ms. Vaughn. I am Mrs. van der Walt, and I just wanted to let you know we delayed the service until you arrived. We are about to begin now."

"Where's her horse?" Cat asked. "Edith said she'd be riding in on a horse."

"I don't know," I said. "We can ask her later."

Just then, a tiny woman who was sitting in front of a huge organ that took up most of one wall started to play a tune I didn't recognize. I panicked and tugged on Edith's pants.

"What?"

"I don't know this song. They haven't taught it to us at school."

"When in doubt, just do what I do, Robs. Hum if you don't know the words."

The pace of the melody began to pick up and the congregation took this as a cue to slowly turn and face the back of the church, and Cat and I swiveled with them. Thankfully, no one started singing—it was one of those songs without any words—and so I could concentrate on what was happening. A throng of men lumbered down the aisle, laboring under the weight of large oak and brass boxes resting on their shoulders. Wreaths of lilies perched atop the boxes, and I breathed in the cloying scent as they were carried past us.

I recognized a few of the men who were huffing and puffing under the strain of their cargo and waved to them, though none of them waved back. *Oom* Hennie, Piet's dad who should have been at the party that night, winked at me as he walked by. Behind him were *Oom* Hans, *Oom* Willie and Uncle Charles, all of whom worked with my dad on the mine. I also recognized Mr. Murray and Mr. Clarke from my mom's office, and a few other faces, but there were no other children. Cat and I were the only ones there.

As the men struggled to lower the boxes onto two stands, Cat tugged at my jersey. "What's in the boxes?" she asked.

I shrugged and then leaned over to Edith to repeat the question.

"What boxes?" she asked.

I nodded in their direction. "Those ones."

Edith's eyes widened. "Those aren't boxes, Robs, they're coffins."

"Coffins?" I bounced the word around in my mind, hoping to shake loose its meaning. I'd never been to a funeral before and since we didn't have a television, I'd never seen a show depicting one. Suddenly, though, something clicked into place.

My parents hadn't let me listen to the scary radio programs, sending me off to bed before they started, but Mabel wasn't quite as strict when they were out. I remembered a show I'd listened to about a man who'd been falsely pronounced dead and then buried alive in a coffin. The sound of him scratching against the lid and calling for help had given me nightmares for weeks.

I looked back to the coffins, and then back to Cat whose expression of horror showed that she'd had the same realization as I had.

Our parents are in there.

Edith turned her whole body to face me, took my hands and leaned in to whisper urgently. "We spoke about this, remember? When we were shopping? I said that we were buying outfits for the funeral so you could say your good-byes."

"Yes, but you didn't say they'd be in coffins," my voice rose shrilly.

Edith shushed me though the organ music was still echoing through the church. "Of course they're in coffins. That's where you put people before you bury them. I thought you knew that."

"They can't bury them," Cat whispered fiercely.

I carried the thought through to Edith. "But what if they're still alive like that guy on the show? That man who was buried alive?"

Edith's grip on my hands tightened as I strained to be released. I could see her alarm and assumed it was because she'd also just realized the possibility that a terrible mistake was about to be made.

"We have to get them out of there. They'll listen to you; you're a grown-up."

Our agitated whispers were starting to attract the attention of people seated near us and the organist turned to give us a dirty look.

Stop making such a noise, I thought as I looked back at her. *I can't hear myself think and I need to come up with a plan. How can I do that with you pounding away like that?*

The coffins had finally been balanced on the stands side by side, and the men were making their way to their seats. *Oom* Hennie blew me a kiss as he sat next to his wife, *Tannie* Gertruida. She attempted a watery smile and a small wave, but I didn't wave back.

You told Mommy I'm a bad influence. You said I can't play with Elsabe anymore.

Mrs. van der Walt, who'd been hovering around the coffins, stepped forward to adjust the wreaths and wipe fingerprints from the varnished wood. I nudged Edith to prompt her into action, and she cupped her hand around my ear so I would hear what she was saying without our neighbors eavesdropping.

"Robs, they're not still alive. They've passed away and those are just their bodies in there. That's what you do when people die, you bury them. I can assure you they're not still alive."

By then, the music had faded away completely and a tall man, with a huge stomach hanging over his belt, appeared from the wings. He was wearing a black suit, but the jacket remained unfastened; there was no way that gut was allowing itself to be tucked away. He carried a large black bible in his hands; the pages' edges had been painted gold, which would have enthralled me at any other time, but I wasn't going to allow myself to be distracted.

Edith turned to whisper to Victor as the minister welcomed the congregation, and I started to panic that the conversation was over. I tried to appeal to her one more time. "Did you see them? With your own eyes?"

The woman sitting behind us hissed at me. "Shh!"

I ignored her and plowed on. "If you saw them and you say they're really dead, then I'll believe you."

"Shh," the woman said again, holding a finger up to her lips.

Victor spun around. "This is her parents' funeral and she can speak as much as she wants to! Try shushing her one more time and that finger is going to end up where the sun doesn't shine. Do you hear me?"

She shrank back.

The minister's voice rose and he began to speak in a booming register, taking long, shuddering pauses between every sentence. "When Noah awoke from his wine, he knew what his youngest son had done to him and so he said, 'Cursed be Canaan. The lowest of slaves he will be to his brothers.' And just as God curses Canaan, the son of Ham, he blesses Japhet.

"Now, the bible tells us very clearly that we whites are the blessed descendants of Japhet and the blacks are the cursed descendants of Ham. They are the 'lowest of slaves.' So the murder of two of God's blessed children, Keith and Jolene, at the hands of slaves is especially despicable in the eyes of the Lord."

I couldn't make any sense of what the minister was saying, but most of the congregation was nodding along with him. All I knew was that I couldn't let Edith get distracted. "Did you see them?" I persisted, shouting at Edith to be heard above the sermon.

As my voice ricocheted across the room, the minister dropped his bible in alarm. He stared at me, and seeing his consternation, the rest of the congregation's eyes traveled from him to me.

Edith lowered her head into her raised palm, and through the netting of her hat, I could see that her eyes were closed. "No, Robin, I didn't see them."

I considered whispering, but the entire church was now so quiet that I could hear my heart racing; the blood whooshed past my eardrums, and I could hear the pews squeaking as a few gawkers leaned forward, craning their necks to get a better look at us.

"Then how can you be sure? On that show, everyone thought they were sure, but then the man woke up and—"

Edith sighed. "What do you want me to do, Robs?"

"We need to make sure," Cat said. "Tell her!

I took a deep breath, speaking for both Cat and myself. "We need to open the coffins up and see for ourselves."

There was a collective intake of breath. One or two people started muttering to their companions but were immediately silenced by those around them.

"If we open the coffins up, and I have a look, and I tell you that they're dead, will you let us go ahead and bury them?"

I considered this and the possibility that Edith would lie to me. She clearly wanted the funeral and burial to go ahead, but I knew she wouldn't allow her sister to be buried alive just to silence me. I wasn't too sure about whether she'd extend the same consideration to my father, given her feelings for him, but reasoned that he'd yell blue murder if he was alive and I would hear him.

"What do you think?" Cat asked.

"I think we can trust her."

"Okay then, let's do it," Cat said.

I turned back to Edith and nodded solemnly.

"You promise you'll let us bury them after that?" Edith asked.

"Yes, I promise."

Edith rose slowly and turned to face the congregation. She cleared her throat and then spoke loudly and clearly. "I'm terribly sorry for the inconvenience, but I'm afraid we'll need to open the coffins up. Just for a moment and then we can proceed."

A fter the funeral, when everyone milling around outside on the steps started to leave and the last people had come up to offer their condolences, Edith pulled me aside.

"Victor is going to take you back to the flat now."

"Why?"

"I've just remembered an errand I need to run."

"I'll come with you."

"No, kiddo, not this time. It's something I have to do alone, okay? I'll be home as soon as I can."

Victor held out his hand and I took it. His palm was softer than my dad's—he had no calluses at all—and I let him usher me away from the church to his green Jaguar. When I looked back, the coffins were being loaded into the back of a strange-looking black car; their polished wood gleamed in the sunlight.

"Where are they taking them?" I asked.

"Umm . . . well . . ." Victor was searching for something to say, something that wouldn't upset me, and I could see the conflict on his face. "They're going to the cemetery, Robin." He admitted it so reluctantly, and with such kindness, that his words were a burr in my heart.

"They're going to bury them," Cat said in a quavering voice.

I dared a peek at her in the rearview mirror. She had her fist shoved up against her lips, stifling a sob. I didn't like how deathly pale she'd grown and how stark her red-rimmed eyes looked in contrast.

"Are you okay, Robin?" Victor asked as he took my hand again. "Edie said I should lie to you, but honestly, I think the lies just make it worse, don't you?"

I nodded.

"They're going to put them in the ground," Cat said.

"I know," I whispered, "but we gave Edith permission, remember?"

"Yes, but—"

"Don't think about it," I whispered. "Just don't think about it."

I'd decided by then that the best way of coping with the situation was not to dwell on it, because as I saw it, we could either tread water or we could drown. Later in life when I became acquainted with psychology textbooks, I was surprised to discover there was a whole branch of study dedicated to what I'd experienced; it wasn't the unknowable black pit I'd thought it was.

There were experts in the world who'd concluded there are five stages of grief: denial, anger, bargaining, depression and acceptance, but while I was stuck in that whirlpool of churning sorrow, my nine-year-old self didn't know anything about coping mechanisms or working through the pain to come out breathing on the other side.

All I knew was that if we only glanced at our loss from the corner of our eyes, if we kept it firmly in our peripheral vision without ever tackling it head-on, if we circled around it rather than forging through, I could keep Cat's tears at bay. That became my only goal from hour to hour and day to day. If I could manage her devastation, I could manage my own.

It was as we were pulling away from the church that Edith's face slid past us. She was in her Beetle and had joined the procession of cars going in the opposite direction. She'd taken her pillbox hat off and an unlit cigarette hung from her mouth. Tears were streaming down her face. I put my hand to the glass of the window—wanting to touch her, wanting so much to wipe her tears away—but then she was gone.

On the way home, Victor stopped for ice cream at the Milky Lane in Hillbrow. I forced the chocolate sundae down and smiled at his silly jokes. Victor, like Edith, obviously wasn't used to being around children and he was doing his best to cheer me up. My kindness to him was pretending that he was succeeding.

When we got back to the flat, Cat disappeared to whatever place Cat went when I wanted to be the center of attention. I liked to think that she had a whole interior life of her own, a magical one I wasn't privy to, and I tried not to feel guilty about the times when she ceased to exist. It's not as if I banished her; she herself sensed when she was needed and when she wasn't.

"Okay, what would you prefer to play?" Victor asked once I'd hauled out all the games in the lounge. "Dominoes, Snakes and Ladders, Draughts or Old Maid?"

"Snakes and Ladders?"

"Good choice! And just between you and me, you might want to get rid of the Old Maid. I'm pretty sure Edith will take it as an affront to her feminist principles just having it in the house."

We played one game and then another as the hours passed until the afternoon sun quietly withdrew and left us sitting in the gloom. I was just teaching Victor Fifty-Two-Card Pickup when Edith finally returned home. She looked terrible—all of her mascara had run and her lipstick was wiped off—but she wasn't crying anymore. Elvis swooped down from his perch at the top shelf and squawked his welcome as he flapped around her.

Dinner was a muted affair with us all picking at the quiche Victor made. The adults communicated in glances, raised eyebrows and shrugs, and I knew if I went to bed, they would finally talk. I excused myself early saying I was tired.

When Edith came to check on me half an hour later, the orange glow of her cigarette tip a beacon in the dark, I pretended to be asleep, breathing evenly and trying to look serene. I waited a few minutes after she left before I carefully peeled the duvet off me, crept out of bed and tiptoed to the door with Cat following close behind. We sat down in the darkness, wedged behind the door and Edith's bedside table so we wouldn't be seen if one of them went to the bathroom.

Edith's and Victor's voices were hushed and I had to strain to catch what was being said. They spoke for a while about trivial things and then there was a lull in the conversation. The silence was broken by the clink of a glass and the snick of Edith's lighter. Just when I thought they'd both dozed off, Victor spoke.

"So tell me. How did it go?"

Edith laughed; it was a joyless sound, jarring in the quiet of the apartment. "Christ, it was terrible. Terrible! I never thought I'd see my baby sister being lowered into the ground, you know? I always thought I'd be the one to die young. Thank God our parents weren't alive for this." Edith sighed. "And thank God as well that you were there to take Robin or else I wouldn't have been able to go to the cemetery. I was wrong taking her to the funeral, wasn't I?"

"No, Edie, no. Not if that's what Robin wanted."

Edith cried out, "I didn't even ask her what she wanted. I just hate being pushed around, you know, hate being told what to do, especially by that kind of repressed, condescending Afrikaner bitch. Some of them really went out of their way to make Jolene's life hell and I wanted to push back a bit, so I just said Robin was going and that was that. Jesus, I'm going to fuck her up, aren't I?"

Victor made soothing noises. "No, you're not. You did what you thought was best. That's all you can ever do."

"Well, clearly I have bad judgment."

Victor sighed. "What arrangements still need to be made?"

"The mine's already replaced Keith and the new shift boss wants to move in, so I told them they could bloody well empty the house out themselves. At least we don't have to go back there. I don't think I could put Robin through that."

"So what are you going to do now? Going forward?"

"Christ, Vic, I don't know. I really just don't know. I've never wanted the husband and the kids and all that crap that goes with it. My lifestyle isn't suited to a child. I'm away more than I'm here and that's the way I like it."

"Can't someone else take her? I know your folks are dead, but isn't there someone on his side of the family?"

"No. I'm her only relative."

"How will you manage?"

"They had a policy that will pay out and that will help, but I don't know what I'm going to do about work. She's too young to be left alone while I'm away and it's not like I have a support system. It's a complete fuckup, and I have no idea what to do about it."

Cat shifted next to me. "We're going to be sent away."

"No we aren't."

"She doesn't want us. You heard it yourself."

I'd suddenly lost my desire for information. I crept back to bed, relieved that I wasn't supposed to cry because I suspected if I started, I might never stop. I climbed out of bed again after a minute or two and headed for my secret hiding place. I reached my hand in and pulled out the mascara tube that had become my most prized possession, and then I crept back into bed where I clutched it against my chest.

Cat covered my hand with her own, and together we drew strength from one of the last things we'd seen our mother touch.

Twenty-one

ROBIN

24 June 1976
Yeoville, Johannesburg, South Africa

There was a knock at the door and I opened it thinking it was probably Morrie coming to ask about the funeral. He'd wanted to come with to take photos of the proceedings, but his mother wouldn't let him, telling him that funerals weren't the kind of occasion you wanted to commemorate.

Instead of Morrie, a stranger stood at the threshold. It was a woman with a large, beaky nose crouched under hooded eyes, and her long pointy chin jutted forward, made more prominent by her shortly cropped gray hair. Her severe face was completely bare of makeup—she didn't even wear lipstick—and her only adornment was a gold pendant on a chain.

"Hello." She smiled. "Is Edith Vaughn at home?"

"No," I said, before remembering that you shouldn't ever admit to strangers that you're home alone. "She's just gone to the shops so she should be home soon."

"You must be Robin," she said. "Keith and Jolene's daughter. I'm *Tannie* Wilhelmina."

She had an Afrikaner accent, and even though it was a lot subtler than Piet's, it was still there like gravel woven through silk. I didn't recognize her as one of my parents' acquaintances from the mine or from the funeral.

"Yes, I'm Robin." I wasn't going to invite her in. Even if she knew my parents, she was still a stranger to me.

"Are you okay, *liefling*? This whole *gemors* must be very upsetting for you, *nè*?" She reached out and cupped my face, searching it for a sign to confirm her assessment that I wasn't coping with the whole "mess."

"*Ja*," I agreed.

"So you're living here with your auntie now? Your mother's sister?"

I nodded.

"Do you like her?"

I shrugged.

"Come on now," she encouraged, "you can tell me."

"She's nice. She let me drink a brandy and Coke last Christmas," I confided.

"*Liewe hemel! Regtig?*"

"Yes, really. And she said she'll show me how to stuff my bra when I'm thirteen."

Before I could say anything more, a throat cleared behind Wilhelmina, and she stepped aside to reveal Edith.

"Can I help you?" Edith asked.

"How do you do? You must be Mrs. Vaughn." The woman held out her hand to shake Edith's.

"Ms. Vaughn," Edith said, drawing out the *zzz* sound at the end. "I've never been married. And who, may I ask, are you? And why are you standing here quizzing my niece about me?"

The woman blushed. "I'm Wilhelmina Labuschagne from the Child Welfare Society of Johannesburg."

Cat was suddenly at my side. Her eyes were wide with fear. "I told you," she whispered. "I told you Edith doesn't want us. This woman is here to take us away!"

"Child Welfare?" Edith asked.

"Yes, we get notified when situations like this arise and we try to make ourselves useful with providing assistance to the new family unit." Wilhelmina stressed the words "situations" and "useful" and they suddenly became heavy with menace.

"Hmm." Edith looked as skeptical as Cat and I felt. "You make yourself useful or you butt your nose into other people's business?"

"I'm a qualified social worker, Ms. Vaughn, as well as a registered nurse, not the local busybody peeping through the curtains."

"I can't say I see much of a difference. I've always thought it takes a particular kind of person who has no life of their own to become a social worker. Why else would they be so fascinated with the lives of others?" She didn't wait for a reply. "Now, if you could please be so kind as to let me get through the doorway of my own home."

Wilhelmina quickly stepped into the passage.

"Next time, I'd suggest you call and make an appointment instead of just showing up. Good-bye."

Before Edith closed the door in her face, I caught a glimpse of Wilhelmina's expression. It was clear that she didn't take kindly to Edith's rude dismissal.

Edith waited a beat—leaning against the door until she heard Wilhelmina's retreating footsteps—before she launched into action.

"Shit," she exclaimed, lunging at the row of empty wine bottles and overflowing ashtrays that were still lined up on the lounge table from the night before. "I should have bloody cleaned this up after Victor left, but I was too tired, and then, this morning, I had too much of a headache to try and deal with it. That's what I went to the shops for. Headache tablets."

Edith carried the bottles to the garbage bin in the kitchen. "God, can you imagine if she'd seen this?"

"That lady scares me," Cat said.

"She doesn't scare me," I said. But, of course, that wasn't true.

Twenty-two

BEAUTY

❧

7 JULY 1976
Houghton, Johannesburg, South Africa

By the time I find the right street in the rich suburb of Houghton, it is much later than I planned to get there. The sun is setting and I am irritated with myself for taking so long to find the address scribbled on the crushed piece of paper that was passed to me under a table in Soweto a few days ago. It is the address of the White Angel, a woman who is reputed to help blacks who are seeking refuge from the security police. It is whispered that she supports our cause and has assisted dozens of our people who have needed to disappear.

The house in Mofolo that the boy told Nothando about was found empty, and the man who was last seen with Nomsa and Phumla has disappeared. That trail has now gone cold and the White Angel is my only hope.

I have been warned the police patrol here at night to protect the rich whites from the threat of the black savage, now even more so after what happened in Soweto. It is said that the whites sleep uneasily in their big beds, even behind their high walls in their mansions, knowing that the blacks rose up in protest on soil that lies a mere thirty kilometers from their utopia. It appears they feel safer knowing that men with guns can protect them from the enemy outside the gate, but I wonder how they feel about the enemy within.

What about the maids and the gardeners and the cooks and the nannies? What about all the black people they so desperately need to keep their big houses clean and their fancy cars polished? What about their staff who sleep on their properties in tiny servants' rooms? Do they think that bad pay, ill treatment and scraps of yesterday's food buy their loyalty? Even a *mampara* of the lowest intelligence knows that if a man starves and beats his dog, the beast will one day turn on its master.

As I make my way down the street with its perfectly manicured lawns and carefully tended gardens, I hope that the uniform I am wearing will help me look like I have every right to be there. I borrowed it from a friend of Lindiwe's. Over several layers of jerseys and stockings, I have donned the pale blue dress that buttons down in the front and have paired it with a white apron and *doek*. I am grateful that Nomsa cannot see me now.

The streetlights start to come on as the whites make their way home in their shiny cars. I pass a few men who look like gardeners and greet them each in the customary way. "*Molo. Unjani?*" One man starts a conversation and says he is not fortunate enough to live on his employer's property and so he is making his way home to Soweto. I wish him a safe journey. "*Hamba kakuhle.*"

When I am about two hundred meters from my destination, I hear the squeal of tires from a car that is traveling too fast. It is a menacing sound, like the high-pitched hunting cry of a bird of prey. I turn around and feel my breath catch in my throat; it is the dreaded yellow vehicle, the *kwela-kwela* van I have been warned of, the one police use for their passbook roundups. I do not have permission from the police to be out of the Bantu homeland of the Transkei. I am in Johannesburg illegally without papers. If they catch me, they will arrest me.

The van comes to a halt beside the gardener I have just greeted. A policeman jumps out of the van, a slinking black dog following behind him, and he shines a bright torch in the gardener's eyes. His voice echoes down the street, but I cannot make out his exact words. I do not have to; I know that he is demanding the man's passbook.

I quicken my pace. I hope that my unfortunate comrade will keep them busy long enough so that I will have time to get to the gate and slip through before the van can reach me, but then the doors slam and the engine begins accelerating. The man must have quickly shown a valid passbook; they are making their way to me. I will be the unfortunate comrade tonight.

I want to run, the gate so near and yet just out of reach. I am still ten meters short of it when the van screeches to a stop next to me and the doors open once again. The pain in my chest that has eased these past few days suddenly awakens.

"You, stop. Where is your passbook?" The order is issued in Afrikaans, which I understand, but I stop and turn around slowly. I raise my hands in the air and pretend that I do not speak the language.

A torch is shoved into my face and I wince from the bright light. The policeman switches over to English and repeats the question, and I shrug, once again feigning ignorance. The man calls out to the van, and the back door opens, this time releasing a black policeman to join us.

I have heard of these men, black men who wear the despised uniform of the oppressor and who work for the police. Men who brandish batons but whose real weapons are far more dangerous than even guns: words that are uttered in our own language, turned against us and used in order to oppress and humiliate us. Traitors who get housing and good pay in return for selling their souls to the white devil. I heard that on the day of the uprising some of the policemen firing into the crowd were black; it turns my stomach to think of such treachery.

The dog follows the black policeman out of the van; it starts growling as it nears me, and I glance down at it against my better judgment. The sight of its large white teeth bared in a snarl takes me back to the day of the conflict in Soweto, and I have to rein in my impulse to turn and run. I force myself to look away from the dog and back at the black policeman.

"Where is your passbook?" he asks in Sotho. When I do not answer, he asks the question again in Xhosa.

I want to spit in his face, but I am too afraid. Being arrested would mean I could be of no help to Nomsa. Instead, I look him in the eye and quietly ask, "Is your mother proud of you?"

I then turn and address the white policeman in English. "I work at this house, right here, *baas*, and I forgot my passbook in my room."

The policeman looks surprised, but before he can comment, the black policeman, angry at my disrespect, speaks first. "You know you must keep your passbook on you at all times."

"I was just quickly going to the shop. I did not think I would need it."

"You are lying. Where is your shopping now, *sisi*, if you went to the shop? Where are your bags?"

"I am not your sister, Judas, and I did not find what I was looking for so I did not buy anything."

The white policeman starts to speak but is cut off when the gate near us suddenly swings open. My blood turns cold. The charade is now up. I was hoping to be allowed onto the property while the police waited for me to return with my passbook, and my plan was to then try to escape by another route. But whoever is coming out will now confirm that I do not work for them.

A black security guard steps out and he greets the police officers with great humility. The sight of the dog frightens him, especially once it starts barking, but he smiles and addresses the white policeman who appears to be in charge.

"Good evening, *baas*. Is there a problem that I can help with?"

"Man, mind your own business unless you also want to be arrested."

"*Baas*, please, this lady works here. She is a maid for my madam who sent her to the shop."

My hopes lift. The guard must have been listening in on our conversation from behind the gate and he understands what I am trying to do.

"Where is her passbook then, hey? Your madam should know that blacks can't be on the streets without their passbooks."

Before the guard can reply, we are all lit up in the beams of approaching headlights, and a car slows before it turns into the driveway. The guard raises his hand in greeting and takes a step towards the car, but the police dog starts growling again so he stays where he is. I can feel the dog's hot breath on my hand and wonder how often it has tasted human flesh.

The car window winds down; there are two people inside. An old white man is driving and a blond woman sits in the passenger seat. She leans forward to speak, but the man puts his hand on her knee, and she seems to understand this as an instruction to be silent.

"Good evening, Officers. Throwing a party in our driveway? How wonderful. Are we invited?" His tone is jovial; it sounds like he is joking with a friend. "How can we help our men in blue this evening?"

The man is distinguished-looking and speaks in a refined English accent that sounds foreign. He is smiling and his friendliness has the effect of relaxing the white police officer who hunches over with an arm resting on the roof of the car to make eye contact with the driver.

"Good evening, sir. Sorry for the problems, but your maid doesn't have her passbook and we should actually arrest her." His voice is stripped of all menace. The policeman obviously views this man as a superior who he does not want to upset.

The old man turns to look at me and I worry again that I will be identified as a stranger. Instead, he smiles and shakes his head ruefully as he turns back to the policeman. "Ah yes, Dora's not very bright, I'm afraid. You know what these people are like."

The policeman laughs at that and nods in agreement.

The old man speaks again, giving me a meaningful look. "Dora, go to your room, please. You've created enough fuss for one evening." He then turns to the policeman, "Why don't you come inside for a moment, Officer? I feel terrible that we've inconvenienced you, and I'm sure that we can offer you something to make it up to you."

The guard takes my arm and steers me through the gates. The policeman smiles and doffs his cap at the old man before turning to the black officer, instructing him to wait in the van until he comes back.

When I am later properly introduced to Maggie—the White Angel—and her husband, Andrew, they will tell me how an imported bottle of brandy from France and a carton of Texan Plain cigarettes paid for my freedom.

I am now in the lion's den, living in the home of white people. I am in the heart of enemy territory, and yet, I feel safe.

Twenty-three

ROBIN

❁

E dith took a week off after my parents died, and once that week was up, she took another to try to figure things out. It seemed that no matter how many times she went over the variables, the figures still added up to her having one more child than she'd had before, and a career that frowned upon loose ends.

Holidays had begun and so I wasn't missing any more classes for the time being. I'd realized by then that I would be starting at a new school a few blocks from my new home, and though my palms got clammy when I thought about the change, I didn't say anything given Edith's own increasing levels of anxiety.

She resigned on the first of July, and for a few days afterwards, friends from the airline called to sympathize and offer encouragement. Edith sounded cheery on the phone, assuring them that she'd be fine and was looking forward to a "normal" job for a change. She must've fooled them because most of the calls died off. She even almost fooled me. The first sign that things weren't all "fine and dandy" as Edith insisted was after another call she received.

"Hello?" Edith answered in her usual bright voice, which softened when she heard who the caller was. "Oh, Michael. It's you. Can you hold on for a moment?" Edith covered the mouthpiece with her hand and whispered, "Robs, come here."

Elvis was perched on my shoulder, nibbling at the whorl of my ear as I walked over to her.

Edith nodded at her purse, which lay on a side table. "Why don't you make yourself useful? Take some money and go get us some milk and bread."

"By myself?" I still hadn't ventured out into the city streets alone.

"It's perfectly safe. It's just a few steps down the road."

"Can Elvis come with?"

"No, you know the rules. He's not allowed outside."

I held two of my fingers up to Elvis and he stepped off onto them. His claws closed tightly around me in a rough embrace that was oddly reassuring, and I ferried him down to the armrest of the couch.

I didn't have to tell Cat that I'd need her on the first errand Edith had ever sent me out on. She was already waiting at the door as I took some coins from Edith's purse. When we returned ten minutes later, charged with adrenaline but proud of managing the task on our own, Edith had changed into a pretty blue minidress, swept her hair up into a kind of beehive and reapplied her makeup. Elvis had also been re-turned to his cage where he was squawking loudly. "Elvis has left the building. Elvis has left the building."

Edith lit a cigarette and bent low to blow a smoke ring at him.

"Devil in disguise," Elvis squawked.

"Oh shush, stop being so dramatic."

"Don't be cruel. Don't be cruel to a heart that's true," Elvis said.

"These cigarettes are imported from France, you know," Edith said, holding up her box of Gauloises. "They're very expensive. You should thank me for sharing them."

"Devil in disguise."

"Come on," Edith said, barely giving me enough time to put the milk and bread away before nudging me out the door. "I have an errand to run and Rachel said she'd watch you while I'm out."

"Who's Rachel?"

"Mrs. Goldman, Morrie's mother."

"But I want to come with you."

"Well, you can't. Not this time. Anyway, I'm sure you'd much prefer to spend the afternoon with Morrie. It sounded like the two of you hit it off the other day."

"Okay. Come on, Cat," I said, motioning for her to follow us.

"No, leave Cat behind. I'm sure she can keep herself entertained."

"But—"

"No buts. It would be rude of you to be yakking away to an empty space while the Goldmans try to avoid sitting on your sister who is, by the way, really underfoot and needs to work on getting out of the way faster." Edith pulled the door closed and called out, "Bye, Cat!" punctuating her parting shot with the key turning firmly in the lock.

A petite woman with curly dark hair answered our knock downstairs and welcomed us inside. She air-kissed Edith and cupped my chin. "Look at that face. Isn't that just the saddest face you ever saw? Such tragedy."

I didn't know what to say to that so I just smiled.

"Look at how brave she is. Will you look at that? Smiling through the pain. Suffering in silence." She released my face and straightened up. "Go sit with the *boychick*. I'll head out with Edith now because I have a hairdresser's appointment, but don't worry. Mr. Goldman is here if you need anything while I'm out. Bye, you two."

"Bye." I sighed and went over to sit next to Morrie who was reading *Treasure Island*.

"Did you get that from the library?" I asked.

"No, my *bubbe* gave it to me."

"Who?"

"My grandmother."

"Oh." I'd never much missed my grandparents until then when I realized how many presents I might have missed out on. "Do you have any Enid Blyton books?"

"No."

"Do you have any books about orphans?"

"No, but I have five books from Willard Price's Adventure series." He pulled a book out from under the couch and handed it to me. "This one is my favorite."

I looked at the lurid green cover showing two boys tied up to something. "*Cannibal Adventure*?" I skimmed over the blurb. "Headhunters and cannibals? Yuck. Boys' books are revolting!"

"*Feh!*"

"Would you stop saying those stupid words?"

"What are you *kvetching* about now?"

"There you go again! Saying those words that aren't even English." In the world of children, there is very little power to be had so supremacy must be seized and lauded wherever possible. I figured Morrie was flinging out his mother's Goldmanese every chance he got just to show off that he knew more than me.

"They're not stupid words," Morrie said. "They're the language of my people."

"The Goldman family needs their own language?"

"Not just my family. All of us," Morrie said.

"All of who?"

"The Jews."

"The juice?"

"Not 'juice.' *Jews*." He spelled it out for me. "I am Jewish."

I had no idea what that meant either, but he said it so somberly that I figured it had to be something really bad. "I'm sorry."

"For what?"

"That you're Jewish."

"Why?"

"It sounds really awful."

He nodded. "It is. My people have been persecuted for centuries."

"What does 'persecuted' mean?"

"I'm not totally sure," he said. "But I think it means no one invited us to parties."

"Wow, that really is terrible."

"I know. And we have to get circumcised."

"What's that?"

"A rabbi cuts our foreskins off."

"What's a foreskin?"

"It's on our willies."

That gave me a lot to think about. I'd have to come back to that once I'd processed it properly. "So, is that language with the funny words Jewish?"

"No, it's Yiddish."

I considered this for a bit. "So your people come from Yidland?"

"Yidland? How do you figure that?"

"Edith has been to almost every country in the world," I said proudly. "She says the Finns speak Finnish and come from Finland. I think that's how it works."

He looked impressed by my knowledge. "I'll ask my dad, but I'm pretty sure we come from South Africa."

I was confused. If the Jews came from South Africa, did that mean I was Jewish too? I suddenly didn't want to carry on with the discussion. I had a feeling that Morrie pretended to know a lot more than he actually did and that he mostly just listened in on his parents' conversations, and then recited bits to make himself look important.

Morrie suddenly stood up and gave me his *Treasure Island*. "Here, you can read this. It doesn't have as many cannibals in it. I want to take some pictures."

I pretended to read but mostly just watched Morrie as he took photos of a dead beetle, a pair of scuffed shoes and a dismembered radio. There were much nicer things in the flat to take pictures of, and I put my book aside to get a better look at them. Every doorway had a strange but pretty rectangular ornament hung up at an angle, and I wondered if Mr. Goldman had got into trouble for putting them all up askew.

Ornate silver frames encasing enlarged black-and-white photos were scattered throughout the flat and I paused in front of each one. A few pictures were of Morrie while others showed old people who I assumed were his grandparents. There was a wedding picture of Morrie's parents and, in it, Mr. Goldman was wearing a strange little hat no bigger than a pancake. The candlesticks then caught my attention and it was one of these that I dropped, bringing Mr. Goldman out from a bedroom.

"What broke?"

Morrie pointed at the broken glass at my feet. "That. She's a real *klutz*, this one."

"I'm so sorry," I stammered. "I'm very clumsy. Everyone says so. I should've looked with my eyes and not my hands." I knew I should have brought Cat down with me; if she'd been there, I could have blamed her for the accident.

"Stand still while I get that cleaned up," Mr. Goldman said, not unkindly, and I got my first good look at him while he was picking up the glass. He was a small, bespectacled man with strawberry-blond hair and a swarm of freckles that made me look positively freckle-free in comparison. He wore thick square glasses and a green knitted cardigan, but there was no sign of the little hat.

When Mr. Goldman disappeared back into his room, I asked Morrie about it.

"It's not a hat, it's a *yarmulke*. Jewish men wear them."

"Why don't you wear one?"

"I do sometimes, when we go to *shul*."

Before I could ask what *shul* was, there was a knock at the door and Edith had returned less than an hour after she'd left. She was brusque. "Come on, let's go. Bye, Morrie."

I stomped back up the stairs behind her, bored and cranky. Unwilling to spend the rest of the afternoon cooped up in the apartment, I asked, "Can we go to the library? You said I could sign up for a new membership."

"Not today, Robin. We'll go another time, all right?"

"That's what you said the last time I asked. Can we go get my bike then?"

She sighed. "Why don't you amuse yourself playing with Elvis or if it's books you want so desperately, here, read some of these." Edith pulled a few of her travel books randomly from the shelf and tossed them on the couch before heading for Elvis's cage and opening the door. Elvis squawked in pleasure. "Thank you, thank you very much!" He hopped out and immediately flew to his favorite perch on the corner of the top shelf.

Edith lifted the ice bucket from the liquor cabinet and took it to the kitchen. When she returned, the bucket heaped with cubes, she thumped it down and poured herself a scotch. She knocked it back in one go and grimaced before slamming the glass down. Edith then started viciously yanking at the clips in her hair and tossing them on the dining room table with the kind of fervor another person might reserve for throwing down gauntlets. She kicked off her heels and poured herself another drink, forgoing the ice tongs to use her fingers to fill the glass.

I looked away from her to the book resting open on my lap and pretended to study a few of its pages. The silence made me nervous. "Edith?"

"Hmm?"

"Do you know that Morrie's been circumscribed?"

She didn't reply.

"It means a rabbit cut his forefathers off, which means he has no willy. Do you think it will grow back again?"

"Hmm."

I tried to engage her again, this time asking the question that I really wanted an answer to. "Who's Michael?"

Edith plucked an ice cube from the glass and popped it into her mouth, crunching it into oblivion before replying. "No one. Michael is absolutely no one." She picked the bottle of scotch up by its neck and went to her room, shutting the door behind her. She didn't come out again that night.

Cat materialized from the shadows and curled herself around me.

"Robin?"

"Hmm?"

"I'm lonely."

"Don't be lonely. I'm here."

"I miss Mommy and Daddy."

"I know. Me too."

"I miss Mabel too."

I nodded as my throat constricted.

"Do you remember when—"

"Let's not think about it. It will only make it worse. Here," I said, "do you want to look at the books with me?"

We fell asleep on the couch, hours later, with travel books splayed around us and Elvis crooning to us from his perch.

In the week that followed, Edith had her first job interview. She ate a modest breakfast consisting of a large cup of coffee (no sugar and no milk) and a single boiled egg with an unbuttered slice of toast. Once she was finished eating, she headed to her bedroom to get ready.

"Make yourself useful, kiddo, and put a record on," she called to me as she disappeared through the doorway.

I went to the shelf where all her albums were stored, and riffled through them for a few minutes before picking out one whose cover showed a man sitting cross-legged in what looked like a giant bubble. Pulling it from its sleeve, I held the record by the edges, as my father had taught me, so as not to get oily fingerprints on it, and then laid it down on the turntable. I gently lowered the needle to the vinyl, my father's voice coming back to me as I did so: "Freckles, the worst thing you can ever do is scratch a record. You may as well throw it out after that."

There were a few seconds of staticky noise before the needle caught the thread of the song, and then the opening strains filled the room. "Sugar man . . ."

Edith's hand appeared seemingly out of nowhere, stretching over my shoulder and yanking the needle from the record, probably scratching it in the process. "Not that one, Robs. Rodriguez is more suitable for a mellow vibe, if you get my drift." She brought her thumb and index fingers together, and then held their squashed tips to her mouth while pretending to be inhaling from them. "We need something a bit more upbeat today." She plucked out an Elvis record, cranked up the volume, and then headed back to our room where she started excavating her closets.

Edith took great care to pick the perfect outfit, and then hunted down shoes and a bag to finish it off. After she laid each item out on the bed, including the underwear she'd chosen, she sat at her dressing table in her gown where she spent ages curling her hair, sweeping it up, painting her nails and "putting on her face."

I was already dressed and sat on the bed watching her in the mirror with the fanciful thought that if I reenacted those last moments with my mother—our reflections communing with one another—Edith's face might magically rearrange itself into my mother's features. When Edith got to the moment where she applied her mascara, I waited, holding my breath to see if she'd open her mouth like my mother did; my own mouth ready to copy the O. She didn't and I felt cheated.

Once Edith was dressed and made-up, she went to the cupboard where she reached into the back of one of the top shelves, pulling out a large ornately carved and painted box. She brought it back to her dressing table, where she set it down gently and opened the lid. A tune escaped like a genie from a bottle and, with it, the smell of Chanel No. 5, Edith's signature scent.

"What song is that?"

"It's 'Greensleeves.' Pretty, even if it's a touch maudlin."

The box had dozens of drawers with tiny gold handles, and as she pulled each one out, I could see they were lined in pink suede and filled with sparkly trinkets. It was a treasure trove of jewels, and without thinking, I reached a hand out. The smooth lacquer of the box, the velvety softness of the lining and the cool sparkle of gemstones was a hypnotic combination and my fingers itched to touch every one of the mesmerizing textures.

Before they connected with anything, Edith uttered a stern, "No!"

I snatched my hand back as though scalded. "I'm sorry."

"This is the one thing that is off bounds to you. You can play with my makeup and clothes and anything else you like, but you must never, ever touch my jewelry. Do you understand?"

"Yes."

"Some of these pieces have huge sentimental value and are irreplaceable. One day when you're grown up and I'm no longer around, they'll be yours, but until then, you must promise me that you'll never touch this box or anything in it."

"I promise."

"Okay then. Good girl." Edith extracted a string of pearls with a matching bracelet, which she put on with expert fingers. After she'd closed the box and returned it to its place, she said, "Let's go."

We were preparing to leave when the phone rang. Edith checked her watch and, with a sigh, snatched up the receiver.

"Hello, Edith speaking." She listened for a moment and then a twitch of impatience tugged at her eyebrow. "Wilhelmina, I'm afraid this isn't a good time for me, I was just on my way out."

Wilhelmina? My stomach twisted into a knot.

"You want to set up an appointment to visit?"

My thumb automatically went to my mouth, and I started to chew on the nail as I listened in on the one-sided conversation. Cat was doing the same on Edith's other side.

"I see. Well, you'll just have to call back another time, I'm afraid. If I miss this job interview, it will be your fault, and I'm assuming you agree that gainful employment would be nice if I was to be Robin's legal guardian. Ta-ta."

Edith slammed the phone down with relish. "Good riddance to bad rubbish. Come, Robin. Let's go."

We headed out in Edith's yellow Beetle without Cat who'd once again been told to stay at home, and I promised to behave once we got to the office. I took a book along (one of Edith's travel ones as we still hadn't gotten to the library), and I was hoping to use it as a prop so I could eavesdrop from wherever I was seated. The job was an admin position and Edith was being interviewed by a senior secretary who came out to the reception area to meet us.

"Good morning. You must be Edith; it's lovely to meet you. I'm Harriet." The woman was much older than Edith, and if not exactly frumpy or overweight, then definitely dowdy in appearance. She wore her graying, uncolored hair up in a severe bun and wore very little makeup. Her nails were cut short and left unpolished. She smiled brightly when she greeted Edith and politely gestured her ahead, but when Edith started to walk in the direction she indicated, Harriet's friendly mask slipped and I could see something akin to contempt cross her face. I'd been well trained by my mother to be sensitive to nonverbal cues, and I could see that this woman had made up her mind within seconds of meeting Edith. She would not be hiring someone who was dressed better than she was, and certainly not a younger woman who looked so glamorous.

Edith didn't seem to pick up on the woman's jealousy and chattered excitedly all the way home. "That went very well, hey? Harriet seems nice and I think I made a good impression. Did you hear how impressed she was about my experience with the airline? I thought it would work against me, but she seemed to get what I was saying about service industries being pretty much the same. How difficult do you think it will be to pick up shorthand?"

Edith was surprised, hurt even, when she never heard back, and I didn't know how to tell her that, like my mother, she was an exotic orchid in a garden of daisies and would often be punished for it. The next few interviews were very much along the same lines, and after her first dozen rejections, Edith replaced Elvis with Dean Martin and took less care with her appearance. Contrary to helping her chances, it only made things worse. The women interviewing her seemed to instinctively know that all Edith needed was to be given a chance before she would rise like a phoenix from the ashes.

The closest Edith came to being hired was by the only man who interviewed her. He asked her few questions and barely looked at her résumé before announcing she had the job. Edith was ecstatic until he casually suggested she meet him at the President Hotel in Eloff Street that night to celebrate. I was listening in on the interview with my back turned, so all I heard was an almighty thwack. When I spun around, Edith was marching out of his office while the man clutched his cheek.

After that, Edith refused to take any calls from her friends, not even Victor, and took the phone off the hook when I complained about having to lie to him about her whereabouts. I was relieved that the phone was out of commission; it meant that Wilhelmina wouldn't be able to reach us to set up a time to do her visit. Cat also relaxed once the phone stopped ringing.

One morning, Edith breezed up to the liquor cabinet and measured out a tot of brandy, topping it up with ice and ginger ale. An hour later, she was back to pour another. After two more drinks, the tot measure was abandoned, as were the ice and mixer, and the tumbler was half filled with pure liquor. By the sixth drink, she'd hauled her travel books down from the shelves, spread them around her on the floor and started talking to them like long-lost friends.

Edith was saying her reluctant good-byes to all the exotic destinations she'd been to and become a part of; the places whose rhythms flowed through her veins. She was mourning not only my mother's life but her own life too, the life she had envisioned but would not get to live. Her sorrow permeated everything.

She began to roam about the apartment at night and sleep during the day, and she wouldn't change out of her nighties or make our bed. "There really isn't any point, is there? Not if I'm not going anywhere."

"Maybe you'll have another interview," I suggested tentatively.

"There'll be no more interviews! There are only so many times a woman can be told she isn't wanted. It's important to know when to call it quits."

I was secretly relieved. I couldn't keep being a spectator to Edith's constant disappointments; I knew she would come to resent me for being the chief witness to her downfall.

A few days after Edith's drinking began, I looked up from picking my cuticles to find Cat doing the same. Our nails had already been bitten down to the quick and pinpricks of blood dotted our inflamed fingertips. It looked like a colony of rats had been nibbling on our hands while we slept. Cat kept shooting Edith nervous, fearful looks, adding up the drinks on her fingers until the day's count exceeded the number of digits on both of her hands. After that, I'd take over, though I was less obvious with my calculations.

No matter how much I tried to assure Cat that everything would be fine, she insisted on obsessing over all the things that could go wrong in our perilous new reality.

"If she carries on like this, we're going to be taken away. It's only a matter of time," Cat said.

"No, we won't," I replied, trying to sound both exasperated and bored with the discussion. There were certain things that were better off not being said out loud and I wished Cat would learn when to keep her mouth shut.

"Yes, we will. If she keeps drinking all day and doesn't get a job, we won't have any money. And if we don't have money, that will mean we're poor, and if we're poor, we won't be able to pay to live here. If they throw us out, we'll be living on the street because that's what homeless people do, and they'll take us away from her and send us to a foster home. That's if that social worker doesn't show up here again first. If she sees Edith like this, she won't even wait for us to be homeless, she'll take us then and there."

I wished Cat would just shut up. All of her chatter, the constant outpouring of her insecurities and deepest, darkest fears was getting harder and harder to ignore. "All we need is to come up with a plan," I said, faking confidence.

"The plan is to not have Edith give us away or have Wilhelmina take us."

"That isn't a plan! That's just what we want to happen. The plan tells us how we're going to do it."

"So then, what's the plan?"

"Could you just keep quiet for a minute and let me think?"

In the blissful silence that followed, I went to get a pencil and some paper. I'd watched my mother draft out her own plans in this way: our family budgets, what we needed to pack and prepare for our holidays, and instructions for how to put together a dinner party. I was pretty sure I could do it, too, because she'd explained each step to me as she went along, emphasizing how important it was to always be in control of things.

"Okay," I said, sucking on the pink eraser at the tip of the pencil. "What could stop us from living here?"

"Edith, obviously," Cat said darkly. "And Wilhelmina."

"She's easy," I lied. "If she shows up at the door again, we just pretend we aren't home. She can't take us away if she can't get inside, so stop worrying about her. What would make Edith give us away?"

"I don't think she wants us," Cat said with a tremor in her voice. "I think she's only taking us because we have no other family."

"So then it's easy. We just have to do stuff to make her want us."

"Okay." Cat brightened. "She's always telling you to make yourself useful so we can do that."

"Yes, but how?"

"Maybe we can pour her drinks."

"Don't be stupid," I said. "We don't want her drinking so much, remember?"

"Yes, but what if we pour the drinks for her but we make them a lot weaker?"

"Good thinking!" I'd seen my mother do that with my father a few times at mine functions and it had worked. "What else?"

"We can make her breakfast for her. And paint her nails."

"Yes, and we can make up bubble baths . . ."

". . . so she has to get out of bed."

"Exactly." My hand was getting sore from scribbling all our ideas down.

"We can also tell her she's pretty."

"That will make her happy."

"And we must be quiet and behave so we don't irritate her."

"You're the one that irritates her."

"I'm sorry, I don't mean to."

"We need to try and cheer her up."

"How?"

"Well, she likes pictures," I said, gesturing to all the stuff on the walls. "We could draw her funny ones."

"And we can tell her jokes."

"And we can hold concerts where we sing and dance like Elvis."

We were both quiet for a moment as we tried to come up with more ideas.

"I wish we could get a job," Cat sighed. "Then we could give her money."

"So let's try and get one!"

"How?"

"Well, we saw her type up her résumé thingy on the typewriter she keeps under the bed. You need one of those to get a job so we'll make up one for me."

"What about me?"

"People can't hire an imaginary person, dummy."

"They can if it's an imaginary job."

"You try and go to the shop and pay for stuff with imaginary money."

"Okay, sorry. You're right. That won't work. Do you think getting a job will really help?"

I thought about it. All of Edith's depression and drinking stemmed from the fact that she couldn't get a job. If we could get a job and help pay for stuff, she'd stop the drinking and she'd cheer up and all our problems would be solved.

"Yes," I said. "Definitely!"

Twenty-four

BEAUTY

❦

23 JULY 1976
Houghton, Johannesburg, South Africa

The late-afternoon sun streams through the window and dust motes swirl in the gentle breeze. My bedroom in the freestanding cottage at the back of Maggie's property is larger than my entire hut in the Transkei; it is larger even than the classroom in which I taught thirty children. I have never in my life seen such luxury as this.

The room has an en suite bathroom with a bath that could hold four people. Filling it does not take dozens of trips to a stream with buckets that then have to be carried back for miles. No fire needs to be made to heat the water. All you have to do is turn the tap and wait a few minutes for the tub to fill. No wonder white people are always so clean. If I lived like this, I would take at least two baths a day.

The bedroom itself is furnished with four chairs, a dressing table, a writing desk and built-in cupboards. The queen-size bed in which

I lie at night, adrift all by myself in its vastness, could hold my entire family. The room is decorated with wallpaper and paintings, and a plush white carpet tickles my feet as I walk. Rows of jacaranda trees line the street outside the window. I wish they were in bloom so that I could see the purple flowers floating like lavender clouds above the wall.

I sit now and bask in the sun's warmth like a lizard on a rock as I read Dr. Martin Luther King's *Why We Can't Wait*. Maggie's collection of banned works is extensive, and it has been a privilege to absorb the philosophy and literature the apartheid government does not want me to read.

Dr. King's words move me exactly because they are a more eloquent expression of my own feelings: "We did not hesitate to call our movement an army. But it was a special army, with no supplies but its sincerity, no uniform but its determination, no arsenal except its faith, no currency but its conscience."

I know that if Nomsa were here and I showed her this passage that underscores my own belief in nonviolent resistance, she would point out that it was a bullet that killed Dr. King eight years ago—less than a year before he could celebrate his fortieth birthday—and that the bullet came from a white man's gun. I can even hear her voice saying, "Maybe if he had picked up a gun and fired first, he would still be alive to fight another day."

Our imaginary conversation is interrupted by a knock at the door. Kgomotso, a young man who works for Maggie in some mysterious capacity, tells me that there has been word of Nomsa. He says that Maggie has just arrived home from work and would like to see me in her office. After almost three weeks of being a part of her "invisible household," I know that Maggie does not mean the large, street-facing office they keep on the ground floor, the one with the walls covered in expensive Pierneef paintings of Highveld landscapes. That office is purely for show and has been stripped of any materials that might cause suspicion. It has also been equipped with a minibar stocked with the exact brands of imported brandy, cane, rum and whiskey that the local police officials prefer.

Instead, I make my way to the secret office at the back of the house on the second floor—the one that can only be reached through a door disguised as one of the bookshelf panels in the library—and slip into the room. Maggie has not yet arrived and I use the time alone to compose myself. The only thing I dread more than hearing what Maggie has learned is not having that knowledge at all.

The room is tiny in comparison to the other rooms in the house, about the size of a long but very narrow bathroom. There are no windows to let in natural light, but the room is made bright with three ceiling light fixtures. A desk takes up most of the floor space and the walls are lined with bookshelves waist high and, above them, dozens of framed photographs.

Instead of sitting down, I try to slow my breathing by studying the images. My favorite photographs grab my attention first. In one, a much younger Maggie sits next to the exiled African singer-songwriter Miriam Makeba. Both women are wearing glittering evening dresses and Miriam's head is thrown back, her mouth wide with laughter. Mama Africa's one hand rests on Maggie's leg in a gesture of affection and friendship that I have never seen a black woman so casually display towards a white one. In another photo, Andrew stands next to Miriam's musician husband, Hugh Masekela. Andrew has a hat rakishly perched on his head and holds a drink in one hand, his other arm flung around Hugh's shoulders.

As I move farther along the wall, I skim past dozens of photographs that, if discovered by the police, would incriminate my hosts to such an extent that no trial would ever be required to send them both to prison. I keep scanning until I notice a photo I have never seen before. Again, Maggie is much younger in it and she is standing next to a tall, handsome black man who looks to be in his thirties or forties. His hair is cropped close to his skull, and he has a neat trimmed beard that accentuates his pleasant features. He looks familiar but I cannot place him, and I assume that he is an American actor or politician.

"I like that picture too," Maggie says as she steps into the room. "It's one of my favorites."

"Who is he?"

She looks surprised that I do not know. "That's Rolihlahla Mandela."

I look at the picture again. "You mean Nelson Mandela?"

"Well, Nelson was never one of his given names, but yes."

"His father did not name him Nelson?"

"No. Apparently a white teacher who couldn't pronounce his Xhosa name gave him the English name of 'Nelson' when he was a child and it stuck. I just assumed that's what happened with you as well."

"No. My mother believed that no good could come of giving me an African name. She thought that the highest ambition I could ever hope to achieve was becoming a maid in an affluent white household. Naming me 'Beauty' was her way of making sure my future employers could pronounce my name, and that it would have positive connotations in their language."

"How proud your mother must have been when you went on to attend university and become a teacher. You went to Fort Hare, didn't you?"

"Yes, I graduated in 1953, just six years before they put a stop to proper tertiary education for blacks. My mother never knew. She died before then." I turn back to the photograph. "The village where he grew up is very close to mine. I have heard so many tales about him, such great stories about such a great man, but I have never seen what he looks like."

"Well, I suppose that's to be expected with the ban on reproducing his image. That's exactly what the government wants."

I turn away from the picture and sit across from Maggie. "It is humbling to learn about my people's hero from a white person."

"It's infuriating that you're deprived of knowing more about him."

"Do you know what 'Rolihlahla' means?"

"No, and do you know, I never thought to ask him."

"It means 'troublemaker.'"

Maggie laughs. "Well, that he certainly is, so he was very well named. See? Now you've taught me something too."

"When was that picture taken?"

Maggie's eyes return to the photograph. "Years ago, long before the Rivonia Trial. I must have been about your age. I met him through Albertina Sisulu who is a friend of mine. He was such a charismatic man. Standing next to him was like being caught up in an electric storm. He was so passionate about liberating his people and so willing to make sacrifices. I can't begin to tell you how much he inspired me." She pulls her gaze away from the picture and looks back at me. "Everything Andrew and I do is aimed at securing his freedom one day. And yours."

"I do not believe it will ever happen."

"You must believe, Beauty, you absolutely must. Or else what is the alternative?"

"Tell me, Maggie, when we have this freedom you are fighting for, who will lead us? Who will stop us from behaving like children with a new toy so that we do not break it?"

Maggie's blue eyes are shining. "Someone great, Beauty, someone like Nelson Mandela. We deserve to be led by a man like him."

"He is not a young man anymore, and after he is gone, who then?"

"There will be other great men."

I shake my head. "There are very few great men. That is exactly what makes the great ones great. And I worry what the power will do to us."

"What do you mean?"

"What is that saying? 'Power corrupts, and absolute power corrupts absolutely.' I do not believe in utopia. There is no such thing and I fear that chasing that dream will only lead to disappointment for us all." And then I can put off hearing the news about Nomsa no longer. If it is bad, I will have to hear it now. "There has been news about Nomsa?"

By this time, I have learned just how extensive Maggie's network is and how far it reaches. Her intelligence is made up of reports from spies, government officials, officers in the police force, social workers, members of the Black Sash, journalists and various other members of important organizations. Most of them use fake names and have never met face-to-face because of the risk involved. She says, though, that her best information comes from her invisible army—the black maids, gardeners and nannies who work for high-ranking individuals and who are able to gather intelligence because of the arrogance of their masters who do not believe their staff intelligent enough to comprehend or use the information they are privy to.

"Yes," Maggie says. "That tip-off about the man in Mofolo proved to be useful. He goes by the nickname 'Shakes' and my sources tell me that Nomsa and Phumla are with him. They haven't left the country just yet. It seems they're hiding out in Venda until they can safely cross the border into Rhodesia."

"That is wonderful news." I had prepared myself for the worst. "And she is unharmed?"

"She was apparently injured during the uprising last month. A bad cut down the side of her face, but they managed to get it stitched up and treated. She's in good health otherwise."

"That is a relief."

"Unfortunately, there's worrying news as well."

"What is it?"

"They say that once she crosses the border, she will be sent to the MK camps where she will be trained."

"MK camps?"

"Sorry, I forget that you're relatively new to all of this. 'MK' is the abbreviation for *Umkhonto we Sizwe* or the Spear of the Nation, as it's also called. It's the armed wing of the African National Congress, and they've set up military camps across a few African countries where they train their operatives."

"Train them as what?"

"As soldiers. It seems that Nomsa and her friend have signed up. Apparently Shakes is a recruiter and that's where he's taking them, to the military training camps."

My heart feels as though the weight of the Drakensberg Mountains has come down upon it. The government has branded *Umkhonto we Sizwe* as a terrorist organization and members, if caught, are tortured for information before being assassinated. In the camps, Nomsa will be trained to kill civilians, which means she will be hunted like an animal every day of her life by the white government's security police who will not rest until she is dead and can no longer pose a threat to them.

"We have to go get her. We have to save her before it is too late."

"We can't. There's another problem, Beauty. A bigger one."

"What?"

"I've received word from my police contact that someone tipped them off about us. The security police have been called in and surveillance will begin on the household soon. The only thing stopping them from swooping in and arresting us all immediately is Andrew's position of power in the international community."

"How much time do we have?"

"A day or two at most before the operation begins in earnest. We've come up with a plan for all the others and they're being moved as we speak, but my contact hasn't been able to get you documents like he has for the rest of them. He's being watched and needs to be careful."

"I do not care about papers. We need to find Nomsa before she crosses the border."

"You won't be able to find her if you're detained and imprisoned along the way. We have to get you a legitimate passbook. It's the only way for you to remain in Johannesburg while we try and get Nomsa back. I've got my feelers out to try and find you a position as a maid so you can get valid paperwork. In the meantime, we need to move you to a safe location until this all blows over."

"I can go live with Andile in Soweto."

"It's too dangerous. The families of the march organizers are under surveillance in case they return. You'll be a new face, which will make them suspicious."

"Please, Maggie. Please tell me where my daughter is."

"I'm afraid I can't do that, Beauty. Forgive me, but it wouldn't be safe for you to travel at this time and I'd be putting you at risk, which I'm not prepared to do. My contacts are keeping an eye on her. She's safe where she is, and if she's moved, we'll know about it. In the meantime—"

The light on the telephone on Maggie's desk lights up to indicate an incoming call. There is no ringer on it; it has been removed so that no noise from within the room can betray its presence. The phone has a dedicated line and number that very few people have access to. Maggie snatches it up and listens for a few moments before returning the receiver to its cradle.

"It's worse than we thought. They're already on their way. You need to get out of here. Hurry!" Maggie calls for Kgomotso and he rushes into the room. She nods at him and he takes this as a sign. Whatever is happening, they have prepared for it and he knows what to do. Maggie is already dialing another number, and calls to me as Kgomotso pulls me from the room. "We'll speak soon."

All of a sudden, someone shouts from downstairs and there is banging at the front door.

"Damn it," Maggie says, slamming the phone down again. "Both of you get back inside here. I'm going to lock you in. Don't make a sound."

As the door slams closed behind her, the thudding of my heart sounds like footsteps over a grave.

Twenty-five

ROBIN

❁

23 JULY 1976
Yeoville, Johannesburg, South Africa

C at and I pulled the typewriter (a baby-blue Olivetti with white keys) from under Edith's bed while she slept, and lugged it to the dining room table where we hefted it up to put next to the huge dictionary Edith occasionally used as a doorstop.

We'd quickly dashed out and canvassed the neighborhood for job opportunities and two positions caught our attention. Mr. Papadopoulos at the fish-and-chips shop and the hairdresser two blocks down both had signs up in their windows saying "Help Wanted" and we figured I'd be perfect for both jobs.

My first job application, after an hour's effort, ended up like this:

```
Dear Mister P̶o̶p̶a̶d̶o̶p̶a̶l̶u̶s̶ P̶o̶o̶p̶a̶d̶o̶p̶a̶l̶i̶s̶,

    I heard you want help at the fish and chips shop. I know

besides fish you make russiens that are not really russien

people but vienas. Edith says russiens say nyet and drink

vodka and dress like pimps.
```

I will be good at the job because:

1. My father took me to the vaal dam and I caught a carp with a stick and some pap because I did not like touching the worms. I will fish for you every day and no worms will be killed.

2. I like chips.

3. I can miss school because my twin sister Cat can pretend she is me.

4. If you do not have money you can pay me in food and wine and nail varnish and lip stick.

5. I am a hard worker and will not hide up a tree and fall out and bleed like I did that time with ballet class.

6. I can speak Greek because Edith taught me. I can say fila mou te kola. I am not sure if I spelled it right because the words are not in her dictionary. They may be bad words because she laughed when she said them.

Please give me the job. We do not want them to take us away because we are poor and have nowhere to live.

Thank you and have a good life,

Robin Conrad

We were impressed with our handiwork and considered retyping it to remove the mistakes, but agreed that it would take too much time. We began the second one instead.

Dear nice lady at the hairdressing place,

You are looking for a hairdresser and I like hair. We are like John and Paul of the Beatles. We are meant to be.

My dad cut a lot of hair so I know how it is done. I also know how to use a bowl to make sure the fringe is straight. I will show you how.

I hope you can explain the tale of the tortoise and the

```
hair to me because it does not make sense that hair can run
faster than a tortoise because hair does not have legs.
Maybe it was magical hair.

    You must pay me with money because we cannot live on
haircuts.

    Your friend with hair,

    Robin Conrad
```

Edith stumbled out of her room once while we were clattering away, her hand raised to her forehead. "What is causing all that racket? It sounds like you're remodeling in here."

I had to think quickly. "Cat and me are writing our own story so we can have something to read."

"Marvelous. I am overjoyed for the both of you. Could you please just keep it down a bit? I have a headache."

After Edith disappeared back into her bedroom, taking a bottle of wine and a bottle of pills with her, Cat and I decided that my job applications had to be delivered straightaway before other people could be considered for the positions. Forgoing *takkies* and jerseys, in case a trip to the bedroom for them made Edith suspicious of our intentions, we tiptoed to the door and then ventured out barefoot in our jeans and T-shirts.

I regretted the decision almost immediately; it was much colder outside than it had been earlier and an icy wind swept down Raleigh Street. The chilled concrete pavement leached what little heat I'd retained and my nose started to run. I had nothing to wipe my nose with (no tissues, my shirt was short-sleeved and Cat wouldn't oblige), so I did the best I could with the back of my hand.

Edith had told me more than once that first impressions were the most important, which is why you had to be the best version of yourself when meeting people for the first time. Looking at my reflection in a shop window, I knew that my dirty bare feet, blue-tinged skin speckled with giant goose bumps and snot-encrusted upper lip wasn't my best look, but I was too cold to care.

I sprinted into each shop, threw my application on the counter and then dashed out again. If nothing else, I hoped that my first impression would be of someone who was quick and efficient. Once the letters were safely delivered, Cat and I dashed back to our building so I could thaw out while we worked on the rest of our plan.

As we walked through the lobby door, we bumped into Morrie who was on his way out with his camera.

"Hello," he bellowed in that voice of his. "Where were you?"

"Just out. Where are you going?"

"To the shop to take pictures of the niggerballs. You want to come with?"

"What's a niggerball?"

"It's a round black sweet that turns white as you suck on it. If you put a few in your mouth, they make it bulge like this." He puffed out his cheeks and bugged his eyes out in an attempt to entice me, but I didn't quite see the charm of a sweet that made you look like that. "They're in a bowl on the counter and sometimes the flies land on them. Want to come see?"

"Yuck. No, thank you." I walked around him to press the button for the lift and he turned and followed me.

"What are you going to do now?"

"If you absolutely must know, we need to carry out a top-secret plan."

"We do? Cool!"

"Not you!"

"But you said 'we.'"

It was a slip of the tongue. I hadn't meant to mention Cat, but now that he was pestering me, I realized that it was probably time to unleash the craziness that Edith had warned me about. If Morrie truly wanted to be my friend, he needed to know what he was getting himself into.

"'We' as in me and my sister."

"I didn't know you have a sister."

"She's standing right next to you."

Morrie looked around, confused for a moment, and then he smiled. "Cool. An imaginary sister!"

I smiled. He'd passed the first test.

"I can help with the plan," he said as he followed us back into the lift.

"How?"

"Well, you'll need to tell me what the plan is first and then I'll be able to say—"

I clapped my hand over Morrie's mouth. "Shh."

I could hear the banging before we'd even reached our floor and I knew that it couldn't be anything good. With an overwhelming sense of foreboding, I crept out of the elevator and down the passage, indicating to Morrie that he should keep quiet as he followed. Once we got to the corner, I craned my neck to peer around into the corridor. The person standing at the door was short and squat. The face was in profile, which made the hook nose and sickle chin look even more pronounced. A gold pendant glinted at her neck.

"It's that horrible lady," Cat said.

She was right. It was Wilhelmina and she was pounding on our apartment door like the dickens.

"Robin? Are you in there? Please open the door." Bang, bang, bang. "Ms. Vaughn? You can't go on avoiding me like this. I keep phoning but the line is constantly engaged so you've forced me to arrive unannounced."

Cat looked terrified. "What if Edith opens the door?"

"I'm sure she isn't that stupid," I whispered back, though I wasn't entirely sure of that.

"She might do it just to shout at her."

"She won't, don't worry."

That's when Morrie decided to join the hushed conversation between Cat and me. With his voice sounding like a foghorn. "What is your sister saying?"

The social worker spun around at the sound of Morrie's voice. "Robin?" She'd spotted us and was already striding in our direction.

"Run," I yelled at Cat but she was already ahead of me making a dash for the stairwell. I had to push Morrie so I didn't fall over him.

Twenty-six

BEAUTY

❦

23 JULY 1976
Houghton, Johannesburg, South Africa

A t first, there is nothing to hear except the sound of our own breathing. There is nowhere to hide, the tiny room itself is our only sanctuary, and so Kgomotso sits in Maggie's chair. With a shrug, he invites me to sit across from him. There is nothing to do but wait, but I would rather pass the time on my feet.

For the first time since I have been in here, the photographs and books do not interest me. I cannot bear to look at the happy faces in the framed pictures or the bound volumes of hope below. My thoughts are an army of red ants that are constantly in motion. They devour everything in their path; allowing them to turn inward would be dangerous.

I want to ask Kgomotso about himself, learn his story about how he came to be in this room with me, but I am too afraid to speak. The "invisible household" has thus far been made up of seven of us, all of whom Maggie and Andrew are helping in one way or another. We are all in danger of being arrested, though I suspect that Kgomotso is in more danger than the rest of us.

It is an unwritten rule that we do not divulge too much about ourselves. What we do not know cannot be used against others if we are tortured for information. Kgomotso has been here longer than we have and seems to serve some kind of security function. A young man, no older than his early twenties, he is ambitious and driven. He fights for what he believes in, just like Nomsa.

I think back to the day she was born; to a time before my husband, Silumko, had to leave the village along with other able-bodied young men to work in the gold mines. He'd been away with the cattle for two days and I expected him back before nightfall. When my pains started, they did not last as long as the other women said they would. The baby struggled to leave the protection of my womb, and I didn't have time to call for the midwife before Nomsa fought her way free onto the floor of clay and dung.

Nomsa did not cry out, she made no noise at all, and I knew then that something was wrong. The cord of life was wrapped around her neck and she could not breathe, could not accept the gift of air that was waiting to fill her lungs. I reached for the panga and I freed my child from the noose that bound us together. I wonder if that cut of the cord that so decisively separates mother from child is nature's way of reminding us that we are no longer of one body and must start learning the process of letting go. If so, does any mother ever truly learn how?

Thinking of Nomsa is like adding wood to a fire whose thirst can only be quenched by painful memories, but I cannot help myself, and thinking of Nomsa makes me think of her father. I wonder if his death two years ago is what fueled her anger and set the course of her life northeast. Did the magnetic field of his death draw her to Johannesburg so she could avenge his death?

I think, too, of my remaining sons, Luxolo and Khwezi, who are being looked after by the elders in our tribe. I always said that I would not allow my children to be raised away from me, yet look at me now: one child in the ground, another on the run from the police and two more across the country without one parent to take care of them.

Voices outside interrupt my thoughts and I instinctively switch off the lights. At first, the murmurs sound like the buzzing of a swarm of flies but then, as they get closer, we can hear the individual words in their muffled entirety.

"As you can see, this is the library. Feel free to check behind the curtains if you think someone might be hiding there." There is no trace of fear in Maggie's voice.

"That won't be necessary, Mrs. Feldman, but you won't mind if we take a look at your reading material?" I am surprised to hear that the policeman is English.

"Of course not. You won't find anything undesirable. This is a law-abiding and God-fearing household."

"Officer Lourens, remove the books from the shelf, just so we can be sure nothing is being hidden behind them."

It is too dark to catch Kgomotso's eye, but I wonder if he is as startled as I am. Do they know about the hidden office behind the bookshelves? Are they looking for a way in? Books crash to the floor.

"Is that absolutely necessary? Some of these books are quite valuable. Isn't it possible to take them down carefully?"

The thudding stops. Another few minutes pass and I am sure that the whole world can hear the beating of my fearful heart.

"There, you've now unpacked everything," Maggie says. "As you can see, there are no hidden safes behind the books either, just like you didn't find any behind any of the paintings. If you'd like, I can take you to the two we do have and I'll open them up for you."

Voices confer and an agreement is reached to carry on the search downstairs. I am just starting to feel light-headed with relief when another voice speaks. "Wait, I want to look at those shelves again."

I am seized by trembling. I cannot imagine how Maggie is maintaining her composure under the scrutiny of those men. A loud bang startles me and I almost cry out. Kgomotso gets up from his chair and slowly walks over, feeling his way to where I am. He wraps his arms around me and allows me to bury my face in his chest. His heartbeat is a hammer knocking against his breastbone. There is another bang and then a few more as someone pounds against the shelves.

"I do hope you won't have a problem giving an account of the damage you are causing my property, as I'll be making sure a full evaluation gets done before we submit the bill to your department."

Finally, the banging stops and the voices retreat. I cannot let go of Kgomotso. He is holding me up, and I am grateful for the support that my own legs can no longer give me. When my strength returns, I allow him to lead me to the chair, which I sink into.

Hours later, I worry that I cannot hold my bladder any longer and wonder how I can relieve it without the humiliation of wetting myself in front of a young man. It brings back the memory of my commute to Johannesburg and the incident with the bathroom in Pietermaritzburg, but before I can relive the sting of that shame, the door to the office is opened. Maggie stands in the doorway; she is backlit and looks like an avenging angel. She switches on the light and I blink in the glare. Maggie is pale but smiling.

"Luck has been on our side. Everyone got away before they arrived and they didn't find anything that could implicate us. Come, we need to get you both out of here before they find an excuse to come back."

Twenty-seven

ROBIN

23 THROUGH 27 JULY 1976
Yeoville, Johannesburg, South Africa

M orrie, Cat and I raced up the stairs of the emergency exit, our footfalls echoing off the walls.

"Who was that?" Morrie yelled.

"Shut up and run," I shouted back.

We'd just made it up two flights when we heard the door slamming below.

"Robin!" Wilhelmina called after us.

We ducked out of the stairwell and raced across the corridor of the fourteenth floor. There were emergency stairs on both sides of the building, and I figured we could start a cat-and-mouse game running up and down both. Wilhelmina was overweight and unfit and had already been puffing when she called to us before. She wouldn't be able to keep up the pursuit for very long even if she knew which direction we'd gone in.

Over the next ten minutes, we ducked up and down and across

seven floors, being careful to avoid our own apartment on the eleventh floor in case Wilhelmina had gone back there.

"Why don't we go hide in your flat?" I suggested to Morrie.

"My father locked me out," he confessed sheepishly. "He has an important meeting and said I would be distracting with the camera's flash going off constantly. Maybe we should try leaving the building?"

"What if she thinks we might do that and is waiting downstairs in the lobby?"

"That's a good point. Why don't we go down to the basement? There's nothing down there but storage rooms and no one ever goes there except George. It's the perfect place to hide."

There wasn't time to ask who George was and I couldn't think of a better plan so we slowly made our way down, listening all the while for Wilhelmina. Once we got down there, we stood in the warren of rooms and caught our breath. Another twenty minutes passed, each minute marked by the jolt of Mickey Mouse's hand on my wristwatch. I'd just decided that enough time had gone by to make it unlikely Wilhelmina was still looking for us, when the elevator started whirring. Someone was on their way down.

There wasn't time to think. I grabbed at the handle of the nearest door, and by some miracle, it opened. It was only after we'd rushed inside that I registered the other person's presence. It was an old man, a brown one who was smoking a strange-smelling cigarette, and he looked just as surprised to see us as I was to see him.

I glanced at his hands, the brown skin of them, and wondered if they'd ever held a knife to a white person's throat. The thought sent an icy tingle down my spine. As I turned to escape, Morrie spoke.

"George! *Howzit?* Quickly, lock the door."

The old man didn't need to be told twice and he was sprightly for his age. He was up in a flash, sorting through a bunch of keys hanging off a chain attached to his belt. Only when the key turned in the lock did I stop holding my breath. The elevator dinged and the doors opened.

"Shh," I said, and he nodded, stubbing his sweet cigarette out on the floor.

"Light," he muttered, indicating the switch above my head. I nodded and flicked the switch. We were plunged into darkness.

Any doubt that it was Wilhelmina was quickly dispelled when she began to call my name. "Robin? Are you down here? Robin, please come out. I'm here to help you."

In the darkness, sounds were heightened. We could hear footfalls and heavy breathing as she passed outside the door, still calling out to me. Another few minutes ticked by, shuffling and rattling noises punctuating the silence, as she tried all the doors along the corridor.

My panic was rising.

We haven't had time to carry out our plan. If Wilhelmina finds us now, she'll force us to open the apartment door and she'll see the terrible state Edith is in.

I looked awful as well, I knew, dirty and neglected like one of those street urchins I'd heard about in a radio story about a boy named Oliver. Cat didn't look much better.

If Wilhelmina catches us looking like this and sees Edith drunk and passed out, she'll take us away for sure. I can't let that happen.

Wilhelmina was getting closer. She was still huffing from the effort of chasing us and each small gasp sent shivers down my spine. I waited for her to reach our door and began to gnaw at the skin surrounding my nails.

She's going to find us. She's almost here.

Then, magically, the rasping sound of her breath died away. I listened harder but there was nothing. All was quiet outside.

She's gone! She's left!

And then the handle of our door was thrust down. I couldn't see it in the dark, but it squeaked. I held my breath until Wilhelmina finally let go of it and moved on.

I don't know how much time passed then. The sweet, musky scent of the man's cigarette permeated everything and my head felt heavy. I was tired and wanted to sleep, and I might have nodded off for a while until I was woken by a flash of light and then another. For a second, I thought it was lightning until I remembered that we were underground and there weren't any windows.

The light was switched back on and the old man was smiling a gap-toothed smile at me.

"*Yissus*, Master Morrie and Little Miss saved King George," he said. "If they found him here smoking *boom*, he would have been fired for sure." He had a strange lisping accent, an odd mixture of English and Afrikaans, and he pronounced his *s*'s as *z*'s: *Yizzus, Little Mizz*. It was like talking to a mosquito that referenced itself in the third person.

Too sleepy to explain that he'd actually saved me, I merely nodded and smiled back. Morrie was distracted by trying to dry the two photographs he'd just taken.

"King George is pleased to make Little Miss's acquaintance." He held out his hand and I took it after only the briefest hesitation. "Any friend of Master Morrie's is a friend of King George."

"I'm Robin," I said, and then pointed next to me. "And this is Cat."

King George giggled and nodded. "This *dagga* is strong, hey. Makes King George see all sorts of *kak* too. This is a kangaroo," he said, pointing off to his side.

"And this is my concubine." Morrie laughed as he wrapped his arm around thin air.

I couldn't help but notice that King George's skin was a strange shade. Too light to be black but too dark to be white, I couldn't quite figure it out. I wanted to ask him how that had happened—if he'd started out black but got paler, or if he'd been born white and then got a deep tan—but couldn't hold on to the thought long enough to express it. Mr. Klopper, a teacher at my old school, once told us that all black people wanted to be white, because they stupidly believed that white people were rich and happy just because of the color of their skin. He said they used all kinds of skin lighteners so they could become white, and we'd all laughed at how stupid black people were. Maybe that was what had happened with King George.

When Cat and I finally got back to the flat after we said good-bye to Morrie, a note had been slipped under the door insisting that Edith call Wilhelmina. We scrunched it up and threw it away. A quick peep into Edith's room confirmed that she'd slept through the ordeal and was still snoring loudly. I was suddenly ravenously hungry, and after I'd finished the last four stale slices of bread, Cat and I curled up on the couch and fell asleep.

The plan to cheer Edith up was put into action the next day. I kicked it off by drawing a few silly pictures for her, mostly ones of the "gatekeepers of hell," which is what she'd taken to calling the women who'd interviewed her. None of the drawings, not even the ones where the women had devil horns on their heads and spiked tails coming out of their butts, made Edith smile when I showed them to her. In an effort to distract her from her misery, I asked for details about her ornaments and even feigned an illness. It didn't work. She just emptied a packet of Grand-Pa Headache Powders down my throat and followed it with a spoonful of Borstol cough syrup. The mixture was revolting and I vowed never to try that tactic again.

Cat and I were forced to get creative with the meals we made for Edith. The only thing she'd popped out for was liquor, and like Old Mother Hubbard, our cupboards were bare. The piccalilli and half-cooked spaghetti concoction we made for breakfast wasn't well received, and neither were the Rice Krispies and tomato sauce cakes we tried for dinner. We tried twice to entice Edith out of her room by filling up the bathtub with an elixir of potions, but each time the bath-water cooled until it was a murky brew.

No amount of compliments cheered Edith up and our knock-knock jokes all bombed.

Elvis was my only company besides Cat, and even he seemed to be suffering from depression. His feathers fell out, at first just one or two and then whole heaps of them, and the only song he'd sing was "Don't Cry Daddy," which would make Edith sigh harder and pour even bigger drinks. We tried blasting Elvis records as loud as we could and then thrusting our hips around and twitching our lips like we'd seen Elvis do at the movies shown at the Top Star drive-in, but Edith just came out of her room, took one look at me, exclaimed, "God help me!" and turned back around and went to bed.

Even though none of our plans worked, at least worrying about Edith, coming up with plans and measuring her decline by the incremental increase in her alcohol consumption gave us something to do. It provided a distraction from our own pain. By then, I'd already worked through a complex process of reasoning regarding what was acceptable and what was taboo as we tried to come to terms with our grief. Talking about feeling sad or expressing that sadness in any way that our parents could see or overhear was not allowed.

"Just think happy thoughts," I told Cat one day when we felt especially lonely and she started crying.

"I have been thinking happy ones," she sniffed.

"Like what?"

"I was thinking about the time Mom read us a bedtime story and she did the funny voices and let us do the funny voices back."

"That's a good one. And what about the times when Dad would sit me on his lap and use a pen to join the dots of my freckles while calling out the names of the constellations he could find?"

"I remember. It made me wish I had freckles just like you."

"If you're thinking of the good times, then why are you still crying?"

"The good times make me sad."

I realized then that too-happy memories led to despair, so they had to be medium-happy ones. It was like being on a seesaw; too much weight on either side of the emotional spectrum could tip the scales. I had to make sure that Cat maintained the equilibrium.

So medium-happy memories became the moments Cat and I were allowed to give the most airplay to, ones in which our family ate meals together, went for drives or planted seedlings in the garden.

"Do you remember when Mabel—"

"No talking about Mabel," I reminded her. "That makes you cry as well!" I had to be hypervigilant.

Even as I tried to stop Cat from crying, I knew how illogical I was being. My parents had never been able to see her, and so any tears she cried didn't really count. It was only my tears that counted; it was only my tears that had to be checked and dried up and held back. If anything, Cat needed to cry; she needed to shed tears and grieve for the both of us, because it helped somehow—it helped ease the terrible pressure in my chest a tiny bit—when I knew Cat was crying. I just couldn't watch her doing it.

I started leaving the apartment and I forbid Cat from following me. My mother's mascara tube went wherever I went; it made me feel braver, like nothing bad could happen to me so long as it was in my pocket.

I began venturing out to the park to sit on the swings or to the grocery store to buy sweets. Mr. Abdul, the owner, looked at me with sad eyes because Edith had told him about my parents, and he would let me buy lollipops on Edith's account, though I suspect he never actually charged her for them.

Mr. Abdul wasn't white but he also wasn't black. He wasn't quite the same shade of brown as King George either, which was confusing.

If people didn't come in the right colors, how would we know who to be scared of?

The hairdresser, Tina, called me into her salon one afternoon when she saw me passing.

"I got your job application, Robin," she said. "I'm sorry that I couldn't hire you because you would've been terrific! I just needed someone with more experience and hairdressing qualifications. But why don't you let me cut your hair for you? I'll do it for free!"

"Okay," I said. I'd never been to a hairdresser before; my father always cut my hair in the bathroom at home. "Thanks. Just don't do anything with my fringe."

"But it's getting so long and you have to peep out from behind it."

"I like it this way," I said but what I actually meant was that I didn't want her messing up my father's cut.

After a quick wash, I sat in the chair—on two pillows to prop me up to the right height—and felt Tina run her hands through my hair. The reality of her fingers blended with the memory of my father's, and I was taken back to the last time he made me sit on a footstool in the bathroom while he sat behind me on the edge of the bath.

"Close your eyes, Freckles," he said just before he sprayed my hair wet, the mist from the spray bottle settling over me like a sigh. The comb's teeth tickled against my scalp as he gently brushed the knots out.

"Keep them closed," he instructed as he placed a bowl upside down over my head.

The scissors were cold against my forehead as my father was guided by the rim of the bowl. The snick of the blades was like a lullaby and it made me sleepy. Strands of hair fell into my upturned palms, and I imagined it was snow settling into them. I drifted off to sleep and was woken by blasts of my father's breath as he blew hard to get rid of the bristles of wet hair caught in my eyelashes.

The memory of my father—of the scent of his aftershave, and the mint of his chewing gum, and the sturdy warmth of him pressed against my back—made me sad, and the traitorous tears began to prickle again.

I have to get out of here.

"I forgot that I don't have the time for this," I said as I hopped out of the seat. "I need to get home."

Tina called after me as I ran out of the salon, my hair dripping wet, but I didn't turn back.

Mr. Papadopoulos, when I went inside to check if he'd read my application, said he wasn't allowed to hire children but insisted I take home free fish-and-chips wrapped in newspaper. He also asked me nicely never to repeat the Greek phrase Edith had taught me. Apparently it was very, very bad. Without a job, I couldn't make myself of any use to Edith and so the last of our plans fell through.

Then one day—sick of Edith's travel books, Cat's blubbering and being on the constant lookout for the social worker—I took some change from Edith's nightstand and caught the bus by myself to the Johannesburg City Library. I hopped off on the corner of Commissioner and Simmonds streets when the driver told me to, and then paced outside the huge Italianate building for an hour before I worked up the courage to go inside.

Once inside, I found the children's section easily enough, and I walked along the rows and rows of books, running my fingers along their spines and inhaling their musty scents. I pulled volumes from the shelves, seeking out my favorite authors and my most beloved characters and tales, and piled them up one on top of the other until my arms ached from the strain. I found an empty table and hefted the pile down, preparing to do what I must have been subconsciously wanting all along; I lost myself in those books. I don't know how long I sat there for, but as I turned the pages, reading snippets and studying the illustrations, I forgot how sad and lonely I was.

Instead, I smiled at the antics of Moonface and the folk of *The*

Magic Faraway Tree, cheered as the Secret Seven solved another mystery and forgot that to laugh was to feel guilty for a stolen moment of happiness.

After I turned the last page of the last book, I remembered the reason I'd wanted to come to the library in the first place. I didn't know where to look though, and the catalog system scared me, so I decided to ask a librarian for help.

When I got to the counter, the librarian was talking to an old woman who had a big cardboard box set down next to her. It sounded as though they were saying their good-byes. After a few minutes of my standing there, the librarian finally excused herself from the conversation and turned to me.

"Yes, can I help you?"

"Hello. I need help finding some books, please."

"I'm in the middle of something right now, but if you could come back—"

"No, that's all right, Karen. I'll help her. This kind of thing is just up my alley," the old woman said.

"But you're on your way out."

"This will be my last book scavenger hunt. I'm just going to leave my things here if you don't mind." She then turned from the woman and looked at me.

Her blond hair was cropped short along her jawline, and she had kind, periwinkle blue eyes that were intensely focused on my face.

She smiled and reached out her hand to introduce herself. "Hello there. I'm Maggie, the head librarian."

I shook her hand shyly. "Hello. I'm Robin."

"How lovely to meet you, Robin. Now, what kinds of books are you looking for?"

"Books about orphans."

"Orphans? Well now, you've picked the perfect subject for some really good classics. Take a seat and let me see what I can find for you."

I went back to the table I'd been sitting at and watched as Maggie moved around the stacks, plucking books from a shelf here and there, and then marching on to the next one. It was clear that she knew exactly where everything was.

"Here you go," she said when she returned, her arms laden with books.

She plopped them down on the table and then sat on one of the chairs across from me, sighing comically as she tried to fold her adult shape into the tiny chair.

"Right. Here we have *The Secret Garden, Heidi, A Little Princess, The Boxcar Children, Pippi Longstocking, Anne of Green Gables, The Jungle Book, Cinderella* and *Peter Pan* to get you started. Do you want to check them out?"

"Yes please, but I only just moved here. I belonged to the library in Boksburg but not this one."

"Ah. Well, we can sign you up here too. Let's go to the front desk so I can get a form for you. You'll just need to get your parents to sign it."

I nodded, eager to please, and then it hit me.

I don't have parents. I don't have a mom and a dad to sign the forms for me.

The sum total of everything I had in the world was one drunken aunt and one imaginary sister. They were the defective safety net separating me from the abyss, the gossamer spider's web I clung to. It came then, seemingly out of nowhere, the crushing weight of my loss pressing against the bones of my chest.

Mommy and Daddy are dead and being dead means you never come back. They promised they would come back. Mommy promised—she promised!— but they never came back and now they never will.

All the weeks of pretending, and filling the silence with chatter, and telling myself not to think about it, all those weeks had been for nothing, because they had led me to that moment in which my heart was breaking. Panicked, I looked for Cat to save me. She knew how deep the well of our grief ran and how bitter the taste of our tears. She knew how corrosive abandonment was and how it rubbed you raw. I needed her to express our pain, to cry for the both of us while I comforted her, but Cat was nowhere to be found.

Without her there acting as the pressure valve to my expanding emotions, the first tear escaped and then the second. I was horrified by how warm and startlingly wet they were, and I held my hands up to my eyes to try to stem the flood.

Don't cry, don't cry, don't cry.

I knew even as I did it that the gesture was futile; I may as well have been raising my fists to stop a thousand waves breaking on the shore. So I did then what I hadn't done in the six weeks since I lost my parents; I surrendered and gave in to my grief, and I sobbed and sobbed like the frightened and abandoned child I was.

Maggie was startled by the force of my emotions that had come seemingly out of nowhere. "Oh, my goodness. Oh, my word," she said. "What's wrong? Robin, are you okay?" She tried to coax my head up so she could see me, but I buried my face deeper under my arm on the desk.

My mother's words came back to me: *You're ugly when you cry.*

"Robin, please can I see your face?" Maggie asked. "Please will you look at me and tell me what's wrong?"

"No," I hiccupped. "Don't look at me!"

"Why? Why not?"

"Because I'm ugly!"

"That's not true! You're beautiful. You're a beautiful little girl." She said it with such conviction, such utter sincerity, that I almost believed her. I wanted so much to believe her, to be as sure as she was.

I dared lift my head.

"That's better. That's so much better. Look at that lovely face."

I smiled through my tears.

"Now, why don't you tell me what's wrong?"

I sniffed and rubbed my leaking nose against my arm, and then I started talking. Maggie kept stopping me with gentle reminders to take deep breaths so she could hear what I was saying, and I'd take in great big gulps of air before starting up again. She held my hands, squeezing them in her own as I hiccupped my way through the relaying of my tale, telling her almost everything since the police arrived until that very morning when I'd walked in on Edith, lying drunk on our bed, her South African Airways stewardess uniform slung across the duvet with photos of my mother flung like confetti over it.

"And now I'm crying," I gasped. "I wasn't supposed to cry."

"Why ever not?"

I shuddered between breaths. "Because my parents are watching and my mom always told me not to be a crybaby and now she'll think I don't love her because I'm not acting like a big girl."

It took further gentle coaxing from Maggie to hear the full story of how I hadn't cried since my parents died; how hard I'd tried to live up to an ideal my mother had tried to get me to uphold mere days before she was murdered; how I'd allowed Cat to do our crying because my mother couldn't see her.

"And when did this all happen, Robin?" she asked. "How long ago?"

"Forty-one days," I said. "It's been forty-one days." Even in my denial and through my constant insistences—*don't think about it, don't think about it*—I'd kept track of every day.

Maggie's eyes glistened. "My dear, dear child," she said, "your mother would never, ever expect you not to cry under these circumstances."

"She . . . she wouldn't?"

"Absolutely not. These are exceptional circumstances, which can in no way be compared to falling and scraping your hand, though, I for one think a good cry and maybe a curse word or two when you hurt yourself is just the ticket." She allowed the thought to sink in before continuing. "Your mother and I disagree on that one point, but I know, beyond a shadow of a doubt, that we would be in perfect agreement on this: When someone you love dies, it causes immense pain, an emotional pain so much deeper than any mere physical hurt, and that hurt is made tenfold when it's both your parents who have died and under such terrible circumstances too. The best way, the only way, to express that pain and show them how much you love them is by crying."

"Really?"

"Absolutely! There's no doubt at all. I know your mother would have no objection, none whatsoever, to these tears because they come from a place of deep, deep love. She'd be happy to see these tears because they show her how very much you miss her. And your father too."

It was all the permission I needed and Maggie held me while I shuddered, the tears shaking me to my core. She stroked my hair and held me close to her chest so my face was shielded from the inquisitive stares of other library patrons. She didn't shush me once, not even when my wails echoed across the bookshelves and into the foyer.

Eventually the sheer force of my sorrow made my nose bleed, something that hadn't happened before. I pulled back from Maggie's embrace and cried out at the crimson patch that was spreading obscenely across her cream blouse. Maggie interrupted my apologies with instructions to lean my head back and pinch my nose until the tide subsided. Once I could stand up without triggering a bloody waterfall, I followed her with my head thrown back as we wound our way out of the library's common areas, through a corridor and into a bare room.

"The ceiling needs dusting," I said in a small, muffled voice.

Maggie laughed and suggested I lie down on the floor to keep my head back. She brought me a few tissues, and I twisted them into points and stuck them up my nostrils. She asked me for Edith's phone number and then our address after I explained about the phone being off the hook. Maggie covered me with a jersey while she set about making me a sweet cup of tea, claiming it was an antidote to just about everything. I was asleep within minutes, and it was the most soundly I'd slept in weeks.

I woke up later as I was jostled about. I felt like I'd been asleep for years. It was dark outside; the moon painted orange and hung low enough to touch over the tops of the buildings. I struggled to free myself and turned to see that it was Edith holding me, and she was straining with the effort of carrying me to her car. She shushed me when I tried to speak.

"Everything is going to be okay. Go back to sleep now," she whispered.

I could see in the moonlight that Edith had been crying. I reached for my pocket and was only able to relax once I felt the reassuring shape of my mother's mascara nestled there.

I never found out exactly what happened between Maggie and Edith, or how she got Edith sobered up and to the library that evening. All I ever knew for sure was that it was Maggie who brought Beauty into our lives and that after that day, everything changed.

Twenty-eight

ROBIN

❁

1 AUGUST 1976
Yeoville, Johannesburg, South Africa

When the knocking returned, knuckles connecting with wood, louder and more aggressively than before, it made my pulse quicken. Bang, bang, bang. Bang, bang, bang. It seemed that only policemen and social workers—people who wanted to take you away—announced their arrival in that way.

I started to rise from the couch, but Edith touched my knee and winked, indicating that I should sit down again.

Bang, bang, bang. "Ms. Vaughn! Open this door at once."

Edith smiled and put her finger to her lips.

"I will break this door down if I have to. I have a right to be here and I will not be kept out!" Bang, bang, bang.

Edith slowly rose from the couch, and sashayed to the door where she waited a few beats before suddenly yanking it open to reveal a startled and red-faced Wilhelmina with her fist raised in midair.

"Good grief, it seems that someone should have attended finishing school. This is not the way guests announce their presence. Their uninvited presence, I might add, but please, do come in since it seems you'll assault me otherwise."

Wilhelmina lowered her fist, glowered at Edith and pushed her way past as though suspicious that the invitation would be revoked. She'd barely crossed the threshold when Elvis started flapping and squawking from his cage. "Devil in disguise. Devil in disguise!"

She spun around to find the source of the insult, and after she'd spotted the parrot, she turned around again and addressed Edith. "*My magtig.* I have been calling and calling, but the phone has constantly been engaged. I know you took it off the hook, don't deny it."

Edith nodded at the phone. The handset was in its cradle and it looked perfectly benign sitting there, as though it couldn't possibly understand all the fuss that was being made about it.

"As you can see, the phone is not off the hook. Perhaps you've been dialing the wrong number the whole time?"

"I have not! And I've visited twice but you wouldn't answer the door."

"Might it not have occurred to you that we were out? My goodness, it seems that you're rather used to people running and hiding when you come to call or why else would you think that?" Edith turned to me. "Wouldn't we have opened the door if we'd been home? Isn't that what well-mannered people do?"

"Yes," I said, nodding emphatically and trying very hard not to catch Cat's eye.

"You saw me when I came the one time and you ran away from me," Wilhelmina accused.

Edith raised her eyebrow. "Robin, is that true?"

"No."

"You see? It must have been another poor child terrified at the sight of you. Would you care to sit down? Can I get you some tea or coffee? A biscuit perhaps?"

Wilhelmina waved off Edith's offers and craned her neck as she peered around the apartment, eyes narrowed in suspicion. Everything sparkled from Edith's earlier cleaning frenzy. The sink full of moldy dishes had been washed, the floor and furniture cleared of books, albums and clothes, and the apartment aired of its stale and smoky smell. Even Elvis's cage glistened from Edith's ministrations.

"Wilhelmina, are you looking for something? A pentagram? An altar for human sacrifice? Pornography, perhaps? I'm not into that kind of thing myself, but don't be embarrassed if you are. I won't tell anyone."

Wilhelmina flushed and horrible blotches of color climbed up her neck like obscene ivy. "I'm within my rights to do a home visit to ensure that this is a safe environment for the child. The child is my only concern here."

"Good gracious," Edith said, looking perplexed. "I'm assuming then that you didn't speak to your boss before you foisted yourself on us today?"

"My boss?"

"Yes, Mr. Groenewald. Lovely man, rather attractive, too, if I do say so myself. I'm sure with him being an eligible bachelor and you being a single woman—I'm assuming you're single based on, you know . . ." Edith flicked her wrist dismissively at Wilhelmina's navy pantsuit and court shoes. "Anyway, you'd be forgiven for having a little crush on him."

Wilhelmina's blush deepened further and I felt an unexpected pang of sympathy for her.

"I saw him on Friday," Edith continued, "and dropped off a whole ton of paperwork that I thought he might need. Keith and Jolene's will indicating their desire for me to be Robin's guardian, their death certificates, character references from various people, my financials, proof of Robin's school registration and so on."

"But," Wilhelmina stuttered. "You don't even have a job. Without employment, you can't possibly—"

"Oh, but you see, I do, in fact, have employment. Rather well-paid employment too in my new position as the secretary to the branch manager at Volkskas bank. Mr. Groenewald has all that paperwork as well, but if something's missing, please tell him to let me know and I'll give it to him next week. When we're meeting for dinner."

It seemed that all at once, Wilhelmina's bluster and fury abated. Her fighter's stance drooped as she went from being a contender to an opponent who's already been defeated. She didn't even put up any resistance when Edith ushered her out two minutes later, nor did she turn around when Elvis piped up again from his cage. "Up your big Dutchman arse! Up your big Dutchman arse!"

I told myself that no good could come from feeling sorry for a person who'd wanted to take me away from Edith.

Later that same day, Edith emerged from the bedroom and clapped her hands. "Okay, kiddo. I'm going to have to ask you to put that away and come sit over here."

Edith patted the seat on the couch next to her, and I closed my coloring-in book and returned my pencils to their tin case. Cat remained seated at the table, her bottom lip caught between her teeth as she concentrated on the picture of a dragon she was working on.

Elvis was perched on Edith's shoulder. The red of his tail feathers perfectly matched her blouse, and he nuzzled her jade earring as he relished the affection she'd been lavishing on him for the past hour. He was clearly over the moon that his mistress had returned to her former self and that her terrible silence had been replaced with the alternating loud bickering and whispered crooning he was used to. She gave his beak a peck and scratched his head with her index finger before she stood up and returned him to his cage.

"Don't be cruel to a heart that's true," Elvis griped as she closed the door.

"Ah, my sweet, don't be that way. You know I can't stand whiny men." She went to the kitchen and returned with a wedge of cheese. She shoved it through the bars and crooned, "How's that? You happy now?"

"Thank you, thank you very much." Elvis hopped from the perch to the floor and started feasting on his windfall.

The sun had just set and the room was cast into a gloomy darkness. Edith switched on the lights and drew the curtains before she returned to the couch, this time sitting across from rather than next to me. She cleared her throat and looked down at her hands, opened her mouth to speak and then closed it again.

She stood, said she was thirsty and offered me a cold drink. I accepted even though I didn't really want one. I knew that it was best to give Edith time to compose herself and gather whatever thoughts she'd need.

While I waited for her to return, I studied all the pictures and art on the opposite wall, my gaze lingering on a brightly embroidered wall hanging from Mexico. It depicted various domestic scenes: two adults and a child standing outside their house; a mother and father working in their garden while their child played with a ball; the sun encircling a couple who were holding hands. It was my favorite, not only because it was done in vivid oranges, reds, yellows and blues, but because it showed a family.

The past few days had been emotional ones. Speaking to Maggie that day in the library had been like lancing a boil; all the infected emotions—the sadness and the anger, the grief and the loneliness—were all finally coming out. They drained through my tears, and when I wasn't crying, I was tipping my head back with toilet paper shoved up my nostrils to stop the nosebleeds. It seemed as though my body didn't feel the tears were enough; it was mourning with blood as well.

It was on one of those days, while riffling through Edith's record collection, that I came across the Dolly Parton album with the song about my mother, "Jolene." I'd only ever heard it once (my father was a staunch Beatles fan and hated country-and-western music, so he would never have played it at home), and I remembered how my mother had blushed as one of the men drunkenly serenaded her with it at a mine *braai* while his wife stonily looked on.

At first, I listened to the song just to remind myself of the lyrics. Then, once I knew the words, I played it repeatedly, my voice rising in crescendo with the chorus as I sang my heart out with Dolly.

It didn't matter that the song was about a woman who didn't look like my mother at all. It also didn't matter that it was about a woman taking another woman's man. I was enthralled with it and relieved that I could get to howl my mother's name over and over again in a socially acceptable context.

Mourning my father left a more permanent mark on me. Literally. I found a purple marker in Edith's bedside drawer, and then sat at her dressing table staring at my reflection. After I'd conjured up the memory so I could be sure to get the shapes right, I re-created the constellations that my father had found hidden among my freckles: the Big Dipper (looking like a kite trailing a piece of string), the Southern Cross (the easiest to draw) and Orion's Belt (requiring the most freckles of all). I didn't know then that mirrors inverted everything, nor was I aware that the marker was a permanent one. All I knew was that I made a terrible mess that took two days of incessant scrubbing to remove from my face.

"Oh my God. You look like the purple people eater from that song," Edith exclaimed when she first saw me.

"I was making constellations like Daddy showed me."

Throughout all of this, Cat remained dry-eyed and silent and either hung back in the shadows or sat next to me holding my hand, depending on whether or not I felt like company. While I cried, Edith made tea, and with each tear I shed and each cup she drank, she was brought back from her own precipice. The daytime drinking stopped and she started taking her friends' calls again. Her grooming rituals resumed. The shock of seeing the old Edith was enough to dry the tears. It seemed that while I'd been leaking sorrow, Edith had been damming the flood of her self-pity.

She took me to visit my parents' graves, but only after she sat me down and asked me if I wanted to go, explaining that we'd be visiting the site where my parents were buried in their coffins. She obviously wanted to avoid another scene and needed to be sure that I was up for it. When I said I was, we climbed into her car and took the fairly short trip to the Westpark Cemetery where she'd insisted they be buried near my grandparents.

The graves were marked by small wreaths without their names on them; it would take another year for the sites to settle and for head-stones to go up. I thought I'd feel closer to them where they were buried since that's where their physical bodies were, but I didn't feel their presence at all as I crouched atop the fresh mound of dirt. I wanted to cry, especially after what Maggie had said about crying be-ing a way of showing them how much I loved them, but I couldn't muster any tears there. Cat was surprisingly stoic as well.

Edith returned with a glass of Coke and placed it on a coaster on my side table. She sat across from me, holding a lit cigarette in one hand and a half-filled glass of wine in the other. I eyed it warily.

"What? It's after dark. I'm perfectly entitled to a glass of wine without you giving me the hairy eyeball. Also Noah in the bible had wine. You heard what that minister said during that miserable excuse for a eulogy."

When I didn't reply, she pointedly took a sip of the wine and car-ried on. "We need to have a talk, you and I, and I think I'll start off with an apology."

I waited.

"I went off the rails a bit and I'm sure that must have scared you, and I'm sorry about that because I know how difficult the last few weeks have been for you. It's just, you know, I don't really have all the answers. I know when you're a child, you think that adults know everything, but we don't. Not really. I know it's your parents who died, kiddo, but your mother was also my sister, and though I wasn't all that fond of your dad, he was my brother-in-law and I didn't want him to die, especially not like that." Now that the words were coming, it didn't seem that Edith could stop them. "That was bad enough, but also having to give up my job, my freedom—"

"You don't want me." The words slipped out. I hadn't intended to say them, but they were a part of the festering pain I'd been working through. It seemed impossible to resolve my despair over my parents' death without resolving my immense feelings of rejection.

Edith reddened. "What gave you that idea?"

"You're only taking me because I have no other family. If there was someone to give me to, you would."

"That's not true."

"It is. I heard you say it to Victor."

She took a drag from her smoke, fingers trembling, and her expression changed, hardening into what looked like resolve. She rammed her cigarette into an ashtray, muttered, "Fuck it," picked up her glass and went to the kitchen where she topped it up. "Do you want some more Coke?" she called to me.

"No thanks."

She returned and took a lengthy sip of her wine. "Okay, since we're being honest, I didn't really want you."

There, she'd admitted it. I thought I'd feel better hearing the truth and knowing that I was right, but I didn't. Edith saw my lip start to quiver and moved to come and sit next to me. She took my hands and waited until I looked up at her before carrying on.

"Well, actually, that's not totally true. It's not you I didn't want. I didn't want the responsibility of a child or the responsibility of being a parent. I never wanted children at all, not even children of my own, and suddenly finding myself having to act like a mother and having to take care of a child? God, that was my worst nightmare come true, and that's what I didn't want. But you . . . you, I want. Can you see that difference?"

I thought about it. I could sort of see the difference. "Do you mean like wanting to eat lots of candy floss at the funfair but not wanting to vomit from it afterwards?"

Edith laughed. "It's a tiny bit like that, I suppose. In all honesty, I'm scared to death that I'm going to mess you up. That I've been given this amazing child, this bright and funny and wonderful child, and that I have no idea how to raise you without breaking you, you know? You haven't exactly come with a set of instructions."

I smiled. "Daddy never read the instructions of anything anyway. He said it was more fun to figure it out himself."

"Christ, typical of your father. He waits to die before letting me know we have something in common."

"You have me in common."

"That's true, that's very true."

We sat in silence for a while and I could hear Elvis ruffling his feathers as he groomed himself.

Edith spoke again. "Here's the thing. In order for me to raise you properly and minimize the damage I'm undoubtedly going to do to you, I need two things. One, I need an income. And two, I need my sanity. Now the first thing shouldn't be that hard to come by, but it seems that I'm not qualified to be any kind of office worker. And to be honest, I'm actually relieved because I just couldn't do those jobs without dying a little inside every day. Can you understand that?"

"But you said you have a job as a secretary!"

"Oh that," Edith snorted. "That was a lie told for Wilhelmina's benefit."

"But you said you gave her boss the paperwork."

"And I did. Very official-looking paperwork, too, thanks to a big favor from a friend. But in order to keep my sanity, I have to keep my job as an airhostess. I love traveling, I love the freedom. It's my life, it's who I am, and if you take that away from me, I won't be any damn good to you." She lit up another cigarette and put it straight back into the ashtray. It seemed that we were coming to the point of the conversation.

"I probably only have another five years or so before I'm too old to be in the air, so I really have to take full advantage of that time I have left." Edith looked to me for understanding and I nodded. "The thing is that I can't travel all the time if I have to look after you."

"I can come with you."

"Ah, kiddo, I wish you could, but that's not how it works. You have school starting next week and I'm not allowed to take you with me, and besides, even if I could, a child needs stability. Even I know that."

"So then what are you going to do? Are you giving me away?" My voice caught. We'd read about orphanages and I knew Cat and I would rather run away than live in one of them.

"Of course not! Get that out of your head immediately. Listen to me, Robs, you are mine and I am yours. Whatever happens from here on out, no matter how much we screw each other up, we're stuck with each other, okay? You can't get rid of me."

I wiped away the tear that had escaped and nodded.

"But I need help looking after you. I'll limit my shifts as much as I can, but I'll still be away a lot, which means I need someone who can look after you when I'm gone."

"Victor can look after me. I like Victor."

Edith smiled. "Yes, Victor is a lot of fun, but I'm afraid that won't work. Victor works and he has his own place and he can't live here and take care of you, and believe me, the sights you'd see at his place would mess you up more than anything I could do."

"What sights?"

"Never you mind. We're getting off track here. I've already found someone who can look after you. Well, actually, Maggie from the library found someone who can look after you."

"Who?" I was heartened by the mention of Maggie.

Edith smiled nervously. "She's a black lady."

"Mabel?"

"No, not Mabel. She's gone back home, kiddo, and I don't think we'll see her again."

"You got another maid?"

"Well, I know it sounds like that, but she's actually not a maid at all. She's unlike any black lady you've met, and it's important that we don't treat her like a maid. She has a university degree from before the blacks were stopped from studying further, and she's incredibly bright. She's actually totally overqualified for this job but that's beside the point. Think of her as a chaperone."

"What's that?"

"Well, it means she'll live here when I'm away and she'll take care of you."

"But I don't want someone else to look after me."

"It's only a temporary arrangement until I can come up with a better solution. Let's just give it a try."

"But we don't have a maid's room. Where will she sleep?"

"She'll sleep in my room. In my bed."

"But that's where I sleep."

"Yes, I know. I wish we could afford to get a bigger place, but we can't for now. We'll move the lounge around and get a partition over here and make you your own room. How does that sound?"

"Why can't I sleep in your room and she can sleep here in the lounge?"

"Because she's an adult, Robin, and she's doing us a huge favor."

"But she's black. Blacks don't sleep inside with us. They sleep outside in their rooms."

"Yes, usually, but this isn't a normal situation. We all need to make some concessions, okay, in order to make this work, but I really think that we can do it. When I'm away, she'll stay here and look after you, and then when I'm back, I'll look after you. I'll still be able to earn an income and do what I love, and you'll be properly taken care of."

"I don't want a black mother. I want you."

Edith frowned. "Like I said, it isn't a permanent situation, it's just for a while and we'll see how things go—" Before she could finish the thought, the phone rang and I leapt to answer it.

"Hello?"

A gravelly voice asked to speak with Edith. I motioned her over, covering the mouthpiece and whispering, "It's a man."

Edith took the phone and I returned to the dining room table where I sat next to Cat trying to listen in as she greeted the caller.

"You've found them?" Edith's perfectly plucked eyebrows rose in surprise. "There were two of them?"

As she listened, I could hear the man's voice coming through the earpiece, but couldn't make out what he was saying. I had to rely on Edith's half of the conversation for more information.

"But what about the third man? I was told three of them had been spotted running from the scene."

Edith listened to his reply and I could see by the expression on her face that she was skeptical about his answer. "And when do you expect the trial to begin?"

Edith frowned at what she heard. The man was still talking but she cut him off. "Hold on, just hold on a second. What do you mean there won't be a trial? We want to see justice done, it's important—"

The voice continued to drone and Edith shot me a quick look. I stared back, waiting.

"They died in custody at Brixton? How?" Edith started tapping her nails on the table before she cried out in surprise. "Both of them? They both had an accident in police cells? How, pray tell, did that happen?"

I didn't really need to hear any more.

Twenty-nine

BEAUTY

❦

1 AUGUST 1976
Melville, Johannesburg, South Africa

I have more possessions now than a month and a half ago when I first made the trip to Soweto. All I had then was one small case filled with a few items of clothing and my bible. I thought it would be a short journey that would end with my returning to the Transkei with Nomsa; instead, it ended with my suitcase's meager contents strewn across a battlefield. I could not retrieve my things from the street that day, as I did not want to invite evil into my life. I even threw away the clothes I had been wearing. How naive I was then to think that bad luck could be shed and that misery would never arrive unannounced.

Maggie replaced everything for me during the time I was with her and then, on the night I fled the Houghton mansion for this safe house in Melville, another gift was bestowed.

"Here, I'd like you to have this," Maggie said, handing across a velvet box.

I opened it and drew out a silver pendant hanging from a chain. I held it up to the light; it was a rendering of a holy man carrying a baby across water to safety.

"I wanted to give you a proper gold Saint Christopher, but I've learnt that expensive gifts can attract unwanted attention," Maggie said. "I give the pendants to the people I've met in the resistance whose friendship I most cherish."

"Thank you, Maggie," I said, touched by her sincerity. "You chose the metal wisely. I could never have accepted gold."

"Because of its value?"

"Because I know the men whose backs break and lungs fill with dust as they dig for it. No object's value should ever be placed above the worth of a man's life."

"You're so right, of course you are. I can't believe I never thought of it that way before. Turn it over," Maggie said.

I did. The back of the pendant was engraved with a single word: "Believe." I asked Maggie to help put the necklace on, and when I turned around again, she wrapped her arms around me. We hugged tightly and it was an embrace filled with love.

"I'll be in touch as soon as I can organize papers for you. After that, we'll arrange a meeting with Nomsa."

But in the week and a half since I have been at the safe house, Maggie's intelligence has lost track of Nomsa's whereabouts. While all of her people were scrambling to ensure they evaded the security police's net, Nomsa was moved from the smallholding and the trail has gone cold. Maggie is confident that it is just a matter of time until a member of her network hears something, but I cannot just sit and wait.

I am befriending everyone I come into contact with and am making my own inquiries through less official channels. What I am hearing makes me nervous. People say the man Nomsa is with, "Shakes" Ngubane, is a dangerous man, that he is violent and has a taste for alcohol and drugs, both of which he sells illegally along with stolen weapons. They say he preys on young girls and it is rumored he runs a brothel. I am more determined than ever to get my daughter away from him.

Within five days, I will move out of the safe house and officially begin the job that Maggie has found for me, the one that has allowed me to get my passbook stamped. This has lifted a great weight from my shoulders as I can travel between Johannesburg and the Transkei without fear. If I am to remain in the city indefinitely while searching for Nomsa, I need to be able to return home as often as I can to see the faces of my sons, and to assure them that I am doing everything in my power to return their sister to them.

Though I am now classified as a maid, I will not labor as so many of our unfortunate sisters do. My employer, Edith, is a white woman, and though she cannot be compared to Maggie, she is also not one of the madams who will have us break our backs to do their work. She is illegally placing her almost-daughter in my care while she leaves the country for her work, and she knows the great responsibility I have accepted. We understand one another, and so far, she has treated me with respect. In the past, my pride would never have allowed me to take up such a position, but now I shed my pride like a snake casting off its skin.

The weather will soon be changing. The wind is blowing and I can smell that the rains are on their way. The time for planting *mielies* and pumpkins is almost upon us, and I pray that Nomsa and I will both be home in time for the sowing of the seeds. I will do as Maggie says and I will believe.

Thirty

ROBIN

❀

2 AUGUST 1976
Yeoville, Johannesburg, South Africa

E dith was in the lounge with the black woman. They weren't whispering exactly, but they were talking softly enough that I wasn't able to eavesdrop from the bathroom. I made a show of flushing the toilet and spraying three long blasts of air freshener.

See? I'm not hiding in here to listen in on your conversation—I have real business to attend to!

When I stepped out into the lounge, Edith's head snapped up and she became businesslike. "Right, I'll leave you two alone to get acquainted. Beauty, I have a meeting with the airline to finalize my new flight schedule, and then I need to get the last of Robin's school supplies for tomorrow. I should be back before supper and I'll pick us up something to eat if you'd like to join us for dinner. I was thinking of pork chops."

"I am sorry, but I do not eat pork, Edith."

"Of course. Sorry, I forgot that you people don't eat pig. Mabel didn't eat it either, hey, Robs?"

"Hmm." I'd seated myself at the dining room table across from Beauty where I could properly size her up. She was older than Mabel, and I could see a few tiny gray curls escaping from her *doek*. Her features were also more sunken and stark than Mabel's. Mabel had been plump while Beauty was gaunt. When I peeked under the table, I saw she wore black court shoes rather than the slippers Mabel wore around the house, and her stockings bunched up around her thin ankles like loose skin. She looked tired but she had bright, watchful eyes. They made me nervous.

Edith pecked me on the cheek and instructed me to behave before heading for the door. She turned back after a few steps and spoke to Beauty. "Maggie said you're staying with a friend nearby until I leave on Friday. Robin's bed and partition will be delivered on Thursday, and I've already bought the extra bedding. We'll be set up in time so don't worry about that. I'm just glad you're able to spend some time with us before then." Edith blew a kiss to me and then left, closing the door behind her.

Silence settled over us. Beauty sat stiffly in her chair, still clutching a small kitbag and looking around the room. The clock ticked nearby.

"She looks nice," Cat said.

"Mabel was nice too," I reminded her.

"Yes, we loved Mabel," Cat agreed.

"She left us." I let Cat feel the pang I'd felt that morning, the utter helplessness and despair. I let her remember what it was like to watch someone you loved walk away from you without so much as a backwards glance. "Do you want to feel like that again one day when Beauty leaves?"

"No," she whispered.

"Good."

My stomach growled and I turned my attention to Beauty. "What are you making me for breakfast?"

Beauty's gaze shifted from the wall of treasures to my face. She studied it for so long that I started to get uncomfortable and was relieved when she finally spoke. "What do you normally eat?"

"Jungle Oats or Maltabella."

"Then that is what I will make. I will call you when it is ready."

"Okay." I hopped off the chair, relieved to have an excuse to escape. Being around Beauty, even for those few moments, brought back so many memories of Mabel that I didn't know how to process. I was learning, every day, how to mourn my parents and how to express the hundreds of ways in which I missed them, but my pain at Mabel's leaving of her own accord was a wound I was still trying to clean and bandage up.

Cat followed me into the bedroom where my new school uniform was hung up in the cupboard. It was a checked white-and-blue all-in-one dress and I thought it was wonderful. Just being rid of the ugly brown-and-yellow uniform I used to wear almost made up for the fact that I'd have to make new friends and meet new teachers. Trying on the uniform and staring at my reflection in Edith's full-length mirror helped distract me from the butterflies that swooped around in my stomach.

"Why can't I come to school with you?" Cat asked.

"Maybe you can. I haven't decided yet. It depends on how things go." What I meant, but didn't need to say, was that it depended on if I made friends or not.

"How are you going to do your hair tomorrow?"

"Don't know yet. What do you think?" We played around with a few practice styles and had just decided that pigtails, rather than a single pony, were the way to go when Beauty called me to come through.

As I made my way to the table and pulled out my chair, Beauty eyed my dress. "What are you wearing?"

"My new uniform." I was about to sit down when Beauty placed her hand on my shoulder to stop me.

"Please take it off before you eat."

"Why?"

"Because you might mess on it."

"I won't mess."

"But—"

"I said I won't mess." I sat down and started eating.

Beauty returned with her own bowl of porridge and sat across from me and started eating. I eyed her warily. It looked like she was eating from the usual crockery, which my mother never would have allowed, but I didn't say anything. She smelled different from Mabel and spoke differently too; she articulated her words better and spoke English very formally.

I miss Mabel-English. I miss Mabel.

"Where's Cat's breakfast?" I asked, purely to fill the silence and distract myself from getting too morbid.

"I put it down in front of her. Can you not see it?"

Edith must have told Beauty about Cat, which was annoying. I wondered if I was being humored or made fun of. "Why don't you wear a uniform?"

"Because I am not a maid."

"Oh. But you look like a maid."

"How does a maid look?"

"Like you. A black lady. So if you aren't a maid, what are you then?"

"I am a teacher."

"There are no black teachers."

"Not at your school, no. I teach black children."

"Black children go to school?"

"Yes, they have their own schools."

"In QwaQwa?"

Beauty looked surprised at my question and impressed by my semi-decent pronunciation. She smiled at me for the first time. "You know QwaQwa?"

"That's where Mabel lives."

She nodded. "I teach in the Transkei."

I persisted with my questioning. "So if you're really a teacher, what are you doing here looking after me?"

"I need to stay in Johannesburg for a while, and in order to do so, I need a passbook. And for that, I need to have a job."

I knew about passbooks; I'd seen Mabel's and had asked my mother to get me one because it looked important and official, but she said white people didn't need passbooks, which I thought was a great pity. "Why do you need to stay in Johannesburg?"

"My daughter is missing and I need to find her."

"Did she run away from home?" I'd tried to run away from home once when I was four. I'd packed a plastic bag full of picture books and told Mabel I was leaving. She bid me farewell and gave me a sandwich for the trip in case I got hungry. Then she followed me for three blocks while I dragged the bag behind me. The bag soon tore and the books fell out, and I made Mabel pick them up before I headed back home, having decided that running away was too much hard work.

"No, she did not run away from home."

I wanted to get to the bottom of the mystery of what happened to Beauty's daughter, but her stony expression told me she wouldn't answer any further questions about it. I'd ask Edith.

"So why don't you find work here as a teacher?"

"I tried but there are no jobs for teachers here."

"Oh." We were quiet again and I searched for something else to say. My gaze fell on her bare hand. "If you have a child, why aren't you married?"

"I did get married."

I pointedly looked at her ring finger. "Married ladies wear gold and diamond rings." The only jewelry Beauty was wearing was a silver necklace with some kind of medallion on it.

Beauty sighed. "White women wear gold and diamond rings. Black

women give up their husbands so they can dig up the gold and dia-
monds to make those rings."

"My father worked on a gold mine."

"My husband worked on a gold mine as well."

"Oh, I wonder if they knew each other. Maybe he was one of my
dad's boys."

Beauty's smile was grim. "My husband was a forty-nine-year-old
man when he died. He was not a boy."

I was about to explain to Beauty that all the blacks who worked
underground were called mine boys just like all gardeners were called
garden boys, but she looked so annoyed, I dropped the subject.

Beauty stood up. She reached for my bowl and I yanked it back; I
liked to lick the bowl clean. As I pulled it, the spoon toppled and
landed against me, messing some of the porridge onto the front of my
uniform. I immediately rubbed it in, not wanting Beauty to see it. She
went to the kitchen where she washed her bowl and spoon, setting
them on the dish rack to dry. When she came back out, Elvis squawked
loudly from under the blanket covering his cage.

Edith had forgotten to uncover him and he sounded tetchy. "Elvis
has left the building. Elvis has left the building," he chirped, which was
his way of saying that he wanted to be released from the darkness.

Beauty clutched her chest, staring at the gigantic cage hidden behind the blanket. "What is that?"

"It's Elvis."

"What is Elvis?"

"Elvis is not a what. Elvis is a who."

"Then who is that?"

"Elvis is Edith's parrot. He's an African gray and she named him
after Elvis Presley." Beauty looked at me blankly so I clarified. "Elvis.
You know? The King?"

"The King? Of England?"

"No! The King of rock 'n' roll. Jeez, and you call yourself a teacher." I walked to the cage and pulled the blanket off.

Elvis bobbed his head and delivered up his usual, "Thank you. Thank you very much." I noticed that his bowl was empty.

"You'll need to give him seed. He's hungry."

Beauty stared at the cage openmouthed. "*Hayibo*. A talking bird."

"Yes, you need to feed him."

"No, I will have nothing to do with a talking bird."

"Why?"

"It is not natural. Only people should talk."

I sighed. "That's just stupid. Fine, I'll feed him. He doesn't like black people anyway." I reached under the pedestal to get the tin with Elvis's seed and scooped some out into his bowl after making sure to throw out all the husks like Edith had taught me.

"Why?"

I was distracted with my task and didn't immediately make the connection. "Why what?"

"Why does the bird not like black people?"

"Because black people kill white people."

"You think white people do not kill black people?"

"No, they don't."

"And those men who the police caught, the ones they say killed your mother and father, how do you think they died?"

"Edith says they fell out of the window at the Brixton police station. It was an accident."

Beauty snorted. "Yes, many black people are accidentally falling out of windows these days."

I didn't know what to say to that.

"You've messed on your uniform," Beauty observed, nodding to the stain of brown on my dress's lapel.

"That's okay," I lied. "I actually prefer it this way."

When I was finished with Elvis, I escaped back to the room where I took the uniform off and inspected the damage. The brown mark looked terrible.

"You look like you pooped on it," Cat said.

"I know," I wailed. "How can we fix it?"

"We can try washing it."

We waited until we could hear Beauty opening and closing cupboards and when she switched the radio on, we sneaked to the bathroom. I opened the tap and put the plug in the drain, filling the basin with water until it was full, then dipped the top half of the dress into it. I reached for the bar of yellow Sunlight soap and rubbed it into the stain.

"It's not working," Cat said.

I rubbed the soap in harder and decided not to rinse it so that the effect of the soap would be more powerful. I took the dress back to the room with me, ignoring the drops of water that marked my trail, and laid the dress over the foot of Edith's bed. I read for a while and then checked on the dress again.

"It looks worse than before!"

The yellow soap had congealed into a paste. I tried to scratch it off with my fingernail, but it stubbornly clung to the fabric. I crumpled the dress into a ball and threw it under the bed.

"Come, let's go," I said.

"Where?"

"Anywhere. The park or for a walk."

"But what about the dress?"

"I don't want to think about that now."

When I returned a few hours later, worried what Edith would say about the dress when she got home, I found Beauty at the dining room table hunched over an exercise book that she was writing in. I wondered what was in it and if she was writing about me. Beauty didn't say anything, didn't acknowledge my return at all, but when I went to the bedroom I found the dress washed and ironed, and neatly hanging up in Edith's wardrobe.

I peeked around the corner, careful not to let her see me because I didn't know if I should say anything. Beauty was smiling. I surprised myself by smiling too.

Thirty-one

ROBIN

❦

6 THROUGH 30 AUGUST 1976
Yeoville, Johannesburg, South Africa

Edith's first trip away was meant to last a week but somehow got extended to six.

"I'm sorry, Robs," her voice crackled down the line after the first nine long days away. "There was a problem with the fuselage and so my flight back got canceled. And then Moira got sick, and since I was already in New York, they asked me to take over her route. I'll be back next week, I promise."

The promise—like most of Edith's promises, I would come to learn—was a loose and slippery one. If other people were shackled by their oaths, then Edith was the Houdini of hers; she always managed to extricate herself from them while you were left trying to figure out how she'd managed the sleight of hand.

Her next call came after fifteen days out of the country. "I've had to pick up another route. It couldn't be helped, Robs. I'm not in a position to be dictating my schedule to my bosses. Anyway, Beauty seems to have everything under control there. How are you? You're not misbehaving?"

"No." I didn't consider mounting regular skirmishes against Beauty to be misbehaving.

"How's school?"

"It's fine."

"Have you made any friends?"

"Yes."

"Just remember what I said about being careful not to tell anyone about Beauty."

"I haven't said anything to anyone," I told Edith, "but people are starting to get suspicious."

And it was true. Each extra week Edith was away was another week that the neighbors saw only Beauty and me coming and going from the apartment; it piqued their curiosity. One night, after we'd run out of the money Edith left for the week she was meant to be gone, Beauty slipped out to the Goldmans' after 8 p.m. to ask for bread to make my school sandwiches for the next day. Upon returning, Beauty had been confronted by old Mr. Finlay who lived three doors down. I listened in from the dining room where I was sitting waiting for Beauty to return.

"What are you doing?" Mr. Finlay demanded, just as Beauty was pushing the door open.

"I work here," Beauty replied. Her tone was pleasant but firm.

"Where are your manners? Hey? You call me '*baas*' when you're talking to me."

I winced. By then, I knew Beauty well enough to know that there would be no bowing and scraping.

"I work here, sir," Beauty said.

"But you're not allowed to be out so late at night. And there are no maid's rooms in these flats."

Thankfully, Mrs. Goldman turned the corner at that moment. "Good evening, Angus," she said.

"Evening, Rachel. Do you know what this coon is doing here so late? Where's Edith?"

"She's sick in bed."

"With what?"

"Women's problems." I smiled at Mrs. Goldman's ploy.

"Oh. But what's the—"

"I've asked the maid to stay over for the night to look after Edith and the girl."

"But the spoonies are not allowed—"

"'Spoonies'?"

He laughed and it was a nasty sound. "Cockney rhyming slang. 'Spoonies' as in 'egg and spoons'? Meaning 'coons'?"

"How delightfully droll."

He must have picked up from Mrs. Goldman's tone that she was being sarcastic because he became belligerent again. "The *kaffirs* are not allowed to sleep inside these flats! This isn't a bloody township, you know."

"Stop *kvetching*, Angus. She won't be sleeping. She'll be up all night playing nursemaid. Does it look like she's in her pajamas getting ready for a slumber party?"

"But—"

"I can't look after Edith, Angus. I've had a long day and I'm tired. Unless you'd like to go in there and keep an eye on her all night what with her ovaries—"

"No. No, never mind!" Mr. Finlay's grumbling voice faded away as he returned to his flat. "Kikes and *kaffirs* . . . all the same."

I breathed a sigh of relief as Mrs. Goldman and Beauty slipped inside. "Mrs. Goldman," I asked, "what's a kike?"

She waved a hand in a dismissive gesture. "It's a bad word, *bubelah*, that bigoted people call Jews. Don't ever clutter up your head with insults. Forget them as soon as you hear them and remember the endearments instead." She turned to Beauty while opening her purse. "Sorry, I wasn't thinking before. Bread's not going to be enough to tide you over until Edith gets back. Here, take this and if you need more, let me know." She put a wad of bills down on the table instead of in Beauty's hands, and I realized that she'd done it that way so that Beauty wouldn't have to clap her hands and curtsey as black people were expected to do when getting anything from whites.

"Thank you, Mrs. Goldman," Beauty said.

"It's Rachel, please. Or else I'm going to start calling you Mrs. Mbali." Beauty smiled and we both bid Mrs. Goldman good night.

After that, Beauty made sure to be locked inside from 5 p.m. onwards so there wouldn't be another incident. She wasn't the only one keeping to herself; I was as well. While I hadn't lied to Edith about making friends, they were very superficial friendships because I had to be careful about keeping my distance. I'd been sworn to secrecy about our living arrangements, and I wasn't allowed to tell a soul (not even if they pinky swore on it) that Beauty lived in our apartment and looked after me when Edith was away. Morrie's parents, the Goldmans, were the only people in the building who'd been entrusted with this information because Edith said they were her friends and weren't racist, but she was paranoid about anyone else finding out. Although I wanted to invite my new friends over to play, I didn't want Edith to get sent to jail if the police found out about Beauty, so I kept my mouth shut.

The problem with being on guard all the time was that it made it difficult to just be myself. I had to think through every sentence before I spoke it in case I inadvertently said something that could bring the police back into our lives, and this hesitation on my part created a wall between me and the new friends I'd made.

At least the schoolwork was easy, and after hours spent diligently getting through all my work in class every day, I could be sure Beauty would be standing outside the school gates waiting for me. This wasn't in any way suspicious as most of the girls had maids who came to fetch them, so at least I didn't have to explain it. I'd grunt at Beauty's greeting, hand over my satchel, and then walk ahead of her all the way home pretending not to know her.

Elvis still made Beauty nervous and so I made sure to let him out of his cage as soon as I was through the door every afternoon. I'd then profess not to know how to get him back inside while he swooped and whooped around the room, making Beauty duck and cringe as he whizzed by. Besides scaring her, Elvis also pooped all over the apartment, which Beauty then had to clean up; he was a very effective weapon in avian form.

For the first few days after Edith had left, I'd made a point of wiping the toilet seat down and scrubbing the bath in protest for having to share them with Beauty, but when the pantomime with the yellow rubber gloves and Handy Andy didn't provoke her, I stopped giving myself the extra work. Same went for rewashing all my crockery and cutlery before I'd use it as it just made Beauty commend me for my wonderful personal hygiene.

Besides, no matter how much I studied the bathroom and the cups and plates, I couldn't see anything different about them after Beauty had used them. It seemed they were in no way tarnished or tainted by her touch. It was confusing because my mother had been so adamant about Mabel never using our things that I was sure she dirtied them in a way that could never be cleaned.

While Beauty didn't leave a mark on our crockery, she definitely affected my relationship with Cat. I began to conduct my conversations with my sister in private when I started to suspect that Beauty was the only person I knew who preferred Cat to me. One conversation in particular tipped me off.

"When will Edith be back?" Cat had asked as we sat at the dining room table doing my homework.

"I don't know. She says it will be another few days."

"But it's already been a week and a half longer than she said."

"I know. She says it can't be helped and she'll be back as soon as she can."

"What if she doesn't come back?"

"Will you stop being such a baby? Of course Edith's coming back! Why would you say she isn't coming back when she promised she'll be back?"

"Mom promised—"

"I know Mom promised they'd be back that night and then they never came back. I know! But that doesn't mean the same will happen with Edith."

Beauty had been scribbling in her notebook while Cat and I spoke, and I wasn't aware she was listening in until she cleared her throat and spoke. "Fear is not a weakness, you know."

"What?"

"You do not need to shout at your sister because she is afraid. Fear is what makes us human and it is in overcoming fear that we show our strength."

"Brave people don't get scared."

"I do not agree with you. I think that brave people do get scared and what makes them strong is admitting their weakness and learning to accept it while still carrying on regardless."

"But Cat is scared all the time."

Beauty smiled. "And so am I. So are most of us."

It unsettled me that she hadn't ridiculed Cat like all the other adults in my life had done. While I didn't want to become too attached to Beauty, I didn't want her preferring Cat either. That's why I bit my lip and didn't comment on how much she used the phone even though my mother only ever allowed Mabel to use the phone once in a blue moon, and then only for a minute or two at a time.

When Beauty wasn't preparing my meals, helping me with home-work or otherwise attending to my needs, she was making calls and taking notes in her journal. Most of the conversations were in Xhosa and so I couldn't understand what was being said, but from the ones conducted in English, I knew that the calls centered on the search for her daughter. I didn't complain either about the calls that came through in the middle of the night even though they woke me up.

I tried a few times to read what she'd been writing in that book of hers, but once she noticed my interest, she stopped leaving it lying around. A surreptitious search of Beauty's cupboard as well as her suitcase didn't reveal the journal, and I realized that she'd taken to hiding it when she wasn't writing in it.

Beauty's constant search for Nomsa didn't impact me much until the day she wasn't at the gate waiting for me after the bell rang. It sent me into a spiral of panic, and I ran home by myself when it became clear Beauty wasn't just running a few minutes late. I had a key to the flat and I let myself in only to see that she wasn't there either. The first tears had just started to build when Beauty came through the door, out of breath.

"There you are."

I turned away so she couldn't see my red eyes. "Yep."

"I am so sorry I was not at the school to meet you."

"I don't care."

Apparently there'd been word of her daughter just after she'd come home from walking me to school. She'd taken the call and then immediately gone out to meet with someone. "The meeting ran later than I expected."

I brushed away the tears, refusing to let her see how much she'd scared me. "It's fine. I didn't even notice you weren't there."

I went in search of King George then, not because I particularly liked his company but because Beauty disliked him. She said he was an alcoholic and a drug addict and I was to stay away from him. I knew that seeking him out would irritate her, especially since the smell of his sweet cigarettes lingered on my clothing afterwards leaving little doubt as to where I'd been. When I got home after visiting him, I ig-nored Beauty for the rest of the evening even while I made sure that she was always within sight.

The next morning, I woke up with a sore throat, but we were mak-ing puppets in art class so I ignored the pain and went to school. By that afternoon, the mild discomfort I'd been feeling spread to the rest of my body. I was hot and it was difficult to swallow.

Beauty took one look at me as I came through the gates and rushed over. "What is wrong?"

"My throat is sore."

Her hand was blessedly cool against my forehead. "You feel very hot."

I wanted to cry. Beauty took my case and slung it over her shoulder and then she took my hand. "Come, we will walk home very slowly and then you can lie down."

"I'm not going to get into bed."

Except, I did.

Thirty-two

BEAUTY

❀

The child is being colonized by a rash. It migrates from her face and neck, over her chest and around her back, dipping below to her navel and then journeying down to her legs. It is rough to the touch, like the bark of a tree, and has the reddish-purple hue of the protea flower, especially in the valleys of her groin and armpits.

Her face is flushed and the only part of it that is not red is a circle that has formed around her mouth. She is hot to the touch, too hot, and her swollen tongue is coated with a white substance. She cannot speak or eat. Swallowing causes her pain. The tears run down her cheeks, but she does not make a sound. My heart is heavy for her.

I cannot help thinking that she is a child without her mother, and I am a mother without my children. I am learning how love wells up and causes great pain when it has nowhere to go. Like breast milk, it has to have an outlet; it can only be nourishing if it is directed away from its source. Does it matter if the child is not mine? Does it matter that she is white? Does it matter that her tongue cannot wrap itself around my language when I can wrap my arms around her? I do not think so.

There is a sunrise of infection dawning across her skin, but I cannot take her to seek medical treatment. A black woman arriving with a white child at a white hospital will raise alarms and invite unwanted attention. The same would happen if I tried to take her to Baragwanath in Soweto. My hands are tied by our secret.

My first thought is to contact Rachel Goldman. She is in the building and will be able to take Robin to a hospital without causing raised eyebrows. It is only as I am dialing her number that I remember they have gone to Cape Town for the week to celebrate her nephew's bar mitzvah. I put the phone down and try not to panic. Rachel is my emergency contact, and with her out of the province, I am at a loss to think of who can help us. Robin needs to see a doctor. Her temperature is almost as high as that boy's in Soweto and he breathed his last breath two days later.

Think. I must think.

Edith has left a number for me to contact her, but it will go through to a person at the airline as I cannot reach her directly. All I can do is leave a message and then wait for Edith to phone me back. Who knows how long that will take?

There is a pitiful moan from Edith's bedroom where Robin is sleeping and I rush to her side. Her hair is damp with perspiration and her eyes roll in their sockets. She wears nothing but her panties and yet she still kicks out at imaginary blankets as she tries to cool herself down. The weight of the air is too heavy against her skin and I fan it, trying to make the air lighter so it will tiptoe over her.

In the kitchen, I pour cold water into a pot and then empty ice from the deep freeze into it. I carry it through to the room and use a white facecloth, dipping it into the water and then gently holding it to

Robin's face. She sighs. I repeat the process over and over again, a dozen times, a hundred times, pressing the wet cloth to the sandpaper of her skin. After two hours, she is hotter than she was before.

I must think. What is the best thing to do?

And then it comes to me. Maggie. *Why did I not think of her before?*

I dial her number with a trembling finger and then have to start again when I fumble the last digit. My breath catches as I listen for the connection and I only exhale when I finally hear the first ring. The phone rings twice and then a third time; I keep count as my panic rises. After the eighth ring, I lower the receiver to its cradle, defeated by my certainty that no one is home.

Who can I turn to now?

A voice echoes across the line just before I break the connection and I snatch the phone back up.

"Maggie? Maggie, is that you?"

"No, I'm afraid Margaret's not in. May I ask who's calling, please?"

I recognize the voice as belonging to Maggie's husband. "Andrew! It is Beauty Mbali. I know I should not call there, and I am sorry to disturb you, but I desperately need to speak with Maggie. It is Robin, the child. She is sick, very sick, and I do not know what to do. Please, I—"

"Beauty? Is that you? Goodness, I couldn't make any of that out. Who did you say is ill?"

I repeat what I have said, forcing myself to speak slowly, and Andrew listens until I am done. He asks questions about Robin's symptoms and his calm tone is reassuring.

"Maggie's just popped out but please don't worry. She should be back in a short while and I'll make sure she calls you as soon as she steps inside. Just keep doing what you're doing because it sounds like you've got it all under control. We'll send whatever help you need."

I have just sat back down on the edge of Robin's bed when the phone rings and I run to snatch it up. "Hello? Maggie?"

"Beauty?" The voice is a man's but it is not Andrew's. I do not recognize it.

"Yes, can I help you?"

"I know where Nomsa is. I will give you the address, but you need to come right now."

Nomsa. The shock of hearing her name renders me speechless. Nomsa.

Finally, after all this time.

I reach for a pen and paper and am about to tell him to proceed with the address when I remember . . . Robin. I cannot leave her.

"Who is this?"

"You do not need to know that. Just come now. The address is—"

"I cannot come now. There is an emergency here and—"

"I thought you loved your daughter. I thought you wanted to find her."

"I do. I do, but—"

The line goes dead.

I cannot believe it. After all these months of silence, finally there is news and yet there is nothing I can do. I have just replaced the phone in its cradle when it rings again. This time it is Maggie and she says that someone is on their way.

"It sounds like Robin has scarlet fever, the symptoms seem to match up, and she'll need penicillin. The doctor I normally use is out of the country, but I know someone with a nursing background. Sit tight. She won't be long."

I go back to the room and pick up the facecloth once again. I do not know if it is helping the child, but it gives me something to do so that I do not give in to the madness of thinking about Nomsa and how I have just given up my only chance to find her. Instead, I move the cloth back and forth, again and again, between the cold water and Robin's feverish skin and I pray.

Finally, there is a knock at the door.

Thank you, Jesus, help has come.

I rush to the door and fling it open. A white woman stands at the threshold. She has a strange expression on her face as she peers past me, but she takes my hand as I step aside for her to enter.

"You must be Beauty. Maggie sent me."

The tears on my cheeks surprise me.

"*Ag*, please don't cry. Everything is going to be all right, okay?" She squeezes my hand.

"Thank you for coming," I say. "Thank you."

"Where's the child?"

"In the room."

The woman rushes past me directly to the bedroom and stands at the threshold looking at Robin.

"Yes, that's definitely scarlet fever," she says and I detect it now: the Afrikaner accent. It would normally make me very nervous, but if she is a friend of Maggie's, I know I can trust her. She turns and the light catches the pendant hanging around her neck. It is a gold Saint Christopher; the one Maggie gives to those she cherishes most. I know that if I turn the pendant around, it will have a single word engraved into the back: "Believe." And I do believe. This woman is going to save Robin, I know it.

She pulls a thermometer from her pocket and walks over to the bed.

Robin opens her eyes and they seem to clear for a moment. She looks at the woman and then she starts to scream and thrash around.

"No. No. No." Robin reaches out an arm and smacks the woman across the chest. "Not you. No. Not you." The child is desperate to get away from this woman and her eyes roll towards me in appeal. "Please. Help. No."

"I am sorry," I say to the woman. "I do not know why she is being like this. It must be the fever."

The woman merely grunts and instructs me to hold the child's arms down. I circle my fingers around Robin's wrists and try to raise her arms up above her head to rest against the pillow, but Robin struggles against me. She pulls her arms from my grasp and I do not know where she gets this strength from. She fights against me and, in her warrior spirit, is my daughter. Robin is so much like my Nomsa that it takes my breath away. I wonder how I did not see it before. Finally, after much thrashing around while the woman and I both try to hold her back, Robin slumps against the pillow, her jaw slack. The fight has gone out of her.

The woman slips the thermometer between Robin's lips.

"Her temperature is forty-one degrees. *My magtig*, that's very high. I'm worried it might cause a seizure." She puts the thermometer down and turns to me. "Where's Edith?"

I am surprised that she knows Edith's name. Maggie usually limits information in situations like these as she says that people cannot betray one another with details they do not have.

"Maggie told you about Edith?"

"No. She just said that a child needed medical help and that the caregiver was a black woman. I've met Edith and Robin before."

Before I can ask the woman the details of that meeting, she checks her watch and then stands.

"I unfortunately can't stay very long because I have an appointment at the courts that I need to get to." She digs in her bag and pulls out a bottle of yellow medicine, which she hands across to me. "You need to give her this syrup every eight hours, exactly on the hour. Try to keep her hydrated. I'm going to give her an injection now that should help her with keeping fluids down. Carry on with the cold compresses and give her cold baths every few hours. If we can get the temperature down, the worst will be behind us."

Once the injection is administered and we are again at the door, I take the woman's hands. "I do not believe that you told me your name."

"It's Wilhelmina," she says.

"Thank you, Wilhelmina. Thank you for what you have done for us. I will never forget this kindness. I hope to see you again one day so that I can repay it."

"Oh, don't worry," she says. "I'll definitely be back."

Thirty-three

ROBIN

❀

1 THROUGH 7 SEPTEMBER 1976
Yeoville, Johannesburg, South Africa

E verything was blurry like looking through a desert haze. Beauty was there with me, a dark smudge, and then she wasn't. I blinked, trying to clear my vision, but that only made it worse. I could make out the white ceiling and the light fitting and the net curtain fluttering against the window, and if I turned my head, the Elvis paintings shimmered at the horizon of the room before they faded into blackness.

The next time I opened my eyes, Mabel was back again after having left me at the police station on the day my parents died. She was sitting next to me, singing softly, leaning over me with something wet and white in her hand. A cloud, she was holding a cloud to my face, and it felt wonderful.

Except it wasn't Mabel after all; it was someone else with skin like darkness. Something silver shimmered at her neck and it dipped down towards my lips every time she leaned in. Up and down and up and down.

When my vision cleared slightly, I saw a disc with a giant of a man carrying a child across the water on it. The giant whispered that everything was going to be okay. His icy breath swept over my lips as he kissed me and then he was gone, and Mabel was gone too and the loss was overwhelming. Mabel had left me. Mabel, who I loved and who called me her white child and who kissed me all over—everywhere except my lips—Mabel had walked away without looking back. Each time I relived her leaving, the tears would run until the vision blurred and faded away, and then I would wake and it would happen all over again.

"Mommy," I whispered.

I want you, Mommy. Please come, please. I'll be strong, I promise. I'll stop crying and I'll smile and I'll be good and you will love me this time. You won't wish I was the dead baby, my real twin sister, the one who wasn't born.

In my fevered dreams, I was six years old again, hiding behind the couch being quiet as a mouse, taking quick peeks and listening in on the grown-ups' conversation. Edith and my mother took long sips of wine, and cigarette smoke escaped from their noses and mouths, making them look like angry dragons. My mother only ever smoked when Edith came to visit.

"God, you're so lucky having the exciting life you lead," my mother said.

"It's not luck, darling. It's called 'birth control.' I told you no bloody good could come of giving up your training and marrying a mine worker. If you'd listened to me, you'd be a footloose and fancy-free airhostess, and the two of us would be jet-setting all over the world like we planned."

My mother groaned. "I know! Don't rub it in. It's not like I planned the pregnancy."

"There were ways to take care of it, but there's no use crying over spilled milk. Robin's very cute," Edith offered in a grudging sort of way.

"I know she is," my mother said. "It's just that she's her father's daughter through and through. They're like two peas in a pod, always ganging up against me and making me feel left out." She was quiet for a moment and then added, "I sometimes wonder about Robin's twin, the one I miscarried . . . if she would've been more my child. More like me."

Edith laughed. "A mini Jolene? What a scary thought. One of you is bad enough, thank you!"

"I'm not that bad! And at least I'd know how to deal with someone like me. Motherhood is hard enough without feeling like you gave birth to an alien. It's like there was a mix-up somewhere and I got given the wrong child."

I'm not the wrong child, Mommy, I can be the right child. I will be just like you and you will love me.

Mabel. Mommy. The giant. They came and went, came and went like the tides, washing over me in waves but none of them cooled me down.

Cat was there with me; she leaned in close and settled against me, falling through the barrier of my skin until she lay snuggled up inside of me. She was my twin, the one who died and the one my mother said she wanted, until I brought her back to life, raising her from the dead like Lazarus. Then my mother didn't want her so much anymore.

Where is the cloud? Where has it gone?

I tried to look for it but the world blurred again.

Later, I don't know when exactly, they came again, the giant and the baby, coming closer and closer until they touched my lips, a benediction. They were cool against my skin, but this time they were cloaked in gold, not silver. When I looked up, I recognized the white face floating above and my blood ran cold.

It's the woman who wants to take me away! No!

I tried to keep my teeth closed so she couldn't hurt me, but I was too weak to fight back. I begged Mabel-Beauty to help me, but she was on the bad woman's side and she held me down. The woman forced a tiny dagger into my mouth and I waited to die.

Cat squirmed in my belly where she was sleeping and then she burrowed into my heart to hide. She would not be helping me, and I was too sick to help myself.

Daddy, come save me. Daddy, please.

When the social worker left after injecting me with poison, she took the gold giant and the child with her. Mabel-Beauty was back with the cool cloud.

"Edith will be back soon," she whispered. "Soon."

That's a lie. I don't want to be fed any more lies.

So many of them already swam in my veins as silver snakes; they were red-hot scaly things rubbing against my skin from underneath making it feverish and raw. Mabel-Beauty poured more lies into spoons and tried to get me to swallow them.

"No more lies! No more snakes! I don't want any more of them." On and on, they whispered to me with their forked tongues.

"Robin," Beauty said as I knocked the spoon of lies from her hand. "My child, I will tell you the truth."

"You will?"

"Yes, I will answer all your questions truthfully. I promise. But then you must let me feed you this truth medicine. It will help take away the snakes and the lies. If you swallow the medicine, I will tell you the truth."

"Yes," I whispered. "Yes." And then I opened my mouth.

• • •

Are my parents in heaven?
I do not know for sure.
Are they watching over me all the time?
I do not know for sure, but I do not think so.
Are my parents buried alive?
No.
Do black people kill white people?
Yes.
Do white people kill black people?
Yes.
Will I go home to get my bike?
No.
Will Edith give me away?
No.
Will someone take me away?
I cannot be sure.
Did my mother love me?
Yes, though it may not have been in the way you wanted.
Did I kill my sister before she was born?
No, your sister was not meant to be a part of this world.
Are all black men bad?
No.
Are all black men good?
No.
Will Mabel come back?
No.
Does Edith love me?
Yes.
Do you love me?
Yes.

Do you love Cat more than me?

No. I love you equally because you are two halves that make up a whole.

Will you leave me one day?

Yes.

C at climbed out of my stomach and lay down next to me. We were both resting on our sides facing each other.

"The snakes are leaving," she whispered. "You're going to get better."

"I know." I could feel it. They couldn't live in a heart of truth because the truth was not a comfortable place to live. They began to slither away and took the heat with them. Beauty's words came back to me.

I love you equally because you are two halves that make up a whole.

And I knew then what I had to do to heal myself and live a life of truth.

"Cat?"

"You don't have to say it. I know."

I looked at her, my sister. She was the best of me and the worst of me. I reached out to her and she reached out to me and we laced our fingers together.

"I'm going to miss you so much."

There were no words left after that. Cat wiped the tears from my cheeks because she was my tears and she was my cheeks and then she was gone. She left in her place not emptiness or an absence, but a fullness I had never known before. I felt complete, like I was finally, finally enough.

Thirty-four

BEAUTY

❧

9 SEPTEMBER 1976
Yeoville, Johannesburg, South Africa

A week passes in which the man does not call again no matter how much I pray for it to happen.

Wilhelmina, however, has been true to her word and is back to check on Robin. After she has satisfied herself that the sleeping child's temperature is down and that her color is returning to normal, she accepts my offer of a cup of tea.

"The penicillin has done its job nicely," Wilhelmina says. "And you've done a wonderful job of caring for her, Beauty. You missed your calling. You would've made a wonderful nurse."

"Thank you, Wilhelmina. Is that how you met Edith and Robin? In a nursing capacity?"

"No. I'm actually a social worker with a background in nursing. I received an anonymous call a few months ago reporting Edith as an unfit caregiver and I tried to investigate those claims. That's how I met them."

She relays the interactions with Edith and Robin that culminated in her being told to leave them alone after Edith reported Wilhelmina to her boss, saying that the woman had a personal vendetta against her.

"She provided documents proving she had a full-time desk job, but I knew there was something fishy about the whole thing. I just couldn't prove it. What kind of a woman just abandons a child like this while she goes off to do her own *blerrie* thing? Huh?"

I go cold as my gratitude turns to fear. Now that this woman has given Robin medical treatment and is aware of the full extent of Edith's treachery, will she take Robin away?

What have I done?

Wilhelmina sees the concern on my face and clucks. "Don't worry, I won't say or do anything in my official capacity. At least, not unless I have to, since I have to consider the best interests of the child. If Edith knows Maggie and Maggie has approved of these living arrangements, then I will respect that even if I don't like the *blerrie* woman. But I will be keeping a very close eye on things."

She reaches out and touches the Saint Christopher pendant around my neck. "It's a small club we belong to, Beauty. It's good to know there are others out there. Sometimes it feels like I'm the only one. *Regtig.* I'm sure it's the same for you sometimes."

As we sit and sip at our tea, we begin to share stories. I do not know what it is about this woman, but I trust her despite the fact that she is white and an Afrikaner, and despite the threat she poses to Robin and Edith through her profession. She is a friend of Maggie's and she saved Robin's life. That is enough for me.

I tell her about my search for Nomsa, and she tells me about the social work that gives her a valid excuse to be in Soweto while she assists Maggie's cause under the cloak of official business. She speaks some Xhosa and Sotho taught to her by an Afrikaner grandfather who she says was violently opposed to the apartheid regime.

I have never heard of an Afrikaner man who would fight against his own people to defend mine and I tell her so. "He sounds like a very brave man."

"*Jinne tog, ja.* He was. He really was. But he died under very suspicious circumstances and so I've come to realize that bravery can be a very dangerous thing. Sometimes duplicity is a much better weapon."

When she is finished with her tea, she stands to go. "Robin is lucky to have you, Beauty. I rest easier knowing you are here with her. Certainly this arrangement is better for her than foster care. And I have a feeling that you and I are going to become the best of friends."

When I hold my hand out to shake hers, she bats it away and engulfs me in a hug. I am too emotional to say anything and so I just hug her back. I am learning that friends can sometimes be found in the most surprising places wearing the most unexpected disguises.

Thirty-five

BEAUTY

❦

20 DECEMBER 1976
Transkei, South Africa

As I walk the sandy pathway up the side of the hill, I am barefoot and I relish the sensation of warm dirt under the soles of my feet. It is this soil more than anything else that brings me back to myself. It is this sand in this place that gives me roots.

When I arrive in the village after my long commute from the Transvaal, the first thing I do is greet my two sons and pull them in close, and then I kick off my shoes. My Western clothes get folded away, and I tuck myself into the traditional ochre-dyed blanket wrap all the women in the village wear. It has become a ritual for me now each time I return for a visit, this shedding of the prickly city and slipping back into the familiar rhythms of my people.

Sometimes in Johannesburg when I struggle to see the stars, I also struggle to hear the voices of the ancestors. I think it is the same for all my people and that is why we are letting go of the old ways.

On the way up the path, I pause under an *umNqwane* tree to take shelter from the summer sun. My sons, who have been racing one another up the hill, stop here. They will not venture any farther and will wait for me to return as there are some things custom does not allow. A warm breeze stirs the leaves but does nothing to cool me down. As I catch my breath, inhaling the sweet scent of grass and baked earth, I look down over the valley and my heart swells at the beloved sight.

Long stalks of feathery thatch grass encircle the village; they dip and sway in the warm breeze, whispering and sighing in waves of burnished copper. Winding streams crisscross between the village and the maize fields, while the pastures corral the grazing livestock. White smoke unfurls from the chimneys of the brightly colored beehive-shaped huts that cluster together to form the residential area, and women and children mill about between the *rondavels* while attending to chores or socializing.

I look out over the place of my birth and my spirits lift for the first time in many weeks. I am happy to trade in the electricity, running water and plumbing of the city for this rural landscape where water must be fetched from the stream, cooking is done over fires and only a candle can cast light into the deepest shadows. It is a place where time stands still.

There are no clocks here; there is no sense of urgency with everyone anxious to be somewhere else. Here, time is measured by the journey of the sun and moon across the sky, and there are no strangers, just clan members I have known all my life. After spending the past few nights sleeping on my mat on the baked floor, the pain in my back starts to ease from weeks spent tossing and turning on a soft mattress. It is good to be home even though the visit will be brief.

I turn and walk up the pathway once more towards the summit. When I reach the burial grounds, I tend to the sites as I do every visit. I kneel down next to them, ignoring the sharp pebbles that jut into the flesh of my knees, and begin by gathering the loose stones into a tight grouping. I begin with the grave of my firstborn son, Mandla, and then I move on to that of my husband, Silumko. I brush insects and dust from the simple tombstones with their sparse inscriptions:

MANDLA MBALI
04/09/1959–08/11/1965

and

SILUMKO MBALI
06/08/1925–19/04/1974

The ministrations are a form of prayer for my hands; they allow my body to speak its grief when words alone are not enough.

When I am done, I wind my way down the path again to the tree where the boys are waiting.

"Mama," Khwezi says, "when are you coming home?"

Luxolo shoots him an angry look. They have clearly spoken of this before, and Luxolo must have warned his younger brother not to ask this question. I look at both of their faces, so serious and so changed in the six months that I have been away. Khwezi has lost the last of his baby fat, and a shadow of hair grows on his lip and chin. Luxolo's face has hardened into that of a man. His jaw is always clenched and he is slow to smile; adult concerns have prematurely carved themselves into his features.

I sigh. I have missed out on their growing up. While I have been in Johannesburg failing to find their sister, my sons have donned the mantles of maturity; I should have been here to witness their informal passage from childhood to manhood. Though neither of them has undergone the *ulwaluko* ritual to officially make them men in the eyes of the tribe, after everything they have been through, I do not consider them boys.

"I promised you that I would bring Nomsa home," I say. "And I cannot return until I have her with me."

I just hope that when that day comes, it is not to lay Nomsa to rest with her father and brother. I will not tend to another grave.

Thirty-six

ROBIN

❁

25 DECEMBER 1976
Melville, Johannesburg, South Africa

E dith says you're not her boyfriend because you're light in the loaf-ers." I was sitting on the champagne-colored brocade chaise longue in Victor's living room. (I'd called it a gold couch as I first flopped onto it, but he'd set me straight.) Elvis was in his traveling cage next to me, and my luggage was still in the entrance hall where Edith had un-ceremoniously dumped it on her way out.

I was wearing bright orange velvet hot pants paired with a white sleeveless turtleneck and white knee-high lace-up boots. The pants were accurately named; even though they barely covered my butt, the velvet (coupled with the thirty-degree heat) made them very hot and uncomfortable to wear. The outfit was supposed to include a white beret, but I'd lost it in the rush from Edith's apartment to Victor's house after the call from the airline came through and she said there was a change of plans.

Edith had bought the clothes during her last trip to New York and said they were the height of fashion. It was the first time I'd been able to wear the hot pants and boots because Beauty had forbidden me from going out in them, saying that I looked like a child prostitute. I'd wanted to look the word up in the dictionary, but Morrie told me that prostitutes were people who'd left the Catholic faith to start their own religion. I didn't know why Beauty would have a problem with that, but I respected her opinion and only wore the outfit that day because it was Christmas and Edith insisted. Victor was nattily dressed, as always, and his mauve fedora perfectly matched his bow tie and socks.

"I didn't know what 'light in the loafers' meant," I continued, "and so I looked it up in the dictionary."

Victor laughed, but he sounded nervous. "And what did it say?"

"It just said that loafers are shoes, which didn't make any sense so I had to go back to Edith to ask her to explain it."

"And?"

"She said you and her aren't a couple because you're a homosexual."

"Well, yes and no. I do love Edie, but I don't think I could've been her boyfriend even if I wasn't queer. But don't tell her I said that."

"She says homosexuals are men who have sexual reproduction with other men."

"Well, there's no reproduction involved per se, but there certainly is the . . . ah . . . sex."

"She says I can't tell anyone because it's illegal and you could go to prison."

"Well, yes. The law is rather draconian, wouldn't you say?"

"What's 'draconian'?"

"Something that's very severe."

"You mean like the apartheid laws?"

"Yes, exactly."

"We're not allowed to tell anyone about Beauty either. If people know she lives with us to look after me, she could also go to prison."

Victor's brow crinkled. "You have an awful lot of secrets you have to keep, don't you? That's a lot of responsibility for a nine-year-old."

"I'll be ten next month."

"Still."

"It's okay. I don't mind keeping secrets." I looked around the living room. It was the most beautiful room I'd ever seen. A crystal chandelier was suspended high above us and every surface—including the walls and floors—was covered with the kinds of luxurious fabrics you want to wrap around yourself and go to sleep in.

"Is Liberace your boyfriend?" I asked.

"Liberace? No, why?"

"Because Edith said your house looks like a scene from a Liberace wet dream."

Victor spat out the sip of champagne he'd just taken. "Pardon me," he said as he wiped at his chin.

"What's a wet dream?" I asked.

"Err . . . well . . . What do you think it is?"

"Is it when you're sleeping and you're dreaming and someone pours water over you?"

"Well, there you go."

"Oh wow, look at your tree!" I'd only just noticed it in the dining room and I jumped up to take a look.

I'd never seen anything like it. It was tall but not that wide, and each of its black twisted and curling wrought-iron branches held multiple glass candleholders that were forged in the shape of stars. Flames from tea lights flickered inside them so that they looked like shooting stars burning up from the inside.

"It's meant to be avant-garde," Victor said. "I'm not sure if I like it. I'm hoping it will grow on me."

It was nothing at all like the traditional Christmas tree my parents used to put up, but it brought to mind the rituals we'd followed every festive season for as long as I could remember. The fake spruce tree would be hauled out from storage in the garage, and there'd be a frantic search for the metal base until someone would remember that it had been broken a year or two before. My father would then find an empty flowerpot, cover it with Christmas wrapping paper and fill it with soil from the garden, and the tree would be wedged into that and put in the corner of the lounge.

Untangling the lights was always the most volatile stage in the decorating process, and if that didn't go well, the rest of it would have to be abandoned for a day or two until tempers had settled down sufficiently for us to continue.

"What the fuck?" my father would say every December, tugging at the knotted cords. "Who put this away last year?"

"You did, Keith," my mother always replied.

"Impossible. I would have made sure they were rolled up properly. This is a gigantic whore's nest."

If the lights managed to be detangled without a dozen globes breaking, or my father having to cut the cord and then re-fuse the wires, we could drape them around the tree and move on to the next step, which was putting up the tinsel. It was usually my second favorite part of the process because I loved the silky texture of the garlands, but it could be fraught with as much tension as the lights.

"Where's the rest of the tinsel?" my father asked one year, holding up only two mangy strings.

"That's all there is," I said, peering into the bag.

"What do you mean 'that's all there is'? We should have at least a dozen strands of this stuff. Where are the silver and gold ones?"

I didn't dare say that I'd taken them without permission to jazz up a particularly dull angel costume in the nativity play, and that I'd then cut them up to use as glitter for the Christmas cards we made in class. I just shrugged as my father had scratched his head muttering about a scourge of fish moths. That year, the tree had been greatly lacking in pizzazz.

The baubles were always the second-to-last thing to go up and had to be hung in a very particular order.

"Globes first," my mother would say. "Gold and then silver, followed by red and green."

I'd reach for a gold Father Christmas and my mother would swat my hand away. "Only the globes for now. Then the stars. Then the candy canes. Then the angels. Father Christmases are last."

There was no use arguing with her, and God help anyone who hung too many of the same ornaments next to each other or left a bald spot somewhere. Finally, once everything had been put up to both their exacting specifications, it would be time for the giant star. My father would slip his hands under my armpits and raise me up so I could place it right at the top of the tree.

"Good job, Freckles! Now let's hope those rumors that Father Christmas was arrested for shoplifting aren't true!"

I hadn't gotten to do any of that this December. Edith didn't do a Christmas tree and her only concessions to decorations were red and green liqueurs and multicolored shot glasses.

"You miss them very much, don't you?" Victor asked quietly.

I nodded, not trusting myself to speak.

He sighed and then put on a fake, festive voice. "So . . . what did Father Christmas bring you?"

"Father Christmas doesn't exist, Victor, but Edith got me clothes and a few records, and Beauty gave me this. Isn't it beautiful?"

I came around to stand in front of him and opened the tiny latch of the heart-shaped locket to show him the black-and-white pictures inside: my dad's face was on the left and my mother's on the right. "The photos were taken on their wedding day. Beauty got them from Edith."

"It is beautiful. What a thoughtful gift."

That's when I remembered that Edith had given me a gift to give Victor. I hopped up and ran to my hastily packed suitcase, pulling out the silver box tied with silver ribbons. "Here you go, this is for you."

"Thank you, but you really didn't have to." Victor took the box and put it down next to him.

"No, you have to open it now. It's Christmas already so you don't have to wait." He looked reluctant and I thought it was because he was intimidated by the sight of all those ribbons. "Here, I'll help you untie them." I picked the box up and set about loosening all the knots. When I was done, I tossed the lid aside and reached in, my hand connecting with something hard and cold. I pulled it out. "Handcuffs? Are you a policeman?"

"I'll take that," Victor said, grabbing the box from me before I could delve any further into its depths. "Robin, I hope you don't mind me asking, but are you comfortable in that outfit? I can't help but notice that you keep tugging at the shorts."

"Hot pants," I corrected.

"Right. Hot pants. Would you like to go change into something more comfortable?"

"Yes please!"

"Wonderful. Go on upstairs; you're staying in the guest room. It's the second door on the left. I'll get Elvis settled down here in the meantime."

As I turned away from Victor, I noticed that the dining room table was done up with all twelve of its places set. Crystal glasses twinkled in the light given off by the Christmas tree, and the multiple sets of gleaming cutlery stood to attention in between the china. At the end of the table was a white plastic chair that had hastily been pushed in at an angle between two other upholstered chairs. It was the only ugly thing in a perfect room filled with perfect things.

Victor saw me looking. "That's your spot. I haven't finished setting it properly, but you'll be sitting next to me at the head of the table."

Up until then, I'd been feeling sorry for myself that my first Christmas with Edith had been ruined by her having to work. We'd planned to go up to the roof and tan all day while listening to Boney M. records. I'd been teaching Elvis to sing "Feliz Navidad" and Edith had even bought a small, inflatable blue kiddie pool that was covered in fish motifs, which she'd said we could turn into a Jacuzzi. The cooler box had already been packed with wine, Coke and ice cream bars when the phone had rung.

It dawned on me then as the heavenly scent of roast chicken wafted through from the kitchen that Edith had offloaded me on Victor without any regard for his own plans for Christmas. That was one of the worst things about being an orphan, not knowing when or if you were wanted.

I had to ask. "Have I ruined your Christmas, Victor?"

"Of course not!"

"It looks like you're having a lot of people over for a fancy lunch."

"Well, yes, but the more the merrier. I am honored to have you as a guest, young lady. Now scram upstairs to change. Everyone should be here any minute. Come down when you're ready."

"Okay." I gathered up my luggage and raced up the stairs to find my room. It was big and beautiful, and the best part was that it was all mine; I didn't have to share it with anyone. The walls were covered in silky wallpaper that had red-and-white swirling patterns on it, and the double bed had giant, round fluffy pillows scattered across it. I climbed up and jumped on it like you would a trampoline, but that only made me hotter than I already was so I had to stop.

I yanked off the hot pants and boots, and then dug around in my suitcase for my favorite denim shorts and the "Free Nelson Mandela" T-shirt Edith had given me for Christmas. It was only once I'd pulled them on and was looking at myself in the mirror that I decided I looked too casual. Victor had gone to so much trouble to make everything perfect that I wanted to look perfect too; I didn't want him to regret having me at his party.

I'd packed a few of the gifts I'd opened that morning and pulled them out one by one to see what might work. After much deliberation, I settled on a red corduroy miniskirt, pairing it with the white boots and turtleneck I'd just taken off. My crotch at least felt a lot cooler in the skirt; it let in a lot more air than the hot pants. My hair was getting very long and my fringe hung over my eyes almost down to my chin, so I pinned it back with a pair of red heart-shaped sunglasses.

I looked good but there was still something missing and it took me a few minutes to figure out what it was. Edith always wore a lot of makeup, and my mother used to put extra on for special occasions. I decided this would definitely qualify as such. My strawberry lip gloss was easy enough to apply, though I licked two separate coats off because it tasted so good. Putting on my mother's mascara was harder, because poking a small stick at your eyes while you try to keep them open is tricky. Also it was a bit clumpy by then. It smudged when I opened my eyes really wide, and when I tried to wipe the black streaks off, it smudged even more.

The doorbell had been ringing intermittently the whole time I was getting ready and Elvis returned its call each time. Voices and delicious smells floated up the stairs and I didn't want to miss out on any of the fun, so I gave up on fixing the mascara mess and followed the chatter down to the dining room. As I made my entrance, twelve men stopped talking and turned to look at me.

"There she is!"

"Doesn't she look groovy?"

"Oh my God, those boots are far out."

"Those glasses are so cool."

"Love the panda eyes. Is that the latest thing?"

Victor called me over to his side, dipping a napkin in some water and gently removing the excess mascara. "Everyone, this is Robin. Edith is her aunt." I loved that he said that. Not "She's Edith's niece," but "Edith is her aunt" as though I was the important one to know. Then he walked me around the room, introducing me to everyone.

The men were all well dressed and handsome, and very different-looking from the burly men my father worked with on the mine. They made a big deal out of greeting me, and some of them kissed my hand

and some my cheeks. I tried to keep track of all the names: Claude (shirt open, lots of chest hair), Sebastian (permed hair), Jonathan (John Lennon tinted glasses), Johan (Afrikaner with a purple paisley waist-coat), Kristoff (another Afrikaner, no moustache), Hans (moustache), Jacques (bald), Samson (smelled like suntan lotion), Gordon (very wide lapels), Nick (cowboy boots) and Shane (red hair).

When Victor rang a little bell, everyone moved to their seats. Johan came around with champagne to top up everyone's glasses and gave me Babycham in a port glass that looked like a wineglass for fairies. "Just a teeny tiny bit. Don't get tipsy, okay?" His Afrikaner accent was gravelly and lyrical; when he spoke, it sounded like he was singing.

The seven-course meal was served over the next three hours; it was a conveyer belt of food that just kept on coming. Avocado Ritz. Cold beetroot soup. Caesar salad. Crab cakes. Lemon sorbet. Roast chicken with roast potatoes and four vegetables. Cheese platter and crème brûlée. It was the best feast I'd ever had, and every time I thought I was too full to take another bite, I'd just wait ten minutes and I'd be ready to go again.

The conversation was steady during the meal, but I didn't feel as though I needed to add anything. I was content to just sit and listen to it as it buzzed all around me, sentences breaking loose in English and Afrikaans to float free like kites in the wind.

"It's disgusting that the All Blacks came out to play here this year. If the Springboks were banned from playing international rugby, you'd start to see things changing . . ."

"Jeremy had a run-in with the police the other day. Something about a complaint from one of his neighbors. A question of his moral values and something to do with . . ."

"I knew there was censorship, I just didn't realize how bad it was. The foreign press reports everything that happens here while we remain deaf and blind . . ."

"Where did you get this recipe from? These crab cakes are divine, simply divine."

After the last course had been consumed and the plates had been cleared away, we gathered in the second lounge, which is how we all eventually ended up crowded around the piano while everyone called out requests.

Victor covered a few Christmas carols before the song suggestions started veering into more modern selections. Johan asked for "Lola" by the Kinks and I listened as they all sang, trying to figure out what the words meant. I didn't know any of the words except the "Lola" part, which I really belted out during the chorus. I was just starting to hum the next bit when there was a loud crash to my right, and the glass pane window disintegrated into hundreds of tiny daggers.

We all screamed as the glass rained down on us, but Johan screamed the loudest as something big and solid connected with his head. One minute he was standing next to me, his hand on my shoulder, and the next he'd dropped, clutching his temple. As everyone crouched out of the line of fire and Victor crawled across to Johan, I reached for the missile that had fallen on the floor next to me.

It was a brick with a piece of paper tied around it. Someone had written "Die you queer freaks" in big block letters. Words once again buzzed over me as the men discussed the futility of calling the police and wondered if another attack was likely. I clutched the brick in one hand and Johan's hand in the other. I was mute. I didn't know what to say in a world where people were hated and attacked for not being the right color, not speaking the right language, not worshipping the right god or not loving the right people; a world where hatred was the common language, and bricks, the only words.

Thirty-seven

BEAUTY

❦

Hᴇʀᴇ, I made you a cup of tea just the way you like it." Robin places the steaming mug on a coaster in front of me, and I smile a weak but grateful smile.

I have only been back for half an hour and even though Edith has told the child not to badger me with questions, she cannot contain herself. I have never met such a curious child, one who has such an insatiable thirst for information. Even though I am tired from the long commute, I do not mind answering her as I like to talk about the Transkei and my family. It makes me feel closer to a life I fear I will never live again.

After Robin serves the tea, she sits next to me and traces the satiny fabric of my dress where it flares out between us on the couch. Her fingers are pale against its darkness.

"How was your Christmas?" she asks.

"It was a blessed time, thank you. It was wonderful to see my sons."

"Did you give them the photo of me?"

I smile and reach for the tea to take a sip. I have promised this child to only ever tell her the truth, but I also do not want to hurt her feelings by telling her that I had no intention of handing her gift across. I keep it in my bible, which is a better place for it than in the hands of two abandoned boys who are resentful of their mother's presence in the white child's life.

I am spared from having to answer when Robin is unable to wait long enough before expressing the next thought that has occurred to her.

"Johan had to go to hospital for stitches."

"Who is Johan?"

The child explains that Johan is Victor's friend, and that he was hurt when someone threw a brick through the window. I wonder where Edith was during this Christmas ordeal, as she was supposed to spend the holiday with the child, but before I can ask, Robin's thoughts veer in a different direction yet again.

"Edith said Silumko died of Tyson? My dad had to go for Tyson tests as well."

"It is actually called 'phthisis,'" I correct her. "You get it from inhaling rock dust underground. Your father would have gone for regular checkups because it is a common mining disease. The black miners weren't always tested."

"Are you very sad? Do you miss Silumko?"

"Yes, I miss him very much," I say, which is true though it is more complicated than that. I have discovered, to my surprise, that grief is a process that gets more difficult, rather than easier, with time. In those first few weeks after Mandla and then Silumko died, my loss had been too great, too much for me to take in all at once. During those early days, I could merely circle around it, tracing its contours as I tried to familiarize myself with its heft. I learned that just as a map of the world only contains rough outlines of countries—their borders and major cities, as well as the rivers and oceans that dissect and separate them—so too would the cartography of my loss at first be laid out as a broad, abstract concept for me to come to terms with.

Only after I had learned those boundaries and generalities of my grief was I able to venture further into the mountains and valleys, the peaks and troughs of my despair. And as I traversed them—breathing a sigh of relief thinking that I'd conquered the worst of it—only then would I finally arrive at the truth about loss, the part that no one ever warns you about: that grief is a city all of its own, built high on a hill and surrounded by stone walls. It is a fortress that you will inhabit for the rest of your life, walking its dead-end roads forever. The trick is to stop trying to escape and, instead, to make yourself at home.

I know Robin will learn this for herself one day, and that it is too much to try to explain to her now, so instead I say, "I will always miss him. Silumko was a good man. A very good man."

The child looks doubtful, and so I reach out and take her hand. I squeeze it gently. "He really was. I know that you find that difficult to believe after what happened to your mother and father. I know you think that all black men are bad, but that is not so. My husband was a kind and decent man, and my sons will grow up to be fine men as well." I stroke her palm with my thumb. "Good people come in all different colors and speak many different languages, bad people too. And sometimes good people do bad things, and sometimes bad things are the only things people know how to do because they do not know any better. One day you will see that for yourself."

The bird suddenly screeches loudly from his perch on the top shelf and I stand to go and tend to him. I stopped fearing him during Robin's illness when I was the only person who could feed him, and I was surprised to find that I missed his constant chattering and singing while I was away.

"Don't worry. I'll do it." Robin gets up and puts Elvis back in his cage. She measures out his seed and tops up his water before coming back to sit next to me. "Why aren't you crying if you miss Silumko so much? You're allowed to, you know. Sometimes it makes you feel better."

"Just because you do not see something with your own eyes, my child, it does not mean it does not happen. I do cry but I do so in private."

"Oh."

I sigh. "The truth is that I have been mourning him for a long time now. Since long before he died."

"What do you mean?"

"Silumko left me more than ten years ago to work in the mines in Johannesburg, and during that time, I only saw him for four weeks a year when he was allowed to come home. Even then, I could see he was not the man I married and I missed that man."

"What man was he?"

"He was still Silumko, but he was also not Silumko. Do you understand?"

The child shakes her head and I try to explain. "The Silumko I first loved many years ago was a very handsome young man with a smile like the crescent moon. He was a person who did not like to be kept inside. He was happiest when he was setting out, sometimes for weeks at a time, to find the best grazing for his sheep, and during that time away, he would sleep on the ground among his cattle with nothing but the night sky as his blanket."

"Didn't you miss him then when he was away?"

"I did, but not so much because I knew he was happy. We both were, during those years when the children were little and we lived by the old ways. But then, Mandla drowned in the floods, and after that, the droughts came and we lost the last of the cattle, and Silumko was forced to leave for Johannesburg." I stop speaking to make sure that the child is paying attention. It is important that she understand this. "Can you imagine what that is like? To be taken from the fields and open spaces and blue skies and sunk down a mine shaft more than a kilometer deep into the earth? To labor sixteen-hour days in damp and darkness, amid rockfalls and explosions? That is when I lost him, because that is when he lost himself. I first started mourning him then."

My throat constricts and I reach for the tea, take a sip and then set the mug down again. "In the first few years, when he was squashed into the cages with hundreds of other mine workers before the sun rose, he would hope that an owl would not be seen on the headgear, because he said that owls were messengers of death and no good could come of seeing one. But then, later, he said that he came to welcome the sightings."

"Why?"

"Because he believed that dying would be better than living in terrible circumstances."

Robin shrugs. "I don't know why he hated it so much. My dad worked on the mines and it didn't sound so bad."

"Where did your father go after work, Robin?"

"He came home."

"Who did he come home to?"

"Me and my mother."

I am trying to be gentle with her. "Silumko couldn't come home to his family. He had to stay in the mine hostels, in terrible conditions, sharing a room and toilets and other facilities with hundreds of other men."

"Oh. My father wouldn't have liked that."

"And how much money did your father earn?"

"I don't know."

"Enough for you to have your own house and a car and new clothes and food?"

"Yes."

"And was your father the boss or was he a worker who got told what to do?"

"He was the boss," she says proudly.

I explain how little Silumko earned and how different his working conditions were to her father's. I want her to understand that two men can be in the exact same place doing the exact same things while wearing the exact same clothes and yet they can still be worlds apart. The serious expression on her face shows that she does understand, at least a bit. I worry that I am telling her too much and that she is too young to understand, but at the same time, I have also promised her honesty.

The phone rings and Edith comes out of her room to answer it.

"Beauty, it's for you." She holds the receiver out.

I make my way to the phone slowly. My muscles have stiffened up. "Hello?"

It is the unknown caller again. "Meet me downstairs at the back of the building in ten minutes. This time, no excuses," he says before the line goes dead.

"Edith," I say, "I have to go."

A white van turns the corner and then comes to a halt in front of me. The name "JC Plumbing" is stenciled across the sides in big red letters.

A tall, muscular black man steps out of the van and walks towards me. After looking around the parking lot and satisfying himself that no one is watching, he pulls a piece of black material from his pocket and holds it out to me. "Put this on."

I take the cloth and shake it out. It is a blindfold.

"Who are you?"

"Put it on. Quickly." His eyes dart around. I am nervous that he will see something to scare him off and that he will leave without me.

I tie the strip of fabric around my eyes, careful to leave my nostrils open. He grips my arm and pushes me to the back of the van.

"Mind your head when you step up."

I duck as I step inside and feel my way to a seat. I do not know who this man is or where he is taking me, but I am desperate to find my daughter. I will go anywhere and do anything if it means I will find her.

The blindfold is untied and falls away revealing a bare, windowless room. The only light comes from a lamp on the floor in the corner. A red scarf has been thrown over it and the whole room takes on the quality of a massacre. I am sitting on a straight-backed chair facing the only other piece of furniture, a two-seater leather couch. The room is stiflingly hot and stuffy; the air settles around my shoulders like an insincere embrace that I want to shake off.

The man walks around from behind me and goes to sit on the couch. A handgun is holstered to his side and the sight of it chills me. He pulls a packet of tobacco from his pants and a pipe from his shirt pocket and sets about preparing it, all the while staring at me.

"Where is—"

He cuts me off by holding up his hand. I keep quiet. We will speak when he is ready. When the pipe is finished and its smoke and cherry tobacco smell has filled the air, the man is ready to talk. "You are becoming a nuisance, do you know that?"

Any hope I had is trampled. This man is not here to help me.

"You are like a tsetse fly with your constant inquiries. Always biting, biting, biting and causing irritation. My people are complaining that you are getting in the way of our cause."

"All I want is to find my daughter."

"And what if your daughter does not wish to be found?"

"Then she can tell me that herself."

"And what if she does not wish to speak with you?"

"If she tells me that herself, then I will accept it."

He makes a dismissive clicking sound, almost as though he is trying to suck an annoying piece of meat out from between his teeth. "Your questions will reach the ears of the wrong people and put her, and the rest of us, in danger. Stop what you are doing. You are not helping anyone."

It finally dawns on me who this man is. "You are Shakes Ngubane," I say, trying to keep the fear out of my voice.

He does not look happy that I know his name, but he does not reply to either confirm or deny it.

"I think you are keeping my daughter from me."

"You seem to be confused, *sisi*. I am not your enemy. The white man is your enemy."

"No one is my enemy, *bhuti*, except the person who keeps my child from me."

"No one is keeping your child from you. Your daughter has made a choice about where she wants to be and you need to respect her decision."

"If she respects her own decision, she will have the courage to tell me of it herself."

"You are wasting your time waiting for that. She is not in the country."

"Then I will wait until she returns."

"If she returns."

"Not 'if' but when. It is just a matter of time. You send them away to be trained so that they can come back to fight your battles here."

"Our battles."

I shrug. "I will wait."

"I thought you were more intelligent than that. I thought you were open to reason, but I see that is not so. I will only talk nicely to you like this once. Carry on making trouble and asking your questions, and the next time, I will not be so nice."

"Are you threatening me?"

"Take it however you will. Just stay out of my way."

Thirty-eight

ROBIN

✿

14 JANUARY 1977
Yeoville, Johannesburg, South Africa

It was the early evening of my tenth birthday, and I'd gone through the whole day without one person wishing me.

I hadn't told my teachers or my friends, because they would've asked why I hadn't brought cake to school or why I wasn't having a party. Edith was away and I didn't know if Beauty knew the significance of the date. It would've been too sad if she didn't—if I'd had to go through our morning rituals as if it was just an ordinary day—and so I'd slipped out to go to school while she was still in the bath. I missed Cat. If she'd been there, I could've wished her and she could've wished me; at least we'd have had each other to celebrate with.

Beauty hadn't been waiting at the gate at the end of the school day, and I'd run all the way home in a panic to find a note on the kitchen table.

Dear Robin,

I have gone out to do some shopping. Please be home by 6 p.m. so we can do your homework.

Love,

Beauty

There was no birthday wish and my suspicion was confirmed: Edith hadn't remembered and she hadn't told Beauty about it either.

After making myself lunch, I went out to practice my surveillance skills because I needed to be prepared for the next time Beauty went on a mission to find Nomsa. Beauty didn't know it, but the night she'd gotten the phone call, I'd snuck out behind her and followed her. As I opened the door to the parking lot, I caught a glimpse of Beauty walking towards a white van with the name "JC Plumbing" on it.

I quickly stepped back so they wouldn't see me, leaving the door open just wide enough so I could peek through. A black man handed across what looked like a piece of material, and I watched as Beauty looked from him to the cloth, seeming to consider her options. After a moment, she nodded and tied the strip of fabric around her eyes. He was making her wear a blindfold.

The man helped Beauty into the back of the van, and as he closed the door and walked around to the driver's side, I felt a wild impulse to make a run for it. If I timed it just right, I could open the back door and hop inside before he pulled off. Beauty hadn't been there the night with Mabel when the police herded us into the van, and so she didn't know that no good could come of being blindfolded and driven away in one. She needed protection, and I desperately wanted to be the one to offer it to her.

But then, I'd allowed myself to think about Edith who was waiting for me and who'd be worried if I didn't come back, and that was all it took—that one second of doubt—before it was too late to act. The van started pulling away, and all I could do was step outside to get a look at the yellow number plate. I made a note of the black letters and numbers that were getting farther and farther way: BBM676T. I turned around and went back inside.

I'd let Beauty down. The members of the Secret Seven and Famous Five would never have hesitated; they would have been in that van in a flash! I was determined to do better the next time, and figured that working on my detective skills would serve me in good stead until then.

I started my training by stopping random people on the street. "Where were you on the night of January the fourth?" I asked an old lady with impossibly thick glasses.

She blinked at me as though trying to figure out if I was real, and then shook her head and walked off.

"Do you remember seeing any suspicious characters around ten days ago?" I asked another three people who all said they hadn't.

When a scary man told me to keep my nose out of his business, I decided to question only suspects I knew.

Mr. Abdul, standing behind the cash register in his shop, narrowed his eyes as he thought about it and then said, "The night of the fourth of January? That's easy. I was in the shop working, always working, never having a rest. And yes, there are always many suspicious characters being about, trying to steal from me."

Mr. Papadopoulos considered it as he wrapped *slap* chips dripping with vinegar in newspaper. "That was more than a week gone by. How I should remember? Suspicious person, you ask? The only suspicious person is my mother-in-law. The Kennedy assassination, you know it? Ask her where she was that day."

I made a note using my secret language in my notebook to follow up on that. The only problem was that my secret language was so secret that I sometimes had trouble decoding it, and so I made a note in English as well.

Tina, the hairdresser, said she was at her boyfriend's house. "Of course, that was before the two-timing son of a bitch decided to start running around with that slut, Vicky, who should actually be called 'Icky.' I'm well rid of the both of them, because you know what? They deserve each other, and another thing—"

"Aha! I've spotted my suspect," I said just so that I could get out of there.

When I finally got back to Coral Mansions, it was 6 p.m. and I couldn't bear the depressing thought of returning to a potentially empty flat. Instead, I went downstairs to look for King George and found him in his room in the basement. I rapped on the door and announced myself, and he called out for me to enter.

King George had knocked off for the night but was still wearing his flatboy uniform. It consisted of a dark blue cotton shirt with a thin red line on the sleeve hems, which was worn with matching trousers. He smelled of tobacco and polish, and was loosening the leather knee protectors he usually donned on floor-cleaning days.

The room was as spartan as I remembered. The only furniture was a small bed and a single chair. A rope was strung up across the one wall and a few items of clothing and a towel were hanging from it. Something was different and it took me a moment to figure out what it was: all the rows of drawings taped to the walls. There were dozens of them, all beautifully rendered in pencil or charcoal on different-sized scraps of paper. Most of them were of faces, but some were of marinas or town scenes.

"Did you draw these?"

"*Ja.*" King George smiled shyly. "King George normally keep them inna box but he decide to hang them up like inna art gallery he see down the road. He like that kind of fancy *kak*."

I skimmed past a few of the portraits and focused on a street scene showing an old-fashioned car parked outside a shop. "Where's this?"

"Home."

I squinted at the name of the store. "You lived in a liquor store?"

"*Ja*, inna back room."

"Huh." I carried on scanning until a drawing of a beautiful girl on the opposite wall caught my eye.

"Wow. Who's that?"

"King George's wife."

"Your wife? This girl?" I didn't mean to sound so scornful, but it seemed highly unlikely that an old man missing a few teeth was married to such a young and lovely woman.

Instead of answering, King George studied my face. "*Jinne* but Little Miss is *dikbek* today. What's wrong?"

I sighed heavily. "It's my birthday and no one gives a crap." I'd wanted to say "shit" but couldn't bring myself to say it. "Crap" was as far as I would go to show how upset I was.

"Must be *lekker* for Little Miss to know when her birthday is."

"You don't know when your birthday is?"

"No, Little Miss. King George's ma was *slapgat* and didn't mark the day down in the bible and the white *ouballie* had made *gat skoon* by then."

This news was shocking. "Your father was white and your mother was black?" I'd never heard anything like it. Was it even possible?

"That's *mos* what King George is saying. King George is a *klonkie*."

"What does that mean?"

"He a colored."

"Oh." That explained his odd color and why he didn't look either black or white.

"*Ja*, and the *klonkies* have it *moerse* hard in this country. The whites hate them because they have black blood, and the blacks hate them because they have white blood. A *ou sommer* can't win."

"Is that why you talk so funny?"

"Hey, don't be cheeky. This is *mos* the way all us *Kaapse klonkies* talk." When I just stared at him blankly, he explained that he was from Cape Town, and that's how all the colored people from District Six spoke. He waved at his drawings when he said this, including all the faces and the scenes in his statement, so that I understood they were all drawn from his past.

"So why are you in Joburg then?"

"The *gatte* came and told the *klonkies* to live in the Flats, *die gat kant* of Cape Town. King George didn't want to live in the Flats, so he packed up his wheels with *sommer alles* he own and came to Joeys."

"Oh." From what I could make out, the police had used violence to move everyone from District Six to a place called the Flats, and King George decided to move to Johannesburg instead.

"You have a car?"

"Why so *geskok*, Little Miss? A *ou mos* needs wheels for business."

"You need a car to be a flatboy?" That seemed highly unlikely. Flatboys mostly cleaned the communal areas, washed windows, polished the parquet flooring and brass-ware, took out garbage and stoked the boiler fires. You didn't need a car for any of that.

"Flatboy is *mos* King George's day job. The real bucks come from the night job."

"Oh, and what job is that?"

"Never you mind."

"So where's your wife then?"

The mischievous expression on his face suddenly gave way to something raw resembling grief; it lasted just a few seconds before King George shook it off and changed the subject. "That's *kak* for Little Miss that no one care about her birthday. Come to King George. He will give you a *drukkie*."

"No, thank you."

"*Jinne*, Little Miss being racist now? Won't let the colored man give her a *drukkie*?"

"I'm not racist. You just stink, that's why I'm not hugging you. When last did you bathe or spray on some deodorant?"

"Deodorant and soap cost money, Little Miss." I turned to go and he called out, "Come visit King George again, *né*? Just don't be so *woes* next time."

"Okay." I decided my birthday couldn't get any worse, and so it was time to call it a day and head home. I let myself into the flat and my spirits sank even further. It was dark inside, which meant Beauty wasn't home yet. I flicked the switch and that's when it happened: people appeared seemingly out of nowhere—from the bedroom and the bathroom, and behind the curtains and couch—and they all yelled, "Surprise!"

Almost everyone who mattered most to me was in the same room: Beauty (smiling broadly), Morrie (hair more poofy than usual), Mr. and Mrs. Goldman (bearing gifts), Victor (wearing an aquamarine bow tie because I'd told him once that aquamarine was my favorite color), Johan (minus his stitches), Wilhelmina (no longer a baddie!) and Maggie (no longer my only guardian angel). Black, white, homosexual, heterosexual, Christian, Jew, Englishman, Afrikaner, adult, child, man, woman: we were all there together, but somehow that eclectic jumble of labels was overwritten by the one classification that applied to every person there: "friend."

Near the end of the night as the festivities wound down, Morrie had his camera out and was taking photos though none of the pictures were of the cake or my presents or even of me. Instead, he took pictures of cigarette butts in an ashtray, discarded wrapping paper on the floor and a deflated balloon. His morbid fascination with all things depressing had still not played itself out. I was just trying to convince him to take a photo of something more cheerful when Victor and Johan joined us.

Johan cleared his throat until Morrie raised the camera from a tear in the couch's fabric. "Good evening, young man. I'm Johan. It's lovely to meet you. May I ask what your intentions are with our lovely Robin over here?"

I groaned.

"Good evening, sir. I'm Morrie and I'm Robin's boyfriend." Morrie put the camera down, wiped his hands off on his pants and shook Johan's hand.

"He's not my boyfriend." A flush of color crept up my neck.

"I'm not?" Morrie sounded hurt.

"No, you're just my friend."

Johan winced. "*Eina*, that's got to hurt."

"But we spend a lot of time together, we like the same things, and you're always telling me what to do. That means we're in a relationship," Morrie insisted.

"It does?"

"Yes. Here, I even got you a present and I spent a lot of my pocket money on it. If you're saying you're not my girlfriend, then I'm not sure I'm going to give it to you."

I looked at the gift he'd pulled out from his bag. It was a rectangular shape and quite thick; it had to be a book. I really wanted it. "Okay then, fine, I'm your girlfriend. Give me the present."

"Glad we got that sorted out," Victor said.

Morrie handed the gift over and I tore the wrapping off. I was right, it was a book! I read the cover: "The Hardy Boys Adventures."

"They're brothers who act like detectives. You'll love it," Morrie said.

"Thank you."

"Don't I get a kiss?"

"Don't push it. I said I'd be your girlfriend, didn't I?"

Coupledom didn't fascinate me like it did other girls. From what I'd seen with my parents and then with Edith and Michael, being in a relationship wasn't all that great. I liked Morrie and didn't want to fight with him as I was sure to do if we went steady, but he seemed really adamant about it.

"It's time for us to go, Morris," Mr. Goldman said as he and Mrs.

Goldman joined us at the table. He was wearing his usual green knit-ted cardigan, and even though Morrie had tried to convince me that his father owned seven identical cardigans, I told him I wasn't born yesterday.

"Can't we stay a bit longer?" Morrie asked.

"No, *boychick*," Mrs. Goldman said. "You didn't finish your school-work today while you were helping Beauty get ready for the party, and your father also has some work to do tonight."

Mr. Goldman was always at home. I thought he didn't have a job, but Morrie informed me that his father ran an accounting practice for various local businesses from their flat. I'd seen a lot of important-looking papers lying in a room he called his office, and his father had a huge calculator that spewed ribbons of coiled paper covered with numbers, so I believed the accountant story more than the one about the cloned cardigans.

"Say good-bye to everyone," Mr. Goldman said.

"Bye, everyone. Good night, Robin."

Once I'd said good night to the Goldmans and thanked them for coming, it was just the three of us left in the lounge sitting amongst the debris of the party. Maggie, Wilhelmina and Beauty were chatting off to the side in the dining room. Elvis had calmed down from his earlier excitement and was hopping from plate to plate nibbling at the leftover cake.

I reached out and touched Johan's forehead. "Does it hurt?"

"No, it's fine. And don't you think I look butch now?" He was joking and trying to brush it off, but I remembered the fear and tears, and his head resting on my lap as we rushed to the hospital.

"Have the police found the person who did it?"

Victor sighed. "We never called the police, Robin."

"Why not? Isn't it a crime to hurt people and throw bricks through their windows?"

"Yes, it is, but getting the police involved will just make things that much more complicated, and that's exactly what we don't need."

"Aren't you scared it will happen again?"

Johan yelled, "Ha! Let them just try," just as Victor said, "Yes."

"But they're bad people. Shouldn't they be punished?"

"It's not as simple as that," Victor said.

"Why not?"

"Because the law thinks we're the bad men and it would probably take their side."

"So then why don't you move?" I asked. "If you go live somewhere else, people won't do that to you."

"You can't spend your life running away from bullies because bullies are everywhere. Sometimes you have to stand your ground and face your fears rather than trying to outrun them."

"So they're going to get away with it? Nothing will happen to them?"

"Not necessarily," Johan said. "There's always karma."

"What's karma?"

"It's this belief system," Victor explained, "that says when you do bad things to people and don't get punished for it, justice will still prevail because bad things will then happen to you in return."

I really wanted to believe that was true.

Thirty-nine

BEAUTY

❀

14 JANUARY 1977
Yeoville, Johannesburg, South Africa

Robin is sitting with Victor and Johan, eating the last of the cake that Wilhelmina baked. Her eyes are shining, and she laughs as Johan licks his teaspoon and sticks it against his nose. It is good to see her happy and I am glad that the surprise party was a success. I turn back to Maggie who is still frowning. I have put her in a difficult position, and for that, I am sorry.

"It's just that those MK guys make up a huge part of my network of intelligence, Beauty. I work very closely with them because we all want to achieve the same goals—"

"They have very different ways of achieving those goals than you do."

"I know that, but at this point, we all have to stick together. And they've made it clear that they aren't happy with your interfering. They say Nomsa has chosen to join *Umkhonto we Sizwe* and that she knows what she's getting herself into. You need to accept that and stop stirring things up."

"Why is it they cannot produce Nomsa? Why can they not show me my child so she, herself, can tell me she is happy and that she will not come home with me? If she tells me that nothing I say or do will make her change her mind, then I will respect that. But all these threats make me think that they are holding her against her will."

"That's not what they do. You can't force a person to want military training or to be committed to a cause. All their operatives are motivated and believe in what they're doing. The only reason they can't produce her is because she's in Rhodesia."

"So they say."

Maggie sighs. "Could you please just back off a bit? Just until I'm able to speak to some higher-ups in MK. I'm keeping tabs all the time, Beauty, and I know that the process is slow and that you're getting impatient, but getting in their way won't help anyone, neither us nor Nomsa."

I do not commit to anything and Maggie does not notice my silence as she excuses herself to say good-bye to Robin and the last of the guests. Once she has left, I remain sitting with Wilhelmina who has been unusually quiet the whole evening. I realize that there is something different about her appearance, and it takes me a few moments to see what it is. She is wearing lipstick and has styled her hair.

"You are looking lovely this evening," I say and she blushes. "Is it for Robin's party or for a man?" I tease gently.

She flushes even more. "A man, if you must know," she whispers and then looks away in embarrassment. She catches sight of Victor and Johan who are talking to Robin, and I am surprised by the expression of dislike that forms on her face.

"Wilhelmina, I would have thought you, of all people, would be less bigoted than that."

"What do you mean?"

"Your distaste for those two is very obvious. I would have thought you would believe that persecuting people because they are homosexual is as bad as persecuting them because they are black."

"*Ag*, please, my brother is a homosexual and I have no problem with that. I just don't like them because they're such good friends with Edith. It shows bad judgment on their part. She's not even here for the child's first birthday since her parents died. *Siestog!* You would think she could've changed her schedule a bit so she could be home today."

I merely smile. It does not help to defend Edith to Wilhelmina or vice versa. I am resigned to the two women hating each other. As long as they both have Robin's best interests at heart, that is all I care about.

"Have you had any more calls about us?" I ask.

"Not since that last one a month ago from that man who calls anonymously."

"Mr. Finlay," I say. "I am sure it was him."

"I told him that I've done multiple home visits, and that Edith has been home every time I was there, and that you don't sleep in the flat."

"Hopefully that will put a stop to his calls."

"I also told him that if he continues to show an unhealthy interest in the little girl, we might need to come and investigate him because perverts are worse than blacks who sleep in white people's flats. I think that's probably what did the trick." She laughs and I laugh with her. I am glad to have her on my side. I rest easier at night knowing that we have Wilhelmina looking out for us and keeping the police away.

"And you will keep an ear to the ground for me?"

Wilhelmina shifts in her seat. "You know I'm not comfortable with doing anything behind Maggie's back."

"We are not doing anything behind her back. All we are doing is gathering information, just like Maggie does."

"But then why can't you just wait to get information from her?"

"I have a feeling she is not telling me everything."

Wilhelmina sighs, not meeting my eye. "Maggie looks out for you. You know she does."

I reach out my hand to take hers. "I know that, but I also know that Maggie has to be careful of whose toes she steps on. She is thinking of this from a political angle, I understand that. But this is my daughter, Wilhelmina. She is first and foremost my child, and I need to be sure of her safety."

She sighs again.

"Please, Wilhelmina. Just keep your eyes and ears open and come to me first before you go to Maggie. That is all I am asking you. As a friend."

She does not say anything, but she squeezes my hand back.

Forty

BEAUTY

❖

11 FEBRUARY 1977
Hillbrow, Johannesburg, South Africa

My wristwatch says it is 11:23 p.m. I have to tilt it at an angle to see where the hands are pointing because the neon sign from across the road casts a pink glow over the watch's surface. There are seven minutes left before I am to leave this room to make my way across the street to where I will meet my contact.

The note was slipped under the door a week ago and gave the address of a place I was to go to in Hillbrow.

I have heard of your search for Nomsa. We must meet. Come on Friday, 11 February. Come alone. Get there at exactly 7 p.m. and go to flat #206 on the second floor. The door will be open. Lock it once you are inside. Stay there until 11:30 p.m. The security police will finish their curfew patrol by 11:00 and will not come back until after midnight. At 11:30 p.m., leave the flat and cross the street. There is a nightclub across the road. Do not try entering it from the main entrance. Walk around the alley to the back and go down the stairs. You will see a blue door next to the rubbish bins. Knock twice then pause and knock three more times. I will be waiting.

I have made so many inquiries and given my details to so many people in the past eight months that I cannot even guess which inquiry has led to this. I tell myself not to worry for my safety. If it was Shakes, he would not direct me to a busy part of Johannesburg on a Friday night to kill me.

Raindrops splatter against the glass. I have been looking out at the nightclub's entrance since I got here and it has been raining almost the whole time. As the writer of the letter said, the police vans drove down the street at 10:45 p.m. checking for any blacks who were out after curfew. The only activity since then has been the many cars pulling up outside the club to drop people off.

Eleven thirty. It is time. I leave the flat and go downstairs, checking the area for any signs of danger before I exit the building. I pull the hood of my raincoat up over my lowered head as I step into the rain to cross the street. The pink neon of the club's flashing sign is reflected in the puddles in the road, and as I near the entrance, loud disco music spills out into the night. I recognize the song as a popular tune that Robin has been listening to on the radio lately.

"Valentine's Day special. Ladies get in free tonight," a large man at the entrance to the club says to a group of white women who are queuing under an awning to get inside. "Drinks are half price until midnight."

"Shit, we better get a move on then and buy as many as we can before twelve," one of the women says.

They are all wearing short skirts and those high platform shoes like Robin has. At least I know Robin is safe while I am out; she is sleeping at the Goldmans' tonight. I step onto the curb just as another car pulls up spilling even more girls onto the pavement.

"Check you chicks inside. I just gotta find a *lekker pozzie* for the wheels," a man's voice calls out after them. "*Howzit, bru,*" he says to the security man at the entrance. "Where's a *shweet* place to park the ride?"

I keep my head down and head for the alley around the back of the building. The blue door is easy to find and I knock using the special code. Nothing happens. I stand for a minute or two and still no one answers. I try the handle but the door is locked. Something clatters nearby and my pulse leaps. I have no valid reason to be here after curfew, and if the police catch me, I will go to jail.

I knock again and this time the door swings open. I step through and am standing in a large, steamy kitchen. Crates of wine and beer glasses are piled up against the walls and dustbins overflow with paper plates and half-eaten food. The young black man who opened the door returns to a huge sink.

"You look like her," he says, shouting to be heard over the music.

"And what is your name, *bhuti*?"

"No names. It is safer that way."

He is a small man, slight but wiry like a lightweight boxer. His head is shaved, but he has a beard.

"It was you who sent me the note?"

"Yes. We do not have much time. I am only alone for half an hour before another cleaner joins me. It is best that he does not see you."

The music from the nightclub overhead is so loud that the floor vibrates. Water runs from my raincoat creating puddles on the floor. I remove it and then cast my eyes around the room looking for a mop.

"In the corner," the man says as if he is reading my mind. I go to fetch it.

I sense that he will tell me more if we are both otherwise engaged. If he is distracted by washing glasses and I am busy with mopping the floor, we do not have to look at one another. Sometimes that makes talking easier.

"How did you know where to find me?" I ask as I mop over the puddle.

"You have been asking a lot of questions. Many people know where to find you."

"And why did you contact me when all those people did not?"

"I admire your persistence. I wish my mother cared as much as you do." He is silent and I sense there is more so I wait. He does not disappoint. "Nomsa spoke about you a lot. I was curious to see the woman who gave birth to such a great warrior."

"And where did these conversations take place?"

"In the MK camps."

"You were training there with her? As a soldier?"

"Yes." He stops washing dishes and dries his hands off on his apron before reaching for a pack of cigarettes on the counter next to him. He lights a cigarette and then returns to washing the glasses, the filter hanging loosely between his lips.

"You are not a soldier anymore?"

"I am finished with my training. Now I wait for my orders."

I want to ask what those orders might include, but as much as I want to know, I also do not want to know. "Is she well, my daughter?"

"She is."

"She is unharmed?"

"What is 'unharmed'? We are all harmed. All of us. That is why we fight."

"But she is healthy and uninjured?"

"Your daughter is one of the strongest and bravest people I have ever met." There is something in his voice that speaks of more than just admiration. I wonder if this young man is in love with Nomsa.

"Is she still with Shakes Ngubane?"

The sound of disgust that he makes in reply answers my question. "On and off. He comes and goes." It is a line of questioning that will make him stop speaking and so I change the subject.

"You said she spoke of me. What did she say?"

"That you are an educated woman, a teacher, and that she admires you greatly."

I cannot stop the bitterness from creeping into my voice. "She has a strange way of showing that admiration."

"Just because she has done things that you cannot understand does not mean that she does not love you."

"Love is one thing. Trust and honesty are another. If you respect someone, you are honest with them."

"Perhaps that is your problem."

"What do you mean?"

"I do not doubt that you are a good woman, but the very fact that you are so righteous might be the reason Nomsa could not be honest with you. Sinners have more forgiving ears than saints."

His words cut me to the quick because I know them to be true. "Where is she?"

"I did not want to meet with you to tell you where she is. Only that she is where she wants to be and that it is people like Nomsa, revolutionaries like Nomsa, who will change the course of this country's history."

I cannot stop myself. "You mean terrorists like you and Nomsa?"

"No, I mean freedom fighters like us. You should be proud of her. Your daughter is a hero. It is a pity you cannot see that."

It is as I leave that the rustle of wings catches my attention; it is an alien sound in the urban setting. I freeze when I spot the large owl perched on a nearby garbage can. This must be a good hunting ground for it; there are a lot of mice and rats in the city.

The owl is tensed up, ready for flight, so I stand completely still. Its yellow eyes stare at me unblinkingly, and I recall what my husband, Silumko, always said about them.

Owls are messengers of death. No good can come of seeing one.

I turn and run.

Forty-one

ROBIN

❦

19 MARCH 1977
Johannesburg, South Africa

I answered the call because I was sitting closest to the phone. We'd just finished dinner, and I was doing my homework at the dining room table while Beauty sat on the couch, her knitting needles clacking against each other as she fed wool to a growing jersey.

"Hello? Robin? Is that you?" The person on the other end sounded agitated.

"Yes. Who's this?"

"It's *Tannie* Wilhelmina. I need to speak with Beauty, please."

"Listen to this," I said and cleared my throat. "*Molo. Unjani?*" Beauty had been teaching me Xhosa—the lessons were her birthday gift to me—and I grabbed every opportunity to practice.

"That's very good, *liefling*, but could you quickly put Beauty on the phone?"

I sighed. Grown-ups could be so boring sometimes. "You want me to put her on top of the phone or call her to the phone?"

"*Jinne*, not now, Robin. This is no time for jokes. Just call her!"

"There's always time for jokes, Willy." "Willy" was the new nick-name I'd come up with for her, but she didn't like it very much.

"*Sies*, how many times must I tell you to stop calling me that? It's a bad word! Now hurry up and call Beauty."

I turned around to shout Beauty's name, but she was already stand-ing next to me holding out her hand. I passed the receiver over and then listened in on Beauty's side of the conversation.

"Hello . . . In Soweto? How do you know? An hour, that is fine . . . I will be waiting at the back for you. Good-bye."

"What did she want?"

"I need to go out tonight."

"With Willy?"

"Yes."

"Is it to do with Nomsa?"

"Maybe, that is what we need to go and find out."

"In Soweto?"

"Yes."

"Can I come with? Please?"

"We cannot take you into Soweto."

"But—"

"Robin, my child, please listen to me. It would be too dangerous to take a white child into the township. It is out of the question."

"But Willy's white."

"She is an adult who works in Soweto and they know her there. She will be fine, but a child would raise suspicions."

"But—"

"I said no and that is my answer."

I was about to protest again when I had an idea. "Okay, fine. I suppose you want me to go to Morrie's tonight?"

"Yes, thank you for understanding. Could you please go down there now, and check with Rachel that it is fine for you to sleep over? I am not sure how late we will be back."

"Fine," I sighed as I stomped to the door, making sure my face looked like a thundercloud because that's what Beauty would expect. All the while, my mind was in a whirl.

And what exactly do I get out of it?" Morrie asked half an hour later when I'd laid out the plan for him in detail and answered all his questions.

"You get to help a friend who's asking you for a favor."

"What you're asking me to do is lie to my mother, which I can get into a lot of trouble for. And then on top of that, you're asking me to spill my sacred Jewish blood for you. I'm going to need more than the satisfaction of helping a friend, I'm afraid."

I groaned. There wasn't much time left until Willy arrived and everything had to be perfect by then. "Okay, fine, what do you want?"

"Ten kisses."

"Ten? That's way too many."

"And you need to hold my hand when we're in public and not make vomity faces behind my back when I tell people you're my girlfriend."

"Ugh, okay, fine then." I didn't want to agree to his conditions, but I didn't have time to argue. I'd just have to figure out a loophole down the line.

"And you need to tell my mother you've thought long and hard about it and that you want to convert to Judaism."

"What? Why?"

"Because my mother said we shouldn't get too serious, because I have to marry a Jew one day and you're a heathen who wouldn't be good wife material."

"What would I have to do to convert?"

"I don't know exactly. Probably learn Yiddish and how to make matzoh balls."

I was already learning more Yiddish than I liked just by hanging around the Goldmans, but I did like matzoh balls. "Okay, fine."

"Excellent. You have yourself a deal."

"If you mess this up, the deal is off."

"I won't mess it up."

"Remember, only come running out once she's doing the reverse turn to get out of the parking lot so—"

"I know, I know. I won't mess it up."

"I hope not. See you down there." With that, I turned and made a run for it in case he demanded the first of his ten kisses immediately. As I was heading out the door, Mrs. Goldman stepped out of the kitchen.

"Robin, sweetie, I didn't hear you come in."

"I just quickly came to lend a pen," I lied.

"Borrow. It's 'borrow a pen.'"

"Yes, exactly. Borrow a pen," I said. "And Mrs. Goldman?"

"Yes, sweetie?"

"I want to convert to Julie-ism. Okay, bye."

S he said it's fine. I can stay over," I told Beauty as I headed out the door with the bulging kitbag I'd hastily packed. "See you tomorrow."

"Come here first," Beauty said from the kitchen where she was making a thermos of tea.

My stomach clenched. If she opened the kitbag, the game would be up. There was no way she could mistake Edith's opera glasses, a bag of bread crumbs, black shoe polish, a balaclava, gloves, my surveillance notebook and a torch for my pajamas and toothbrush.

"Why?" I tried not to look or sound guilty.

"Are you okay?"

"Of course," I enthused. "Why wouldn't I be okay?" I added a toothy grin for good measure.

Don't look in the kitbag. Please don't look in the kitbag.

"I thought you would be more upset. About being left behind."

Of course! I'd made the mistake of not acting sulky enough. That's why she was suspicious. "I want to come with you, but if you don't want me there, I'm not going to beg." I cued the angry expression again, and it seemed to satisfy her because she came over to hug me.

"It is for your own safety that I am not taking you with."

"Okay. If you say so." I squeezed Beauty back halfheartedly and then waved as I headed for the door. "*Sala kakuhle. Ube namathamsanqa,*" I said, making Beauty smile. Go well. Good luck.

"*Hamba kakuhle,*" she replied. Stay well. But, of course, I had no intention of staying anywhere.

I was in position in the parking lot hiding behind a yellow Ford Escort, peeking over its boot while looking out for Willy's *bakkie*. The pickup she used for work had a canopy attached to the bed of the truck so things could be securely stored in the back. She was always carting supplies back and forth, and I was counting on it being as cluttered as it usually was so I could hide without her spotting me in the rearview mirror.

I couldn't see Morrie anywhere. I didn't know if that meant he was a good hider or if he was running late or had chickened out. There wasn't time to find out because at that moment, the *bakkie* roared around the corner into the parking lot and came to a squealing halt close to the back door. Willy hooted once and the door opened. Beauty stepped outside and headed for the passenger door.

Once Beauty was inside the car, there was a crunch as Willy found reverse and the *bakkie* shot backwards. It was showtime. If Morrie didn't time it right, he'd either be killed or he'd be too late to stop them from leaving.

The truck stopped inches away from where I was hiding; the canopy door just within my grasp. The gears protested again and as the first gear finally engaged and the *bakkie* started to accelerate, Morrie appeared from out of nowhere, running in front of the car. There was a loud bang as he slapped his hand down on the bonnet, and the van immediately lurched to a halt.

Morrie let out a bloodcurdling scream and I almost dropped my kitbag. He was either a really good actor or he'd been seriously hurt. Both doors opened and Beauty and Willy bailed out, rushing around the front of the car to tend to him. That's when I crept forward and gently turned the handle on the back door. I'd told Morrie to make as much noise as he could so that it would mask any sounds I might be making, and he was doing a good job.

"Oh my God. The pain! The pain! Is that a light at the end of the tunnel I see? Have I died?"

The handle refused to budge. I tugged down on it again, but it still wouldn't give.

Morrie was wailing and Willy's raised voice joined the cacophony. "*My magtig*, I didn't see you! I'm so sorry, I didn't see where you came from. Are you all right? Can you stand?"

I closed both hands around the handle and pulled with all my might. Still nothing. If Willy had locked it, there was nothing that could be done and I'd have to call the plan off. I peeped around the car and saw Morrie standing, which was a relief. He was being held up by Beauty who was dusting him off.

"How many fingers am I holding up?" Willy asked. "Are you bleeding? Do you think anything is broken?"

I was running out of time. In a last desperate effort, I tried pushing the handle up instead of down, and the latch immediately engaged and the door swung open. I crept inside, keeping myself as low as possible, and then pulled the door closed behind me. My luck was holding out; the back was stuffed with overflowing boxes and bulging black garbage bags. I squirmed my way as close to the front as I could and made myself a nest. Everything had worked out perfectly.

S *joe*, look here, my hands are still shaking."
     Wilhelmina's voiced floated out to me from the open glass partition separating the back canopy area from the front seats.

"Watch the road," Beauty replied.

"*My magtig!* I thought I'd killed the child. Did you see where he shot out from?"

"No, but I suppose that is how accidents happen. He is fine though. Concentrate on your driving."

"Don't you think we should have taken him back to his mother?"

"He said he was fine, but I will speak to her about it later when I see her."

The sun had set and the headlights of the cars behind us lit up the *bakkie*'s roof in waves.

"What did you find out?" Beauty asked.

Wilhelmina exhaled a long, shaky breath and then replied, "One of my contacts was at an illegal bar in Meadowlands two nights ago. What do they call those places?"

"A shebeen."

"Yes, a shebeen, and he heard talk of three women, all operatives, who were about to arrive back from their training. People are talking about it because it's unusual to see MK soldiers who are women."

"And where are we going now?"

"To the same shebeen. He said it sounded like the women would be hidden there for a few days. It's worth us seeing if Nomsa is one of them."

"Have you told Maggie of this?"

"Not yet. I thought I'd wait."

"Thank you, Wilhelmina."

"*Ag*, that's okay. I just hope we find her."

"You cannot come inside with me."

"No, I already thought of that. I'll park a few blocks away at one of our orphanages' care worker's houses. She knows I'll be there. Just be as quick as you can."

W e lurched to a stop and the car was switched off.

"Okay, it's the house I showed you on the right. The she-been is called Fatty Boom Boom's. You must pretend to be a customer, because if you go in there asking lots of questions, everyone will just clam up and Fatty will chuck you out because that's bad for business."

"Yes, I know," said Beauty.

"Luckily it's a Saturday night so they should be quite busy, which will help you blend in more. Mpho said he'd come back again tonight and he'd look out for you. You can sit with him and pretend you're also a teacher."

"I am a teacher."

"*Ag*, you know what I mean. It will just look less suspicious if you're sitting with him than if you're a woman there alone. He's quite light-skinned and he wears glasses. He said he'd wear a blue tie as well so you'd recognize him. I told him your name is Patience."

"Patience?"

"What's wrong with 'Patience'? Patience is a virtue, you know. I just don't want it getting back to Maggie that you've been asking more questions so a fake name seemed like a good idea. I'll see you when you get back. I'm just going to pop inside and tell Gertrude that I'm here."

"Thank you, Wilhelmina. Thank you for everything."

"*Ag*, that's okay. Good luck."

One door slammed closed and then the other. I assumed that Beauty was on her way to the shebeen place, and Willy was headed for the house to check in with the owner. I only had a small window of opportunity to get out of the car so I could follow Beauty without Willy seeing me.

I shuffled to a side window and cracked it open so I could peer out. It looked like we were parked in a short driveway with a sand road behind us. Luckily, no one was out on the street because I didn't want to wait for the coast to clear in case I lost sight of Beauty. Being lost and alone on the streets of Soweto, the scary place I'd heard so much about, didn't appeal to me.

Rummaging in the kitbag, I felt around for what I needed. There wouldn't be time to cover myself with black shoe polish, and so I pulled the balaclava over my face and then put my gloves on. A white child would stand out like a sore thumb in Soweto and so my only hope was covering my skin as much as possible so no one could see it. Finally, I grabbed the bag of bread crumbs and eased my way out of the car as quietly as I could.

There was a sudden bang and I froze thinking I'd been shot at until I realized it was just Willy knocking on the person's door. Another knock and then the door opened. I used the cover of their voices to mask the sound of the canopy door closing as I slipped out of the driveway and into the street. There weren't any streetlights, but the moon was full and I was able to see Beauty's silhouette slip around the corner at the end of the street. I set off after her trailing bread crumbs behind me so I could find my way back.

The only window that looked into the front of the house where Beauty had entered was around the corner at the far side of the yard. It was small and narrow and very high up, tucked in just under the tin roof. There was no way I could reach it unless I found something to stand on. At least it was out of sight of the main entrance where people were constantly coming and going from; I'd had to duck past really quickly to avoid being seen.

I looked around the sandy yard for a ladder or table, and even though it was almost as cluttered as a junkyard—filled with rusted beds, car parts, broken appliances and other strange metal objects—I couldn't see any furniture that would be able to elevate me high enough. I poked around some more and finally found a few beer barrels and oil drums stacked up against an outhouse.

If I stand on one of those with my tippy toes, it just might work.

Music and laughter from inside masked the sound of my alternately dragging and pushing an empty drum across to the wall. It took a while to navigate it around all the junk. The exertion made me perspire so that the woolen balaclava scratched against my face, making it hard to resist the temptation to yank it off. When I finally had the drum in position, I hopped up. Even standing on my toes, the drum wasn't high enough, and I jumped down again to see if I could find something to prop me up further.

It was while I was digging around at the back of the property that I saw it: the white van with "JC Plumbing" stenciled across its side with red letters. It was parked in the shadows away from the street. I checked the license plate just to be sure. BBM676T. I was right; it was the car driven by the man who'd blindfolded Beauty that day.

What's he doing here? Is he here because he knows Beauty's here too?

She'd never told me what happened with him, and I'd never asked as that would have been admitting that I'd spied on her, but I didn't have a good feeling about his being anywhere near us. Something about that man made me very nervous.

I sped up my search, quickly circling the van, and spotted a gate in the fence leading to another property. A small pile of bricks was heaped just on the other side, so I unlatched the gate and darted through. I carried six of them across in three trips, alternately running and pausing to listen out for any danger, and then latched the gate closed again. The double layer of bricks on the surface of the drum gave me the extra few inches I needed, and when I hopped on again, I could finally see into the room.

Forty-two

BEAUTY

❀

The room is dark and grimy. Its avocado-green walls look black in the corners where the light from the candles does not reach. Cigarette smoke rises up to the roof, and as I walk through the haze, a few heads turn to look at me. I am quickly regarded and just as quickly dismissed, which suits me. The room is already half full and I cannot see anyone matching Mpho's description.

I need to decide where to sit. The couches in the corner look too relaxed, and I know my stiff-backed nervousness will be too obvious if I try to lounge in one of them. The grouping of beer crates around a low table looks uncomfortable; something that young men would play cards and dice around. Instead, I choose one of the proper tables lining the wall and sit down facing the door.

A white candle is wedged into a green wine bottle on the bare table. The flame gives off a subtle, unassuming heat. It is not hostile in the way of shops that have been torched and police cars set alight; it does not burn like dreams going up in smoke. There is a light breeze in the room and the tiny flame is swaying. It does a languorous, almost sensual dance around the wick as if the fleck of fire is dancing to the beat of my thundering heart. The sight is mesmerizing: the orange and gold and yellow and blue and green of its light, the purple of its core; its tapering tip struggling upwards either in supplication or hallelujah. I watch the tendrils of smoke as the fire consumes itself.

"*Sawubona, mama.*" I am snapped out of my reverie by the young woman who has appeared at my table. She speaks Zulu, but I am able to understand her. All our languages overlay one another like blankets of mist on a mountaintop.

"Good evening, my child."

"What will Mother have to drink this evening?"

"I am afraid that I am not much of a drinker. I am just waiting for a friend."

"Everyone who comes to Fatty Boom Boom's is a drinker, Mother. Otherwise Fatty herself will show you the door."

"In that case, what do you have?"

"Wine, gin, whiskey, brandy, *umqombothi*—"

I cut off her recitation. "I will have a small glass of *umqombothi*."

The girl laughs. "Fatty is a big woman, Mother, and she believes in big glasses. You will find nothing small here."

The home-brewed traditional African beer I have ordered is illegal, just as the shebeens are illegal, because the government wants to make money off its state beer sold at its beer halls. The revenue from their beer goes to the state treasury and so I will not drink it on principle. Many believe the apartheid government has not banned Africans from drinking alcohol because they are compassionate enough to allow the black man that one pleasure. In actual fact, the state encourages drunkenness in the townships because it knows that oppressed and exploited people, who are always spending their hard-earned wages on drink, are people who are easier to control and keep down.

The young woman returns with my sorghum brew, wiping my

table before setting the glass down. Just then, the familiar strains of the pennywhistle uncoil from the record player in the corner as Elias and His Zig Zag Jive Flutes launch into "Tom Hark." I take a tentative sip of the sour beer and my foot begins to tap under the table. By the time Dolly Rathebe starts singing "Meadlowlands," I am halfway through my beer and feeling much more relaxed.

After a while, a man wearing a blue tie pauses at my table as he looks down at me. "Patience?" he asks.

I almost shake my head before I remember the false name Wilhelmina gave him. He is light-skinned and wearing glasses, just as she described him, and I nod. "Mpho?"

He smiles and pulls the chair out to sit down. "I'm sorry I was late, but I had to take the long way to get here. The *tsotsis* are out in packs with it being Saturday night and everyone coming home with their weekly wages."

"I am glad you got here safely," I say. "Please excuse my drinking. They would not let me sit here without ordering one."

Mpho smiles. "I'll order the same and then I'll tell you everything I know."

Once Mpho's drink arrives, he leans in close and begins to relay his story in a hushed voice. The room is noisy and I wish he would speak louder, but I know he is nervous about being overheard. He tells me of being in the shebeen two nights ago and the conversation he overheard about the women MK operatives.

"Wilhelmina had asked me to keep my ears open in case there was any talk of them. You are looking for one of the women?"

I nod as I straighten my back to relieve the tension caused from leaning in so close. I am about to answer when something catches my eye over Mpho's shoulder. It is one of the serving girls. She looks exactly like the girl from the photo that Nothando Ndlovu showed me a few days after the uprising. It is Nomsa's best friend, Phumla. I am sure of it.

My heartbeat quickens, pounding like a drum, and I take a few deep breaths to steady my nerves. If this girl is back from the MK camps, then maybe Nomsa is back with her. If this girl is here tonight in the same room as me, my daughter could be here too. This is the closest I have come to finding Nomsa after more than nine months of searching, and I am light-headed with the possibility of being reunited with her.

I stand so quickly that I upend my chair and it clatters to the floor. I do not stop to set it right again. If I take my eyes off the girl, I fear she might disappear. Ignoring the startled faces that turn towards me at the sound of the commotion, I begin to make my way to where Phumla is standing. Weaving through the tables, I duck around patrons and chairs as I try to find the quickest route to her.

When I am a mere few footsteps away, a man rises from a table and blocks my path. He struggles to put his jacket on, and by his uncoordinated movements, it is clear that he is drunk. I wait a moment and then another, but when Phumla turns to walk away, I touch the man's back.

"Excuse me, I need to get past you, *bhuti*."

He turns and squints at me. "What is the rush?"

"There is someone over there I need to speak to."

Still he struggles with the jacket, putting the wrong arm in the wrong sleeve, and under his flailing arm, I can see Phumla walking away. I cannot lose sight of her! In desperation, I tug at the man's lapel and he staggers to the side.

"Shit!" He curses as his hand connects with the candle on the table. I push past him as he snatches his palm back.

Just as Phumla is about to slip through a doorway, I reach out and grab her arm. She turns at my touch, frowning. When she sees I am not a young man who has had too much beer and is trying to accost her, her expression softens.

"Yes, Mother? Can I help you?" She smiles.

"Phumla?"

Her smile wavers. "No, Mother. My name is Zinzi."

"No, you are Phumla. You are Nomsa's best friend. I recognize you." My voice has risen.

She shakes her head. "You are mistaken. I do not know a Nomsa. You must go."

"But—"

"Now. You must go, Mother. Please."

From the record player, Miriam Makeba's plaintive voice calls out to me as she croons. "*Khawuleza, mama. Khawuleza.*" Hurry, Mama, hurry. Don't let them catch you.

Forty-three

ROBIN

❁

19 March 1977
Soweto, Johannesburg, South Africa

From my position on top of the drum peering through the window, I watched Beauty grab the arm of one of the serving girls. When the girl turned around, the white mark that extended down her chin and into the collar of the blouse came into sight. A spark of recognition flared but quickly fizzled out.

I've seen that girl before. But where? And when?

At first, the girl smiled at Beauty, but then her smile fell away and she took a step back and shook her head. She was strongly disagreeing with or denying whatever it was Beauty was saying.

A man from a nearby table suddenly staggered up to Beauty and shoved his hand in her face. It looked like he was shouting at her. Luckily, her companion, the man she'd been sitting with earlier, raced up and came to her rescue, pulling the man away from Beauty. It was during this commotion that the girl slipped away. She looked scared as she rushed through the side door, and I wondered what Beauty had said to spook her.

Just as the girl fled through the door leading into the house, an enormous woman stepped out. She was brightly dressed in colorful wraps and wore a towering red turban. Her presence was welcomed with loud cheers and a few of the patrons called her over. She merely waved at them, and then directed her attention at Beauty and the two men.

After a few moments of discussion, Beauty and Mpho returned to their table while the woman called a towering man over to escort the drunken man out. She then began circulating through the room, stopping at every third group to talk to her customers. It was clear that Beauty was waiting for the girl to return, because she kept looking past Mpho towards the door.

I wondered then if there was another window at the back of the house that might give me a look into what was happening in that other room. Hopping off the drum, I hoped I wouldn't have to drag it all the way around the house. Once I turned the corner at the back of the property, I could see two windows along the back wall. They were at a normal height so the drum wouldn't be necessary. I crouched as I scampered across and peeped into the first window I came to.

The room looked like some kind of bar and crates of beer were piled up everywhere. Two long tables took up most of the room and the serving girls bunched inside, grabbing drinks from three men who were doing the pouring. The girl with the white mark wasn't in the room. I hunkered down again and scrambled across to the next window. When I peered inside, I spotted the girl standing behind a closed door. She wasn't the only person in the room; a man was in there with her.

I recognized him immediately. He was the tall, stocky man who'd come to fetch Beauty that one night, the one who drove the van and had made her wear the blindfold. He was holding the girl by the upper arm as though restraining her. Something caught the light at his side. It was a gun in a holster. The girl's eyes were wide with fear, and I began to panic. Just as my mind raced to figure out what to do next, a hand reached out from the darkness and grabbed my wrist. I looked up to see the towering black man who'd escorted the drunken man out.

"*Ufuna ntoni?*" he growled.

I snatched my wrist away and my glove came off in his hand. He looked at my white skin, shock written on his face, and I used that moment to kick him in the shin as hard as I could before I took off running like the hounds of hell were snapping at my heels. And at least one hound was; the same scrawny one who'd eaten my trail of bread crumbs, and who wanted what was left in my pocket.

I managed to find my way back to the right house despite my trail of crumbs having been devoured and slipped back into the *bakkie* easily enough though getting rid of the yapping dog was harder. It wouldn't quiet down and soon a door opened.

"Who's there?" It was Willy checking what the noise was about. I'd forgotten to close the *bakkie*'s side window that I'd opened earlier and was nervous Willy would notice it.

There was no answer for a moment or two. The dog was quiet again and had probably been spooked off by Willy's voice. I was just hoping she'd go back inside without coming to the car to investigate when Beauty returned. I'd made it back just in time.

"Did you see Mpho?" Willy asked.

"Yes, he—"

Before Beauty could answer, another voice cut through the night.

It was a girl's voice and she was out of breath. She spoke in Xhosa, and I couldn't understand what she was saying but her tone was urgent.

"Phumla?" Beauty asked.

The girl started talking again but then stopped abruptly.

"This is my friend Wilhelmina. You can speak in front of her." Beauty was speaking in English and the girl then thankfully switched to English as well.

"But she is white."

"Even so, child. I trust her."

There was a pause before the girl started talking again. "I am sorry about earlier, but Mama Fatty does not like us to use our real names and forbids personal issues from affecting our work. I need this job and do not want to get fired."

"Please tell me you know where Nomsa is, my child. I know that you crossed the border with her many months ago to join *Umkhonto we Sizwe*, and now you are back. Has she returned with you?"

"No, Mama. It is true that I crossed over from Venda into Rhodesia with her to join MK, but after four weeks of training, it was too much for me. It was too difficult, all the running and the drills and the lack of sleep. We were starving without food and I was exhausted." There was a pause before she continued in a softer voice. "I was not strong enough and so I quit. They allowed me to come back."

"And Nomsa?" Willy asked.

"Nomsa was stronger than me. She has the courage of a lion, that one. She worked so hard and was an excellent soldier. She would not come back. She wanted to stay."

"Is she still in Rhodesia?"

"I do not know. We have not spoken since then and no one from MK will tell me anything because they say they cannot trust me."

"And the man?" Beauty asked.

"What man?"

"The tall man. The one they call 'Shakes'? Do you know where he is?"

"No, Mother. I think he is still with Nomsa and the other MK cadres."

Five minutes later, Beauty and Willy were back inside the *bakkie*, the engine starting up as we began our journey home.

I wondered why Phumla had lied to Beauty about where Shakes was and decided it was probably because she was scared of him. I was actually relieved about her duplicity. I didn't want Beauty anywhere near him; he was clearly a very bad man who we had to keep away from.

I must have fallen asleep after that, lulled by the motion of the van, because I woke up when we lurched to a halt outside our building.

"Thank you, Wilhelmina. I could not have done this without you," Beauty said.

"*Ag*, that's okay. I'm just glad it wasn't a complete waste of time."

"Come inside for a cup of coffee."

"No, that's okay. I'm not the one who's been drinking beer all night long," Willy teased.

Beauty laughed. "It is a long drive back to the West Rand. A cup of coffee will help wake you up."

"Okay then. Just one cup."

Once they were both inside, I slipped out the back once more and headed up to Morrie's flat. I was relieved to see he'd left the door unlocked just as we'd arranged, and I locked it behind me before tiptoeing to his room. He was sleeping on a bed he'd made for himself on the floor, and the duvet of his single bed was turned back, waiting for me.

I leaned down over him and kissed him without waking him. One down, nine to go.

Forty-four

BEAUTY

❀

The phone rings just before midnight. I am still awake as I have been writing in my journal, but I snatch it up so that it does not wake Robin.

"Hello?"

"Stop what you are doing."

"Hello? Who is this?"

"You must stop asking questions or he is going to do something bad to you." The voice is a woman's and she is whispering.

"Nomsa? Is that you?"

"No."

"Then tell me where Nomsa is. Please."

"Just stop it or she will not be able to protect you any more than she has."

The line goes dead.

Forty-five

ROBIN

❧

5 MAY 1977
Yeoville, Johannesburg, South Africa

One chilly afternoon in early May when the air held more than a rumor of winter, Morrie and I were sitting in the huge oak tree in the park. It was our usual after-school spot and I loved leaning my back against the tree's thick trunk while stretching my legs out on the fourth branch from the top. I enjoyed being suspended like that, not on the ground but not quite untethered either; floating instead between the two elements as the tree's maternal canopy of leaves held up the sky.

I pulled my lunch from my bag and dropped the tinfoil-wrapped peanut butter sandwiches to Morrie who was sitting one branch below me. "Hand over the cheese blintzes." We often swapped food, and since I'd become especially partial to the Jewish crepes, the whole Julie-ism conversion wasn't looking that bad after all.

"Why have you got your food already?" Morrie asked.

Since I'd turned ten and insisted I was old enough to walk home with friends, Beauty didn't fetch me at the school gates anymore. Instead, she'd meet us in the park in the afternoon to hand over my lunch and take my school case home while Morrie and I caught up for an hour or two before we headed inside.

"She had to go out today, so she gave me the sandwiches this morning."

"Where did she go?"

"Don't know."

"Not much of a detective then, are you?"

"I couldn't follow her. I had to go to school," I protested.

"Yes, but you could've just asked her."

"I did, but she was vague about it."

"Do you think it has to do with Nomsa?"

"Not sure. Maybe."

We finished our lunches, and I pulled one of my Secret Seven books out just as Morrie took his camera from his bag.

"I saw a dead rat over there that I want to take a picture of," he said as he slung the camera around his neck and started climbing down.

I didn't even bother replying. Nothing I said could encourage Morrie to take photos of flowers or sunsets or anything even remotely pretty. Half an hour later, I checked my Mickey Mouse watch and saw it was time to head home. I gathered my things up, and climbed down to join Morrie who was standing waiting for me. As I dropped down, I noticed that my school bag was gone from the place I'd left it at the base of the tree when I'd climbed up earlier.

"Where's my case?"

Morrie smirked. "Well, since you like mysteries so much and rate your Secret Seven so highly, why don't you figure it out?"

I cast my eyes around, knowing Morrie was lazy and wouldn't have carried my heavy bag too far. I spotted a dark shape in the nearby bushes, but instead of rushing straight for it, I pretended to follow footprints in the dust that served as clues. Morrie's face fell when the "footprints" led me to the hiding place. "Mystery solved," I shouted.

"Okay, that one was easy. That doesn't make you a real detective." Morrie had been really snarky lately, probably because I reneged on the ten kisses deal.

"Excuse me," I said, "but when last did you sneak into a car without the people inside knowing you were there? And when last did you see all kinds of stuff you weren't meant to see when you were doing surveillance? At least I have some *chutzpah*!"

"That hardly counts. All you did was *schlep* with. You didn't exactly solve the mystery of where Nomsa is!"

"But I saw that man, Shakes, threatening that girl, and that's more than Beauty knows because she thinks he's with Nomsa."

"And yet you haven't even told her about it, so how is that helpful?"

"You know why I can't tell her! I wasn't supposed to be there and I'll get in trouble!" That was the official excuse I was giving, but my real reason for not telling Beauty was that menacing man, Shakes. I was scared of what he might do to her if she found out the girl, Phumla, had lied, and if she went back there asking questions again.

"Have you even remembered where you know that girl from?"

"No, but I will." The knowledge flitted like a moth around my mind; it was always just out of reach. The smell of sweat and smoke came to me whenever I thought of her, but I still wasn't able to connect that to a specific memory.

"Just admit it. Your surveillance didn't turn up anything useful at all. Ergo, you're not a real detective."

"'Ergo'? You can't just make words up."

"It's a real word."

"No, it's not. It's 'ogre' spelled backwards. Stop reading that stupid *Lord of the Rings* book. It's making you see those ugly ogre things everywhere."

"They're not ogres, they're orcs."

"Orcs shmorcs. You're just cross because I still prefer the Secret Seven books to the Hardy Boys who are stupid, by the way."

"Firstly, 'shmorcs'? What are 'shmorcs'? Talk about making words up! Then, that book was a gift and you didn't even kiss me to say thank you for it."

"Aha! I knew it. I knew you were cross about the kiss."

"Ten kisses actually."

"Only nine to go," I corrected him.

"What?"

"Never mind." I wasn't about to tell him about the kiss I gave him when he was sleeping.

"Anyway," Morrie said, "that's beside the point. I bet you couldn't even solve a real mystery."

"What kind of real mystery?"

"Like . . . like if something really valuable goes missing."

"Bet I can," I said.

"Bet you can't."

Forty-six

ROBIN

❀

8 May 1977
Yeoville, Johannesburg, South Africa

Edith carried her suitcase into the room and my stomach knotted.
I knew that her coming-home ritual included taking off her jewelry and putting it all away, before unpacking and then drawing a
bath. I hovered outside her door.

Please be distracted and don't go to your jewelry box.

I started biting my nails as I tried to make out what she was doing.

Any hope I'd harbored was shattered when her cupboard door
opened and the familiar tinkling strains of "Greensleeves" filled the
air. The tune had always struck me as being very melancholy, but now
it sounded ominous, and I rushed into the room in a desperate attempt
to divert her.

"How was your trip, Edith? Did you see any famous people
this time?"

Edith turned slowly and her face was a mask of disbelief. I swallowed hard.

There will be hell to pay! I'm going to be skinned alive.

"Robin?"

"Yes?"

"Have you been playing with my jewelry box?"

The moment of truth had come, and I knew if I answered honestly, I'd be in big trouble. Edith's jewelry was off-limits at all times; I wasn't even allowed to play with it when she was there. But, technically, it wasn't me who'd gone into it and taken stuff so I wouldn't really be lying.

"No."

"Are you sure?"

"I haven't!"

She studied my face and I willed myself not to flush. Edith walked to the bed and sat down, patting the empty space next to her. "Come here and sit down."

"Why? I'm actually quite busy—"

"Robin."

I groaned. "Fine." I dragged my feet over the short distance and then flopped down next to her. "What is it?"

"This is very important, okay? I need you to be completely honest with me. Tell the truth even if it's unpleasant."

I wanted to point out her hypocrisy and give examples of the many times she'd lied to me, but I knew that would just make me look guiltier, so I just nodded.

"Did you take any of my jewelry?"

I knew I couldn't hesitate. I had to maintain eye contact and answer immediately. "No."

"You're sure? Absolutely sure?"

"Yes." She was interrogating the wrong suspect and asking the wrong questions. She would make a terrible detective.

"Okay. Will you call Beauty for me?"

"Beauty?"

"Yes. And then go to the lounge and close this door."

"But why—"

"Please just do as I say for once."

I considered blabbing and confessing our sins right there. Surely anything would be better than dragging out the torture of the punishment that would surely follow.

"Now, Robin!"

I peeped at Edith before dashing out the door. She looked stricken.

My thoughts raced as I tried to figure out how to buy more time. Morrie had taken the jewels two days before, leaving a ransom note on my bed with clues directing me to where he'd hidden them. I realized now that showing him the jewelry box had been a big mistake, and I wouldn't have done it if he hadn't goaded me by telling me he knew the combination to his father's safe, and that Edith obviously didn't trust me if she wouldn't tell me where the box was. He'd been setting me up and I stupidly fell for it, leading him straight to Edith's most precious possessions.

I'd tried for two days to solve the clues, but either Morrie was a terrible clue-writer or the Secret Seven were better at solving mysteries than I was. My pleas to him the night before to just give me the jewelry before Edith came home were met with, "Only if you admit that Enid Blyton writes stupid girly stories that don't teach you to solve mysteries at all. And that the Hardy Boys and *The Lord of the Rings* are way better." Of course, I couldn't admit that.

He then smiled slyly, running his hand through his thick mop of hair. "Okay, I'll enter into negotiations with you. I'll give the jewelry back if you give me the ten kisses you owe me. Right now."

"No way!" And so the jewels remained missing.

I found Beauty in the kitchen, standing at the counter surrounded by ingredients. An iced chocolate cake was pushed to the side to make space for Beauty to work. I squealed, briefly forgetting my troubles, as I ran to it intending to scrape some of the icing off with my finger.

Beauty swatted my hand away and laughed. "Leave it. We will have it later."

Cakes weren't regular fare in our flat, mostly because Edith was always on a diet for the weigh-ins she had at work. The last cake I'd had was at my party. "Why are we having cake?"

"Because it is my birthday today."

My spirits fell. I knew what it was like to have everyone forget your birthday. "Is it really? How old are you?"

"Fifty."

"Wow, that's really, really old. Happy birthday, Beauty!" I felt bad that I didn't have a gift or anything to give her, especially considering the thoughtful gifts she'd given me for Christmas and my birthday. I decided I'd make a gift for her later. "*Uthini* 'happy birthday' *ngesi-Xhosa?* I asked, wanting to know how to wish her in Xhosa.

Beauty smiled. "Your Xhosa is coming along nicely. You say, *Min'em-nandi yokuzalwa.*"

"*Min'emnandi yokuzalwa!*" I repeated and hugged her.

"Thank you," Beauty said, returning to a page of a cookbook and slowly running her index finger along the page. It looked like a recipe for a roast chicken with crunchy golden potatoes. My stomach rumbled. It was going to be a wonderful dinner.

"Robin!" Edith called from the bedroom, and I remembered what I'd come to the kitchen for.

"Beauty, Edith wants you."

"Tell her I am busy with this recipe."

"Yes, but she wants you. Now."

Beauty slid the book away and stood up, heading to Edith's room. I tried to follow her in so I could tell Edith about Beauty's birthday, but Edith blocked my way and again instructed me to go to the lounge. I hated being left out of things and she knew that. I shot her a dark look. "But, I wanted to tell you it's—"

"Just go!"

I stomped out again and came to a halt just outside the door and held my breath.

"Not outside the door, Robin! Go to your room."

"It's not actually a room, you know. If you're going to send me to my room, I will need an actual door and my own walls and not just a partition."

"Just go!"

I huffed in an injured tone and went to the lounge where I stepped behind the partition and fell onto my bed. When I was sure Edith hadn't followed me out and I'd heard her bedroom door close, I quietly tiptoed back and lowered my ear to the keyhole.

"It is good to have you home again, Edith. I am preparing a special—"

"Beauty, I'm only going to ask you this once and I want you to be completely honest with me. Do you know what happened to my jewelry?"

"What jewelry are you talking about?"

"My two rings, the one with the sapphire and the one with the emerald. And my diamond earrings and my jade necklace. Where are they?"

"What do the rings look like, Edith?"

"I told you, the sapphire ring and the emerald one."

"The blue and the green rings?"

"Yes."

"I have seen you wearing them, but I do not know where they are now. Where did you put them?"

"I put them where I always put them when I go away." Edith's voice had risen and it bordered on shouting. "I put them here in my jewelry box. But as you can see, they're gone. I want to know where they are."

"I do not know where they are, Edith. I have not seen them since you were gone. Did you not take them with you?"

"No, I didn't," Edith shouted. "What have you done with my jewelry, Beauty?"

"You think that I have stolen your jewelry?"

"Well, it was here when I left and now it's gone. Has there been a robbery you forgot to mention to me?"

"No, there was no robbery."

"Then I'm forced to reach the only logical conclusion, Beauty. You are stealing from me."

There was a long silence before Beauty replied. "Have you asked Robin if she has seen the jewelry?"

"Yes, I did and she said she didn't touch it. She knows she's not allowed to. I can't believe you would steal from me, Beauty. Not after everything we've been through."

"Edith, I—"

"You don't have permission to call me Edith anymore. That offer was extended in friendship. Friends do not steal from friends."

"Madam," Beauty said, making the word pregnant with contempt, "I did not steal from you. I have never stolen anything from anyone in my whole life. I am not a *tsotsi*."

"I pay you a fortune compared to the other maids—"

"That is because I am not a maid, madam."

"If you needed money, all you had to do was ask me and I would have—"

"The only money I need is the money I work for. I did not steal from you. That is the last time I will tell you that."

"I can see this is pointless, Beauty. If you would just be honest with me, I could consider forgiving you, but it's the lying I can't stand."

"You want to forgive me?" Beauty sounded incredulous.

"I know you think you have me hostage because of how much I need you, but I absolutely won't harbor a traitor and a thief. You have left me no choice but to fire you. I think it's best that you leave immediately. The only thing stopping me from going to the police is your relationship with Maggie and how highly she regards you, and how much Robin cares for you."

The door was wrenched open and I hopped aside as Beauty stormed out. She walked a few paces before she stopped. She didn't turn around; she just stood there with her back to me, waiting. I wanted to apologize to her and tell her the truth, which I was sure she suspected anyway, but the words stubbornly refused to come.

Beauty waited another moment and when I didn't speak, her squared shoulders drooped slightly. Her bearing was no longer righteously angry but injured. I was the reason that the proud woman standing before me looked broken.

"Beauty," I said, and she twitched in response. When I didn't say anything more, the words crumbling to dust in my mouth, she continued to the kitchen where her packed bag was already waiting in anticipation of Edith's arrival.

I heard Beauty close the recipe book and pack away the ingredients that had been laid out on the counter. When the sound of opening and closing doors finally stopped, I stepped out from where I'd been standing immobile outside Edith's door and saw Beauty lift up her bag and head for the door. It was the simple act of her raising a hand to her face that broke my silence.

I knew the language of sorrow, my body had spoken it many times, and I knew how shamed she was by the tears she did not want to cry. It didn't matter that the difference in our skin color separated us more than the span of the forty years that stretched out between us, I recognized myself in Beauty; I was like her and she was like me. We were so very different and yet we were exactly the same, and it was in her tears that I recognized our shared humanity.

I didn't have the words then to articulate what I was feeling, but on some level I'd understood that tears are neither black nor white; they are the quicksilver of our emotional turmoil and their salt flavors our pain equally. It was this sense of kinship that finally jolted me from my inertia.

"Edith!" I called, the words torn from my chest. "Beauty didn't steal your jewelry! I did! And also it's Beauty's birthday today. She's fifty!"

I ran to Beauty then and wrapped my arms around her waist. "*Ndicela uxolo. Ndiyakuthanda. Ungandishiyi*," I said, struggling with the clicks and twists of the language. I am sorry. I love you. Do not leave me.

Some good-byes are as gentle and inevitable as sunset, while some blindside you like a collision you didn't see coming. Some good-byes are schoolyard bullies you are powerless to stop, while others punctuate the end of a relationship because you decided: enough. Some are heartbreaking, leaving you a little more damaged than you were before, while others set you free.

I would go on to experience all of them during the course of my life, but on that day in May in 1977 when I was just ten years old, I'd had enough of good-byes. And so I confessed everything and threw myself at their mercy.

Beauty forgave me more quickly than I deserved, probably because she sensed how damaged I was and how much I needed her absolution. Morrie, upon realizing the repercussions of his actions and how close Beauty had come to being fired, issued an immediate and sincere apology to both women, handing the jewelry back before dragging his feet home to accept his punishment from his parents. Beauty forgave him swiftly too.

It would take many weeks, however, before she forgave Edith, or at least until she stopped calling her "madam" in that pointed way, but Edith accepted her punishment graciously. She threw a belated surprise birthday party for Beauty a month later and invited Morrie, his parents, Maggie and Victor to join us in the celebration. She was so desperate for Beauty's forgiveness that she even invited Wilhelmina. Edith wasn't a good cook and so the food was terrible and the cake flopped, but no one said anything about it. Edith didn't comment either when Wilhelmina went out to her *bakkie* to fetch the backup cake she'd baked just in case.

Beauty opened her modest pile of presents with a guarded smile, though the smile dissolved into tears when she unwrapped my gift. It was a drawing I'd made of Beauty and Nomsa holding hands; Edith had paid to have it framed. I drew Nomsa as a warrior princess because Beauty said she was the bravest person she'd ever known. I knew, though I never said, where Nomsa got her bravery from.

Against all odds, we had become a family, the three of us, and though it was probably the most unusual family the country had ever seen, it was all I had and it was worth fighting for.

Forty-seven

BEAUTY

❧

It is 16 June 1977, the first anniversary of Robin's parents' deaths and a year since Nomsa disappeared. We are the ones who have been left behind, Robin and I, and the past year of our lives has been filled with grieving and waiting; how is it that invisible burdens and torments such as these are the heaviest to carry and the hardest to endure?

Edith is off on a trip once again and so, when the evening's darkness gathers, Robin and I gather with it in the lounge to build two small altars of memories. We each clear one of the side tables and carry them around to set in front of us so we can get to work.

The first item Robin places on her altar is a black-and-white photograph of her parents taken on their wedding day. In it, they are standing next to a three-tiered cake that is topped off by a miniature plastic bride and groom. Robin's father holds a knife in his one hand and, in the other, a slice of cake he is tenderly feeding to her mother. It is one of only five remaining photos from that day.

Robin places her mother's mascara tube next to the photo along with the locket I gave her for Christmas; she's opened the clasp and her two heart-shaped parents stare back at us. She looks at her collection of three items critically and then goes to Edith's record collection to search for albums that her parents liked. She adds two Beatles records and the Dolly Parton album with the "Jolene" song on it.

"It still doesn't look like very much, does it?" Robin asks, and before I can reply, she heads for Edith's dressing table. When she returns, she is holding up a small bottle of Charlie perfume that Edith hasn't worn since her sister died.

"This was the perfume my mom used to wear." She sniffs it, smiles sadly and then adds it to the collection.

I have only one photograph of Nomsa. It is a group photo of fifteen of the schoolchildren and me gathered in front of the small room that served as the entire school in our village. A Russian sociology professor (who was doing a study of apartheid education in the Bantu homelands) took the picture one day, and it arrived in the mail a year later; he had sent it to me just as he had promised.

Nomsa is one of the older children in the group and she stands in the back row. She looks too serious for a child of fourteen. Her face is slightly in the shadows and it is difficult to make out her features. I place the photo in the center of the table propped up against a glass.

The next item I place on the altar is the last letter I received from Nomsa, written a month before the march. The letter is still in its slit envelope. I do not need to open it to remember what it says because I have memorized every word of it. Seeing her looping handwriting is always a shock. It is like catching sight of her across a busy street and it makes my heartbeat quicken. I also include the framed picture that Robin drew of Nomsa and me for my birthday, and a rag doll that Nomsa used to play with when she was just a child.

"What else can I add?" Robin asks.

"I do not think you need anything more. That is enough."

"No, wait. My mom liked apples." With that, Robin runs to the kitchen where she plucks an apple from the fruit basket. "Here," she says as she walks back, "she'll like this."

As Robin places the apple on the altar, the bird suddenly swoops down from his perch and starts pecking at it.

"Birdy num num. Birdy num num."

Robin swats him away. "Leave it, Elvis. That's not for you! Leave it."

The parrot takes flight and alights on a chair for a moment before flying back. His flapping wings disturb the lighter mementos on the altars.

"Take the apple away," I say gently. "You have enough without it."

When Robin returns from the kitchen, she looks down at her table with a serious expression on her face. She is still worrying that she does not have enough and I am about to reassure her once again, when she says, "I wish I had something for Mabel too."

She does not often speak of Mabel, her old maid, and it is a reminder to me of how much this child lost in such a short space of time.

"You do not need anything of hers," I offer. "You can just think of her."

She nods but then her brow furrows again. "No, never mind."

"Really, it is fine. You do not need things, what is important is that you remember—"

"No! Mabel wasn't taken from me like my parents were. She chose to leave. It's different. I don't want to think about her now."

How wounded this child is. Will she ever truly heal?

"Okay, what's next?" Robin asks.

I place a candlestick on each of the altars and light the white votive candles we bought for the occasion. They are scented and the smell of jasmine rises up to greet us.

"Shall we hold hands?" I ask Robin and she nods. "Would you like to say a few words?"

She shoots me a nervous look. "Like say a speech?"

"Not a speech, no. Just a few words from the heart. Things you would like to say about your parents."

She thinks about it for a moment and then nods. "I'll go after you."

"I will say a prayer for them then," I say and she nods again, closing her eyes. I keep mine open so that I can be sure my words do not cause her distress.

"Dear Heavenly Father," I begin. "We pray for the souls of your dearly departed children, Keith and Jolene."

Robin flinches when I speak her parents' names.

"What is wrong?" I ask.

"Nothing."

"Something is wrong. You can tell me."

She is reluctant to speak and so I have to coax her. "Remember what we agreed about honesty, Robin? I promised to tell you the truth and so do you not think it is only fair that you do the same with me?"

She swallows hard. "It was just a shock to hear you say their names, that's all."

"Why?"

"No black person ever called them by their first names before. It was always '*baas*' or 'madam.' My dad wouldn't have liked it if anyone did it. He would have called them 'cheeky' and told them they needed to learn some manners."

For the first time, I wonder what Robin's parents would think of the arrangement I have made with Edith; how they would feel about their only child being raised almost solely by a black woman who uses the same toilet and cutlery and crockery as their daughter, and who doesn't take orders from a white child like Mabel did.

As if reading my mind, Robin says, "Do you think heaven changes people?"

"What do you mean?"

"Do you think it makes them forget about skin color and invisible germs that only certain people have and who the boss is and what's cheeky and what isn't?"

I know what Robin is really asking. She wants to know if heaven has made her parents grateful that she is being raised by a black woman who cares for her, or if my race is still an issue in their afterlife. She is wondering if heaven is also divided with a section for whites only and a section for blacks, and if prayers go up to God color coded so he knows which ones are more important and which ones should be ignored.

"I think . . ." I trail off, careful to find the right words that will reassure her. This child is burdened with too much worry and I want her to find solace in this. "I think that heaven makes people forget about the things that used to worry them when they were alive. And so the people in heaven are happy when we are happy. That is what is important to them. All your parents want is to see you happy and loved and taken care of. The rest doesn't matter anymore."

Robin nods slowly, letting my words sink in.

"Instead of my saying a prayer for them, why don't you just go ahead and say something yourself?" I suggest.

Robin clears her throat and then looks up to the ceiling. Finding no inspiration there, she turns her head instead to the altar where she sees her parents' faces looking back at her.

"Mommy and Daddy, I miss you very much. I wish I had more photos of you because some days it's hard to remember what you looked like, and when I can't remember, I feel bad." Her voice catches and she swallows before continuing. "I hope you still remember what I look like and that you have photos of me in heaven." The child turns to me for reassurance and I nod for her to continue. "I want you to know that I'm happy and I'm very well taken care of. So you should be happy too. I love you very much." She is done.

"Are you going to say a prayer for Nomsa?" Robin asks.

"I am," I say, "but I am going to say it quietly in my head."

"Okay, I'll say something in my head too."

I bow my head then and think of my daughter. My feelings are so conflicted that I know whatever I say will contradict whatever else I say, but still, I forge ahead.

Nomsa, I am so proud of you for standing up for your people and for fighting for what is right, and yet I am ashamed of you too for joining an army and plotting to cause harm to others. I love you so much for the warrior you are and for the fire that cannot be extinguished in your soul—the fire that so many of us have lost—and yet I am angry with you for your betrayal.

I am angry with myself as well because I should have known what would happen when I allowed you to go to Soweto. I should have known my own flesh and blood well enough to know that you would not be able to resist a call to arms. And so I apologize for letting you down and for not seeing the danger you could not see. I ask for your forgiveness, my child. Please come home.

I tell myself that at least I have hope. Robin knows that her parents will never come back to her and she is saying her last good-byes. I will not say good-bye, and I will never give up hope because that is all that remains. Hope is what fuels my broken heart.

Forty-eight

BEAUTY

❀

1 AUGUST 1977
Yeoville, Johannesburg, South Africa

The note was slipped under the door.

Robin spotted it from where she was sitting on the couch and ran to grab it before opening the door to see who had dropped it off. No one was there.

My name was on the blue envelope and so she passed it to me. I put my knitting down so I could open it.

> *You do not learn. I thought you were clever.*
>
> *I saw you meet with Comrade Mashongwe in the park in Braamfontein last night. He will not be meeting with anyone ever again because of you. Are you happy now?*
>
> *This is your very last warning to stop asking questions and return to the Transkei.*
>
> *After this, not even Nomsa can save you.*

It chills me to think that it was probably Shakes who stood outside the door, mere steps away from Robin, a few minutes ago. If it is true what he has said about Edward Mashongwe who I did meet with last night, then my life is probably also in danger. These are not empty threats.

I think of the man with the hat who took the letter from me in the park as he cast his eyes around nervously. He patted my hand before slipping the envelope inside his jacket pocket.

"I will make sure to get this letter to Nomsa when I return to the camps," he said. He would not offer me any further information nor tell me what camp Nomsa was at. "I am a loyal soldier and I will not put anyone at risk by confiding that."

"Then why are you helping me? Why take the letter at all?"

"I am of a generation that does not believe a woman's place is in an army. The female operatives are never as good as the men and they are a distraction. My motives are purely selfish. I hope whatever is in this letter will convince her to go home to where she belongs."

When we had parted ways and I was walking in the opposite direction as him, I felt the prickle of eyes upon my back. I spun around to see if Edward was following me, but he had already disappeared from the park. I turned slowly in a circle, searching for the person who was watching me, and after I saw nothing on the ground, I cast my eyes upward. There, in the lowest branch of a large oak tree, was an owl.

It was smaller than the one I'd seen in Hillbrow and I could not make out its color in the darkness, but its eyes glowed orange in the moonlight. It launched itself into the night just as I turned to flee. I wonder now what has happened to Edward. I did not like the man, but I would never have wished him harm. I can be sure the letter will not find its way to my daughter.

"Who's it from?" Robin asks leaning over my shoulder. "What does it say?"

"It is just a note from a friend to arrange a visit."

"Oh," she says, returning to her book.

I have been trying to ignore the threats, but I cannot any longer. The owls seem as much warnings, harbingers of death, as the notes and phone calls. All this time, I thought the owls were foretelling Nomsa's death. Now I know they are warning me of my own.

It is time for me to get my things in order in case something happens to me. I turn to one of the last pages of my journal and begin:

My Dearest Robin . . .

Forty-nine

ROBIN

❦

The spine of my book was wedged open under my porridge bowl, and I was careful not to splash milk onto the pages while I ate. Beauty usually didn't let me read during meals, but she was in her and Edith's room changing the linen. Edith was due home that morning after three weeks away, and I was hoping to see her before I left for school.

I'd just stood up to take my bowl to the kitchen when the key turned in the lock. I raced to the kitchen to put the bowl down so I could free up my hands. I wanted to take Edith's suitcase from her when she walked in but when I turned back, intending to meet her at the threshold, I was frozen in place by the sight of her. Edith was pale and looked like she was in shock.

"Edith?" Her eyes focused when I uttered her name. She turned her head to look at me but she remained silent. "Edith, what's wrong?"

She blinked and then shook her head slowly in disbelief. "He's dead."

"Who?"

"Elvis."

I looked to the cage and Elvis was still there, exactly where I'd put him before I had my breakfast. He was squawking loudly as he always did when Edith came home.

"No, he isn't. He's fine."

"He is?" Edith perked up. She looked so hopeful that I nodded vigorously and walked to the cage to let him out again.

"Here he is, see? He's not dead."

She turned to look at where the parrot was swooping around in circles and then her face crumpled. "Not him. The real Elvis. The King. I just heard it on the radio, but I was hoping it was a hoax like that time with Paul McCartney. They said it happened yesterday."

Beauty came through from the bedroom then. She must have heard enough to know that something was wrong, because she came rushing towards Edith and grasped her hand, leading her to the table. I closed the door and carried Edith's suitcase inside before I went to sit next to her.

"He was the only man I've ever truly loved," Edith whispered.

"Who are you speaking of?" Beauty asked.

"Elvis," I whispered.

Beauty looked to the parrot, who'd alighted on Edith's chair and was nipping at her ear, and then she looked back at me questioningly. I shook my head and went to Edith's record collection, pulling a few albums from their place and handing them to Beauty.

Beauty looked from the pictures on the records to Edith. "This is the man who has died?"

Edith nodded mournfully, a single tear running down her cheek. She stood to go pour herself a drink.

"Did you know this man?" Beauty asked.

Edith nodded again from the liquor cabinet. "Yes. I knew everything there was to know about Elvis. I was his biggest fan."

Beauty tried again. "But did you ever meet him?"

Edith returned to the table and sat down, her glass of scotch clutched in her hand. She shook her head sadly. "And now I never will."

Beauty clucked and stood. "*Hayibo*. White people are mad." She snatched the glass from Edith's hand and took it to the kitchen. "Robin, go to school. You are going to be late. Edith, stop crying over a man you have never met and go wash your face. There are papers from the school I need you to sign and things we need to talk about before I go. And someone put that bird back in his cage."

It was just over a week later that a cough jolted me from the adventures unfolding in my book and brought me back to the park. I was propped up against the oak tree, reading while I waited for Morrie.

I looked up. A young black woman stood a few paces away. A raised purplish scar ran from her hairline to her left ear; it was as wide as a finger and bisected her left eyebrow. It almost stopped her from being pretty, almost, but not quite. She was very thin, almost to the point of starvation, but she looked strong and muscular. I knew she wasn't a maid, because she was wearing a Western-style dress instead of a uniform and *doek*, and her hair was braided into cornrows.

"What are you reading?" Her voice was pitched low, almost a whisper.

I held the book up and showed her the cover. "*Anne of Green Gables*. Have you read it?" I'd finally gotten around to checking it, and all the other orphan books, out of the library.

She shook her head and didn't say anything more. I rushed in to fill the silence.

"She's an orphan too and she also has lots of freckles that drive her crazy. It's one of my favorite books because she's just like me."

She didn't say anything in response and the conversation was starting to feel a bit one-sided. "What's your favorite book?" I asked.

"They do not write books for people like me."

That was sad. Everyone should have books they could see themselves in.

"Do black people have freckles?" I asked because I didn't know what else to say. "Do you just not see them because the freckles are dark and your skin's dark too? Wouldn't it be funny if black people had white freckles?"

She didn't seem to want to talk about freckles so I tried another question. "What's your name?"

She glanced around and then uttered it, sharing a confidence. "Nomsa."

"Nomsa?" My heart started to jackhammer in my chest. "Are you Beauty's daughter?"

She nodded.

I threw my book aside and scrambled up while dusting myself off. Beauty had told me so much about her that it was as if I knew her; she was like the real sister I'd never had. I stepped forward, wanting to hug her, but she thrust an arm out to ward me off. "No, do not touch me."

I looked at her hand as she withdrew it and saw that it was trembling. When I looked back to her face, she wasn't looking at me. Her eyes were darting all around the park.

"I'm Robin," I clarified. "Beauty lives with—"

She cut me off. "I know who you are. I have been watching."

This new development thrilled me. While I just read about detectives and played childish games, Nomsa was a real-life spy who had been following me. My fledgling admiration turned to hero worship.

"Where is my mother? She is late today."

Beauty usually brought our lunch to the park, but I knew she wouldn't be there that day. She'd told me before I left for school that morning that a friend of hers was in the Transkei to bury her child who'd died from a snakebite, and she needed Beauty's help cleaning her employer's house. Her friend, Dorothea, was worried she'd lose her job while she was off and hoped that sending a replacement maid would make her madam less annoyed with her for going home. Beauty expected to be home after 6 p.m. and had sent me to school with my lunch already made.

When I told Nomsa this, I wasn't expecting the look of absolute defeat that crossed her face. It looked like she might cry. Beauty had always described Nomsa as being so strong, and I didn't think a warrior would crumple so easily at such a small disappointment.

"It's okay, don't worry. You can just come to the flat and wait for her there. She'll be back tonight and you can see her then."

Nomsa shook her head and clucked at my apparent stupidity. She cast furtive glances around the park once more. "I cannot wait." I could see that her mind was reeling; she was talking to herself more than she was speaking to me.

"Well, can't you come back tomorrow? I'll make sure she's here then."

"Have you not heard me? I cannot just come again whenever it suits you." Her voice was strangled, and I was beginning to get scared. I didn't know what to do. I wanted to help her because she looked so cornered and skittish, but her level of anxiety was rising and I didn't want to say anything more to upset her.

After a moment or two, she seemed to reach a decision. "I need a pen and paper. Quickly." She pointed to my school case and snapped her fingers as I scrambled to open it.

"I only have pencils. They don't let us use pens yet—"

"Quickly!"

I handed her a pencil and one of my exercise books, and watched as she propped it up against the tree as she wrote. She looked up after every few words to glance around and then carried on scribbling. I used the time while her attention was diverted to get a proper look at her and noticed for the first time that her left foot was bandaged.

"What happened to your foot?"

She shushed me and I kept quiet until she finished. Her paranoia had by then rubbed off on me and I was looking around as well. I was relieved not to see any police cars go by and I told her so. I was hoping she would praise me for being helpful. Instead, she ripped the paper from the book, folded it up and thrust it at me. "Here, give this to my mother. Tell her I will come back to see her here on Sunday at two o'clock." She looked around the park and then added, "Make sure you give that to her. It is very important. And she must not be late. Two o'clock on Sunday. And do not tell anyone else that you saw me. Not even that little boyfriend of yours." With that, Nomsa turned and limped out of the park towards Rockey Street. She didn't even say good-bye and I had to stop myself from calling out after her that Morrie wasn't my boyfriend. There'd been an edge of menace to her tone; I knew not to mess with her.

Looking around again, I couldn't understand what had scared her because there definitely weren't any policemen in the park, only a few people in normal clothes. A moment later, Morrie came ambling over.

Speak of the devil.

His camera was hung around his neck and he was shaking a photo to dry the ink.

"Who was that?" he asked.

"Who?"

"That lady?"

"Oh her. She was just lost and asking for directions."

"What's that?" Morrie said, pointing to my hand.

"Nothing. It's just a stupid letter from a girl at school," I said. Then, in an attempt to change the subject, I asked, "What did you take a picture of?"

"The two of you," he said, handing the photo over. "She looked unhappy and I'm trying to capture negative emotion, because my grandfather says I'm ready to move on from inanimate objects."

I took the photo but didn't look at it. "Have you got my lunch?"

Morrie slapped his forehead. "I forgot. Wait here, I'll be back now." He turned and ran back in the direction he'd come from. As soon as he was out of sight, I checked around the park to make sure there weren't any police nearby and then quickly looked at the photo. It was very clearly Nomsa and me. I couldn't allow Morrie to hang on to the evidence, so I slipped the photo into my dress pocket before unfolding the letter. There were a few paragraphs of Xhosa written in a hurried looping script. I could only recognize a few of the words: "mother" and "I love you"; the rest of it may as well have been hieroglyphics.

I carefully refolded the page, happy to have it and the photo as evidence of the encounter. The meeting had been so surreal, and Nomsa had behaved so strangely that if it weren't for the proof, I would have thought it had all been a daydream.

B eauty arrived back at the flat just after six that night. I was sitting at the dining room table doing my homework and she joined me there, looking relieved to be off her feet for a few minutes. I was playing one of the kwela records Edith had brought back from America for Beauty. She'd been teaching me how to dance to her African music, and I'd begun to listen more to Beauty's records than Edith's, though Beauty warned me to play her music very softly so no one could overhear the banned albums.

"*Molo, makhulu*," I said. Hello, Granny.

"*Molo, mtwana*," Beauty replied. Hello, my child.

"Thandiswa," I reminded her. I'd asked Beauty to give me a Xhosa name and she chose "Thandiswa" because it means "the loved one."

"*Molo*, Thandiswa," Beauty corrected herself.

"*Unjani, makhulu?*" How are you, Granny?

"*Ewe, Thandiswa. Sikhona!*" Yes, Thandiswa. I am well! Beauty then swapped over to English. "How was your day?"

"It was fine."

"How was school?"

"Also fine."

Beauty looked at me for a long moment. "Is everything all right?"

"Yes."

"Were there any problems with my being away?"

"No, everything was fine."

Beauty sighed. "Okay then. I am going to bathe," she said, "and when I am done, I will make us dinner."

I nodded without looking up or meeting her eyes. "Okay."

Once the water had stopped running and I could be sure Beauty was in the bath, I slipped the letter and photo out from under my mattress and hid them both in my secret compartment under Edith's dressing table. I told myself that it was only Thursday and I still had a few days to give them to Beauty along with Nomsa's instructions, but the truth is I'd made my mind up as soon as the excitement had worn off and Nomsa's intentions had dawned on me.

She was obviously on the run from the security police and had been there to fetch Beauty. She planned for them to head back to the Transkei because Beauty had always said Nomsa would be safe there. There was no other explanation for Nomsa's sudden reappearance, her crazy behavior and her desperate need to see Beauty after more than a year away.

The decision came easier to me than I would've thought, and so 2 p.m. on that Sunday came and went. Beauty, oblivious to the significance of the afternoon and her prodigal daughter's presence a mere block away, spent those hours watching over Morrie and me in the Goldmans' apartment while Morrie's parents went to a matinee at the Market Theatre in Newtown. I claimed to want to spent the afternoon there because the Goldmans had just bought a television set, but I actually wanted to make sure we weren't in Edith's flat if Nomsa came looking for Beauty.

I waited all that next week for the knock at the door or the phone call that would take Beauty away, but none came. I stopped going to the park and pretended to be sick so I wouldn't have to leave the house to go to school. All the while I was keeping watch over Beauty to make sure that Nomsa didn't get to her, I allowed my relief to stifle my guilt.

If Nomsa cares about Beauty as much as I do, if she truly wants to be with her, she would have found a way. She wouldn't have given up so easily. The one who fights the hardest is the one who loves Beauty the most.

Fifty

BEAUTY

❦

B eauty, would you like some tea?" Robin asks.

"No thank you, my child."

"Would you like to listen to one of your stories on my Bugs Bunny radio?"

"I am happy just sitting here in silence, but thank you."

Robin goes to the kitchen and starts running water. "What are you doing?" I call.

"I'm washing the dishes."

"Leave them. I will do them tomorrow."

"No, it's fine. I like helping you," she says.

When she is done with the dishes, Robin disappears into the bedroom and returns with my slippers. "Why don't you change out of those shoes and wear these instead?"

I do not have the heart to tell her that the slippers are too hot on a night like this. Instead I let her put them on my feet and then I pat the couch next to me. When she sits down, I pull her in to my side and kiss the top of her head. "You are too good to me," I say.

She does not say anything. She just leans in closer and clings to me. I wonder what my boys are doing right now. I wonder if they miss me as much as I miss them.

The child has dark smudges under her eyes that look like bruises. She looks tired, and her nails are bitten down again like they were when I first met her. She says she is sick and I have kept her home from school, but she does not have a fever and shows no physical signs of illness, only sleeplessness and worry.

"Is something wrong, my child? Is something troubling you?"

She smiles. "No, I'm fine."

There is a knock at the door and I stand to go answer it, but Robin pushes past me.

"Ignore it. We're not expecting anyone," she says looking nervously between the door and me.

"My child, let me see who it is." Unexpected visitors make me nervous. Shakes has been here once before; he could come again.

Whoever it is knocks once more.

"No, really," Robin says. "I have a bad feeling. Let's just pretend we're not home."

A voice calls out from behind the door. "Robin, open up. I know you're in there."

It is Morrie, and when I open the door, he stands there scowling, looking both injured and angry at the same time. "Hello, Beauty."

He steps past me and addresses Robin. "Where have you been? Why don't you come to the park anymore?"

Robin shrugs. "I've been busy."

"Doing what?"

"Just things. I'm spending time with Beauty." She looks at me with a guilty expression.

"Okay then, I'll join you." Morrie walks towards the couch. "I have some new photos I want to show you."

Robin blocks his way. "Another time, okay?"

Morrie throws his hands up in exasperation. "When?"

"Maybe next week."

"You promise?"

Robin nods. When Morrie has gone, she comes and sits next to me, resting her head on my shoulder.

Fifty-one

ROBIN

❀

They say bad things happen in threes, so I probably should've realized it was the beginning of the end after that first thing happened when Morrie convinced me to leave Beauty and the apartment.

We spent the afternoon at the library stocking up on our supply of books.

"Isn't this a bit old for you?" The librarian frowned at one of the books I'd handed across to be checked out. "This is meant for adults."

I'd put the Agatha Christie book, *A Murder Is Announced*, in the middle of the pile of children's books and hoped the librarian wouldn't notice it.

"It's for her aunt," Morrie chirped in. "She asked Robin to get it for her." He was standing next to me with his own pile of books that he'd had processed at another counter.

The librarian considered this for a moment and then stamped the checkout page. "I'll let you do it this time, but tell your aunt to come in herself and get her own books next time."

"Okay. Thanks." I kept a straight face until we were outside, and then I let out a theatrical sigh and laughed, thanking Morrie for his quick thinking.

"No problem. It's good to see you smiling for a change. I wish you would just tell me what's wrong."

"Nothing's wrong. I keep telling you," I said. "Do you want me to kiss you to prove it?"

"There! See, now I definitely know something's wrong."

We boarded the bus and Morrie handed over our tickets. Once we were seated and I had my books on my lap, I reached for my pocket. It was an instinctive action by that time, almost as natural as breathing, and I was startled to find that there was nothing in there. I shifted in my seat and pulled the fabric of the pocket inside out to make sure it really was empty—it was. I patted my blouse's pocket; there was nothing there either.

Morrie frowned. "What's wrong? What are you looking for?"

I leaned out into the aisle, hoping to spot a glimpse of pink and green, but when I didn't see anything, I got up to look under the chair.

"What is it, Robin? What did you lose?"

"Her mascara." That's all I needed to say; no further explanation was required.

"Come on," he said. We hopped off the bus at the next stop and retraced our steps back up to the library's entrance. Once inside, we split up and did a search of all the sections, even the ones we hadn't been through, and then split up again to double-check. We didn't find it. After an hour of frantic activity passed, the panic I'd been trying to control threatened to overwhelm me and I started to hyperventilate. The mascara was my last link to my mother and the life I'd lived before my parents died. It was irreplaceable and it was gone.

I headed outside to get some air, walking quickly because running wasn't allowed, but the air didn't feel any less soupy there than it had inside. I sank down onto the steps and started to cry.

Morrie shuffled up next to me and put his arm around me. "Here, rest your head on my shoulder."

I tried, but I got a crick in my neck from dropping my head so low. We gave up on that, and he patted my back instead, whispering words of comfort until my hiccupping breaths slowed and all the tears had dried. Then he reached into his pocket, pulled out a linen handkerchief and instructed me to blow my nose.

When I arrived home again, relieved to be back, I'd only just closed the door behind me when the phone rang. "Hello?"

A moan that sounded like an animal in pain returned my greeting. My heartbeat quickened.

"Hello? Who's there?" Every missed call, every hang-up made me think of Nomsa. Was this her now?

"Robin?" The voice was tremulous, but it was clearly a man's.

"Yes, who's this?"

"It's Johan."

"Johan? What's wrong?"

He said something inaudible that was more of a gasp than a word, and I asked him to repeat himself.

"Victor's in hospital," he managed to get out.

"What happened? Did he have an accident?"

"No . . . They beat him up."

"Who?" But, of course, I already knew.

There was a shuddering intake of breath, and then Johan sniffed and exhaled to steady himself. "We don't know. There were at least four of them. Probably the same people as on Christmas Day. He's in a bad state, Robin. Very bad. They left him for dead in his driveway and then urinated all over him. Can you imagine that? What kind of animals do that to a person?"

The kind who throw bricks through windows at people singing around a piano.

He carried on. "I'm calling to see if you have a contact number for Edith so I can let her know."

I reached for Beauty's notebook and read off the numbers to Johan, explaining that he would have to leave a message for Edith to call him back. I promised to pass on the message if Edith called us in the meantime. "What hospital is he in? Can I come visit?"

"He's at the Joburg Gen, but they won't let children into the ICU."

"Please tell him . . . tell him . . ." But before I could think of the words to say, the line went dead.

"What's wrong?" Beauty was at the door holding a shopping bag.

I opened my mouth to speak, but the words wouldn't come. Instead, I answered her with tears.

"Come here, my child." Beauty held out her arms and I rushed into them. "Has something happened to Edith?"

"No," I sobbed. "It's Victor, he's in hospital."

There was a knock at the door and Morrie's face popped around the corner. "Robin? Edith wants to talk to you. She phoned my mom about something and I said I'd run up to call you."

I looked at Beauty.

"Go, child. Run. Tell her about Victor."

"What about Victor?" Morrie asked.

I was rooted to the spot. I didn't want to leave Beauty.

"Robin?" Morrie pressed.

"Go, child."

And stupidly, I did.

F orty minutes later when I came back after speaking to Edith, Beauty wasn't in the lounge or the kitchen.

"Beauty?"

There was no reply, and so I went to look for her in the bedroom. Beauty had her back to the door, but I could see in the reflection in Edith's dressing table mirror that she was holding something. It looked like a piece of paper. My breath caught between my throat and lips. I looked down. The photo I'd hidden away was lying on the floor next to what looked like Beauty's journal.

She turned around slowly and I could see her hands were shaking. "Where did you get this?"

I couldn't look at her and I lowered my eyes.

"Robin." Her voice was raised. "Where did you get this?"

I swallowed to try to wet my mouth. "Nomsa gave it to me."

"Is that when the photograph was taken?"

I nodded.

"When was this?"

My lip started quivering, and I had to clear my throat a few times before I could speak. "She came to the park last month looking for you, and when you weren't there—it was the day you were helping your friend, I don't know if you remember—she asked me for that paper to write you a letter."

Beauty closed her eyes and I could see she was trying to make sense of what I was telling her. "But I do not understand. What is the letter doing hidden away? Why did you not tell me that you saw her?"

"Nomsa was coming to take you away back to the Transkei. And I didn't want to lose you. I wanted you to stay with me."

Beauty didn't speak; she just continued to look at me in that puzzled way. Her hand had drifted to her chest and she was rubbing it slowly, making small circles over her breastbone.

"I'm sorry, Beauty. I should have told you, but I knew if I did that you'd go back to the Transkei with her. And she doesn't need you, not like I do. She's grown up and she can look after herself. I need you. I love you."

Beauty was looking at me like she didn't recognize me, her face a blank mask. She took a shallow breath and then another, deeper this time, and her shoulders rose and fell as she struggled to get enough air into her body. No matter how deeply she inhaled, she seemed unable to breathe and her eyes widened in panic. Her right hand had stopped circling around and around her chest, and she suddenly raised it to her throat, fingers closing around her Saint Christopher pendant. She tugged at it, trying to free her throat of any obstruction that might slow the air's journey into her lungs. The chain snapped free of her neck, but she still gasped as she tried to suck oxygen down.

"Beauty?" I was rooted to the spot, unsure of what to do to help her.

I took a step towards her and her face suddenly contorted in pain, her eyes pinching closed. She groaned and crumpled in upon herself, a cry of pain dying on her lips as she hit the floor. I ran to her and tried to pick her up, linking my arms under her armpits and hefting with all my might, but she was a deadweight and I wasn't able to budge her.

"Beauty? Beauty," I said, kneeling down and tapping the side of her face, her skin like tissue paper against my fingers. "Beauty, say something, please. I'm so sorry. Please be okay, Beauty. Please. I'm sorry."

Still she didn't move or open her eyes; her mouth hung slack. I jolted upright and ran for the phone, dialing the number I'd been taught to use for emergencies. "Please, come quickly," I said as soon as someone answered. "Beauty fell and she's not waking up!"

The calm voice asked me for an address and then asked me who Beauty was.

I started to call her my *makhulu*, but stopped myself just in time. "She's my granny," I said. "Please hurry!" I put the receiver down and then ran back to Beauty. She was very still and her skin had taken on an odd gray pallor. "Please don't die," I whispered, kneeling down beside her and taking her hand. The Saint Christopher came free of her grasp and dropped into my palm. I squeezed her hand, the pendant trapped between our fingers, but there was no pressure in return. "Hold on, please. Help is on the way."

Beauty suddenly convulsed, and a stream of vomit gurgled out her mouth and down her cheek. She coughed and made a choking sound, and I quickly turned her face to the side to give the vomit somewhere to go. It pooled around her chin and soaked into the carpet. I leaned over to the bed, dropped the pendant, and tugged at a blanket, pulling it down to the floor so I could clean Beauty's face. I wiped and wiped and whispered that I loved her and that everything was going to be okay. Some of the vomit had trickled down to her collarbone, and I dabbed it away before bending over and kissing her clammy forehead.

I don't know how long I sat there whispering to Beauty—it felt like hours—but there was finally a commotion outside the flat. I jumped up to open the door, getting there a split second after the first knock. There were two men standing outside, and I grabbed the hand of the closest one, pulling him into the bedroom. I was crying by then, sobbing with fear and regret and relief and guilt. I wasn't able to speak, so I just pointed at Beauty, trusting that the man would know what to do.

Instead of springing into action, he looked down at Beauty with his brow furrowed. He nudged her with his foot, his scuffed black shoe digging into her ribs. "Who's this?"

"Help her," I cried. "Please help her." It came out as a squeak.

"But where's your granny? The one you phoned about?"

I took great big gulps of air so I could speak clearly. "This is her. This is Beauty."

The other man rushed into the room behind us; he'd been slowed down by a big, heavy bag he was carrying. I knew that whatever was in it could save Beauty. "Hurry, please. Help her."

"But she's black," the first man said, still just standing there, doing nothing.

"Is this the woman?" the second man asked, incredulous.

"Do you see anyone else here?"

The second man dropped the bag with a thunk and left the room.

When he returned, all the urgency had gone out of him. "Come, there's no one else here. Let's go."

"What are you doing? Why aren't you helping her? Do something," I pleaded, lunging for the bag and tugging at the zip.

"Leave that alone," the first man swatted at me, grabbing the bag away.

They turned to go and I jumped in their way, blocking the doorway of the bedroom. "No, you haven't helped her. You have to help her."

"We don't answer calls for *kaffirs*, girlie. Stop wasting our time." And with that, they pried me loose of the doorway and left without looking back, leaving the flat door open behind them.

Once I'd gotten over the shock of their leaving, I rushed back to Beauty and crouched over her. "Beauty?" She was so still that I couldn't tell if she was breathing.

I raised myself from my haunches and raced out the door to the stairwell, screaming all the way down the stairs to the Goldmans' flat. "Help! Please help!"

Mrs. Goldman opened the door before I got to it. "Robin? What's wrong?"

"It's Beauty," I panted. "Come quickly."

"Why, what happened?"

"Just come!" I turned and raced back the way I'd come.

Mrs. Goldman's voice rang out behind me. "Anthony! Come quickly, something's happened."

I didn't wait to see if they were following. I dashed up the stairs again, taking two at a time, and turned the corner. Mr. Finlay stood at the threshold to our flat, peering inside.

"What's all the racket about? What's going on?" he demanded.

"Nothing," I panted, trying to brush past.

"The hell with that! Something's happened and you'd better tell me what it is."

I tried to duck under his arm that was obstructing the doorway, but he blocked my way with his knee.

"Please, Mr. Finlay. Please get out of the way."

"Not until you tell me what's going on."

"Mr. Finlay, could you please just—"

"Has something happened to that *kaffir* bitch? I knew she was trouble from the moment I laid eyes on her, but no one would listen. What's the spoonie gone and done? Should I call the police?"

The anger welled up in me then, a cyclone of white-hot fury. "*Kaffir* bitch." How could he call Beauty that? How dare the vile man speak of Beauty that way?

"You know why God made them all brown, don't you?" he continued. "So they'd look exactly like what they are. Worthless pieces of shit who—"

Before he could finish his sentence, I was charging down at him, my head lowered like a rugby player preparing to scrum. The top of my skull connected with his stomach—a rock launched into a bowl of jelly—and he yelped in surprise. While he stood there swaying, winded and gaping at me, I disengaged and took a few steps back and then I tackled him again, knocking him to the floor. No sooner had he landed on the hallway carpet with an "Oof" than I jumped on top of him, pinning his abdomen to the floor. I took potshots at his stomach; my thumb was tucked tight against my fist, and not caught inside it, just as my father had taught me.

"Help! Somebody get this maniac child off of me!"

Mr. and Mrs. Goldman rounded the corner and stopped dead in their tracks, the shock of what they were seeing rendering them speechless.

"Don't. You. Dare. Speak. About. Beauty. That. Way." I delivered each word along with a punch to the solar plexus. A hand at the scruff of my neck pulled me up, and frustrated to have the man out of arm's reach, I started kicking out, lashing at Mr. Finlay as he lay on the floor, his arms raised up to protect his head.

"What is going on here?" Mr. Goldman demanded, pulling me even farther out of reach.

"That crazy little bitch attacked me, that's what happened."

"Robin?"

"He said . . . he said . . ." I was panting and it was only when I uttered Beauty's name—one of the few fragmented words I could catch hold of to explain the situation—that I remembered that she was still inside lying on the floor. "Come." I grabbed Mr. Goldman's hand and pulled him inside, leaving Mrs. Goldman to help Mr. Finlay up.

"She's in here," I said, and Mr. Goldman followed me into the bedroom.

"What happened?" he said, and he crouched down next to Beauty, touching two fingers to her neck.

"She was struggling to breathe and rubbing her chest and . . . there was pain . . . and she fell and the ambulance people wouldn't take her . . . you have to do something."

There was a loud gasp behind me. "Anthony? Is she . . ." Mrs. Goldman's voice trailed off.

"She's still alive. We need to get her to the hospital."

"I'll call an ambulance," Mrs. Goldman said, turning to head for the phone, but Mr. Goldman cut her off, relaying what I'd already told him.

He bent down, extending one arm under Beauty's thighs and the other under her back, and scooped her up. She flopped in his arms like a marionette whose strings had been cut. "Thank God she isn't heavy," Mr. Goldman puffed as he turned at an angle to get Beauty through the door without hurting her. "Get the car keys, Rachel, and meet me downstairs. I'm going to take her to Bara."

Mrs. Goldman used the stairs while we took the elevator to the basement parking. Mr. Goldman's face was red with the strain of carrying Beauty, thick veins bulging in his neck and forehead, as he hefted her to his blue Rambler Hornet. The doors were unlocked, and I opened the rear left one and then stepped out of the way so that he could lean in and lay Beauty down. I rushed to the other door and got inside, using my lap for a pillow for Beauty to rest her head on.

Mrs. Goldman had returned with the keys by the time Mr. Goldman had closed the doors.

"You stay here and wait for Morrie to come back from the shops," Mr. Goldman said to her.

The engine roared to life and our tires squealed as we accelerated out the garage. I looked out the side window. Mrs. Goldman had her palms joined together, pressed up against her mouth, her eyes filled with tears.

Fifty-two

ROBIN

❦

2 OCTOBER 1977
Yeoville, Johannesburg, South Africa

Three days had passed since Beauty's heart attack. She hadn't re-gained consciousness after her surgery but she was alive.

During the drive from Yeoville to Soweto, I'd cradled Beauty's head in my lap and wrapped my arm over her body to prevent her from being jolted when Mr. Goldman made sharp turns. I couldn't feel any movement at all, no gentle rising and falling of her ribcage as proof that she was still breathing, but I refused to believe that she might be dying. I spoke to her the whole way, telling her that everything was going to be okay and that I loved her and that she had to hold on.

Once we arrived at Baragwanath Hospital, there was a flurry of activity as orderlies and nurses rushed to pull Beauty from the car and strap her to a gurney. I tried to follow her inside, but a security guard stopped me from charging through the doors that led to the inner sanctum.

"Please let me through. Please! I need to go with her, please!"

"Only medical personnel are allowed beyond this point."

I kicked a wall in frustration, stubbing my big toe in the process. Once I'd calmed down enough to take in my surroundings, I noticed a waiting room off to the side and I headed for that, intending to stay as close to Beauty as I could. No sooner had I sat down than Mr. Goldman came to take my hand.

"Come, Robin. Let's go."

"But I want to stay with Beauty."

"They won't let us in to see her, and I think it will be quite a few hours until there'll be any news."

"I want to wait here."

Mr. Goldman looked around the room. His gaze slid over the other occupants, making me notice them for the first time. We were the only white people in there, our paleness making us as conspicuous as a full moon in a dark sky. One man, who sat three chairs down, was holding up a rust-colored T-shirt to his forehead to try to stop the flow of blood. Another's shirt was ripped open, displaying a jagged flap of skin across his side. Two men sat across from him talking in angry voices. One of the men, when he caught me looking, cracked his knuckles and glared back. A raving drunk was sitting off to the side, yelling obscenities.

"This isn't a safe place to wait. We'll go home and phone for updates."

"But—"

"Come, Robin."

There was no use protesting; I could see he'd made his mind up. When we finally got back to our building, I went directly to our flat telling Mr. Goldman that I was going to pack clothes and a few other things for the night. The first thing I did though, as soon as I was through the door, was to gather up Beauty's journal, Nomsa's letter, the photograph and Beauty's necklace. I packed everything away in a kitbag, and then filled it with the clothes and toiletries I'd need.

A niggling feeling plagued me, making me double-check that I had everything. I did, but still the feeling persisted.

I ignored it and was just pulling the flat's door closed when I realized what was bothering me. I needed to solve the mystery of how Beauty had found my hiding place. I went back inside to Edith's dressing table and knelt down. My secret compartment was open and everything was gone. It didn't make any sense; how had Beauty known where to look or what she might find? I crouched even lower and saw another cubby just above mine. A gentle nudge against the plywood revealed another compartment, one that was the perfect size to hold Beauty's journal. She hadn't been looking for my secret spot at all; she'd been meaning to return her own cherished object to a different hiding place.

I spent a sleepless night listening to Morrie snoring on his bed on the floor. It seemed that I'd barely closed my eyes before Mrs. Goldman woke me to give me the news. She'd called the hospital and was told that Beauty had come out of surgery. She was apparently in a stable condition.

"Can we go see her?" I asked.

"I'm sorry, sweetie. They said only family members are allowed to visit."

"But I am family! She's my granny. Did you tell them that?"

"I think we'll have a tough time getting them to understand that. But I promise to keep calling for updates."

It was frustrating having to rely on the phone calls for news (especially when all they'd tell us was that Beauty was stable), so I was excited when Willy called to say she'd managed to use her nursing contacts to arrange admittance to Beauty's ward. She came to see us straight afterwards with an update.

"They won't know anything more until she wakes up properly," Willy said that night as she sat next to me on the Goldmans' couch, "but they're worried because it should have happened already. *My magtig*, I can't understand it. Beauty has always been such a fighter, but it's like she doesn't want to regain consciousness." Willy placed the teacup and saucer down with a loud rattle, and started dabbing a handkerchief at her swollen eyes.

They looked strange, as if something black had leaked around them, and I blurted out the first thought that occurred to me. "Are you wearing makeup?"

Willy flushed and turned to me. She ignored my question and posed one of her own. "Can you tell me again what happened?"

"Is the makeup for Mr. Groenewald, your boss? Because he liked Edith and she wears makeup?"

"Robin! Tell me again what happened."

I withdrew my jagged thumbnail from my mouth. "I told you! Morrie came to call me to the phone. I went downstairs and spoke to Edith and told her about Victor. She then said she had to phone Johan and we said good-bye. When I got back to the flat, Beauty wasn't in the lounge, and when I went to the room she was gasping for air and then she fell."

"And nothing happened before then? She didn't get a phone call or something that could have upset her? No bad news?"

"Yes, I told you! She was upset about the phone call from Johan."

"*Ja*, I know, but was there no other news? Nothing about Nomsa?"

I shook my head, not trusting myself to speak.

Willy sighed. "Then the call from Johan was probably what did it." She blew her nose and then looked to Mrs. Goldman. "Has there been any word about Victor?"

"Yes, there's some good news on that front, at least. He's been moved out of ICU. I'm taking Robin there later. Hopefully he'll feel up to seeing her."

"That will be nice, hey, Robin? Something to cheer you up a bit, *liefling*? Just don't say anything to Victor about Beauty, okay? We don't want to upset him."

I nodded. I had no plans of giving someone else a heart attack.

"Why do things like this happen?" I asked.

"What do you mean?"

"Why do kind people like Victor get beaten up and wonderful people like Beauty have heart attacks?"

"*Ag, liefie,*" Willy said, "it's not for us to understand it. The Lord moves in mysterious ways."

K iddo, it's me." Edith sounded breathless and very far away when she called late that afternoon. "I just heard about Beauty. I can't believe this happened just after Victor. Are you okay?"

I wasn't, but I didn't trust myself to speak without crying.

"Hello? Are you there?"

I sniffed. "Yes, I'm here."

"You mustn't worry, I've arranged with Mr. and Mrs. Goldman to take care of you for now and—"

"You're not coming home?"

Edith sighed. "No, I—"

"You're never here when I need you. You're never here when bad things happen. You're always away!"

It was a relief to find a target for all my anger and pain; I needed someone to blame. What had happened with Beauty wasn't just my fault; it was Edith's fault too. If she'd been home taking care of me like she was supposed to, if she'd made me a priority in her life and didn't just keep handing me off like in a Pass the Parcel game, none of this would have happened.

"Oh, Robin."

"I need you here."

"Kiddo, you know that I'd be there if I could. But the Goldmans are—"

"I don't want them! I want you!"

"Come on. Cut me some slack, will you? I already take off more time than I'm allowed, and I was told in no uncertain terms that if I take off any more, I'll lose my job."

"I hate you and I hate your job too."

I slammed the phone down and furiously batted away the hot tears that spilled down my cheeks. Edith wasn't coming home because her job was more important than I was. Without Beauty, I was more alone than I'd ever been.

J ohan led me to the private room and nudged me inside. "Take as much time as you want. I'll be outside waiting for the doctor to get an update."

I didn't want him to leave me, but I didn't know how to explain that I was afraid of being left alone with Victor. Instead, I watched Johan disappear down the long corridor, his shoes squeaking on the shiny floor, and then I took a few tentative steps towards the bed.

The thing lying there didn't look anything like Victor. Its whole face was distended and bruised so that its nose and cheekbones all blended into one giant purple moonscape. The jaw wasn't right either, it was way too big, and I could see cavernous space lying behind the cut, swollen lips. Bandages were wrapped around its head, and tubes of clear liquid fed into its arms. The thing looked like a monster, and I was light-headed and nauseated standing next to it. The beeping and flashing of machines only served to make the whole scene even more nightmarish.

I was about to step back and turn away when the thing's eyes fluttered open. Its gaze flitted around the room like restless moths before finding my face and settling on it. Its eyes were so raw, they looked as if they'd been cross-stitched with red thread, but they were unmistakably Victor's hazel eyes. Even in that state, even as pain clouded them, their kindness shone through, and I watched in horror as they welled up with tears.

"Please don't cry," I whispered. "It's just me. It's Robin." I snaked my hand through the tubes that fed into the top of his hand and slipped my palm under his so that his fingertips were resting on the pulse point of my wrist. His fingers curled and he squeezed my hand, just the faintest pressure, and I squeezed back.

I wanted to wipe away the tears that were running down his cheeks, but knew that removing the evidence of pain wasn't the same as taking the pain away, which was what I actually wanted to do. I didn't want him to be embarrassed by his tears either, so I smiled and allowed my own tears to fall free.

I couldn't believe how broken Victor looked. His one leg was in a cast and raised up by a hoist, as was his one arm. He looked to be na-ked under the blanket that was pulled up to his armpit, and thick black hair coiled up his chest and under his bruised neck. A beard had started to grow on his misshapen chin, and blood crusted in one of the top whorls of his ear.

You should've listened to me and moved away. You should've been a coward and run away, because then you wouldn't have been beaten up, and you wouldn't be lying here looking so awful and being in so much pain.

As I took all of his injuries in, I noticed something else. The mountain range of Victor's knuckles was swollen, and scabs were just beginning to crust over the raw wounds on each ridge. The sight took me back to one night when my father had stumbled inside after an evening spent at a mine function, one of the many that women were not invited to attend. I'd watched from my bedroom door as my mother gasped at the sight of his bloodied hands, accusing him of drinking rum, which made him aggressive and pick fights. Victor's hands looked just as my father's had that night.

Victor fought back.

And with that realization came the memory of the conversation we'd had the night of my birthday party. Facing your fears is always better than trying to outrun them, Victor had said.

He was right. Instead of facing my fear of losing Beauty, I'd tried to run away from it. Instead of raising my fists against an unknown future and facing whatever a Beauty-less life would entail, I'd lied and hidden the evidence of Nomsa's return, and then I'd run and run and run. But you couldn't outrun your fears because that was the thing about fear: it was a shadow you could never shake, and it was fit and it was fast and it would always, always be there just a split second behind you.

Victor had said something else that night, too, I recalled, something that had been niggling at the back of my mind the past few days. Karma is when you do bad things to people, and then bad things happen to you in return as punishment.

The realization came in a breathtaking flash of insight. Everything that had happened—losing my mother's mascara, Victor getting beaten up and then Beauty's heart attack—all of it was my fault. I'd done something really bad the day I decided to hide Nomsa's letter away from Beauty, and now karma was making sure I'd be punished for it.

It didn't matter that I'd told myself that I was doing the right thing by trying to hang on to Beauty. It didn't matter that I'd believed Nomsa didn't need Beauty as much as I did. None of that justified my actions. Hadn't my parents and Mabel been taken from me and hadn't I suffered through the pain and the loss of it? Didn't I know better than anyone what it felt like to lose the people you loved most in the world? And yet, despite all that, I'd purposefully kept Beauty and Nomsa apart. Knowing full well that all Beauty wanted was to find her daughter, I'd made sure that wouldn't happen.

It wasn't Edith's fault that this had happened. This had nothing to do with the fact that she was never home. This wasn't God moving in mysterious ways like Willy had said. I'd been looking for people to blame when the blame lay with only one person: me. Both Victor and Beauty were in the hospital fighting for their lives because I'd done something unforgivable, and I was rightfully being punished for it.

Along with the guilt and the burden of responsibility came another thought.

If my doing something bad caused this to happen, then surely my fixing it will make it all better.

And suddenly, I knew exactly what I had to do.

Fifty-three

ROBIN

❦

3 OCTOBER 1977
Yeoville, Johannesburg, South Africa

S o," I concluded, "I have to find Nomsa and bring her to Beauty."
Morrie and I were sitting on his bedroom floor. I'd just confessed everything, telling him the whole truth about how I'd caused
Beauty's heart attack, and giving him all the details going back to the
day of Nomsa's visit.

Nomsa's letter and the photo Morrie had taken of the two of us
were cradled in his lap, proof of my betrayal. I wore Beauty's Saint
Christopher pendant on a new chain around my neck because I'd been
unable to fix hers where it had snapped. The pendant hung next to the
heart-shaped locket Beauty had given me for Christmas, the one with
my parents' pictures inside, and it felt as though I was carrying everything I'd ever need around my neck. It gave me courage.

Morrie hadn't said anything the whole time I spoke. His eyes had
just widened steadily with each new revelation.

"Could you please say something?" I pleaded, plucking up the
photo and looking down at it so I wouldn't have to look at the shock

on his face. Would he still so desperately want to be my boyfriend now that he knew what a terrible person I was?

"How are you going to find Nomsa when Beauty, Maggie and Willy have all been searching for her for more than a year without any success?" Morrie asked.

"I don't know," I sighed. "But I can't just do nothing." I looked down at the picture, studying it while wishing with all my heart that I could go back to that scene and change it. If I could do everything differently, I would. Seeing Nomsa and me together like that shamed me; it was as if Morrie had captured one of the worst moments of my life and pinned it to the photograph for all eternity as proof of what a monster I was.

"There has to be someone who knows where she is. Maybe Maggie will know where to find her."

"Maybe," he said but he sounded doubtful.

I still couldn't look at him and my gaze lingered on the photo. I couldn't look too closely at myself or Nomsa either, and so I skirted around us, studying the rest of the picture instead: the giant oak tree, my school case, the swings in the distance, the sun-dappled black woman standing off to the side in the background.

"I think you'll have better luck with the letter," Morrie said. "I bet you it tells us where Nomsa is."

"Hmm," I said, my attention focused on the woman I'd noticed in the photo. I held it up closer to have a look. The marks I'd thought were spots of sunlight streaming through the leaves didn't make sense because she wasn't standing in the shade.

"We just need to find someone who can read Xhosa to translate it for us." Morrie was still talking about the letter.

"Hmm." And then I recognized the marks for what they were. "Look, Morrie," I yelped, showing him the photo. "I've only just seen it. See this girl to the side with the sun splotches on her face?"

"It's called 'dappling' not 'splotching' but, yes. What about her?"

"That isn't from the sun; it's white birthmarks. That's the girl from the shebeen! Nomsa's friend."

He squinted more closely at the picture. "The one who said she didn't know where Nomsa was?"

"Yes, but she was in the park with Nomsa just a few weeks ago, so she must know where she is now."

"But why would she tell you the truth if she even lied to Beauty?"

My bubble of excitement began to deflate. He was right. There was no reason why the girl would tell me where Nomsa was when she'd lied to Beauty about where that man, Shakes, was. There was no reason why she'd—

And then it clicked, and I finally, finally remembered the very first time I'd seen her. The knowledge that had been just out of reach the whole time came to me in a flash of vivid images: a police station; a half-naked girl with her arms crossed over her chest; a man's shirt ripped open barely covering her; the smell of sweat and smoke; a white hand offering a blanket and a black hand taking it.

"Maybe she'll tell me because," I said as I jumped up, "I did something nice for her once and hopefully she'll remember and do something nice for me too."

I found King George in his usual spot in the basement storeroom smoking one of his sweet cigarettes.

"You want King George to take Little Miss where?"

"Meadowlands in Soweto," I repeated. "To a shebeen."

"A shebeen? Isn't Little Miss too young to be *dopping*?"

"It's an emergency, King George. Please. Beauty's in hospital and she might die, and I need to find her daughter so Beauty can get better and . . ." I was panicked and babbling.

I reached into my backpack past Beauty's journal and everything else I'd packed, and pulled out a handful of notes; it was the last of the money Edith had left for us while she was away, and I'd taken it all from the biscuit tin in the kitchen. I'd also broken open my piggy box and had a bank bag full of coins from that. "Here," I said, shoving the notes and the bag at King George, "I have money. I'll pay you. Please, please just take me."

He looked down at the money resting in the palm of his hand and whistled. *"Jussus!* Where did Little Miss get this money? She rob a bank?"

I shook my head, but before I could reply, King George shoved the money back at me. I wanted to scream from frustration that he was refusing to help me.

"Keep the bucks, Little Miss."

I groaned and turned to go. I had no hope of finding Nomsa if I couldn't even get to Soweto. There was no way Willy would take me to the shebeen, and if Mr. Goldman wouldn't even sit in the Bara waiting room, he definitely wouldn't go into a Soweto suburb. Maggie and her husband had gone into exile in London after the police raided their house again. There were no buses for whites that went to Soweto, and King George had been my only hope of getting there.

When my hand touched the handle, King George called out. "Wait! Where is Little Miss going?"

"You said you won't help me, so I need to try and come up with another plan."

"King George didn't say he won't help Little Miss. He say he won't take money. Little Miss don't need to pay King George. Friends *mos* help friends out."

"So you'll take me?" I asked, cautiously optimistic.

"Ja, if it *mos* means so much to Little Miss."

"Thank you! Oh, thank you so much." I launched myself at him, hugging him as tight as I could.

"Jinne, now you make a *ou* wish he rubbed some soap over hisself this week."

• • •

"Is Little Miss hunnerd percent sure no one is sending the cops after King George looking for Little Miss?"

I ducked my head out from the blanket that was thrown over me where I was hiding on the backseat. "Don't worry. Morrie is covering for me."

We'd told the Goldmans that I wasn't feeling well and wanted to go to bed early. Mrs. Goldman had been busy all day with preparations for Sukkot and so she hadn't been paying that much attention to us as she cooked and got everything ready for that night. The plan was that Morrie would wait for me to sneak out, and then he'd stuff pillows under the duvet and switch the light out. After they'd returned from the synagogue, he'd pretend to check on me every hour or so, and report back to his mother that I was sleeping soundly so that she wouldn't get suspicious.

"*Orright.* What shebeen is King George going to?"

"Fatty Boom Boom's."

"*Jinne*, but Little Miss *mos* knows her shebeens, *jong*! King George *smaaks* Fatty's place. Such a big woman, that one. *Lekker vettetjie!* King George can't touch sides if he wrap his arms around that *tjerrie*, and that's *mos* how King George likes it."

I ducked my head back under the stained blanket and kept enough of a gap open so that I could get air. I was breathing through my mouth because the blanket was so stinky it made me want to gag. The streetlights had come on by then, and they whizzed past overhead in flashes of sickly yellow. King George switched on the radio; nothing but static came out. He gave it a few smacks, but that didn't fix it.

"*Ag* well. King George will just *sommer* sing rather. Little Miss will *smaak* it. Listen." He cleared his throat a few times, paused and then cleared it again before warbling his way into a very loud and impassioned song.

I listened for a minute or two out of sheer politeness, but eventually couldn't stand it anymore. "Stop! Stop that noise!"

"Noise? *Jinne tog*, King George not making noise. King George singing opera. Little Miss not like it?"

I didn't know what opera was, but since it sounded like a tomcat having a seizure, I knew I didn't like it. "No, it's horrible. And it doesn't even make sense. Those weren't real words."

"*Ja*, is real words. Is 'Nessun Dorma' which is *mos* a very famous opera by Puccini. It all fancy and *kak* in Italian."

"Don't you know any English songs?"

"*Ja*, Little Miss. King George thought it be *lekker* to have some classy music, but he can also sing *anner* songs." With that he burst into a loud rendition of "Pretty Belinda."

He was butchering the lyrics and I yelled at him to stop once again so I could correct him.

"It's not a goat house. It's a boathouse."

"A boathouse? What *kak* is that?"

"It's a house that's a boat."

"*Nee, fok*. That not a real thing, Little Miss. A house can't *mos* float."

"It is a real thing. A goat house isn't a real thing."

"*Ja*, it is. Is a house where goats live."

There was no setting him straight so I gave up and hummed along softly, buoyed by the knowledge that I was finally doing something to try to fix the damage I'd done.

"*Fokkit*." King George's singing ended abruptly and his curse was uttered with a twinge of panic.

"What? What is it?"

"Roadblock just at the exit. Lotsa cops. Quick, off the seat and on the floor. Pull the blanket over Little Miss proper, *orright*."

I did as he told me, fighting off the claustrophobia and pulling the blanket close. King George reached his arm around and wildly patted at my head to make sure it was covered. He started flinging things from the footwell over me and onto the backseat. The car was a mess of bottles, wrappers, newspapers and other junk, and it felt like he was trying to turn me into a human garbage heap.

"Little Miss must stay very still and be very quiet. They find Little Miss in this car and King George is *moer-toe*."

He continued to curse as he slowed down and must have lit up a cigarette because I smelled smoke. It wasn't sweet like his normal cigarettes; it smelled like one of Edith's regular ones. Our crawl soon halted to a stop, and the window squeaked as it was wound down. A light shone inside; it must have been bright because I could make it out even through the blanket.

"Good evening, Officer, and how's the officer tonight?"

"Pull over to the side of the road and wait for me."

"Yes, Officer. King George do as the officer say."

King George used a sickly syrupy voice with the cop, but he cursed again as soon as we pulled away. I could hear the fear in his voice and it made me start to tremble. When we came to a halt again, I could make out other sounds: choppy voices magnified through walkie-talkies, the crunch of tires, cars whizzing by on the highway, the beeps and wails of sirens and the barking of dogs. A few minutes went by with nothing happening. I couldn't take it any longer; I had to know what was going on.

"What's happening—"

"Shh," King George hissed.

A few seconds later, a voice instructed King George to get out of the car. His door creaked open and then slammed closed. I could make out most of the conversation coming in through the open window.

"Good evening, Officer."

"Where's your passbook?"

"No, Officer. Coloreds don't *mos* need no passbooks. *Jinne*, they not quite as low as *kaffirs*."

"You're colored?"

"Yes, Officer, colored. Has the officer *mos* never seen a colored *ou* before? King George know there aren't a lot a *klonkies* in the good old Transvaal coz they all live inna Cape. Has the officer gone to the Cape? *Lekker* mountain and *kwaai* beaches, not that King George really know coz the *klonkies mos* aren't allowed to sit on the *blerrie* sand for a minute with their brown *gatte*. Only the whites. But the officer will *mos* like it. Does the officer know how to swim?"

"Where's your proof that you're colored?"

"Proof, Officer? Can the officer *mos* not see King George's skin? It look like weak coffee with lotsa milk, can't the officer *mos* see? Where that torch? King George will *mos* shine it on his skin so the officer can see *lekker.*"

"Whose car is this?"

"Is King George's car. Does the officer like it? Is *mos* only twenty years old. Says ninety thousand *kays* onna clock but the clock reset at a hunnerd thousand. Reset about three times already. The car is a *skadonk*, but it *mos* get King George where he need to go."

"I want to see your identity document and ownership papers."

"Yes, Officer. King George will get them from the car."

There was the crunch of gravel and the creak of the car door again. I could hear him opening the glove compartment and digging around in there. I hoped it was neater than the rest of the car or he'd never find what he was looking for. While he was searching, a bright light suddenly flashed just above my head; its halo shone right through the blanket, and I closed my eyes against the glare. The policeman was shining the torch into the backseat.

"What's all this shit in the back?"

I tried to hold my breath, scared that the cop would see the blanket rising and falling over me.

"That *kak*? It *mos* just a *moerse* mess, isn't it? Garbage and *anner kak*. King George must clean it, but he a *vuilgat*. Here the papers, Officer. King George found them."

The light shifted and I could hear papers rustling as the policeman looked over them.

"Where are you on your way to?"

"Eldorado Park, that *mos* where King George live. He first just quickly making a *draai* at a lady friend if the officer must know the truth. But the officer *moenie* worry *nie*, the *tjerrie* is also a *klonkie*! King George *mos* know all about the Immorality Act and he *mos* don't stick his light brown stick in white or black holes. King George needs to visit his *stukkie* once a week with *geld* and presents, or she'll *blerrie* move on and find another man. The officer *mos* know what *tjerries* are like. A good-looking *ou* like the officer must have a few *stukkies* hisself—"

"Listen, stop talking shit to me. I'm not your friend, okay? Shut the fuck up and do as I tell you. Open the boot."

"*Orright*, Officer. Sorry, Officer."

A key turned and the lock surrendered with a click. The boot popped open.

"Just more *kak* as the officer see. *Jammer* for the *gemors*—"

"I'm not going to tell you again. Shut up."

"*Orright*, Officer."

There was grunting as things were shifted about. Finally, it closed again.

"Is that all, Officer? Can King George go?"

"Not yet. I want to look at the backseat."

An iciness spread across my skin, an earthquake of fear that made the blood rush past my ears, almost blocking out what was being said.

"The backseat? But King George *mos* told the officer that it just full of *kak* and—"

"Now! I want to see it now. Get out of my way."

"But—"

"If you touch me again, I swear to God I'll break every finger on your hand."

"Sorry. Sorry, Officer."

"Step back."

My heart was thudding so loudly that I was sure the policeman could hear it. I tried to slow my breathing and take shallow breaths. The handle by my ear yielded and the door opened with a rush of cool, blessed air. I waited for the blanket to be ripped off of me, but there was no movement at all. Everything was still. Finally, the seat behind my head creaked as pressure was placed on it, the vinyl making a noise like a fart.

The policeman was so close that I could smell the aftershave he was wearing. It was cloying and made my nose twitch; the scent was so strong that I could smell its strange mixture of spice and musk through the stink of the blanket. There was a thunk as something hard connected with the papers behind me and I flinched.

"What was that?"

"What, Officer?"

"That movement. Something moved."

"Really? *Fokkit*, King George *mos* thought he rid of that thing."

"What thing?"

"It a hell of a big rat. *Moerse* long teeth like knifes. King George *mos* checked it out a few times and tried to *skop* it *dood*."

"No, I don't think so. What's this under—"

The sound of gunshots suddenly tore through the night and the policeman cursed. Voices nearby started commanding someone to stop running, and another round of shots was fired.

"Let the dog loose," someone ordered and the policeman cursed again, slamming the door shut behind him.

There was a lot of commotion with men shouting and dogs barking. A squeal of tires was followed by hooters being blasted. It sounded like someone had made a run for it, trying to escape across the lanes of the highway. Before I could figure out exactly what was going on, the engine fired up and we were reversing.

"*Jurre, fok* that was close. King George almost *kakked* hisself."

With a roar we were off, and by the sounds of things, the cops had enough on their hands without trying to stop us. I jumped up from my hiding place, desperate to get away from the rat.

Fifty-four

ROBIN

❦

3 October 1977
Soweto, Johannesburg, South Africa

There she is!" I was so relieved to see Phumla that I almost fell off King George's shoulders. He'd hoisted me up so that I could see into the room without having to drag the drum out again.

"That the girl Little Miss must speak with?"

"Yes." I didn't know what I would have done if Phumla wasn't working that night; I simply hadn't thought that far ahead.

"*Orright*. King George will go inside and tell her Little Miss needs to speak with her."

I was about to hop down when something else caught my eye. I yelped in frustration and brought my foot down on King George's ear.

"*Eina!*"

"Sorry!"

"*Klim af,*" he ordered and I obeyed, jumping down.

He rubbed his ear, wincing as he did so.

"Sorry!"

"Is okay. Now tell King George what the problem is."

"I saw that man inside. The one who blindfolded Beauty and then made Phumla lie to her. I think Phumla's scared of him, so she won't talk to me while he's here. I need to get her by herself."

"*Orright.* What his name and what he look like?"

I gave King George a description along with an explanation of where he was sitting. He scrunched up his wrinkled old face and then nodded a few times. "Okay. *Orright.* King George think he can do it. But he going to need funds."

"Funds?"

"Some bucks," he said, rubbing his thumb and index fingers together. "Moola. Dough. *Geld.*"

"Oh, you need money?"

"*Ja*, but is not for King George. Is so King George can spend it on his new *chommie.*"

"Who's your new friend?"

"That *ou* inside. Shakes."

"But he's not your friend!"

He winked. "Not yet, but after a few drinks, he will be."

"Okay." I slung my backpack down and opened it up, handing across the money King George had previously refused to take.

"Right, now Little Miss must find a *lekker* hiding *pozzie* and wait there, *orright?* King George needs time and *dop* and maybe a little bit of *boom* to work his magic. When the girl comes outside here, then it means is safe. Okay? Little Miss mustn't come out before then."

"Okay. Good luck!" I turned and headed through the yard cluttered with scrap metal to the back fence where I'd found the gate the last time I was there. It was dark and hidden behind trees, so no one would be able to see me there unless they were looking. Most importantly, I'd be able to see the yard for when Phumla came out. Once I was in place, I watched King George square his shoulders, tuck the money into his pants pocket and casually stride inside.

• • •

A half an hour later, I was still leaning against the fence with my chin resting on my knees. The metal wire was beginning to bite into my flesh, and I could feel each individual diamond-shaped link making an imprint on my back. I leaned forward to ease the strain.

It was a warm spring evening and a half moon hovered overhead. The sky was free of clouds and I looked up, trying to make out a few constellations through the tree's branches, but I couldn't see many stars at all. Either the moonlight was too bright or the township's wood smoke was too thick, but all I could see was the lights from the occasional plane flying over. Seeing the planes made me think of Edith and I quickly batted those thoughts away. She'd made it clear that she'd chosen her job over me, and that was a pain I'd have to deal with another time when I was feeling stronger.

A sudden burst of laughter pulled me from my thoughts, and I looked to the shebeen's entrance where three people were just coming out. Music filtered out into the night with them like phantom stragglers, and I listened to their voices trail away until only the chirping of crickets remained.

I desperately needed to wee by then and wedged myself as far behind a peach tree as I could to squat down. The wee took forever to come because I wasn't able to relax, and when it finally did, the stream was so strong that some of it splashed back at me, warm and wet against my bare ankles. When I got back to my backpack, I pulled out a tissue and wiped it off as best as I could. I sat down again to take up my vigil.

I wish I'd brought a sandwich with. Or a chocolate bar.

I hadn't eaten before we left and the smell of meat and onions being browned over wood fires nearby made my stomach grumble. I clearly wasn't the only hungry creature in the vicinity; the dog that had eaten my trail of bread crumbs the last time I'd been to Soweto suddenly materialized next to me as though my thoughts of food had attracted him. He sniffed me and my backpack, but when he realized I wouldn't be a source of any sustenance, he gave a disgruntled whine. I was happy to have some company and reached out to pet him, but he scampered off and I was left alone once again.

Another fifteen minutes passed, and I was falling asleep when a loud voice jolted me awake.

"There plenty more where that came from, *chommie*. And is good *boom* too. Not that *kak dagga* they sell at petrol stations with that Doom and *kak* sprayed all over it. Is *giftig* that *kak*. It will *mos* poison you dead." It was King George and he had his arm slung awkwardly over a tall man's shoulders. They staggered off towards where the cars were parked, and when they passed under a light, I saw that the man he was with was Shakes. They got into the white van, the one I'd first seen Shakes take Beauty away in, and then they drove off.

Before I'd had time to panic about King George leaving me all alone, the back door of the shebeen opened and a figure stepped outside. It was Phumla. She looked around nervously, and then took a few tentative steps in my direction before pausing to listen. She stood still for a few moments, expectant and waiting for something to reveal itself to her.

"*Molo*," she whispered. "*Ufuna ntoni?*"

I stood up at the sound of her voice and came out from my hiding spot, stepping from the darkness of the shadows into the silvery light cast off by the moon. Phumla's head snapped in my direction, her eyes widening and their whites glowing when she saw me. I could only assume, from the shocked expression on her face, that King George hadn't given her any context about who wanted to speak to her. Whatever she'd been expecting, it wasn't a white child.

"Hello," I said. "I'm Robin. And you're Phumla."

She looked around again, as though searching for the person who was playing the joke on her. I was nervous that she'd turn and leave to find King George so he could explain himself, and I cleared my throat to hold her attention. I'd prepared a whole speech but in that moment, as my heart thudded wildly in my chest like fists beating against a door, all I could come up with was, "I need your help to find Nomsa."

Her eyes narrowed. "Nomsa?"

"Yes, Nomsa Mbali."

"What do you want with Nomsa?" She took a step forward, her eyebrow raised as she regarded me suspiciously. Before I could answer, she stepped forward again and grabbed my wrist. "You! You are that girl from the park that day. The one Nomsa spoke to, the one her mother looks after."

"Yes." I nodded, relieved that she knew who I was.

"She wanted to see her mother to speak to her, but her mother never came."

"No." She was hurting me. I couldn't put a proper reply together while her fingers were wrapped around my wrist like a vise.

"Why did her mother not come?"

I hadn't prepared myself for having to explain the whole situation to Phumla. I thought it would be enough to tell her that Beauty needed Nomsa, and then—if I had to—I'd tell Nomsa the truth about what I'd done. The words caught in my throat as I tried to free myself of her grip.

"Why was her mother not there?" she demanded again, and when I didn't reply, her free hand went to her mouth as an upsetting thought occurred to her. "Did you tell someone about seeing Nomsa that day?"

"No."

"Did you report it to someone? Seeing her?" She shook my arm. "Did you?"

"No, I didn't," I said, though without much conviction. The girl was frightening me. Her anger was so intense that it bordered on hatred. I'd never done anything to her so why would she hate me?

"Have you led the police here?" There was now an edge of panic in her voice, a hissing urgency that made me feel like I needed to pee again.

"What? No!"

"How did you get here? Who brought you?"

"I came with King George, he—"

"What happened to Nomsa's mother? Where is she?"

"She's . . . she's in hospital," I stammered.

"Because of you?"

Her accusation took me off guard. How could she know of my culpability when no one else knew that I was to blame? How could she know my darkest secret when I'd only confessed it to Morrie? "Yes, but—"

"You will not find Nomsa, do you hear me? You little spy! You white people are all the same; the treachery is in your blood from the day you are born." Her eyes glowed with righteous indignation and her words, along with her intensity, brought a glimmer of understanding.

"No, Phumla, you don't understand—"

"I do not understand? Why? Because I am uneducated? Because I am a barbarian and a savage who cannot understand the way of the white man? I understand only too well. Now get out of here! Go, before I call our security." She stared me down and when I didn't turn and flee, she turned and started walking back to the shebeen. "In fact, let me fetch them now and you can explain what you are doing here asking your questions."

Every impulse told me to run. And I did run then, but instead of running away from the danger, I ran towards it.

Fifty-five

ROBIN

❧

3 OCTOBER 1977
Soweto, Johannesburg, South Africa

I got to the door a few heartbeats after it had slammed closed and yanked at it, scared that Phumla might have locked me out. The door opened with no resistance at all, and I stumbled backwards from using too much force. Once I'd righted myself, I rushed through and followed Phumla's retreating form down a long corridor. A serving girl suddenly stepped out from one of the side rooms, her drinks tray laden, and we almost collided.

"Sorry!" I said, looking back to see her grabbing at the glasses and bottles to stop them from toppling over. When I was sure everything wouldn't come crashing down around her, I kept going only to see that Phumla had disappeared ahead of me. I'd hoped to reach her in the safety and anonymity of the corridor, but she'd already exited into the main room where all the customers sat. There was nothing to do but follow her in there.

I tried to slip in quietly, staying close to the wall in the hope that no one would see me, but it was too much to expect that my arrival would go unnoticed. Even though the patrons were mostly jaded people who'd seen just about everything in the course of their lives, the arrival of a ten-year-old little white girl in an illegal drinking establishment in a blacks-only township was akin to an alien sighting.

The person sitting closest to me, a young man hunched over his beer, did a double take when he spotted me, his mouth dropping open in shock. Two older men who were seated at a table next to him were more vocal in their surprise, crying out so that other people turned to see what the commotion was. The room wasn't as packed as it had been the first time Beauty had come there; it was only a quarter full, which allowed a large enough space to open up around me, making me the center of attention.

Some people craned their necks while others farther back in the room stood up to get a better look at me. The record that was playing abruptly stopped, the needle scratching against the vinyl as one of the servers cut the music. Once the pennywhistle died, all I could hear was angry muttering throughout the room, as well as my breathing, which suddenly sounded abnormally loud.

"You see," someone called from the shadows. "I told you I saw a white child here weeks ago, but you all said I was drunk and seeing things. Look! It is the white child again!"

Phumla ignored the speaker. She was searching through the room for someone and I knew who that someone was. I was grateful to King George for getting Shakes out of there.

"Phumla, please," I said, ignoring everyone else and making my appeal directly to her. "Please just listen to me so I can explain." The room quieted down, all eyes on us.

Phumla let off a string of angry words in Xhosa that I couldn't understand because she was speaking too quickly. The group's muttering started up again. The room was thick with cigarette smoke; it insinuated itself around me, tickling my throat and making me want to cough. Its haze was oppressive, making me even more nervous than I already was in that room full of black men, and as I shifted my feet, my *takkies* stuck to something sticky that had been spilled on the floor.

It was hot in there and I wished I'd worn something lighter than my jeans and jersey, yet as uncomfortable as I was, I knew I had to ignore everything else and focus on my words if I stood any chance of getting through to Phumla. Before I could implore her again, a voice boomed out from behind me. "What's going on here?"

I turned. The large, turbaned woman was standing behind me, one hand on her cocked hip and an incredulous expression on her face.

"Mama Fatty," I said.

She blinked in surprise and her glossy mouth curled into a smile. "Well, my dear, it seems that I'm at a disadvantage in my own shebeen. I have a rather unusual guest who knows who I am and yet we haven't been formally introduced." She stepped forward, her bulk swaying as she advanced. She held out her hand and a dozen bracelets jangled at her wrist. "Let's do this properly, shall we? I'm Mama Fatty, the Shebeen Queen of this very fine establishment. And who, my dear, are you?"

"I'm Robin. Robin Conrad, and it's a pleasure to meet you, Your Highness." I took her hand and shook it before I remembered that you had to curtsey to royalty. Dropping her hand, I dipped low and bowed my head. There were a few titters from the crowd.

Mama Fatty laughed and the rolls under her chin jiggled about. "'Your Highness,' did you hear that? The child knows royalty when she sees it." There was laughter, but I didn't join in because I didn't get the joke. "Now tell me, what's a white child doing in my shebeen?"

"I came to speak to Phumla, Queen Fatty."

She looked from me to Phumla, frowning. "Zinzi," she said pointedly and I remembered that's what Phumla was called in the shebeen, "please explain yourself."

Phumla spoke in Xhosa, but once again, it was too rapid for me to understand any of it. Whatever she'd said caused agitation to ripple through the room and there were one or two shouts. Mama Fatty raised her hands up as though conducting an orchestra, and right on cue, everyone settled down. She turned to me.

"Zinzi accuses you of being a spy and of working with the security police. Is that right?"

"No, Queen Fatty, no. That's not right at all."

"Liar!" Phumla had switched back to English. "You said yourself you came here to find Nomsa, and that you have already put her mother in hospital."

There was a collective intake of breath. Even Queen Fatty was frowning and I spoke quickly before she turned against me. "Yes, but I'm not looking for Nomsa because I'm a spy or with the police. Really, I'm not like other white people."

There were a few laughs and Phumla joined in. "That is funny because you look just like other white people to me. In fact, you look just like the kind of white child who is used to getting her own way, and who thinks that she can come into the township and make demands like she would in her house in the suburbs. You think we are your servants here, but we are not."

A few people heckled me, hissing their support of her.

"No!" I shouted in a shrill voice. "No, I really don't think that. I'll prove to you that I'm just like you," I said, desperation creeping into my voice as I struggled to pull off my jersey.

I revealed my T-shirt and twirled around so everyone could see it properly. "See? This says 'Free Nelson Mandela' and there's a picture of him on the back. I could get arrested for wearing this shirt but I don't care." I frantically tried to remember everything Beauty had told me about him so they could see I knew all about their hero. "Rolihlahla is a good man, a freedom fighter, and he shouldn't be in prison for the rest of his life. I hope he will lead us one day and that he will heal us all so that we can live together as equals."

I was saying the right things because there were murmurs of agreement. I used the brief moment while the crowd was on my side to go to the record player. "This record that was playing before it was stopped? It's Spokes Mashinyane's 'Meva.' I have the record at home. Beauty taught me how to dance to kwela music."

I put the needle back and the record suddenly came to life, the pennywhistle loosening my muscles and filling me with hope. I looked around the room for a dance partner, but the grown men scared me. I was relieved, instead, to catch sight of a boy who looked only slighter older than me. He was leaning against the wall, a mop and bucket at his feet.

"*Ungathanda ukudansa?*" I held out my hand to him.

He looked around the room after I issued my invitation to dance, and a few people whistled and called out encouragement. He shrugged and then stepped forward, taking my hand in a gallant way. He tapped his feet, leading us into the dance, and then we swung into it, knees loose and arms bent. The kwela was part rock 'n' roll, part jive, and was punctuated at different points with fingers snapping or jazz hands waving. Even when we separated to do the moves individually, the rhythm kept us bound together so that our legs bent and kicked in unison as our hips and shoulders swayed together. The music was wonderful; it was something alive and pulsing through me, and when I smiled at the boy, he smiled back.

The audience was appreciative, and as we worked our way through the steps, circling each other, twisting and turning, dipping and sway-ing, they rose to their feet and started cheering. There was clapping and hollering, whistling and stomping, and the faces blurred as I whizzed and spun past, but I could see that they were smiling. When the song faded, I was breathless but elated, and my dance partner bowed to me and I bowed back.

Once the applause died off, I looked to Phumla, hoping that I'd made an impression but she just shook her head impatiently. "So, you have a Nelson Mandela T-shirt and you speak a bit of Xhosa. So you have learned one of our dances. So you are a little performing monkey. So what?"

My elation drained away.

I'm not winning her over. What else can I do?

I raised my hand to my locket, something I unconsciously did when I was nervous, and my fingers connected instead with Beauty's pendant. It gave me hope and I tugged on it, holding it up to the light.

"See this? This is a Saint Christopher pendant given to my *gogo*, Beauty, by Maggie, the White Angel. Maggie is white but she fights for black people's freedom. See the word on the back? It says 'Believe' because Maggie says we must believe that the black man will one day be free. Maggie is my friend, and she wouldn't be friends with a bad person, she just wouldn't!"

"You know the White Angel?" Mama Fatty asked, looking impressed.

"Yes." I nodded. "I do."

There was more murmuring, which Phumla's voice cut through. "Child, you pretend to be one of us, but you are not one of us. You will never be one of us and I have no reason to trust you. What are you doing here, really? What is it you want with Nomsa?"

All my bluster faded away in the face of her questions. I had no more ideas, no more plans that I could put into effect. I had no tricks or reveals, nothing left in my repertoire to try to convince her that I was a good person. And even as I was crushed by that knowledge, I realized that I was failing because it was a lie and she could see through it.

I'm not a good person. I'm not someone who doesn't hurt black people because didn't I hurt Beauty in the worst possible way?

I was an imposter and a hypocrite, and all that I sincerely had to offer her was the truth. I just never thought I'd have to offer it up like that, in such a public place in front of a jury of people who would judge me harshly without mercy, but then again, I couldn't expect kindness and forgiveness because I simply didn't deserve it.

So I did as Victor had told me to do. I faced up to my fear of finding out that I was unlovable after all, and I bared my shame and told my darkest secret. I told the truth. "Beauty didn't meet Nomsa because I didn't give her the letter."

"Speak up, child," Queen Fatty commanded, and I tried to dislodge the fear that was constricting my throat.

I looked straight at Phumla so that she could see how sincere I was. I hoped that my vulnerability would succeed in getting through to her where my bravado had failed. "Beauty didn't meet Nomsa that day because I didn't give her the letter. I hid it away and didn't tell Beauty that I'd seen Nomsa because I didn't want Beauty to go back to the Transkei with her." I'd started crying by then. I was so ashamed of what I was saying, what I was revealing about myself, that I couldn't hold back the tears. I knew my face was made ugly by grief, but I sniffed and kept on talking, determined to get it all out no matter how terrible it was.

"My parents were killed on the day of the Soweto uprising, the same day Nomsa went missing. They were killed by black men after a party. My father was a shift boss on the mines. They say the men didn't know my father, but I don't know if that's true. My dad was a good dad and I loved him very much and he loved me, but he wasn't always nice to black people." I felt like a traitor saying that about him, but it was the truth, and by this moment, I'd made up my mind to reveal everything.

"After they died, I was sent to live with my aunt, but she didn't really want me and wasn't able to look after me properly. I didn't want to get sent away to an orphanage and so when Beauty came to look after me, I started feeling safe again. She . . ." I trailed off, trying to get air into my lungs because the tears were making it hard to breathe.

"She looked after me and she loved me and that's all I wanted was for someone to love me and for someone to stay. So when Nomsa came, I didn't want Beauty to leave and go back to the Transkei. So I didn't tell her. And then she found Nomsa's letter and she had a heart attack."

Phumla gasped, but I couldn't stop to take in her shock. I had to keep going. "And Beauty might die, and I don't want her to die without seeing Nomsa because that's why she stayed with me. Not for me, not really, even though I told myself that's why. She was always honest with me and she told me that she'd leave me one day. She was only staying so she could find Nomsa and now I have to bring Nomsa to her. It's the only way to make things right."

The room was deathly silent. The only sound besides my voice was the record spinning round and round, all its music wrung out of it just as all my emotion was wrung out of me.

Phumla shook her head as though trying to clear her thoughts. "Why should I believe you? How do I know that this is not a trap and that as soon as Nomsa gets to the hospital, she will be arrested?"

A few people in the crowd murmured their agreement.

"Phumla, I know you don't believe me but I helped you once. Can't you help me now?"

"You? Helped me?" Her face had become hard again.

"Yes, don't you remember?"

She made a dismissive clicking sound. "When did this happen?"

"That night of the uprising, at the Brixton police station. I was there because of what had happened to my parents and I was sitting in the waiting room, and you came in, and you had no clothes, just a torn shirt and your underwear, and—"

"You gave me the blanket to cover myself."

"Yes."

Her face had softened at the memory. "That was really you?"

"Yes," I pushed on, "and I was hoping you'd help me now."

She didn't speak. I could see she was conflicted and I held my breath, too scared to say anything. The silence stretched out into what felt like an eternity.

Finally, Phumla opened her mouth with an answer. "No, I am sorry. I cannot help you."

I couldn't believe I'd failed Beauty once again.

Fifty-six

ROBIN

❧

3 OCTOBER 1977
Soweto, Johannesburg, South Africa

No one was in the parking lot when I came running out and I was relieved to find King George's car unlocked. I slipped into the passenger side and closed the door behind me. He'd said the story about the giant rat was a lie to throw the cop off, but I wasn't so sure. I pulled my legs up and rested my feet on the seat, cradling my backpack in my lap.

I let out a shaky breath, crushed with disappointment. I'd been so sure Phumla would help me and now I was at a loss for what to do. Without Phumla's help, there was no way I could get a message to Nomsa. There was nothing for me to do but give up.

The minutes ticked by and the music started up again inside. I wondered how long King George would still be gone for. I wanted to go home, get into bed and forget that this night and my humiliation in front of everyone had ever happened. My eyelids began to droop and I forced myself awake because falling asleep there wouldn't be safe.

The radio still didn't pick up any reception and I wished I'd brought a book with—something to distract me and keep me awake while I waited—but the only reading material in my rucksack was Nomsa's letter and Beauty's journal. In desperation, I dug the journal out. Trying to translate words from Xhosa to English would, at least, keep me alert.

I flicked through the first few pages and only understood a handful of words, not enough to decipher any kind of meaning from it, and then I skimmed through the rest. Beauty's handwriting filled the pages, and the familiar sight of it saddened me so much that I couldn't bear to look at it. I slammed the journal shut intending to put it away, but as I did so, something caught my eye. It was on the last few pages, an entry that was in English. More than that, it appeared to be a letter to me.

My Dearest Robin,

I find myself at a crossroads where I need to make a decision: to give up or to keep fighting. Giving up and backing down will mean that my safety is guaranteed. Continuing to fight will almost certainly place me in harm's way.

I always used to think that Nomsa was the fighter in our family. I would look at her and the way she took on the world with her fists raised, fighting the battles that needed fighting, and I would wonder where she got it from, that fire that burned in her veins. Silumko, my husband, was a brave man but he was not a fighter. I thought, perhaps, it was a trait passed down to Nomsa from my father or my father's father; they were both difficult men who insisted on having their own way.

Yet, here I am at the age of fifty discovering for the first time that the person who Nomsa has taken after all these years is me. Upon being given two choices, I have discovered that giving up is not an option. Perhaps if the person I was fighting for was myself, I would be more likely to step down. We are always so much more ready to give up on ourselves than those we love. But I am not fighting for myself. I am fighting for Nomsa, for her safety and her future.

My daughter is young, she is only nineteen years old, and she still has her whole life ahead of her. Once she is older, has an education, and has seen more of the world, if she then decides to take up this fight, I will respect that choice no matter how much I hate it. As it is now, she is too young to know the implications of what she is doing. She has been led astray by a man she trusts, one who has no moral compass and who is using her as a weapon against the world. I will not have it. I will not have her used as a pawn that he is willing to sacrifice.

It does not matter how often I am told that Nomsa is where she wants to be and what a good soldier she is. I know my daughter. I know that under the passion and the aggression beats a heart that knows the difference between right and wrong; a conscience that will grapple with the implications of bombing train stations and municipal buildings; a heart that will question the morality of hurting innocent people to make a political statement.

When I set out from the Transkei after I received my brother's letter, I promised my sons that I would bring their sister home. I am a woman who keeps her promises. In the meantime, now that I have decided to push on, there is a very real possibility that something might happen to me. There is no point in telling you who would be behind my disappearance. I do not want to put you in harm's way in a quest for justice, and the police will not care about another black woman who has gone missing.

I am writing this letter to you in my journal because I know if I disappear, you will look for clues as to what happened to me. I do not doubt that during your search, you will find my diary and this letter buried inside. It will be easy enough for you to find as it is the only entry written in English.

I want to assure you that if you wake up one morning and I am gone, it would not be because I left you willingly. It breaks my heart

*thinking that you might be waiting for me to come home one day, and
if that does not happen, you will think that I am one of the many
people who have left you without saying good-bye and without
keeping their promises. That would never be the case.*

*You remind me so much of Nomsa that I sometimes feel as though
the Gods took my daughter away but gave you to me in her place. You,
too, are a fighter like us Mbali women. When I think of how much life
has taken from you at such a young age, I can only marvel at your
strength and resilience. The courage you have shown in letting me into
your life and allowing me to love you—and I dare say, loving me in
return—shows bravery, Robin. I do not think it is brave to pick up a
gun or to carry a bomb, but it is brave to open yourself up to the
potential for loss and disappointment when you have already felt too
much of its sting.*

*I see greatness in you. I see great things in your future. You are
going to grow up to be a woman of substance, and I am proud to have
known you and to have shared a part of your journey. Never doubt
your strength and never doubt that you are worthy of love.*

I love you very much. Do not ever doubt that either.

Beauty

It wasn't like reading a letter at all. Instead, it was as if Beauty had
enfolded me into an embrace; each word was a caress, lips pressed
against a wound. I heard her voice speaking to me, and it spurred me
on as nothing else ever could have. I wouldn't give up because I was a
fighter, and Beauty believed in me even though I didn't deserve it. I'd
let her down so much already, I couldn't—I wouldn't—do it again.

I'd go back inside and find Phumla. This time, I wouldn't take no
for an answer. It didn't matter how much I humiliated myself or if she
threatened violence; it didn't matter if the crowd was on my side or
baying for my blood. As Beauty had said in her letter, we fight for the
ones we love and we don't give up. I'd force Phumla to tell me where

Nomsa was, whatever it took, because I could never live with myself if I didn't make things right.

The door met with resistance when I tried to push it open. I'd been so distracted by the journal, I hadn't noticed anyone making their way to the car.

"I've been looking for you." A face appeared at the window and I started.

It took me a moment to realize it belonged to the boy I'd danced with earlier. I rolled the window down.

"It's you," I said stupidly. "Why have you been looking for me?"

"I want to help."

"You do?"

He nodded.

It didn't make sense. I'd thought that my only chance at salvation was through Phumla, because I'd done something to help her once that might've made her likely to help me in return. I didn't know the boy—I'd never met him before our dance—and he didn't owe me anything at all.

"But . . . why?"

"I met Beauty once. It was when my brother was dying," he said. "She tried to get my mother and her friends to take Sipho to the hospital for treatment, but they wouldn't listen." He was quiet for a moment before continuing. "Beauty was kind to my brother. She'd found Sipho lying in the road after the police started shooting on the day of the uprising. He was bleeding and afraid, and she stayed with him to comfort him. I never thanked her for that. If she wants to find her daughter, then I want to help her."

"Your brother died?"

"Yes, he was my twin."

I wanted so much to tell him that I'd had a twin as well and that she, too, had died, but I knew that his real loss was greater than my imaginary one. "I'm so sorry."

"Thank you."

"But, you're just a child, like me. How can you help?"

"I've been asking a lot of questions since the uprising, and I've been following the movements of the man Nomsa has been with."

"Shakes?"

"Yes, that's him." His voice was flat and hard.

"So, what do you know about him?"

"I know you've arrived just in time. One more day and you would've missed them."

"Why?"

"Their trip was delayed, which is why they're now only leaving tomorrow."

"What trip?"

"Shakes and Nomsa were leaving for Moscow."

"Where's Moscow?"

"In the Soviet Union."

"Is that a Bantu homeland?"

"No, it's a country very far away where they're happy to fund the training of communist soldiers."

"Why was the trip delayed? What happened?"

"The security police caught wind of it. Someone tipped them off and they raided Shakes just before they were planning to leave."

"Someone?"

"Me," he confirmed after a beat.

I gasped. "But you're black. How can you report one of your own people to the security police?"

"Shakes is a bad man. He recruited many young children for the march. He knew it would be dangerous and what was going to happen, but he didn't care because their lives meant nothing to him. I was there the day he threatened my brother with violence if he didn't join the students' movement. My brother would still be alive if it wasn't for Shakes. I want him to suffer for that." He glared at me, challenging me to disagree with him. When I didn't, he continued. "They managed to escape before the police got there, but luckily didn't find out who'd tipped them off."

That explained Phumla's paranoia and her insistence in believing that I'd only come to find Nomsa to turn her over to the police; it explained why she thought Beauty being in the hospital was a trap to lure her to waiting security officers. She thought I'd used Nomsa's letter to tip off the police. Now, with only one day to go until Nomsa left, Phumla wouldn't betray her best friend's whereabouts to someone she didn't trust.

"After that," the boy continued, "Shakes delayed their departure until it was safe again. I've heard that tomorrow is the day."

"Is that why you work here? To spy on people and get information?"

"No, I need money to support my mother. The information is an added bonus. Children are invisible because we're thought to be powerless, so people say things in front of me here that they wouldn't say otherwise. The drinking loosens their tongues too."

"Your English is very good."

His face broke into a smile as wide as the one he'd given me while we were dancing earlier. "Thank you. I've been studying it outside of school. It's important to learn other languages."

I nodded in agreement. "I've been learning Xhosa, but I'm nowhere near as good as you. Maybe one day." A bottle broke nearby and we both turned in the direction of the noise to see if anyone was coming. When no one appeared, I pressed on. "So you can help me get a message to Nomsa?"

"No."

My spirits dropped. I knew it had been too good to be true.

"I can do better," the boy said. "I can tell you where to find her so you can deliver your own message."

"Really?"

The boy nodded and then looked away before continuing. "Can I ask you something first?"

"Yes, of course. Anything!"

"Why do white people hate us?"

We were separated by the car door that was closed between us. I opened it and got out so that I was standing next to him.

"What's your name?" I asked, realizing that he hadn't told me.

"Asanda. I'm sorry if the question has offended you, Robin, it's just that you're the first white person I've ever met. I told myself it was a question I'd ask when I got the chance."

"I wish I could tell you, Asanda, but I honestly don't know. I've been trying to figure it out myself, but I just keep going in circles. First, I thought it was because black people kill white people, but then I found out that white people kill black people too. I was told black people are lazy and stupid, and that they're dirty and have germs that we don't, but none of that's true either." A thought occurred to me. "How old are you?"

"Fourteen."

"See? And yet you have a job working late nights and then you go to school the next day. You work hard to study and you're clearly very clever. And Beauty . . . Beauty is the nicest, kindest and most intelligent person I've ever met and she's black." I shook my head in frustration. "Maybe it's that the whites need the blacks so much and that puts you all in a position of power that scares us. Or maybe it's just that everyone needs someone to hate, and it's easier to treat people terribly if you tell yourself they're nothing like you."

"Just promise me one thing."

"What?"

"Promise me you will not grow up and become one of them."

"One of who?"

"The whites who hate us. Don't grow up and forget how much the same we are, you and me. Promise?"

He was right; we were the same. Asanda and I had more in common than any other person I'd ever met. We both liked kwela music and loved to dance. We'd both had a twin sibling who we'd lost, and we both spied on people and acted like detectives. Both of us loved learning new languages and we both respected Beauty and wanted to do right by her. Each of us was also trying to make things right in our own way. In another time and place, Asanda and I could have been best friends; in another lifetime, he could've been my boyfriend.

"I will never grow up to be one of those people."

He was taller than I was, and so I had to stand up on my tippy toes to brush my lips against his cheek, white skin against black, to seal the promise.

Fifty-seven

ROBIN

❁

D rive straight," I shrieked as King George veered off the road. "You're going to get us killed."

"It's *mos* no use, Little Miss," King George slurred in reply. "King George is seeing three roads where *jussa* one road should be." He tried squinting with first one eye closed and then the other, but it didn't improve his aim.

When he'd gotten back into the car after finally returning to the shebeen, I'd ambushed him, yelling that we had to follow Shakes to wherever he was going. Now, with Shakes only a few hundred meters ahead of us, I could see he wasn't doing much better at driving than King George was. The van was careening all over the place.

"Sorry, man. King George has never been this *poeg-eyed*. *Jurre,* that's what six *zols* and eight beers will do to a *ou*."

"Just watch where you're going! We can't lose him."

"Why we following him, Little Miss? He *mos* a dangerous *ou* that carry a big gun. He like killing *mense*. He told King George hisself."

"He'll take us to where Nomsa is. Watch out!" A goat had darted into the road. After we swerved to miss it, it disappeared from the headlights as quickly as it had manifested.

"How 'bout Little Miss steer and King George do the pedals and gears?"

"Well, I can't be worse than you, I suppose. Quickly pull over." I scooted across to sit on his lap. "Okay, go!"

Shakes was luckily driving very slowly, and King George was able to respond relatively well to my instructions to brake, slow down or speed up. The steering wheel was much harder to turn than I would've imagined and required both of my hands and a lot of exertion.

We followed Shakes through a maze of streets, down a dip through open marshy *veld* and then up into another neighborhood that was built on giant boulders. We passed a few other cars without incident though one of them honked their hooter when the van swerved into oncoming traffic. Finally, Shakes turned right into a yard and came to a stop.

"Brake," I yelled and King George responded. I switched off the lights.

Shakes opened the van's door and staggered out. He bent over for a moment in the yard and then stood up again, disappearing around the side of the house.

"Are we there yet?" King George asked.

"Yes, this is the decoy house."

"Huh? Decoy house?"

"Yes, Asanda told me Shakes parks here and then walks around the side of the house pretending to go inside. If the security police are following him or staking him out, they'll storm this house, but it's empty and rigged with some kind of bomb."

"*Jurre!* So where he really go?"

"He jumps over the back wall which you can't see from here, and then heads to his real hiding place, which is another house a few hundred meters down that road. Asanda described it to me."

"King George is *jus* gonna get inna backseat and rest his eyes for a *klein bietjie*. Little Miss wait for him to wake up before she go, *orright?*"

He was snoring within seconds. I cranked the window open to let in some fresh air. The alcohol fumes, coupled with the general stink of the dirty car, was making me nauseated. After five long minutes of waiting, I got out of the car and headed for the house. When I got to the yard, I stood behind the protection of the van for a beat and then rushed around the side to the wall Asanda had told me about. Luckily it was a low one and I was able to jump over without any hassle.

There was an empty lot on the other side, and I cut across it heading left towards the grouping of three houses on the opposite side that Asanda had described. When I got to number twenty-one, I knew I was at the right place and crouched low in the shadows. Nothing stirred and after a minute or two I ventured forward. Either all the lights in the house were off or Shakes didn't have any electricity. The rest of the windows of the houses in the street were similarly dark.

The house was built from cinder blocks and had a tin roof like so many other houses in Soweto. It was a small rectangular shape, which probably meant it had a bedroom at the back and a lounge and kitchen in the front. The bathroom was an outhouse at the back of the property. Unlike Mama Fatty's shebeen, this garden was completely bare; there were no trees and no junk piled up, which meant there was nowhere to hide.

I decided to take a chance and skirted up to the only window that faced out onto the street. I tried to peer inside but the room was pitch-black, and all I could see was my frightened face reflected back at me in the glass. A sudden flash gave me such a fright that I stumbled backwards, landing on my bum. A halo of light shone out above me, and I realized that the flare had been a match being struck to light a candle. I dared raise myself up on trembling legs and peeped inside again. Nomsa was a few feet away wearing a nightgown. Shakes wasn't in the room with her.

Once I was sure that he wasn't just out of sight—once Nomsa sat on the couch with a book in hand and the candle balanced next to her—I tapped on the glass. Her head snapped up. Within two strides she was at the window looking out, her eyes wide with shock when she saw my face. I raised a finger to my lips and then beckoned her out, heading back to the car so she would follow me.

After Nomsa had exited the yard and was looking around, I flashed the headlights. She jogged towards me, her nightgown flapping behind her, and when she reached the car, I unlatched the driver's door for her.

She peered into the back of the car and saw King George passed out. She must have decided that he wasn't much of a threat because she slipped inside.

"Robin? What are you doing here? Who is this man?"

"He's a friend and he brought me."

"How did you know where to find me? Were you followed?" I could see by the moonlight that her right eye was puffy. It looked like someone had recently hit her.

"No one followed us and, believe me, it wasn't easy finding you. It's a very long story that I don't have time to get into right now. I came to take you to Beauty."

"Beauty?"

"Yes, she's in Baragwanath Hospital. She had a heart attack."

Nomsa's hands flew up to her mouth. "A heart attack? When?"

"A few days ago. She's still alive but she isn't getting better. We don't have time to waste."

My news didn't galvanize Nomsa like I'd expected it to. She didn't spring into action or agree that there wasn't any time to waste. Instead, she simply hung her head and sighed. "My mother does not want to see me."

"What? Of course she does!"

"No, she did not come to meet me after I wrote that letter. That was a choice she made and I need to respect that. Forcing her to see me now could just make her condition worse—"

"I never gave her the letter," I blurted.

"What?"

"I never gave it to her. I hid it away because I didn't want you to take Beauty away from me back to the Transkei. But then she found where I'd hidden it, and after she read it, she had a heart attack. Here," I said, reaching into my rucksack and pulling the letter out and giving it to her. "See? I still have it."

Nomsa took it from me, her eyes wide with hope. "She never got my letter? That is why she never came?"

"Yes, exactly."

She was silent for a moment. "You thought I came to take Beauty back to the Transkei?"

"Yes, why else would you have wanted to meet with her?"

"You do not know what the letter says?"

"No, I'm learning to speak Xhosa, but I can't read very much of it. Why? What did it say?" If Nomsa hadn't come to take Beauty away, why had she come?

Nomsa slowly unfolded the letter and began to read in her soft, oddly toneless voice:

My Dearest Mother,

I have to see you.

I have been chosen to go to the Soviet Union to complete my training. It is a great honor to be selected as one of the elite, but I know that in order to be an effective soldier, I need to completely turn my back on you and everything you have ever taught me. There are things that need to be done, terrible things, and many people will be killed. The few acts I have already committed keep me awake at night, and make me question who I am and the person I am becoming. It is my greatest fear that one day I will wake up and be someone you would not recognize, or even worse, someone you could not love.

Nomsa paused and I looked up to see why. Her eyes had filled with tears and she brushed them away impatiently with the heel of her palm before continuing.

> *My own people have been watching me. They are suspicious and doubt my dedication, because I have been naive enough to voice my doubts. Traitors are killed because they are a threat to security, so we will need to be very careful when we meet.*
>
> *If you do not come, my mother, I will know you have given up on me and I will not blame you. I will then depart for Moscow without doubts because if you do not think I am able to be saved, then I know you are right and I will continue on this path I chose a year ago.*
>
> *I love you,*
> *Nomsa*

By the time Nomsa had finished reading, I was crying too. I'd been wrong all along. All the lying and the deceit in order to keep Beauty was all for nothing; Nomsa had never intended to take her away.

"When she didn't come, did you think it was because she didn't love you anymore?" I asked.

Nomsa's sob answered my question. She couldn't speak, she just nodded.

"I'm so sorry, Nomsa. She would have been there if she'd known you were coming. If I gave her your letter and told her to meet you there, there was nothing that would have stopped her. Nothing. It's all my fault."

She looked up at me with watery eyes and I could see how lost she was, how desperately confused, and how much she'd needed the anchor of her mother to keep her from drifting off in the riptide of her competing desires. It was obvious how conflicted she was; no matter how hard she'd searched, she could find no middle ground.

"Do you really believe that?" she asked. "That she would have come?"

"Yes, I know it!" I reached into my backpack again and pulled out Beauty's journal. I suspected it documented her entire search for Nomsa, as well as her overwhelming love for the daughter she refused to give up on. I knew, too, what Beauty had written in her letter to me. She'd said she knew her daughter well enough to know that she'd question the morality of her actions and she'd been right.

"Here, take this."

"What is it?"

"It's your mother's journal. That will tell you everything you need to know. All she cared about was finding you."

Nomsa looked at the journal as though too scared to open it. Perhaps she felt that while she didn't know exactly what was inside, she could still believe it held all the affirmations she so achingly needed. Perhaps she believed the actual words would only lead to disappointment. She riffled through the pages without looking too closely at any of them. "It is a lot of writing."

"Yes. You can read it all later. We need to go now."

"Go?"

"To the hospital. Don't you see? It might not be too late."

"What do you mean?"

"You wanted to speak to your mother before you left and you haven't left yet. If . . . if Beauty is still alive . . . if she's woken up . . . then none of it is too late. You can go see her and speak to her and ask for her advice and she'll tell you the right thing to do and . . ." My words trailed off. I'd been watching Nomsa's face as I spoke and it wasn't in any way affected by what I was saying. She still looked sad and defeated. "What? What's wrong?"

"It is too late," she said.

"No, no. It's not. She's alive, I know she is and—"

"I married Shakes."

"What?"

"When I did not hear from my mother, I thought she had turned her back on me. But Shakes was there even though she was not. And he has always taken care of me. On the day of the march, he got me away from the police and hid me in a secure place. He made sure I had medical attention and then he got Phumla out of jail. He is the one who has been there for me the whole time and . . ." Her voice trailed away.

"But . . . but . . . Shakes is a bad man. He made Phumla lie to your mother about where you were. And he blindfolded Beauty and took her away without taking her to you."

"He was trying to protect me. He said she was causing trouble looking for me and that the security police would take notice of her questions. He said that seeing her would bring the police to our door."

"But if you thought it would be dangerous to see her . . . then . . . then why did you come to the park that day to find her?"

"I was desperate and willing to take the risk, because things had happened that made me question what we were doing. Shakes made me do—" She cut herself off and shook her head impatiently before carrying on. "I did things, terrible things, and I began to question if they were the right things. Shakes said they were the right things and that we had to do them, but I was not sure. I had to see my mother no matter the risk because I knew she would speak the truth."

Yes, Beauty always spoke the truth. "Did Shakes know you came to see Beauty that day?"

Nomsa shook her head.

"So that's who you were scared of. Not the police, but Shakes. He hits you."

She shook her head but she didn't contradict me. "I need to go back inside," Nomsa said. "If he notices that I'm gone—"

"No!" I grabbed her hand. "No. We have to go to the hospital now while he's passed out."

"No, I can't."

As she resisted, my stomach hollowed out with disappointment. "Nomsa, it's a sign, don't you see?"

"What is a sign?"

"You should've been gone by now. You should've been in Moscow. And I tried to keep the letter from Beauty, but she found it anyway. There were delays and things happened to stop you from going, and then you should have left tomorrow but I came tonight. If I came to-morrow, I wouldn't have found you. I was meant to find you tonight. Don't you see? You were meant to see your mother. Please, Nomsa. Please come with me."

Still she didn't move. She just sat there looking at me, her face unreadable.

Think, Robin. Think. You have to make her understand.

I unclasped the chain I was wearing and held it out to her. The Saint Christopher pendant, given to her mother for her courage and bravery, had delivered Beauty to me; it had also safely carried me across the tempest of my fevered illness. I hoped it would give Nomsa strength. "This is Beauty's. She'd want you to have it. Please don't let her die without seeing you, Nomsa. Please."

She took it from me and regarded the silver pendant. "I—"

Her reply was cut short by a cry that tore through the night. Our heads snapped up in unison. Shakes stood a hundred meters away just outside their house. He held something in his hand that he waved around as he yelled an angry tirade in Xhosa.

Nomsa tensed next to me. "I should have hidden that away."

"Hidden what?" But then I saw it.

It was a gun and Shakes was pointing it at us. He was unsteady on his feet but trying to find purchase.

"Oh my God. He's going to shoot at us, he's—"

I'd barely got the thought out when a blast of light flared from the gun and we heard a thwack nearby. The recoil unbalanced Shakes and he stumbled backwards but recovered quickly. With his feet planted apart, he took aim once more.

"Nomsa! We have to—" I didn't need to finish the sentence. The car roared to life as Nomsa turned the key in the ignition.

Shakes got off another shot that barely missed us as Nomsa slammed the car into reverse. We shot backwards at a terrifying speed.

"You can drive?" I asked stupidly. I'd never known a black woman who could.

She didn't reply. Instead, she spun us backwards into a ninety-degree turn, tires squealing as we barely avoided yet another bullet. King George snorted once from the backseat but didn't wake up. Movement out the side window caught my eye. Shakes had started to run after us.

"Quick! Let's get out of here!"

Nomsa put the car into first gear, but when she tried to accelerate, the car stalled. She cursed and turned the key again but the engine didn't respond.

Shakes was gaining on us. Even though he was staggering more than running, he was only fifty meters away.

"He's coming, Nomsa! Hurry!"

She turned the key again. The car made a sickly sound and then fell silent. Shakes was close enough now for me to see the fury in his eyes and the sweat beading down his face. I started winding up the window I'd opened earlier for fresh air.

"Bitch," he screamed. "You bitch! Nomsa!"

"Come on, come—"

The engine finally took. It turned once, twice, and then the car roared to life.

I gasped with relief. "Go, go, go."

Nomsa hit the accelerator and we lurched forward just as two hands suddenly reached out from the darkness. Shakes's long fingers slipped through the gap of the window I hadn't yet managed to fully close. They clung on, even as we started to pick up speed, and then pressed down hard so that the glass slid all the way back again.

I screamed in terror and slapped at his knuckles. Still he hung on. I started punching instead, ramming my closed fists at him with all my might. Finally, he let go. I uttered a cry of triumph and Shakes grabbed at me, his fingers closing around the scruff of my jersey. My head slammed against the side of the car as Shakes yanked me towards him. I tried to scream but couldn't breathe. I was being strangled by my own jersey. I punched out but didn't connect with anything. Shakes's grip was tightening and everything began to swim before my eyes, blackness closing in.

And then a foot, appearing seemingly from thin air, struck out from inside the car and connected with Shakes's head. He let go of me and air flooded my lungs.

"You *orright*, Little Miss?" King George had finally woken up and come to my rescue.

I nodded, my throat too tender to speak just yet.

Nomsa reached out and patted my leg. "Hold on," she said.

And then we rocketed forward into the night, and for a wondrous moment as we shot over a bump, we were airborne, and I knew what it felt like to fly.

Fifty-eight

ROBIN

❀

4 October 1977
Soweto, Johannesburg, South Africa

Dawn was holding its breath when I finally found the right window.

When we'd arrived at Bara, Nomsa convinced the nurses to allow her to see her mother even though it would still be hours before the first official visiting time. They agreed to the visit in part because they were already doing their rounds and busy with that predawn flurry of activity to check in on patients before the doctors arrived. It was Nomsa's desperation, though—and the fact that she was barefoot and in her nightgown—that swayed them; her need was that of a person who'd been swept far out to sea and the nurses recognized a drowning woman when they saw one.

Before Nomsa was led through to Beauty's ward, she came outside and told me that the room was on the ground floor of Ward C, and I'd be able to look inside if I wanted to. I'd spent half an hour since then skirting around the building from window to window while King George slept in the parking lot, and I was just beginning to doubt I'd ever find it when I spotted Nomsa standing next to Beauty's bed. It was two beds down from the window on the left-hand side, and although I couldn't make out much more of Beauty than her outline under the blankets, I could see Nomsa's lips moving. My heart ballooned with joy knowing that Beauty was awake and aware that Nomsa was finally, finally there.

As I watched them, there was a part of me that wished I was standing next to the bed with Nomsa because there was so much I needed to tell Beauty. I wanted to say that I was so sorry for the terrible things I'd done and that I loved her so very much; I wanted her to know that she'd saved me with her love and brought me back to myself when I thought I'd be forever lost; and I wanted to tell her that I'd never, ever forgive myself for the hurt I'd caused her and Nomsa; but I needed to ask anyway if there was some tiny way that she might find it in her great big heart to forgive me. Even a little.

I wanted to find the words to express that I thought I was coming close to understanding the nature of love; that love can't be held captive, and it can't be bestowed by a prisoner on their captor, even if the prisoner is in a glass cage and oblivious to its captivity. I wanted Beauty to know that I understood that love can only be given by one who is free to choose, and that I was forever freeing her of her obligation to me.

More than anything, I wished Beauty could truly understand how much the past fifteen months I'd spent with her had changed me. In the darkness of my grief, she'd taken my hand and walked with me through the crucible. She'd brought love and life and color into my world, and I'd never see things in simple black and white again. She'd helped me realize that life wasn't the kind of story that had a happy ending. In fact, the more I thought about it, the more I'd come to believe that a story that ended happily was just a story that hadn't ended yet.

I'd been so terrified of Beauty leaving that I'd done everything in my power to prevent that from happening, and it was in trying to outrun my fears that I'd manifested them; it was in trying to keep Beauty that I'd lost her, and it was in trying to hold on that I was now forced to let go. I wished she could know all of that and more, but I knew that this was their moment, not mine, and I'd already intruded upon their lives too much.

It was time for me to step back into the shadows so that they could write their own story, and I wished with all my heart that it would be different for them, and that they would have their happy ending, or at least one that wasn't too sad. I took one last look at the mother who never gave up and the prodigal daughter who found her way home, and it gave me hope that we imperfect creatures can find other imperfect creatures through the power of the imperfect emotion we called love.

I didn't know then what the future would hold. I didn't know that the story Beauty and I shared was far from over, nor did I know that the winding paths our lives would take—mine and Beauty's and Nomsa's—would go on to become so entangled that all these years later, I'm finding it impossible to pick apart the knots to separate them. But that's another story for another time.

So I left them there like that, fingers entwined, and I turned and headed for where King George had parked. The sun had risen by then, setting the horizon alight and making the Johannesburg mine dumps glow in the distance. The morning was hushed; all I could hear was the chirping of crickets and the whoosh of cars on the highway. A sleepy moon still lingered, as reluctant to let go of the night as I was.

"Robin!" The cry cut through the stillness.

For a wild moment, I pretended it might be Beauty risen from her bed to keep me from leaving; hope can make you believe crazy things like that. But I recognized that voice, there was no mistaking it, and I turned and shielded my eyes from the glare. Even backlit, I knew the figure running across the parking lot was Edith. Trailing behind her was the rest of the rescue party: Morrie and the Goldmans.

Edith swooped down on me, laughing and crying at the same time, and I ran with arms outstretched to meet her. She swept me up, spinning me around so that the sun and the hospital and the landscape all blurred into one.

"Robin, baby. You're okay. Oh, thank God you're okay."

And I was because Edith had come after all. She'd come to take me home.

Acknowledgments

There's an African proverb that says it takes a village to raise a child, and in much the same way, I believe it took a village to bring this book to life. I would never have been able to write it without the encouragement and support of the many wonderful people in my life.

The first big thank-you goes to the amazing instructors and staff at the University of Toronto's School of Continuing Studies Creative Writing Department, especially Lee Gowan, Jen Cooper, Michel Basilieres, Susan Glickman, Glenda MacFarlane, Mark Brownell, Catherine Graham, Ken Murray, Terry Fallis, Dennis Bock and Don Gillmor. I wrote the entire first draft of the manuscript while attending their classes for my Certificate in Creative Writing, and I'm extremely grateful for the opportunity to have studied with such talented writers. An extra big thank-you goes to Rabindranath Maharaj who was my mentor on my final project submission. I would have given up on the manuscript early on if it weren't for him; I am hugely indebted to him for teaching me so much and for encouraging me to keep going.

I have been incredibly lucky throughout my entire life to have the best teachers anyone could ever wish for; there are too many to thank them all individually, but I'd like to thank Lyn Voigt who was my high school English teacher and who mentored me from when I was sixteen years old. She always pushed me to do better and had such faith in my abilities that it ignited a lifelong passion for writing. Thank you to her for that, as well as the editing she did on the early drafts of the manuscript.

It was during my studies at U of T's SCS that I met the most fabulous group of fellow aspiring writers. Thank you to all of them for reading and rereading every new draft of the book; for their unfailingly kind words; for providing a safe space and supportive community; as well as for their honesty and insight. I'd especially like to thank Lisa Rivers, Jenny Prior, Kath Jonathan, Emily Murray, Caroline Gill, Susie Whelehan, Andie Duncan, Cristina Austin, Ben Brown, Gillian May and Brenda Proulx. Their fingerprints are all over the final draft, and none of them will truly know how much their support, encouragement and friendship sustained me through the toughest days.

I'm also very appreciative of the wonderful writing community, in Toronto and farther afield, which has been so supportive. Thank you to them for welcoming me, inviting me to readings, being so generous with their praise and advice, and making me believe I could do it. There are too many of them to thank individually; hopefully they all know who they are.

For assistance with translations and research, I'd like to thank everyone who shared their memories and expertise, especially Bongani Kona, Professor Russel Kaschula (Rhodes University), Dr. Jadezweni (Rhodes University), Phokeng Mohatlane, Thabani Sibiya, Simpiwe Balfour, Bridget Thomas, Peter Barnard, Chris and Lynda de Vries, Wayne Bailey, Joppie Nieman (the South African Airways Museum Society) and Rachel Townsend.

A great big thank-you goes to the world's best literary agent, Cassandra Rodgers, who picked my manuscript up out of the slush pile and was kind enough to fall in love with it even when it needed a lot of work. I could never thank her enough for making all my dreams come true. Thanks as well to Sam Hiyate, Olga Filina (who rocks), Diane

Terrana (who helped in ways she can't imagine) and the rest of the agents, editors and interns who make up The Rights Factory team.

I am enormously grateful to my amazing editor, Kerri Kolen, for giving the book such a spectacular home, and for making the manuscript so much better than I ever could've imagined. Her insight and guidance have been invaluable, and she has been an absolute joy to work with. I'd also like to thank Anabel Pasarow, as well as the rest of the fabulous Putnam and Penguin Random House team. I still have to pinch myself every day because I can't believe I have such a brilliant publisher.

To the people of South Africa—the wacky and wonderful; the white, the black and everyone else in between; those who speak one of the eleven official languages and those who speak a language all of their own; the children of the rainbow nation; the born-frees and those who paved the way before; the ones who live in mansions and the ones who live in shacks—I thank each and every one of them for inspiring this book and being a part of the rhythm that flows through my veins. You can take a South African out of South Africa, but you cannot take South Africa out of a South African.

I don't know what I did to deserve such wonderful friends and family, but I am blessed beyond measure to have so many special people in my life. In fact, too many to mention them all. I'd like to collectively thank my friends—near and far, old and new—and my family—immediate and extended—for their enthusiasm and kindness; for reading all my early attempts at writing and still telling me I was talented; for their unwavering support and blind faith; and for being the best cheerleaders anyone could ever ask for. I'd especially like to thank my sister-in-law, Mandy Marais, for believing in me so much that she submitted my previous manuscripts to every publishing contact she had. I'd also like to thank my amazing parents, Chris and Lynda, for buying me my first typewriter; for encouraging my creativity from when I was knee-high to a grasshopper; and for always believing in me and telling me I could be anything I wanted to be. Thank you as well to my incredibly special friend, Charmaine Shepherd, who has read every draft of this book (and every draft of every book that came before), who cheered me on tirelessly and would not let me give up. There are no words to express how grateful I am to her for everything she has done and for her steadfast presence in my life.

My final thanks goes to my rock of a husband, Stephen, who in making me laugh every day has made the world an infinitely better place. I am so thankful for all the many sacrifices he has made so that I could pursue my dreams. I will never deserve him but that won't ever stop me from trying.